RATTLE MAN

BOOK I OF THE YMIRAN CHRONICLES

E.H. GASKINS

For Allie, whose fiery spirit could challenge
that of the fiercest Viking

PROLOGUE

IN ALL THE OLD STORIES, Death has many names. So why, then, do we call him Death? Well, it is because that is the name Death itself gave.

"I'm Death, and I make sure everyone is equal."

Piper DeRache knew these stories well, and she'd seen Death, but never had she come so close to knowing him as in this moment.

Her ears rang so loudly it drowned out all the chaos around her. She could see it all—the explosions rupturing through the walls of the *Thialfi's* command deck. She could see the shrapnel tearing through her crew, leaving melted flesh in its wake. She could see the growing crack in the reinforced glass, and the hulking form of the *Aegir* capital ship in the distance. Any second, the glass would give way, and they would all be ripped into the void. She could see her ship collapsing around her, smell the sulfurous fumes of gas fires, feel the heat and smoke on her face. But she could hear none of it.

Then the ringing faded, and she prayed to all the gods for it to return and never leave again.

There were many sounds of chaos, but three distinguished themselves. The first was more explosions, though these were distant—likely fuel lines rupturing near the engines. They sounded so small compared to the blast from the *Aegir's* warhead. The second sound was the moaning and wailing of the crew she knew she could not save. The last sound was a voice. Piper knew it was speaking to her, yet it felt so far away. She glanced toward it to find Bronson, her first mate, screaming something at her, but with the percussion around them, she couldn't quite make out the words.

"Captain!" she finally understood. "We have to go!"

"It was supposed to be easy," she muttered to herself. Her hands were wrapped around the command station railing, white-knuckled and squeezing ever harder. "It was supposed to be an ambassador ship."

Bronson's stare narrowed. "We have to get to the shuttles, Captain!"

Piper found his gaze, and all the shock from the blast washed away. It was replaced by a single thought—*help them survive.* She had to get as many of her crew off the *Thialfi* as possible. They would carry on the ship's legacy... *her* legacy.

In a voice edged with unyielding command, she announced to the deck, "Abandon ship! Anyone who can still walk, help one who can't. Bronson, you're with me."

The still-able crewmembers sprang into action, helping what comrades they could to their feet. Their movements were fueled by the confirmation that this was it. The *Thialfi*, the scourge of Knörr Loop, was going down.

Piper made toward the hatch into the throughway, grabbing Bronson by the arm and tugging the bull of a man with her. He'd looked ready to start helping people on the

Command Deck get to safety, but they didn't have time for that. "There are enough here to help. Elsewhere our brethren may not be so lucky."

Bronson's brow creased, and he nodded. "Lead the way, Formathur."

Formathur—Captain. It was a term reserved only for those leaders most beloved and admired by their clan. Piper had proven herself in many battles, and she loved her crew more than family. But in this moment, there was no part of her that felt she deserved her crew's love. She'd led them into the mouth of a giant, into the sights of the *Aegir*.

Those thoughts couldn't hinder her now. They had to move; had to get every soul possible off the damned ship. They sprinted into the passageway, and Piper aimed for the next room. They'd check all of them: the crew quarters, the common areas, the battle stations; every place where there could be stranded crew.

Barely a breath passed before an explosion erupted behind them. It was the Command Deck, where they'd been only moments before, now spewing brilliant white flame. They heard the agonized screams of two dozen men and women burning alive. Then, the containment doors slammed shut, and the voices were snuffed forever. Piper and Bronson were left in the passageway with the sound of distant explosions, and the nauseating fumes from burning fuel tinged with charred flesh and hair.

There was no time for more regrets. No time to mourn. There were still others who needed help. But still, she couldn't turn away from those containment doors, from the latest batch of comrades she'd let die under her watch.

"Captain, we have to go," Bronson said, tugging at her shoulder.

Piper bared her teeth and held back the tears of rage

threatening to spill over. Throwing aside her hesitations, she lurched past Bronson toward the next room. It was the armory, and Piper had no doubt the armorers, Keyes and Hardy, would have been inside when the warhead struck.

The hulking titanium doors didn't automatically open when approached.

"Override it!" Piper commanded, pointing to the control panel beside the door then swiveling to scope out which room they'd clear next.

"Panel's busted," Bronson growled, slamming his fist against the wall above it.

"We'll have to pry it open," Piper replied, scanning for anything they could use as leverage.

A jagged length of pipe that had escaped the Command Deck explosion provided the best answer. Together, Bronson and Piper wedged the pipe into the crack of the armory door and pushed, but even with their combined strength, it proved impossible to budge.

"Jammed," Bronson hissed.

"Keep pushing!"

"Captain," Bronson said, sweat pouring off his brow. "They could already be dead."

"Just push!" Piper ordered, the faces of the late command deck crew flashing through her mind.

Every vein in Bronson's exposed forearms bulged as he pushed, and she pulled. Piper's jaw was clenched tight, her motley-colored leather jacket glistening with the sweat dripping from her own forehead and the shaven sides of her head, the long mop on top drenched-through. The door budged just the slightest bit, not even enough for them to properly see inside.

"Help!" a female voice Piper recognized as Keyes said from within the armory. "Help us!"

"We're coming!" Piper yelled back. "Just hold on!"

Piper braced her foot on the metal door and released a war cry, straining every muscle to its limit. Bronson echoed, and the duo felt the door start to grind open. They dropped the pipe and grabbed the edges of each panel, pulling as hard as their bodies would allow, opening it just a few inches. Piper was immediately struck by the smell of hyrrine gas and knew it had to be leaking from a ruptured line within.

She looked through the gap they'd formed, trying to gauge the situation from her limited perspective. She could make out a massive rifle rack that had detached from the wall when the warhead struck. Keyes was desperately throwing rifles aside, and Piper saw why. Hardy was pinned underneath the mountain of metal. By the look of things, she'd just cleared enough rifles to start trying to move the rack itself.

"Come on, Keyes! We have to go!" Piper yelled, gesturing for Bronson to start pulling again.

They resumed tugging on the door panels but barely got them to move another inch. Still, they kept pulling. Piper knew they had mere seconds before something sparked the hyrrine and the emergency containment doors shut. So, she pulled harder. The door moved another half an inch, still not near enough to let a body pass through.

Piper looked back inside, seeing Keyes had freed Hardy, supporting the lanky man as they hobbled toward the door.

"Let's go!" Piper ordered.

Keyes and Hardy quickened their pace as much as they could, but it wasn't enough. Piper noticed the busted light panel in the far corner of the room, and not a second later, a hail of sparks erupted from it.

The *Thialfi* captain felt the breath squeezed from her and her eyes went wide, her mouth open in helplessness.

Piper looked at Keyes and knew the girl understood exactly what her expression meant, as panic overcame the young armorer. The room erupted, an empyreal fireball raging forth, consuming all in its path. Keyes opened her mouth to scream, but the fire engulfed her and Hardy before she made a sound. The containment doors activated and slammed shut, but not before the force of the blast struck Piper, sending her crashing into the metal wall across the passageway behind her, thrusting her into darkness.

PIPER CAME to as Bronson finished strapping her into the seat of an escape pod, barely able to move or speak due to the pounding in her head, and her vision was blurry. She could, however, deduce one thing. The escape pod, designed to fit a dozen crew, was empty save the two of them.

"Where..." She tried to ask where the others were, but the words were impossible to form.

"It's all right, Cap," Bronson said. "We're going to be okay."

Something snapped in the back of Piper's mind, reminding her of the gravity of the situation. "No!" she said with as much vigor as she could muster. "I have to stay. I'm the captain."

"None of that," Bronson said. "There aren't many of us left, Cap. We might be the only two—" The words caught in his throat. Then, his brow furrowed, and he continued. "We might be the only two left who can give Volkner what's comin' to him."

Piper shook her head, the motion making her so dizzy she could have vomited.

Bronson was about to latch into the command seat when he whipped his head to the rear of the pod, still connected to the *Thialfi*, as a scream rang out. Piper looked as well but could barely make out the details of the passageway, apart from the evident, rapid decay of it.

"I'll be right back," Bronson said, making his way off the pod to help whoever had screamed.

Piper reached after him weakly and tried to say his name but couldn't manage it.

Bronson was still in view, having just stepped out of the pod, when fire and shrapnel tore through the wall panels on his immediate flank. The ensuing haze and smoke hid her first mate from Piper's view as she tried desperately with uncooperative fingers to unlatch her safety harness. She couldn't get a single strap undone.

Piper DeRache—Piper the Red or Piper the Bloodless—was completely and utterly helpless.

When the smoke cleared, she saw Bronson slumped against the wall housing the escape pod's on-ship control panel. He was conscious, but bright crimson poured from his head, and she could see more red peppering his torso. But his look was not one of pain or fear. Despite the grim outlook and near-guarantee of death, her first mate was smiling with bloodstained teeth.

The battered man reached up to the control panel to a switch cover labeled EMERGENCY EJECT.

Bronson, she wanted to say, but the words were far away.

Her first mate flipped up the cover and laid his palm on the large red button beneath.

"We are the axe," he said, with all the strength and confidence of a raging boar.

Then, he pressed it, and the escape pod was launched into the void.

Piper didn't look out the front viewing screen. Instead, her eyes were on the *Thialfi*, stagnate and littered with tiny explosions. The massive capital ship behind it launched a missile, a second warhead. It collided with her ship, and the two became light forged in silent thunder.

Piper DeRache, a captain, left alone with no crew nor ship, descending toward the ice planet Jotun, the remains of the *Thialfi* raining down behind her, let herself slip back into the void. She didn't care whether or not she ever woke again.

PART ONE

CHAPTER
ONE

Tiny smoke wisps swirled each time Mila Messer touched the soldering iron tip to the loose connections on the old reactor battery. She'd found the thing in the pit a few weeks ago. Each day since, Mila had tried to fix the nonfunctioning hunk of metal. Each day since, she'd failed.

But that wasn't enough to discourage her. The battery was the key, after all—the key to freedom. If she got it working again, it would produce enough power to fuel the rusty hoverbike in their shed. Mila wanted nothing more than to feel that hoverbike purr; to toss a leg around it and press the accelerator to max speed. It had to be the hoverbike. Her father's jet truck was too expensive to drive, running on low-grade hyrrine, the most common yet rapidly depleting fuel source in the Ymiran system. Plus, the truck was bio-encrypted to him, so she'd have to cut off his hand if she wanted to even start the thing.

The hope of leaving her father's farm swam in her head. Then it was ripped away as a shockwave of pain flooded her arm. The soldering iron clanked on the metal table as Mila's hand stopped obeying her.

"Odin's eye," she cursed, quickly grabbing a nearby tinkerer's screwdriver.

The device in her arm, a potent nerve stimulator called an elerex, was acting up again. It looked like a silver medallion planted in her forearm, just below the edge of her rolled-up coverall sleeve. The only breaks in its smooth brushed metal surface were two tiny screws one might expect to find in eyeglasses and a small etching of a Neunorse rune—mannaz, which looked like a simple, three-branched tree. The screws were mismatched both from themselves and the elerex, and the metal around them held faint scratches, evidence of years of removal for repairs.

It had been only a few months after her mother died when the accident happened, and the memory of the event was laden with fog. She'd been helping her father work on a dead reactor array on the farm. The device had started up unexpectedly with her arm inside and nearly killed her. The physician who'd come to perform the surgery said she was very strong and such a shock would've stopped the heart of Thor himself. She was lucky to have only lost the use of her right arm, since the experimental elerexes could help restore its function. Her father had poured almost all the money they had left into the elerex and the procedure. He hadn't let her forget it since.

Most of Mila's memories of the accident and the surgery were foggy, as if she saw them through frosted glass. The same could be said for her memories of her mother. She remembered the warmth of her, and occasionally scents of honey cinnamon would evoke images of golden hair in her mind. But her mother's face, her gait, her form, those memories were lost to Mila.

The elerex was a finicky thing, however. Six years after Mila had gotten hers, reports started coming out about their instability. Some people, like Mila, experienced varying degrees of shocks followed by the loss of function. The jolts were more annoying than anything, and the elerex could be fixed with a quick adjustment. Others weren't so lucky with their malfunctions. Mila had heard of more than one case where a damaged elerex became unstable and released energy in large enough doses to kill their bearers. After the reports emerged, the devices were discontinued. Mila knew if she ever lost hers, it meant losing her arm.

Mila sat back in her creaking steel chair and huffed. She eyed the reactor battery and a brief desire to smash it with a hammer passed through her. Maybe the stubborn thing was really busted for good.

Her workshop was nestled behind a low hill on the southern edge of their property. It was far enough away from the house that her father rarely took the time to venture to it. This allowed Mila extended periods to work on the various pieces of equipment strewn about the workshop. It looked nothing more than salvaged sheet metal and bits of wood holding it up on the outside. However, upon closer inspection, perceptive eyes would notice the energy shield battery bolted onto the roof and the shimmer of the invisible forcefield surrounding the ramshackle building. The shield was primarily used to keep the blistering Vidarin cold out of the shack while she worked, but it also served well against alien beasts, woodland insects, and drunk fathers.

She'd found the shield battery in the same salvage pit she'd found the most recent reactor battery. The pit was hidden in the small forest a few hundred yards east of the workshop, at the foot of the Heiser Hills. Though, she referred to them as the Howling Hills, since the wind sweeping off them sounded like just that—a wolf howling.

Sometimes, the winds would blow so strong, Mila felt the world itself was rumbling.

Before the shield battery, Mila had relied on her thick farming thermals to keep her warm in the shop. But they could only do so much. She'd thought about trying to convert the battery for use on the hoverbike, but the device was simply too bulky and weighed nearly eighty pounds; far too heavy for a bike. So, she'd repaired it and put it to its intended use.

The pit was filled with obsolete military equipment, such as the shield, as well as the occasional exciting bobble. Mila expected it was left behind by some long-past research exhibition, back when most of Vidar was still foreign to the humans. In fact, the shop was overflowing with eccentricities she'd scavenged from the mechanical graveyard. There was an analog clock with iridium-lit hands and only twelve hour marks. It was bolted to the wall of the shed above the entrance. There were two digital photobooks. One displayed a carousel of some former soldier's wife or girlfriend, a fair-skinned woman with black hair and laughing eyes. The other cycled pictures of her as a child performing various maintenance tasks around the farm with her father. She knew the pictures had been taken by her mother, but the only evidence of her was a golden-tan arm caught in a timed photo that snapped a few seconds too early. The next picture was a corrupted file.

On the bench by the door of the shack was another bobble she'd received from the pit. It was a holobook entitled *The Nightwalkers*—a book of new fairy tales written after the discovery of the Ymiran planetary system. The metal-cased text was displaying the lyrics to a common children's nursery rhyme called "Rattle."

In night black, cold and rain,

comes a man without a name.
Lost souls knock upon your floor
when he's standing at your door.
Slither lips and silver tongue,
hear his words, too late to run.
Your given call to him is chattel.
Never give your name to Rattle.

Mila's most prized recovery, however, was the old Earthen radio nestled in the corner of her shop table against the wall. Its digital face was blank, and the speakers were staticky at best, but Mila was especially proud of the thing. She'd found it clogged with dirt, and many of the internal pieces rusted to nonfunction. But, after clearing out the plastic casing, replacing some of the copper coils and gears for the dials, and finding a new power cord, she'd been amazed to discover the thing actually turned on. Of course, there were no FM or AM signals; they'd done away with that technology after the migration. Even so, Mila had managed to salvage some of the internals from a Hermod-grade interplanetary communicator to upgrade the relic. It had worked surprisingly well, and she could easily pick up transmissions from Idun.

Mila often listened to DJs playing old Earthen music, her favorite songs from the rock legends of old. When she wasn't listening to music, she listened to the news stations from Idun or Jotun. Vidar had no public news stations of its own, and Hod's transmitters weren't powerful enough for her tech to pick up, even though it was their neighbor planet.

A verse-heavy song by a man named McLean was currently playing, every fifteenth word or so masked by a touch of static. Mila had been humming along before she burned her finger. Now she sat, still sucking on the fresh

wound, irritated by her carelessness. She took it out of her
mouth to inspect the angry red flesh along the bridge of her
pointer. Nothing serious. The pain was already beginning
to fade, and the burn itself would only last two or three
days.

"All right, let's try that again," she said as she picked the
soldering iron back up and resumed her humming.

Mila leaned in close to the old reactor battery to get a
closer look at the connection she was trying to repair. The
tip of her tongue peeked out to the right, a trait she'd gotten
from her father, and her brow was furrowed. She was just
about to touch the end of the iron to her solder when the
music abruptly stopped.

"Breaking news," a newscaster's voice said. "We've just
confirmed that the *Thialfi* pirate vessel has been shot down
by a Jotun fleet. At 2700 YST, a fleet headed by the capital
ship *Aegir* engaged with the *Thialfi*. The Jotun fleet
sustained no casualties. There are believed to be no
survivors among the *Thialfi's* crew."

The transmission blipped out, returning to the sounds
of *Bye, Bye, Miss American Pie*.

"Huh," Mila said to herself. "How about that? The
scourge of trader's belt is gone, just like that?"

Mila had always had something of a savant's fascination with the void pirates of the Ymiran star system. To
most, they were villainous, traitorous dogs with no alle-
giance to anyone but themselves. But Mila had always
thought of them as creatures of passion, who wanted
freedom above all things, who were only loyal to others of
their kind, like a family. There was something admirable
in it. She had a particular interest in the *Thialfi*, named so
because of its speed. And her captain, Piper DeRache,
was practically legend. Stations had called her Piper the

Red and Piper the Bloodless. It was strange to think her gone.

Mila could never speak of her fascination to anyone, least of all her father. He despised the pirates almost as much as he despised the Vidarin president. She knew he'd had run-ins with them during his time in the Navy, but he'd never told her more than that.

As she thought about the fall of the *Thialfi* and DeRache, she heard her father's voice echo from across the farm, muted behind the sounds of the humming shield battery and the radio. "Mila!" he called. "Sundown! Time to work!"

Mila huffed as she took off her goggles, leaving their outline in thin oil around her eyes, and unplugged the soldering iron. There was something particularly irksome about a farmer who hadn't farmed a day in the past four years telling her to get to work. But she had no choice. The crops were their only source of income—their emaciated cash cow. Even if he could tend the crops, the fool would kill them, and she'd be forced to live in the jet truck with him when they lost the farm. No one wanted that.

Mila donned her farming thermals over her black tank top and zipped up her oil-stained olive coveralls. Then she stepped out into the fresh Vidarin night and headed toward the crop fields.

◇—◇·············◇—◇

MILA'S RESPIRATOR mask clicked with each exhale. Its triple-filtration system was designed to keep her safe from the growth hormones she sprayed on the crops. The crops themselves were fungi. More specifically, they were titan mushrooms—massive organisms discovered upon settling

Vidar. They were one of the only humanly-edible crops found on the planet that could be tamed in the 18-hour northern Vidar nights.

The species was naturally resistant to the near-freezing temperatures of Vidar and required little water. They also had an uncannily similar taste and texture to beef, so their meat became something of a luxury once the last of the bovines died nearly sixty years prior. However, despite their hearty nature and relatively simple upkeep, titan mushrooms were notoriously chaotic. A crop could grow with heads as small as thumbtack heads or diameters longer than an adult's arm. With help from the growth hormones, the farm's current yield was about the size of dinner plates. But, its numbers were low—lower than last season, which had already been lower than the season prior to that. Mila could see the trend and suspected their soil was near the end of its growing life. It was a common issue in Vidarin farmlands, and a grim sign for the Messers' livelihood.

"Mila," her father said from behind her.

He was close, and his voice too clear. Mila turned to find, as she expected, that he wasn't wearing his mask.

Her father, Hans Messer, was a man who looked as if he could be sixty as easily as forty. His forehead and eyes were prematurely wrinkled, and his gray hair thinned more every day. Now he was wrapped in his canvas-material jacket lined with thick synthetic wool. It was the same olive color as Mila's coveralls. His keys rattled in his hand.

"I'm headed to town to get some supplies. Need anything?" he asked.

Mila shook her head. He wasn't actually asking. If she said she wanted anything, he'd make some backhanded comment about how much she cost him, even though she was the only reason they had any money at all.

"All right," he went on. "I should be back in a couple hours. Have midmeal ready by then?"

Mila nodded, her eyes empty. She knew better than to expect him back in *a couple hours*. It would be half the night before he was back, and there wouldn't be supplies. What there would be was a drunken disappointment of a father lucky to have driven his jet truck home in one piece. That was the ritual.

Hans started to turn and walk away when he began coughing violently, covering his mouth with a fist.

"You really should wear your mask out here," Mila said. "The chemicals aren't healthy for your lungs."

"I'm fine." Hans waved her off. "I'll be back in a bit."

She watched as he lumbered off to his truck. If he stood upright, Hans would be well over six feet tall. But, he hadn't stood straight in years, and his hunched form was short and sad. Mila had gone back to spraying the crops by the time she heard the compact jet engine of the truck crank. She could hear it float away from the property with a hissing roar.

Tending to the rows of moonlit fungi, Mila listened to a narrated book through a set of old in-ear communicators she'd retrofitted. The static-masked narrator read the *Tales of the Ymiran Stargods*.

"Chapter One: The Neunorse. It was the *Thökk* that reached Ymir first, and so it was their radars that detected the signatures. Signs of life that floated in empty space. The *Thökk* counted ten such signals before their mysterious disappearances. This left the crew wondering what they were. Was it a radar malfunction? Did their systems mistake an inanimate space object for something organic? Or was it something more?

The top Ymiran scholars soon declared these were the

signs of the gods and the Neunorse prophecy had come to
pass. The *Thökk* had found Ymir, and somewhere hidden
within, is Valhalla."

Mila couldn't help but laugh when the narrator said,
"scholars." Religious fanatics desperate to revive an old
Earth religion, more like. Still, she prayed to the gods just as
everyone else did. She prayed to the Matron, Freya, for good
fortune. She prayed to the Storm, Thor, to bring her the
strength to press on another day. She prayed to the Allfather, Odin, to keep her safe from her father. And, just like
everyone else, she did not dare question the gods.

CHAPTER
TWO

To say the jet truck hummed or purred would simply not be accurate. No, it was not a honed performance machine. It was not fast, like the phase racers of Idun. It was not practical, like the ice runners of Jotun. It wasn't even reliable, like the ramchargers of the Tyran desert. The truck sputtered down the road, growling like a rabid dog, and threatened to putter out on Hans Messer at any time.

The feral engine all but drowned out Hans' music. As always, he had the volume dial cranked all the way to the right. The old, earth-style speakers, which Mila had repaired for him at least a dozen times now, screamed a staticky tune. To describe the music, one must imagine folk combined with synthesized sounds. There were heavy drumbeats behind raspy, soulful vocals masked by electronic chords. The style had become popular a couple of decades before, fading from the public ear within a few years. But, as with many things in the past, Hans clung to it.

Hans had heard the songs so many times he sang along even when the roaring thrusters overpowered both the sound from the speakers and his own voice. There were moments, however, when the engine sputtered. In those brief half-seconds, the music and Hans' singing were as loud as a concert.

The engine sputtering was a sign of mechanical failures to come. Hopefully, they would be mild and cost little. More likely, the old motor would die completely, and there wouldn't be a thing Hans, Mila, or any mechanic could do about it. Like the roaring of the engine, Hans' voice was also interrupted in spurts. Except, where a certain quiet calm came along with the engine's pauses, Hans' interruptions were crude and painful. They came in the form of violent coughing fits. Each time they'd start, he'd raise a dirty rag he kept in his back pocket and cover his mouth. When he brought it down, there were always tiny specks of blood.

As he drove along, singing his favorite outdated synth-folk, a particularly intense bout of these coughs reared its head. Just as the engine sputtered, leaving that shallow second of silence, Hans filled the air with a wretched hacking noise. He covered his mouth tightly with the dirty rag. With every cough, he felt something try to break loose within him. He coughed and coughed until his vision went black. When he came to only a moment later, the jet truck was diving headlong into the roadside ditch. He yanked the wheel up violently, almost overcorrecting and forcing the floating craft upside down. He pushed back down and slammed on the brakes, crashing his forehead into the wheel consequently. There was no doubt he'd have a bold purple bulb above his right eye come morning.

Hans took a moment to catch his breath, fighting off the building urge to cough again. When he could fight it no more, he started looking desperately for his rag. Hans spotted it on the floor, but it was too late. He was already coughing again, almost as violently as before. With each cough, he spattered mucousy crimson on the truck's dash. Finally spotting his rag in the truck floorboards, he bent over, still coughing, and picked it up. With his mouth covered, he coughed for a solid minute without stopping. When the fit finally stopped, he pulled the rag away and hesitantly inspected it. He found what he expected, more blood. Except now... now there was so much more. The crimson was not in specks but deep stains. It confirmed something he'd known to be true for a while now.

Like the truck, his motor was sputtering.

Like the truck, Hans was dying.

HANS STAGGERED between the poker tables of the local mead hall. It was named Tröllaskegg, after the great beards of the Norse giants. There were six tables in total, and none of them sat more than three patrons, despite their seven chairs. In the corner of the room sat a pair of Vidarin soldiers—easily identifiable as officers by the bits of polished silver and brass on their collars. They had similar haircuts, shaved to the skin on the sides with short braids on top. On the sides of their heads were tattooed in bright colors Neunorse runes, though Hans' blurry vision, both from his swelling eye and the spirits in his bloodstream, couldn't make out exactly which they were. The duo was having a conversation just loud enough for Hans' drunk ears to distinguish.

"Heard the last brandr refiner died at work today," one said.

The other shook his head. "You think the president will send us to raid Hod again?"

"After last time? Not a chance. Not with the Iduans backing them."

"Yeah, but if we got Jotun on our side. You never know."

"Well, he'll have to do something. Without a brandr refiner, our fuel will run dry soon. No doubt Brandt's scrambling for another master refiner as we speak."

Hans' attention turned from the conversation as he eyed one of the tables that sat only one player opposite the dealer. The player wore a peculiar ensemble; an old, Earthen pinstripe suit with a matching fedora hat. It was vastly different than the farmer overalls and stained shirts most of the regulars sported. He was older as well, perhaps twenty years Hans' senior. His face was wrinkled with years of smiling. A cane laid against his chair with the largest emerald Hans had ever seen as its pommel.

Hans took a seat at the table, slamming his tankard of moonbrew down so hard it foamed and overflowed onto the felt. The dealer rolled her eyes. It wasn't the first time Hans had stained a table in Tröllaskegg.

"What's the game?" Hans asked. His words were slow, trying to avoid a slur.

"Poker," the dealer replied. "Founder-style. Ten mark buy-in."

"Good," Hans said, pressing his thumb into the table's print reader, authorizing the charge to be put on his rolling tab. "Simple game, poker. Earther's knew how to make a good gambling game."

"I couldn't agree more," the man in the pinstripe suit said. His voice was smooth, clean—just like his attire.

The thumbprint reader beeped aggressively, its back-lighting flashing red.

"Looks like your tab's full, Hans," the dealer said.

Hans shook his head. "No, no. I paid it off last week."

The dealer gave him a knowing look. "Yes, you did."

Hans slumped in his chair. His tab cap was two hundred marks. *Two hundred*. More than the farm made in a week, and he'd filled it again in only five days.

"I'll cover him," the suit man said, taking out an old earth-style leather wallet and pulling out glowing cash.

Hans gaped. Actual Vidarin marks were a rarity these days. Almost all money was exchanged through digital accounts from the government banks. It was a clever way to ensure every Vidarin citizen paid their taxes. Well, clever if you were a supporter of the Brandt regime. Most others would call it oppressive, but only in whispers, and only to those they trusted most.

"I play for the sport of it anyway," the man continued, throwing ten marks on the table as if it were pennies. Then, he handed another ten marks to Hans. "This good man can pay me back in due time."

The money felt heavy in Hans' hands. He was already two hundred marks in debt to the mead hall. Did he really want to dig himself deeper by accepting money from this man? He wasn't given the time to decide before two cards sat before him, face down. He picked them up to find a seven and a jack. Hans passed on the first round of betting and waited for the dealer to lay three cards on the table. A nine, a five, and a jack. Hans smiled at the jack. On the second round of betting, he went all-in with the suit man's ten marks. The suit man matched him, showing not an ounce of emotion. Hans had a distinct feeling he was bluffing.

The dealer placed another card on the table. An ace. She followed it with the last card—another ace. Hans smirked and laid down his cards.

"Pair of jacks," he said, his smirk growing into a cheesy grin.

The suit man put his own cards down and said, with a coolness that could snuff a forge, "Three aces."

Hans gritted his teeth, looking at the cards. He did indeed have an ace. What dumb luck.

"Lucky bastard," Hans said. "Buy me in again. I'm sensing a change."

The suit man happily obliged. Before Hans knew it, he'd played eight hands, losing all but one to the suit man. Yet, he wanted more. Every time he felt like it was time to call it quits, he'd win, and his enthusiasm would be restored. And the man kept feeding him the money to continue, as well as kept the moonbrews coming every time Hans emptied a tankard.

"I think that about does it for me," the suit man finally said as he stood and grabbed his cane. Hans saw now that it was purely an accessory, as the man had no difficulty moving.

"How murch der I owe yer?" Hans spat. He was struggling to keep his eyes open.

"Oh, not terribly much," the man replied. "I think we came in at just under six hundred."

Hans was struck with frightening sobriety. "Six hundred? I... I can't pay that."

"Perhaps you can work something out," the man said. He took a step close to Hans and whispered in his ear. "You know, I hear brandr refiners are in high-demand right now. Rumor has it, Volkner Brandt will pay a pretty penny upfront for anyone who can provide a master. I heard he'd pay half a million marks."

The suit man left Hans in his stupor, tipping his hat to the dealer as he exited the mead hall. Hans tried to sit back in his chair, but his core and back wouldn't cooperate. Instead, he planted his elbows on the table and cradled his head in his hands. *A master brandr refiner? How in Hel's name does that help me?* He glanced back to the soldiers at the table, who looked as though they were finishing up.

Hans couldn't remember getting up. He couldn't remember stepping toward the officers' table without a plan. He couldn't even remember what he'd said to get their attention. But, he was standing in front of their table now, and they were both looking at him, their expressions preaching impatience.

"Yes, go on," one of them said. "We haven't got all night, old man."

"Umm," Hans muttered. He couldn't find more words than that.

"Come on," the other said. "He's a drunk fool. He doesn't even know where he is right now."

"Wait," Hans said. "No, I'm no fool."

The bigger officer, a first lieutenant according to his rank insignia, started to stand. "You're wasting my time," he said. "I don't take kindly to drunk idiots wasting my time."

The First Lieutenant stood a full head above Hans. Despite his annoyed tone, his face held a subtle smirk. Even as drunk as Hans was, he knew that smirk meant nothing good for him.

"I—," Hans began without a clue of where his sentence was going.

"Gjalp's piss," the First Lieutenant cursed impatiently. "Just shut up." The officer stepped out of the booth. He was an exceptionally muscular man, his presence dwarfing the Vidarin farmer. He glared down at the farmer and said, "Here's what's going to happen. My comrade and I are going to take you out back and make the left half of your face match that ugly right side. Then, we're going to drag you to our headquarters. You're going to be the new dummy for our men's combat training. They could use live practice."

The First Lieutenant grabbed Hans by the throat and lifted him half a foot off the ground. The room was deadly silent as the other patrons watched in horror.

"Please," Hans sputtered. "Wait, I—"

"You what? You're sorry?"

"I know a brandr refiner."

The First Lieutenant's head cocked, and he looked closely at Hans with one eye squinted.

"Liar," he growled.

Hans was flailing, his intoxicated mind panicking at the encroaching doom. The First Lieutenant was squeezing hard, harder. Hans' brain fought for air. In its desperation, it clung to one person. Mila.

"My daughter," he forced out.

It seemed, for a moment, he might snap Hans in half right then and there. Then, he apparently thought better of it and set the farmer down. Hans collapsed to the floor, coughing blood onto the hardwood. The First Lieutenant glared around the room, a silent instruction for the patrons to go about their business. They obeyed.

"Talk," the officer commanded.

Through his strangled coughs, Hans managed, "My daughter can refine brandr." The lie felt like sand coming out of his mouth. "She can refine anything."

His coughing continued, and the other officer, a second lieutenant, squatted beside him, looking at the ground. "Look, Sauer. Blood," he said to his superior, inspecting the crimson on the floor. "You sick?"

"I don't know," Hans replied.

"It doesn't matter," the one called Sauer said. "Tell us more about the girl."

Hans knew it was too late to take back what he'd said. His thoughts turned toxic with the idea of his daughter. How he'd been left to watch over her alone. How her busted arm had left them penniless. How she judged him every single time he came home from the mead hall. He convinced himself what he was doing was good, that he could be rid of her and the money from the Vidarin government would pay for the effort he'd put into his daughter, even if there was no chance in hel she could refine the brandr. It didn't matter. With half a million marks, he wouldn't even need to pay off his tab at Tröllaskegg or repay his debt to the suit man. No, he could leave all of that behind. He could smuggle himself to Jotun or Idun and live out his days a rich hermit. But then, he'd tried that once... a long time ago.

He looked up at the officers, finally suppressing his cough. "Yes, she's a prodigy; the skill of the old dwarves resides in her. I swear it by the grace of the Matron, the hammer of the Storm, and the spear of the Allfather."

This was one of the most sacred swears a follower of the Neunorse religion could make. Sauer looked down at him pensively, his arms crossed and his eyes narrow. Then, he bent down close and said, "I don't believe you, old man. But it doesn't make much difference if I do or not. We'll come to retrieve your daughter in three days. If what you say is true, you'll have made us all rich men. If not, I'll snuff the life from you with my own hands. Either way, I win. Understand?"

Hans nodded.

"Good." The First Lieutenant stood and headed out of the mead hall, followed closely by his second lieutenant.

Before exiting, he looked back and repeated, "Three days."

———————

HANS SAT in the driver's seat of the jet truck, staring at the leather-rot steering wheel. His thoughts were swimming with Mila and her mother.

She left me alone with her, to fend for both of us myself.

Mila's drained me of every penny, and what have I seen in return? Nothing.

Nineteen years she's been a burden. Nineteen years I'll never get back.

Hans' hands were clenched in a white-knuckle grip around the wheel. He tried to keep his thoughts of Mila angry and resentful. Every problem in his life was *her* fault. But then, he couldn't stop the rogue memories of her as a child, innocent and hopeful, slipping in between the cracks. They pressed in like unwanted guests. She was still hopeful. She was still innocent. As much as he tried to deny it, a part of him knew she held none of the blame for their situation.

Hans couldn't help himself. Rage welled up inside him, and he slammed his fists on the steering wheel. He was angry at the officers, at the mead hall, at the man in the pinstripe suit. He cursed the thought of Mila's mother, the farm, himself. But, he remembered who he wanted to blame... who it was easy to blame.

Mila.

He would tell himself that lie the entire drunken drive home.

THREE

IT WAS MIDNIGHT, which, on the Vidarin clock, meant it was time for lunch, or midmeal, as they called it. Mila was in the kitchen making sandwiches with sautéed mushrooms. This was an everyday meal for the Messers. Bread was cheap, and mushrooms were the only thing they had in excess supply. Though not as much as tinkering and inventing, Mila did enjoy cooking. It was something else she could do with her hands—something productive. And when every meal you eat consists of some type of mushroom, it helps to get creative with seasonings and cooking styles.

She heard the sporadic roar of the jet truck engines as her father returned. After the engines spun down, she heard the unusually loud slamming of the truck door. She whispered a prayer to the Matron that her father wasn't too drunk. Still, she braced herself for whatever profanities and curses he would hurl at her tonight.

When the door to the kitchen finally opened, it was not the stumbling fool Mila expected. Yes, it was her father. And yes, he was drunk. He also had a nasty bruise forming above his eye and his clothes were more disheveled than usual. But there was a certain calm about him—a dangerous calm. She'd never known her father to be docile when stinking of moonbrew.

Hans Messer made his way to the kitchen table—an archaic thing constructed of cheap metal. The chair screeched along the floor as he pulled it back and sat down. He rested his forearms on the table and maintained his silence, his eyes not once making their way to Mila.

Mila didn't know whether to start a conversation. His quiet filled the room, leaving only the sound of sizzling mushrooms. She'd been ready for drunken insults, slights, and blame. That would have been normal, bearable. But, this... this seemed so much worse. She opted to leave the silence there and finished making the sandwiches, not looking at him when he finally spoke.

"You know, I could've probably retired by now," he said, his voice flat. "I could've been living easy in a cottage in the west. My money from the military could've paid my way."

Mila had heard this spiel before, but always in exaggerated anger. Like a cartoon character waving their hands around and complaining about the sun being yellow. But this was far different. Hans always thrived on his yelling fits, challenging her to a contest of who could make the most noise. This time, volume was not his objective. This time, he seemed truly angry. Mila didn't want to respond; didn't want to light whatever fuse was lying in secret. But it appeared Hans would give her no choice in the matter.

"Well, say something," he spat.

Mila was still facing away from him, looking at the plates in front of her. "Midmeal is ready."

Hans laughed, but there wasn't an ounce of real joy in it. "You think *lunch* is going to make this right?"

"Make what right?" Mila finally turned to find Hans' eyes boring into her.

"This," Hans said, gesturing all around him. "This ugly house. This failing farm. This decrepit life we have!"

Mila stepped toward the table, plates in hand. "I wasn't trying to fix any of that with sandwiches."

"You're not *trying* to fix any of it at all. That's the problem, Mila. You always take."

Mila had heard the words a thousand times. Yet, this time, they struck her harder. There was a distinct seriousness to him. He meant it, all of it.

"I always take?" Mila said, her voice starting to swell with anger. "I've been the only thing keeping this godsdamned farm afloat for years."

"You're a stupid, naïve girl. Nothing you've done has helped anything. It's only postponed the inevitable."

"Well, at least I'm doing *something*!" Mila yelled, her face going a harsh scarlet. "What do you do? Drive off into town for 'supplies,' then come home drunk as a dwarf? Then scream at me because you lost all of our money gambling?!"

"I drink because of you!" Hans stood up so forcefully it knocked the table back. The screech was like fingernails on a chalkboard. "I drink because it makes me forget how disappointed I am in you. I drink because that damn thing in your arm broke us. I drink because you drove your mother away from me."

Hans' hand flew up before either of them knew what had happened. His thick hand swiped the plates from Mila's hands. She quickly covered her head, ready to be struck by fallen porcelain. It never came, as she heard them crash onto the floor.

Hans stepped back, then looked up and glowered at

Mila. Mila felt her eyes filling with tears but refused to let them fall. That last thing, about her mother, he'd never said before.

"What do you mean, I drove her away?"

Hans' anger seemed to fade, as if he hadn't really realized he'd said that. "I... nothing. I meant nothing."

"You told me she got sick. You said she went to a hospital and died," Mila hissed. "I've *prayed* to her."

"Mila," Hans said, the rage now completely gone from him.

Mila didn't care. She didn't want to speak to him anymore, not right now. She made her way out of the kitchen and into the Vidarin dark, taking special care to slam the door behind her. There'd be more time to ask more about her mother when the bastard was sober. Right then, looking at him disgusted her.

⟡────◆────⟡

Two and a half days passed without a word between Mila and Hans Messer. Mila hadn't bothered farming any crops in the time. Her sorry excuse for a father could cover it, or they could go completely broke and starve. It didn't make much difference either way to her at that point. She was close to finished with the reactor battery. Just a couple more stable connections and it would be fixed. She could plant it into the hoverbike and ride away from the farm. Far away. And now there was the chance her mother could be alive somewhere. The thought of finding her, of reuniting with her, it brought tears dangerously close to Mila's eyes.

She listened to the retrofitted radio as she worked on inserting a new conductor rod into the reactor battery. A news anchor was talking about the wreckage of the *Thialfi* found scattered throughout the snowy wastelands of Jotun. Though scouting parties had expected to recover weapons, raw materials, and other valuable goods, they'd only found destroyed scrap. The *Aegir* capital ship had unleashed pure hell upon the pirate vessel, it seemed. No wonder no one survived.

Mila's eyes were set on the reactor battery, and the tip of her tongue peeked through her lips. She slid the conductor rod into place with a guardian's care, making sure not to scratch any connections. It fell into place with the softest *clink*. Then, she took the soldering iron in her hand, taking equal care to put just the right amount of solder in just the right places. Too much in one area would shift the rod, making the other connections impossible. Too little, and the bonds would be weak and brittle. No, the reactor battery was a sophisticated, specific, careful design. Only sophisticated, specific, careful repairs would do.

Mila made the connections at a painstakingly slow pace, tiny wisps of smoke rising with every touch of the iron tip. She'd made three without issue. Time for the fourth and final. In one hand, solder. In the other, the iron. She was so focused on making the exact right placement, she hadn't even noticed the bead of sweat crawling down her forehead. It had pooled into an orb just between her eyes. With every passing moment, gravity threatened more and more to make it drop. And just as Mila made the final connection, it did, splashing just left of the solder. Any farther right, and it would have ruined the painstaking work. She would have needed a new conductor rod, which not easy to come by.

But, it had landed to the left of the connection, and Mila watched with a child's delight as the pale light of the battery's power ring flickered on.

Mila could have cried, could have screamed. She could have danced or died with overwhelming excitement. It worked! It really worked! She'd fixed it, and now only one step remained: the hoverbike. She decided the scream would be the best celebration, but as she started to let it out, she heard her father's voice call out from outside her workshop.

"Mila!" Hans Messer called. There was something about his voice. It was softer than usual. Was it apology, contemplation? Was it regret? "I've made dinner. Would you join me?"

Made dinner? He hasn't made dinner in years. She considered the offer for a moment.

"Sure," she finally replied. "I'll be there in a minute."

Mila had already made up her mind; she was leaving after dinner when Hans would inevitably drink himself into a comatose sleep. She'd share this dinner with her father, but that was it. It would be the last one they'd ever have together. Tucking the reactor battery into a slim metal case she'd specially designed for the device and stashed it in her cargo pocket, Mila headed into the late Vidarin night.

She was surprised to find Hans was not back at the house but instead right outside the workshop. He wasn't wearing his regular dirty overalls and stained shirt, but rather his... Navy uniform? The polished golden buttons strained at the seams of the royal blue dress jacket. His hair was cut short on the sides, reasonably clean, but not perfect. Clearly, he'd done it himself. It was styled on top with a Vidarin war-braid, and his face was shaven smooth.

"What's all this?" Mila asked skeptically.

"I wanted us to have a nice dinner and, well, I wanted to look the occasion." Hans scratched the back of his head, and Mila could see the buttons shake, trying to hold the blouse together. "Turns out I don't really have any nice clothes besides these old rags."

"The occasion?"

"An apology. I... I didn't mean what I said the other night."

Mila could feel there was something he was holding back; a strange hesitancy in his voice. Perhaps it was that the old man wasn't used to apologizing. But Mila felt there was something more. She just couldn't pinpoint what it was.

"I'm afraid I don't have any nice clothes to match," Mila said.

"I've taken care of that," Hans replied, smiling.

None of this felt even remotely natural to Mila. Her father hadn't attempted a nice gesture in... well, she couldn't actually remember how long it'd been. They'd had plenty of fights over the years, and while what he said the other night did introduce new barriers between them, she'd never expected anything like this. She'd expected time would pass, she'd ask about her mother, and he'd refuse to tell her anything. She'd expected any chance of discovering more about what happened would rely on her searching for the information. But this, the tone of Hans' voice, the clothes... maybe he was ready to tell her more. Maybe.

Mila followed Hans back to the house. The walk felt much longer than usual while they walked at Hans' pace, and Mila couldn't help but look around at the surroundings, ready for some trap to be sprung. They made it to the kitchen door, no surprises. Nothing more unexpected than her father wanting to have a nice dinner.

The surprise her father's formals had given her paled compared to that which she felt when she saw the kitchen table. Atop a linen tablecloth Mila had never seen sat a feast. There was a half roast three-tusk boar, buttered potatoes, and seasoned squash. There was a pitcher of golden mead almost overflowing. On the kitchen counter sat bowls of fresh fruits, chocolates, and nuts. None of the food was commonly found on Vidar. All of it was more than they could afford.

"What... How did you—," Mila started to ask.

"It seems my fortunes may be changing," Hans replied with an awkward grin.

"Enough to afford... *this*?"

"That and much more," Hans replied.

"How did you possibly manage that?" Mila asked, her critical eyes fixed on her father.

"A long-overdue pension from the Navy."

There it was again, that strange beat in his words. Nerves perhaps? No, he wasn't telling her something. Or worse, he was lying. But she couldn't fathom what he'd have to lie about. Unless...

"Are we losing the farm?" Mila asked, her voice direct, unyielding.

"What?" Hans asked. A look of genuine surprise stretched across his face. "No, why in Thor's name would you think that?"

"This, all of this," Mila said, gesturing first to his clothes and then to the food. "Something's off."

"No, I promise, everything's fine, Mila. Just know I've made a lucrative deal that will make both our lives much better."

As Mila was about to challenge further, Hans interrupted.

"Wait, before you say anything else, I've got one final surprise."

Hans hurried out of the kitchen. He was gone for about five minutes. In that time, Mila couldn't help but pluck up one of the chocolates and plop it into her mouth. Well, maybe it was more than one. No matter her father's angle, the food was there and shouldn't go to waste.

When Hans returned, he held one of the most beautiful garments that Mila had ever seen. It was a dress, dazzling white trimmed with green and a sash of flowing gold. She'd seen it before, over a decade ago.

"Mother's?" Mila asked, taking a hesitant step forward.

Hans nodded. "The last thing I have of her. You look just like her, you know? Well, except for that dark hair of yours."

Mila suddenly remembered the burning question raised by their last argument. "What happened to her?"

Hans' smile flickered as he paused, as if trying to see if silence would make the question go away. When Mila's gaze didn't let up, he said, "After dinner. Let's just have a nice meal together, then I'll tell you about your mother."

Mila thought about arguing, pressing her father for the details. But she also remembered this was their last night together. After dinner, she was still putting the battery in the hoverbike. After dinner, she was still leaving the farm for good.

FOUR

M ILA STOOD in her barren bedroom, taking in the sight of herself in her mother's dress. She was used to her coveralls, to smudges of grease on her night-pale cheeks. But now she was washed, and the dress was as clean as spotless. She'd never given much thought to her appearance. She didn't see the purpose, and she was nothing if not practical. Despite this, she couldn't deny she liked how she looked in her mother's dress. And why shouldn't she? She was gleaming. And the slim metal case she'd strapped to her thigh with an old belt wasn't even a little noticeable. She didn't want to risk leaving the arc battery unattended, even for a second.

When Mila emerged from the room, she found Hans readying their mead horns. He stopped mid-pour when he saw her and gaped.

"Does it look all right?" Mila asked hesitantly. She could swear tears were forming in the old man's eyes.

Hans looked away, wiping his eyes as he said, "Yes, beautiful."

They are tears. Mila had seen her father cry before, but it was always when he was impossibly drunk—when all his woes came out of their dark crevices. She'd never seen him cry like this. It seemed his tears flowed with joy, or memory, perhaps? But then Mila noticed another pause that was just too long. Too out of place. It was the length of time it took him to look back at her. It was the way his soft threat of a tear trod dangerously close to a sob. There was something else in it.

Regret.

"What is it, father?"

Hans finally turned back to her, rubbing his red eyes on his royal blue sleeve. "Nothing, you just look so splendid."

"No," Mila said, her tone growing sharper. "There's something else. What aren't you telling me?"

"Mi, I promise," Hans began, but Mila quickly cut him off.

"Stop it! We've barely spoken to each other these past years. We've struggled on a cent. And now, what? You suddenly get a few marks in your account, and you make a grand peace treaty? All of it's washed away?"

Hans tried to cut in, but Mila didn't hesitate.

"Is it about mom? Is she alive?"

"No... I don't know. It's not about that."

"Then what is it about?!"

The house went deadly silent. Mila could feel the blood pulsing through the veins in her neck. She was through with this display—through with her father's false gesture. Every inch of her was stiff, serious, demanding answers. Hans was over twenty years her senior, but right now, he looked like a scorned puppy.

Mila was about to press him more when she heard it. Distant at first, but approaching very fast. It was a loud, unbreaking hum. Unmistakable. Hover thrusters.

What is a hovership doing all the way out here? There

were few hoverships on Vidar. Unlike Idun, where most people's vehicles ran on advanced magnetic hover propulsion, hoverships were reserved for only the wealthiest in Vidarin society, most of them politicians or retired flag officers. Well, the wealthy, and the military. There was no denying the effectiveness of a hover-thruster dropship, able to take off like a helicopter and quickly shift into void-traversing speeds. Mila couldn't fathom why one would have made its way this far into the rural lands. That is, until she noticed her father.

Hans' face was ordinarily pale. But, at this moment, it was white as bone—bloodless.

"What is it?" Mila asked, her eyes narrow.

Hans shook his head, refusing to speak.

"Why is there a hovership headed for our house, Father?" Mila's fingers curled into fists. The hover thrusters were close enough now she could make out the subtle pulsations in their humming.

Hans dropped into one of the kitchen chairs, the weight of whatever he was hiding clearly pushing him down. He grabbed his mead horn with a trembling hand and gulped deeply.

A chill made its way up Mila's spine as she realized her anger was quickly shifting into fear. "Odin's bane, Father. Why are they here?!"

Mila suddenly felt trapped. She hadn't the slightest idea why the hovership was there, but her father was not hard to read. Whatever the vessel's reason, it was not going to go well for one of them.

Mila considered running, trying to make it to the hoverbike. But, if they were after her, the bike would be no match for the ship. Even if the battery brought it to life instantly, she'd be caught in a matter of minutes.

The humming of the thrusters was blocking out every other sound now. She could feel the house shake in rhythm with the pulses. Dishes rattled on the table and counters. Mead splashed over the rims of their cups. A glass bowl full of salt danced its way to the edge of the table. Mila tried to reach out and save it, but her arms felt weak, nonresponsive. It was time to wake up from this nightmare.

"I'm sorry," Hans said just loud enough for Mila to hear.

She looked at her father, and her heart turned inside out. Tears were streaming down the man's face. The glass bowl teetered over the edge.

"I'm so sorry."

The bowl shattered on the kitchen floor just as the sound from the hovership died, and the world was thrust back into that dangerous silence.

THERE WERE seven of them in total. Six wore armored suits uniquely carved with Nordic runes, save the rune of Mjolnir stamped in gold on the breastplates. The helmets were designed in the old Viking style but covered their entire heads. Mila knew they were likely equipped inside with holo-displays and the suits with minor life support systems. All of the armor was painted the black and crimson of Volkner's regime.

She could identify the leader immediately for the fact he was not wearing combat armor. Instead, he wore a service uniform of fine black cotton. With the gold and red trim and the silver bars on his collar, it was clear he was an officer. He wore his hair long on top, slicked back into a tight knot, and shaved close on the sides, displaying runic tattoos that mostly represented Thor.

Mila couldn't wrap her head around why a military detail would travel all the way out here, nor did she understand why her father had stood and saluted the officer when he entered their house. As one of the bearded guards set up what appeared to be the base for a large holoscreen, the officer turned his attention to Mila.

"Are you Mila Messer?" he asked with nothing but directness in his voice.

Mila instinctively took a step back. "Yes," she questioned.

The officer took out a holotablet and began to read. "Mila Messer, you are hereby enlisted into the service of the Vidarin government. Your official occupation henceforth is Master Refiner. You will receive all appropriate hospitalities and compensation for your service. Full details of your new appointment will be provided once you arrive to your assigned duty station, the *VOS Gjaller*. Your president and your people thank you for your commitment to Vidar."

"Father," Mila said, taking another step back. "What is he talking about?"

Hans looked as though he were about to reply but was interrupted as the holoscreen flashed to life. Hans quickly took a knee and bowed his head, as did the soldiers. Mila was the only one left standing. On it, Mila saw the larger-than-life depiction of the president himself, Volkner Brandt.

He looked just like he did in the propaganda images that often interrupted Hans' shows on the house's holoscreen. Groomed silver-white hair and a black beard beneath sharp cheekbones. His cedar eyes were flecked with bits of gold, a known trait of Brandt's lineage.

The president was so still Mila wasn't sure if it was a video feed or a static image. Then, those shimmering eyes moved. His eyes slowly made their way around the Messers' kitchen. He took in each detail, as observant as Heimdall the All-Seer. He seemed to look at everything except Mila. Finally, after he'd seen enough, he focused on Hans.

"Nice home, Corporal," he said. Even through the minor static of the holoscreen speakers, his voice was powerful, like a blacksmith's hammer on steel, but as refined as a carefully honed edge.

"Thank you, my Vini," Hans replied, head still bowed.

"It feels like a millennium since we've talked. Get up, please. And drop the Vinis, and Yfirs, and sirs. No need for that kind of formality between old friends."

Old friends? Father knows the president?

Hans rose, his eyes fixed on the image of President Brandt.

"You look well," Brandt continued. "I see your wife has been keeping you fed."

"Actually, it's just me and my daughter."

"I see," Brandt replied. His gold-laced eyes flicked to Mila. Though he wore a soft smile, Mila felt like nothing more than a piece of fresh roast lamb. "So, this is our new Master Refiner?"

"Father, what did you—" Mila began, but Hans cut her off.

"Yes, this is her," he said, speaking as fast as a running hare. "We've been working on honing her skills for near a decade. She's a speedy learner."

"Interesting," Brandt replied, his eyes still fixed on Mila.

Mila instinctively took another step back. It was abundantly clear now who was being taken. *The hoverbike, the shed. A couple hundred yards, and maybe I can manage an escape.*

"Stop," the president commanded, his tone cool yet fierce.

The armored men went on alert, their plasma carbines half-raised. Mila didn't dare budge another inch. Hans seemed to go rigid too. Mila could see the muscles in his jaw flex as he clenched his teeth together.

"You're not trying to back away from your president, are you, young one?" Brandt said coolly. "Without dismissal, that's considered a capital offense."

"She wouldn't try that," Hans said, raising his hands defensively. "She's just nervous, is all."

"I hope that's true, Corporal," Brandt replied. Pins prickled the back of Mila's neck as the president spoke. "Even though we are old comrades, I need you to know, if I found out you've lied to me, that your girl is not a brandr refiner, I will have to send her to the brandr mines as payment. That's after I've seized your farm and had you publicly sacrificed. Is that clear?"

Hans shuddered. "Yes, my Vini."

The edge in Brandt's voice dissipated as he said, "Good. Now, enough with the pleasantries. We will meet soon enough, young Mila."

The holoscreen blinked out of existence, and the officer stepped forward.

"Miss Messer, if you will please come with us," he said, waving her to him.

Mila didn't move. She looked at her father, "Father?" her voice was too soft—too close to breaking. The single word was the unspoken question. *Are you going to let them take me?*

Hans looked back at her but could only keep her gaze for a moment before dropping his head. There was no question in it now; Mila was going, and there wasn't a thing her father was going to do to stop it.

The officer advanced, shackles in hand. Mila ground

her teeth. No one but the occasional neighbor and taxman came to their home; it'd been that way since Mila could remember. Now, when they show up, they're soldiers armed to the teeth prepared to take her away in chains? Mila closed her eyes for a time-stop moment.

No.

The thought of going to the *Gjaller,* acting like she could refine brandr only to fail and be sentenced to life in the mines... No, that wasn't happening.

The chill Brandt had left down her spine began to tingle and bud into warmth. It wasn't courage or calm or control. No, what Mila Messer felt starting to course through her veins was rage. Rage at her father. She would not be his golden goose.

The officer was upon her now. "Miss Messer, it's time to go."

She looked up at him, and the rage peaked. There was no strategy in what happened next. She was not thinking about the next step, the hoverbike, or the consequences. In fact, she was not thinking at all. What she felt was instinct, primal and raw. Surviving was the only goal now, and once she was on that ship, there would be no escape.

She aimed for the officer's nose with her fist, feeling all that unnatural warmth pour into her arm. The strength of it was overwhelming; she'd never felt so much power. Her knuckles flew toward him but, before they found their mark, she felt a shock like the lightning of Thor rampage against the energy flowing into her arm. It was the elerex, protesting at the most inopportune moment. The shock was more intense than any she'd felt before, and it was the last thing she remembered before the world went black.

CHAPTER
FIVE

WHEN SHE WOKE, the ceiling above Mila wasn't the cracked plaster of their kitchen. Instead, it was metal scratched from years of scrubbing with steel pads, lit by too-white light. The floor beneath her was metal as well—cold and ungiving. She sat up and found she was in the back of what she expected was the hovership. Her mother's dress was stained and ripped in places, and there was a light but precise scabbing scratch on her right forearm. Two of the Viking-armored soldiers sat in the seats lining either side of the small room.

"Where are we going?" she asked.

One didn't budge, while the other looked down at her but did not speak. Instead, he grunted and pounded a gauntlet against the forward bulkhead. A moment later, the doors leading to what she assumed was the cockpit hissed open. The officer who'd demanded her come with them walked through, his hands behind his back.

Mila tensed and pushed herself away from him until her back was against the rear cargo door. The officer shook his head.

"Trying to run off again?" he said. "I assure you it will go even more poorly than your first attempt, Miss Messer." His tone was polite, but Mila felt the venom in the words. "You've been sleeping for quite a while. Enough time for me to fully update your citizen chip with your new credentials... and your correct name."

"My correct name?"

The officer nodded. "That's right. Looks like your dear old dad tried to mask your digital profile. Did you know that's an offense against Brandt's law?"

Mila didn't answer. Of course she knew that tampering with chip credentials was illegal. In fact, it was one of the most serious offenses a Vidarin could commit, just under lying to the president himself. She looked at her wrist where her citizen chip had been embedded like all Vidarin citizens. Mila didn't know why Hans had tried to alter the contents of the chip, nor why he would lie and say she was even remotely capable of refining brandr, but the thought that the chip would now read she was in the employ of the government sent her stomach twisting.

"Where are you taking me?" she asked, trying to ignore the lump in her throat.

"We're en route to the *VOS Gjaller*, on schedule to dock in less than ten minutes."

The *Gjaller*. The Eye of Vidar. The planet's notoriously expensive ODIN command station. Mila didn't know much about starships and battle stations, but it was said when the station was constructed decades before, it had been the only thing that kept Vidar safe from Jotun invaders. A station with the firepower and defense capabilities of a half-dozen capital ships. A fortress.

The officer stepped closer and reached out a hand. "Apologies if I have been rude. You are President Brandt's

most coveted guest; I suppose we should treat you as such."
He flashed a viper's grin. "I am Lieutenant Sauer."

Mila refused the hand but got to her feet. "I'm sure he'll
be thrilled to know how you managed to get me on this ship,
then."

The Lieutenant's smile didn't fade. "We were simply
following our orders to bring you to the president. I carry
out my orders by whatever means necessary."

"And what if you'd killed me?"

Sauer looked Mila up and down. It made her flesh
crawl.

"That would have been a shame." He leaned in too-near
her ear and whispered, "Would have been a pretty corpse,
though."

Mila would have given anything then for the cargo door
behind her to fall open and let the void take her. That was
the preferable alternative to spending any more time with
the officer.

"You best take a seat," he continued, pulling away.
"We'll be docking soon, and it can be a bit bumpy."

The doors hissed again as Sauer took his leave back to
the cockpit with the other armored soldiers. In the brief
second the doors were open, Mila could see out of the front
visor. In the distance, she saw it. There was no mistaking
the sheer size or the vast array of cannon and turret systems
she could already make out. The VOS Gjaller. Five stacked
circular levels, all connected by a single shaft. The smallest
circles were the polar points, about the size of twenty
Messer houses. The middle rings, the largest by far, were
staggering. Mila estimated it nearly a mile in diameter,
perhaps more. There was no denying the imposing presence
of such a craft.

Mila now understood precisely why the Jotuns had

thought twice about their invasion after the *Gjaller's*
construction. It was a floating fortress, in every sense of the
word. The perfect defensive installation. In addition to the
outrageous armament, Mila also saw the tiny sheer flickering in the empty space around the station. She knew the
phenomenon well. It was the aura the shield battery on her
shop emitted, albeit on a much larger scale.

Yes, this was it. The *Gjaller*—the Eye of Vidar and a
symbol of Volkner's power. It was also the last place she'd
see in the light before her life of darkness in the brandr
mines.

◇—•————————•—◇

THE LIEUTENANT HADN'T LIED about the landing. Once
the hovership was in the *Gjaller's* docking beam being
pulled toward the latches, it felt like Odin himself decided
to use the craft as a rattle. With a final stomach-lurching
drop, the ship was docked with a sharp clang.

"On your feet," one of the armored soldiers
commanded.

Mila obeyed. What else could she do now?

She heard a hiss again and could smell the heating
hydraulic fluid as the cargo door began to drop. She recognized that smell from her countless tinkerings with old
equipment from the pit at the farm. It reminded her of both
the shop and the shack, particularly of the hoverbikes
braking manifold.

The hoverbike. The thought of how close she'd been struck
Mila like an axe in the gut. If only she'd fixed it sooner. She
could have been halfway across Vidar, working on other hoverbikes and jet trucks to live and finding out what other things

the world had to offer beyond her father's farm. She now faced a life of misery and forced labor—a gift given so graciously by her own father. If only she'd got that damn battery working.

The battery. The arc battery. She could feel it, still strapped to her leg under her now-filthy dress. They hadn't frisked her in her unconscious state, apparently. Whether out of respect or the belief that a young girl wouldn't have something of note on her, she didn't know. Either way, they were foolish to not have checked.

The cargo door finished its descent to reveal another soldier standing on the *Gjaller's* deck. He seemed to be waiting for them. However, unlike the others, he was not posed in any military stance Mila recognized. No, in fact, he was leaning on a metal crate, looking so bored he literally yawned.

He was... curious. His uniform was like Lieutenant Sauer's, except he wore it much more casually. The collar was loose, and his sleeves were tightly rolled to just below his biceps. These revealed arms laced with lean muscle, one of which was etched with words in a language Mila did not recognize, though the symbols in it were similar to Neunorse runes. The same language emerged from his collar, traveling up the shaven side of his head. His hair on top was shaggy and unkempt, as if he didn't have time to bother with it, and his beard was kept short—little more than stubble.

"Go on," one of the soldiers ordered, pushing Mila roughly forward. She caught her foot on the lip of the cargo door and fell forward, splitting her chin on the brushed metal. "Get up," the same soldier barked.

"Stand down, Sergeant," the man at the crate said.

He didn't yell, or even raise his voice. In fact, he'd said it barely loud enough for Mila to hear. Yet, it was strewn with confidence.

"Yes, yes, sir," the soldier replied.

Was that a stutter?

"Help our guest up and apologize," the mysterious officer continued.

Mila felt the guards' hands curl around her arms with almost motherlike care. "Please, forgive me," the one who'd shoved her said.

The officer had doused these men with fear, and he hadn't even looked up. That wasn't just confidence. No, it was dominance.

The cockpit door opened behind Mila and the guards. "Ah, Schafer, come to welcome me back," Sauer said, walking past Mila and down the cargo door.

"I've been put on personal escort duty," the man called Schafer replied.

"Have you now. And for whom, may I ask?

"Her."

Sauer looked back at Mila and scowled before turning back to Schafer. "You must be mistaken. I received the same assignment from Capta—"

"I received the orders from Brandt himself," Schafer interrupted. "So, you can save it. If by some gods-damned miracle she can actually refine brandr, then she's a high-value asset. Protection details like that go to experienced fighters, not raven starvers."

Sauer practically growled. "This... this is ridiculous. I'll speak with President Brandt myself."

"Then do it," Schafer said, finally stepping away from the crate. "Let's see how he likes you questioning his orders. He hasn't sentenced anyone to a good blood sacrifice in a few months. Maybe he'll think it's time to change that."

Sauer looked at Mila again, still scowling, but then that wicked smile returned. "You know what, it's fine. I have more important tasks to see to than babysitting duty anyway."

Sauer signaled his men and left Mila alone in the hangar bay with Schafer. Seeing him up close, she noticed a slight glimmer in his pale blue eyes. If she didn't know better, she'd swear it was tiny pixels flashing.

"Well, come on then," he said, gesturing at her to follow.

As he turned, she noticed the glint of two strips of metal interrupting the tattooed flesh on the side of his head. It was something under the skin, part of his skull—evidence of repair to some past trauma, perhaps.

When he walked, it was not straight and proper like Sauer. No, his gait was that of a predator. He held his head forward but was not slouching. The way his shoulders shifted under his shirt reminded her of a wolf stalking prey. He seemed ready to strike or parry at any given moment. Mila imagined he knew how to draw and fell a man with the archaic hatchet on his hip in a single breath.

They left the hovership's private docking hangar and entered another bay infinitely larger. Mila could barely see the other side of it. It was bustling with hundreds of people making their way back and forth. Forty-foot supply containers were being pulled in with high-torque hover-carts. Armored soldiers were patrolling in droves, some doing random checks on passing merchants. Officers and other military in non-armor uniforms held holotablets, checking in various civilians and ordering cargo inspections. The civilians were primarily traders, but their garb ranged from simple Vidarin working wear to the silken robes worn by wealthy Tyrans and the thick furs of Jotuns. Not a single

person was still. Everyone looked like they had somewhere
to be.

"Hurry up," Schafer called.

Mila was suddenly aware she was not walking at the
soldier's pace. She'd fallen into awe of the sheer activity of
the cargo deck. She'd simply never seen so many people in
one place. The most she could remember was a town hall
gathering her father had taken her to shortly after her
mother had left, and that was only a few dozen people.

She hurried to catch up to him and didn't let herself fall
back again. They came to the central shaft in the massive
circular room. When she'd glimpsed the *Gjaller* through the
hovership visor, the station rings dwarfed this main connec-
tor. But now, looking at it as they approached, it was
hundreds of yards in diameter itself.

There were dozens of personnel and cargo lifts built
into it. Mila's mechanical intuition told her its core housed
the power highway for the ship, transporting energy from
the reactors to the various rings. It likely carried breathable
air and other life support elements as well. It was the
vascular system of the colossal station.

Most of the lifts allowed traffic to move freely. However,
the lift door Schafer led Mila to was flanked by two guards
in the carved Viking armor. As they approached the pair,
they snapped to attention and saluted with a fist over their
hearts.

"Command Hall," Schafer said, lazily returning the
salute.

One of the guards punched a code into a keypad beside
the lift and took out a digital device that looked nearly iden-
tical to a long iron key. They were alone in the lift before
long.

Standing behind him, Mila noticed, for the first time,

the scent of Schafer. He was like her workshop—midnight air and rusted metal. He stood like stone, so statuesque that Mila questioned if he was even breathing. She felt the lift jump, and they were off.

"Private lift?" Mila asked. There was a nauseous knot forming in her stomach as she remembered who exactly she was about to meet. Nervous. She'd never been nervous before, not that she could remember anyway. When every day is a repeat of its predecessor on a farm that never changes, why would you be nervous? Now, everything was unknown, unsure. So, she was nervous. Apparently, she talked when she was nervous.

Schafer didn't reply.

That made the knot tighten a little more. In the hangar, when he'd corrected the soldier, she thought there was the slightest chance this man would be her first ally on the *Gjaller*. Now, she feared he'd be even more hateful than Lieutenant Sauer.

She looked down at her mother's dress, remembering how filthy it was from the manhandling. "Is there some way I could change before we see the president?"

Schafer stayed the statue.

"I mean, I'm kind of dirty," she continued, hoping to evoke some response.

Still nothing.

"Odin's bane, you're a stoic one."

"And you talk a lot for someone facing a life in the brandr mines."

Mila felt her face go numb and cold as her blood drained. "What are you talking about?"

Schafer didn't bother turning toward her. "You're about to meet a host of powerful people that mostly believe you're a *master brandr refiner*. I say mostly because I know at least two people who don't think you'll successfully process an ounce of the stuff. In fact, it will probably kill you."

Mila shook her head. *Dammit, Father. What were you thinking? Drunken fool.* "You're obviously one of the non-believers. Who's the other?"

"President Brandt." The words that rolled off his tongue were hot coals against her ears.

"You're not serious," Mila said.

"Why wouldn't I be?"

"Why would he bother bringing me up here?"

"I expect you'll be able to answer that yourself soon enough."

The lift started to slow. Even with its no-doubt electro-magnetic braking system, it still managed to jolt violently right at the end. The shock nearly took Mila off her feet.

When the doors opened, there was not a massive open space like in the cargo hold. Instead, a large hallway stretched out before them. It was lined with closed door-ways on either side which opened every now and then to let pedestrians through. As they walked down the passage, Mila noticed three types of people.

The first type was soldiers, almost every one as old or older than Mila's father, and nearly all officers. There were some inspecting holotablets as they walked and some walking unhindered and with purpose. Very few walked in pairs or groups; they all seemed to have somewhere else to be. Mila knew very little about military customs and rank-ing, but she was not entirely ignorant. She knew a lieu-tenant, like Schafer, was one of the lower-ranked officers. She also knew traditionally subordinates saluted their seniors, and she saw soldiers exchanging the gesture even now. That made it curious that Schafer didn't salute a single one. More than that, they didn't seem to mind. In fact, it was almost as if they did anything they could to avoid looking at the young officer.

The second type of people were civilians. They wore various kinds of semi-formal wear, mostly decorated with colorful aiguillettes, medals, or pins. Mila guessed these were politicians. Most of the clothing beneath the bobbles were suits striped with the crimson and gold of President Brandt's regime. These were likely council members or advisors, and many of them stole glances at Mila, Volkner's new prize refiner. The few who wore other colors, such as the pale blue and white of Jotun, or the red and burnt orange of Tyr, were likely ambassadors. The foreign politicians were not shy about looking at Schafer. She saw pairs of them whisper to each other, and others even pointed. Schafer didn't seem to take notice. He just walked on, looking for all the world like a wolf on the hunt.

The third type of person was drastically different from the first two. They were men and women who wore flowing silks of that same gold and crimson. Most of their skin was tan; not so tan as that of the Tyran traders and politicians, but much darker than any Vidarin. Their clothing was not modest. The men's tops were little more than open vests, revealing the flesh of their chest and abdomens. The women's silks were draped in a triangle around their chest, just enough to cover their breasts. Every single one of the people dressed this way bore a tattoo on the left side of their neck. It was the rune Othala, which could mean noble or wealthy. However, it had a different meaning as well. Property. No, this third type of person was nothing like the first two.

Many other hallways intersected the one that they tread, but Schafer never turned. The metal panels of the walls were showing their age, with rust creeping around their edges. Many odes to the Neunorse religion were carved in the steel as well. Most were runes and symbols of the Storm God, Thor. There was no rust on the carvings. In fact, they showed signs of regular scrubbings and polishing. They passed a few of the servants with the Othala tattoos on ladders tending to the runes of Thor.

The farther they walked, the faster Mila's blood pulsed. Every step was a step closer to Volkner Brandt. Every step a step closer to the brandr mines.

Schafer finally stopped when the passage ended at two massive titanium doors with four Viking-clad guards posted. These guards bore armor different from the others, coated in gold broken only by thin accents of crimson and silk shoulder capes. Their helmets were like the others, except they had curved horns jutting from the sides. Mila saw they each had plasma repeating pistols strapped to their thighs, but those did not seem to be their weapons of choice. No, that job seemed to go to the spears they wielded. They resembled the weapons of the ancient Vikings from the old Earth that Mila had learned about from holobooks found in the pit. But Mila's keen eye for mechanics noted the slight breaks and indentations that suggested they had some kind of power core which likely fueled a superheated plasma edge around the blade.

"Lieutenant," one said as Schafer approached.

"Major," Schafer replied, this time saluting with his fist over his heart. He didn't remove it until the guard returned the gesture.

"This the one?"

"Yep, this is the latest *refiner*."

The major turned to Mila. Like Schafer, he stood over a head taller than her and was made even more imposing by that golden armor and the fact she couldn't see his face. She had no idea what his eyes were doing behind the tinted visors.

"A bit young, isn't she?"

Schafer grunted in agreeance.

Mila tried her hardest to keep her face straight, unconcerned. But she knew she was failing.

The Major looked at his wrist where a holopad appeared from hidden projectors. He typed a quick code, and his helmet face shifted apart, revealing his gray-bearded grin beneath. Mila was surprised to find his smile warm and his hazel eyes kind.

"Worry not, young one," he said. "They may doubt your abilities, but you've got to prove them wrong, eh?"

Mila was shocked. This man was rooting for her?

"Yes, sir," she replied.

"Call me Adel," he said, offering his hand. Mila accepted, and Adel added, "But only when the president isn't around, okay?"

Mila nodded. "I'm Mila. Mila Messer."

"Well, Mila Messer, allow me to welcome you to the *Gjaller*. You shouldn't have much trouble here, what with a berserker as a personal guard."

Berserker? She'd heard of them, fabled warriors who were more machine than man. *But they're all dead, aren't they?*

"And if he gives you trouble, you just let me know," Adel finished with a wink.

"As if you'd land a single blow, old man," Schafer said.

"You still think your speed and strength are a match for my experience?"

"I think I'd fell you in a single movement."

There was nothing serious in their tones. It was more like a father talking to a son.

"You'd try," Adel said as he punched in another code to his wrist, and the helmet face snapped back shut. "But that is a challenge for another day. Best not to keep our president waiting."

Adel fell back in line with the other guards and nodded to the one closest to the door. The guard turned to a holopad and began typing a code just as Adel had on his armored wrist. For the first time, Mila was aware of the door itself and just how big it was; nearly twice as tall and wide as any other she'd seen on the ship. It wasn't rectangular like the others, either. It was a pointed arch, like in ancient earthen buildings, built ornamentally. On the doors themselves was inlaid another carving, though not runes this time. No, this was a work of superior artistry.

It was a battle scene, and Mila recognized it as the duel between Thor and Hrungnir. She knew Thor by his flowing cape, braided beard, and the hammer Mjolnir raised above his head, calling down lightning from the heavens. Hrungnir she recognized by the giant's stone armor and the whetstone he wielded against the Storm God. It was a masterpiece through and through.

As the guard finished typing the code, every drop of fascination with the art on the door evaporated. Instead, she felt someone had tied a rope around her stomach and twisted it tighter and tighter until she was on the verge of vomiting. The doors opened, and the cruel invisible rope-handler cinched what remained of Mila's hope from her.

CHAPTER
SIX

MILA'S FATHER had never spoken well of Volkner Brandt. Deceitful, war hungry, fanatical, and cruel were but a few of the countless ways Hans had described him throughout the years. He'd preached to her that Brandt was president in title only, but dictator was more accurate. He'd also said the man fancied himself a king. Mila never knew why Volkner irritated her father so much, nor did she even know how much of his rantings she could believe. Now, looking in this room, it seemed that bit about the king rang true.

The "Command Room" was the finest room Mila had seen in her entire life. The middle was pronounced with a gold-trimmed crimson rug that was well over fifty yards long. It was flanked by titanium-plated pillars emitting artificial flame, though their heat was very real. It ended at stairs leading up to an ornate metal commander's chair motorized so its occupant could swivel from the massive viewing window spanning the far wall and back to the carpet with ease. There were chairs in a straight line on either side of the commander's chair, though they were all lower. The commander's chair was carved with only one rune, Thurisaz. It was the rune of action, the rune of power, of potency and strength. It was the rune of Thor. Despite what the politicians may say, this was no chair. Nor was this simply a command room. No, it was a throne, and this was the great hall of Volkner's palace—a throne room. And the king himself was sitting high, looking down on Mila and Schafer as they approached with golden-flecked eyes.

Each of the chairs around the throne was filled with political types or the highest-ranking military advisors. One seated Mila recognized as Volkner's Gothi, a priest of the Neunorse religion. He was a stocky man with a white, pointed beard and robes that fit too tightly around his midsection. She'd heard the Gothi's voice on the radio in propaganda ads plenty of times, spouting zealous calls to join the Volkner regime in its quest to please the gods.

Every one of the men seated in the room was Vidarin... except one. There sat a single man in pale blue lined with gray, complete with a shoulder cape of stark white fur. Expensive clothes, no doubt, but in no way military. A politician, then. He was well older than Mila, but still much younger than the president. His snow-white skin and silver-blonde hair, along with his garb, told Mila he was from Jotun.

Every eye was fixed to Mila. Every politician and military man were sizing up the young rural Vidarin. A few whispered to one another in tones too soft for Mila to make out, though their conspicuous pointing and skeptical squinting made the subject of their conversations evident. But none looked more fiercely at her than Brandt himself.

As they reached the last fire pillar, the whispering ceased, and only the soft beeps of the command room equipment were audible. Mila stopped, only a few feet separating her and the stairs that led to Volkner's throne. She had to crane her neck to look up at him.

Schafer smacked his bootheels together and presented his fist over his heart. The politicians and military leaders rose and returned the gesture. The president did not acknowledge the salute. It didn't even seem like he knew or cared that the Berserker was standing beside her. Mila was the only thing in this room that Volkner Brandt cared about in this moment.

"Welcome," Volkner said, rising from the commander's chair.

Everyone, including the soldiers going about their duties, went silent. Volkner was grinning, but Mila found no comfort in the lupine smile. He descended the stairs, his bootsteps echoing through the room. He was wearing a fine military coat — black, trimmed with the crimson and gold of his regime. It was unbuttoned to reveal expensive strapped leathers and at least two armed holsters. An ornate runed hatchet swung from his belt, in easy reach of his right hand. When he reached the carpet, Mila realized the man stood almost as tall as Schafer, and she could see the knotted muscles in his neck, the small scar of some recent wound the only blemish on the skin. Those gold-flecked eyes seemed to glow as he peered down at her.

"Mila Messer, daughter of the *fabled* Hans Messer." Mila didn't know the president or his tones, but she could swear he was being sarcastic. When a few of the generals chuckled under their breath, her suspicion was confirmed.

Before Mila could react, Volkner grabbed her hand with almost inhuman speed, and then slowly rose it to his lips. "And our savior," he continued, raising her hand in the air, and spinning around to the other politicians, presenting her like a champion fighter. "The last *master brandr refiner* in the system." More sarcasm.

Some of the politicians caught his tone and smiled, carefully laughing softly. Others, mostly generals, either grunted or gave the briefest clap. Only one stayed completely silent. It was the Jotun ambassador. He neither applauded nor chuckled, rather he kept his eyes on Mila, examining her.

"More like the newest brandr *miner*," a younger politician sitting on the outer edge of a row said.

Everyone went deadly silent again. Volkner sighed and stretched out his neck. "What was that Mister Fischer?"

Mila could feel everyone else in the room go stiff.

The one called Fischer stood. "Sir, I doubt she'll refine an ounce of brandr."

Volkner's attention was now wholly on Fischer, as he approached him with the calmest gait. "And why would you say something so rude?" The words were as calm as his motion. Too calm.

Fischer seemed to recognize it too as he took a step back. "I didn't, my Vini... that's not..."

It happened so fast Mila could hardly register it. In one graceful yet brutal movement, Volkner drew the hatchet from his belt and cleaved open Fischer's throat. Crimson sprayed the president's face, and the only other sounds were Mila's gasp and Fischer choking on his own blood. It was only a few seconds before the horrible gurgling stopped, but to Mila it was an unbearable eternity.

"Shame," Volker said, wiping the blade on a clean patch of Fischer's clothes. "He had ambition."

Volkner turned around and Mila saw his face splattered with wet red. With his gold-flecked eyes and golden halo, he was truly the embodiment of his own regime.

"But he questioned my judgement," he said, shrugging.

Mila wanted to turn and run; to get as far away from Fischer's body as possible. To get off this horrible space station and away from these vicious men. But she knew she wouldn't even make it to the door before being hit with a stunner.

"However, I can't deny that I, too, question your abilities, Miss Messer. A girl barely old enough to wed and a master of brandr refining? You're either a prodigy or the victim of your father's drunken foolishness. I'd bet my right eye it's the latter, knowing him."

Mila's fear started thawing into anger. Her father was a drunken fool, but hearing him insulted so blatantly... That same hot rage that filled her in their kitchen started flowing up her spine.

"Everything he promised you is true," she said, barely realizing she was speaking.

Volkner huffed a laugh. "Is that so? Well, we'll find out in the morning, won't we?"

"We will," Mila echoed. Her words had an edge she'd never used, not even with her father. It was a confidence she knew she had no right bearing. *What am I doing?*

Volkner ascended the steps to his command chair and sat. "You'll be given control of the refinery tonight. We'll provide a barrel of crude brandr which I expect to yield at least twelve gallons of hyrrine. You'll be monitored by Lieutenant Schafer and his detail throughout the night, so you don't try anything stupid."

"Excuse me," a voice said in an accent that was refined, yet subtly foreign. It was the Jotun ambassador who'd risen from his seat to address the president.

Volkner's eyes went wide in disbelief that someone was so blatantly interrupting him. Most of the others in the room went stiff again, and Mila felt her stomach trying to lurch. But when Volkner looked down at the foreigner, he seemed to release the bloodlust that had filled him.

"Yes, Mister Úlfljótur?" Volkner asked with trained patience and respect. Mila had yet to hear him take this tone with anyone.

"Perhaps the young lady should not be supervised. She is not military, and soldiers make civilians nervous. And you can't expect a master refiner to expose the secrets to their technique, can you?"

Volkner's expression was thoughtful, calm. But Mila saw his nails starting to rake against the arm of his chair. "A fantastic idea," he finally said. "The guards will post outside the door and Miss Messer will have free reign of the refinery. We expect no less than a dozen gallons of hyrrine in the morning. If we do not receive that, the lands of Hans Messer will be forfeit to the government, Miss Messer will be sent to a brandr mine, and Hans Messer will be sentenced to death. Understood?" His eyes were set on Mila as he finished.

Mila wanted to scream—to curse the bastard in front of her. He said such horrible things as if they were everyday occurrences. To sentence a man to death and his daughter to a life of forced labor, these were things that should weigh on a president's conscience. But then, Mila saw clearer than ever that Brandt was no president. No, he was a tyrant—a tyrant that fancied himself a king.

Her only reply was a nod.

———◇———◇———

THE WALK back down the *Gjaller's* command deck passageway was long and wordless. In less than five minutes, Mila had met the most powerful men in all Vidar, seen the most powerful of them kill another, and been threatened by the same. She still felt shellshocked by the whole encounter.

When they were descending in the lift, Mila stared at the holoscreen above the door, watching the names of the various levels go by with a chime for each.

Fyrsty, Command Deck.

Annar, Executive Lodging.

Thrir, Defense Operations.

Mila read them all, but just barely registered it. Her mind was caught on President Volkner and the young politician. Fischer, she'd never spoken to, but Mila felt she'd never forget that name. Nor would she forget the image of him grasping his hemorrhaging throat, unable to beg for his fleeting life as the blood clogged his throat.

"Can you do it?" Schafer asked, his voice level.

Mila was caught off-guard by the sudden break in the monotonous beeping. "Do what?"

"Can you refine the brandr?"

Mila cocked her head. "Did you not hear me up there? Of course I can."

Schafer turned, peering down at her with those soft-glow eyes. It was in that moment Mila remembered exactly what Adel had called him. A berserker. A warrior of modern legend honed and reinforced for elite combat. More machine than man, many would say. Many would also say they were the strongest, fastest, and most cunning warriors in human history. Mila suspected those digital eyes presented Schafer with a heads-up display, but had no idea what it told him about her. Though he seemed to be searching for something.

He kept searching without a word. Mila felt like she was shrinking under that gaze.

"Good," he finally said, turning back to the door. "We have too many *prisoners* in the mines as it is."

"How many?" Mila managed to ask.

A muscle flickered in the Berserker's jaw. "Too many."

The short reply made it clear he wasn't about to discuss the matter further. Still, Mila couldn't help but wonder why a berserker would care how many people Volkner sent to brandr mines.

The descent was long and quiet after that. Mila kept watching the levels change on the monitor, each one with its own beep.

Sétti, Visitor Lodging.

Sjaundi, Supply & Logistics.

Átti, Docking Bay.

They passed a level called *Níundi, Storage,* and then the beeping ceased for a long while and the monitor went blank, though the lift was still moving at full speed.

"Get ready," Schafer said. "It jolts a bit."

"Can't be any worse than docking," Mila said, laughing nervously.

Schafer grunted in what may have been a laugh, but Mila wasn't sure. She could feel the electromagnetic braking system starting to slow the lift, expecting a cushioned stop like they'd found on the command deck. It was anything but. The lift jolted to a halt seconds before the command deck stop had. Even with Schafer's warning, Mila wasn't ready. It sent her straight to the floor with enough force she was worried she bruised her tailbone.

"You'll get used to that," Schafer said, not bothering to offer her a hand.

As Mila got her feet, the holoscreen above the door beeped one last time.

Gjósa, Refinery.

The doors opened to reveal a passage near-opposite of that on the command deck. It was dimly lit by only a scattered few ceiling lights. Those that did work flickered on and off in their final effort before death. Where the hall leading to Volkner's throne room was scrubbed, this hall had not been cleaned in years. The old runes carved in the steel were caked over with rust, and Mila recognized none of them; not even the parts she could see. They looked older, as archaic as the runes on the axe at Schafer's side. These were carved by someone who knew the old Norse, not followers of the Neunorse.

Fresh boot prints interrupted the caked dust and flaked rust on the floor. She followed Schafer down the same path. They passed several doors, all as rusty as the walls, most of which appeared to be welded shut, and Mila wasn't sure she wanted to know what had been sealed away.

Mila paid close attention to the turns they took, memorizing the route back to the lift. She knew there was little chance she'd escape, but if she could get past the guards and back to the lift... Well, it would be a start. No matter how far-fetched, it was the only sliver of hope she had.

They turned a corner into a hallway where the red-brown walls blended with gray streaks. Four human figures were just visible in the dim light at the end. With every step, the gray streaks grew darker and wider, eventually cascading into something wholly black.

"What happened here?" Mila asked, surprised at how her soft tone carried through the near-vacant hall.

"Accidents," Schafer replied shortly.

"What kind of *accidents*?"

Mila suspected she already knew the answer. She hoped she was wrong. When Schafer didn't reply, only looking back at her with a slightly raised brow, she knew she wasn't.

They were close enough now for Mila to recognize the four figures as guards clad in Viking-class armor, though none were wearing helmets. In fact, they seemed much more at ease than any guards she'd encountered so far. Three men and a woman. She could just make out their conversation echoing through the hall.

"Think some fanatic did it?" one asked. He sounded young, and Mila could see he had a short-trimmed beard and blond hair shaved close on the side with three distinct knots on top. "I've heard of some old-school extremists sending threats against Neunorsemen. Could have one onboard."

"Unlikely," another replied, his voice gruffer. Mila saw his graying beard was braided halfway down his chest. She couldn't help but wonder where he stored such a thing when his helmet was on. "Too neat."

"He's right," a third one said. This one wore no beard, nor any hair at all that Mila could distinguish. Not even eyebrows. "Vandal wouldn't take the time for something like this. And in such an obscure place? No point in it."

The fourth didn't speak. Instead, she leaned up against a wall with her eyes closed. When they were close enough, Mila could make out the concentration creases in her forehead. She wore her hair very short and very clean. Her tan-brown skin told Mila she wasn't Vidarin-born, but perhaps Hodian or Tyran. She looked the youngest of the group as well; still a teenager, if Mila had to guess.

The three talking guards were looking up at the only new-looking metal she'd seen on the refinery deck. It looked like someone had only recently bolted a fresh steel plate above the scorched refinery doors. In it was carved a runic eye—the symbol of the Allfather.

"More likely old Volky had it put up there for good fortune," the blond one said.

"Old Volky?" Schafer said in a commander's tone.

The focus of all four soldiers was suddenly on the approaching duo.

"Little nickname for our Vini," the blond one replied quickly. "Thinkin' I might try it out on him next time I see the old twat."

"I think that'd almost guarantee you a one-way ticket out an airlock," Schafer replied.

"Maybe even a certified blood eagle if Waren says it sweet enough," the older one said, shoving the blond one. It was a playful gesture, but that didn't stop the younger soldier from stumbling over and almost falling.

"I suggest you keep your *nicknames* to yourself," Schafer said. "Never know who might be listening."

"Cameras and audio are out on this level," the hairless one said, pointing at a blackened camera hanging by its wires from the ceiling. "Not worth the upkeep."

Schafer scowled at the camera. "Is the refinery even operational anymore? Did the bastard even send engineers to check?"

No one answered. The older one shrugged.

"Thor's blood," Schafer cursed, shaking his head.

"Well, I suppose someone was here," Waren said, nodding toward the fresh steel panel.

The older one barked a laugh. "Yeah, I'd bet Baldur's golden balls Volkner had that carved as a prayer to Odin instead of spending any real marks on refinery repairs. Not when it's just gonna blow up again."

Mila tensed at that.

"Shut it," Schafer snapped.

The older guard suddenly looked serious. His eyes flashed to Mila, as if realizing she was there for the first time, and then back to Schafer. "Right. Sorry, Niko."

Niko?

"Just let her in," Schafer said, not acknowledging the apology.

Waren wiped off a smudged panel beside the door and pressed in a code. It took almost a minute because of the flickering, malfunctioning holoscreen. Finally, when Waren pressed the final key, the doors began to open.

There was not a hydraulic hiss, but a growl as old pumps began to work again. The doors did not slide quietly or gracefully, but ground apart with all the elegance of iron scraping rock. The room within was blackness, emptiness.

The troops made their way inside, locating an oversized lever labeled *Master Power* in faded red letters. The older guard grasped it and pulled, attempting to push it into its upward position. He grunted and it was easy to see the veins bulging from his temple. His forehead went beet-red, and pearls formed on his brow.

"Skadi's tits," he swore, wiping his brow. "Waren, make yourself useful."

Waren grabbed another part of the lever and they pulled together, but it still wouldn't budge. They pulled until Waren was sweating, and the elder guard was heaving heavy breaths.

"Move," Schafer commanded.

"I don't think Thor himself could move that," Waren said. "It's like it's welded into the wall."

Schafer walked to it, grasped it with one hand, and pulled. There was a loud scraping, a crack, and rusty powder fell to the deck. Then, the lever cranked up as easily as if the Berserker were flicking on a light switch. The sound of a cold motor cranking filled the walls, sputtering like Hans' jet truck before it could kick on. Schafer cracked his neck, which had a distinct metallic clink, and looked at his men. They made a point to inspect everything in the room except their lieutenant.

The motor kept sputtering and kicking until it made a high-pitched wailing sound which morphed into a low hum. One by one, the fluorescent lights above flickered on. They went back and back, farther and farther, revealing a room at least four times the size of what Mila expected. Every surface was blackened or rusty, including the array of outdated machinery lining the left side. Mila saw vats and massive pots, generators, hoses, and pipes. There were barrels on a pallet by a large cargo door on the far side of the room, a modest lifting cart beside them. The right wall of the room was almost completely concealed by junk and scrap that reminded Mila of the pit on the farm.

Most everything that wasn't a part of the room itself was bent, twisted, or broken in some way, from what Mila could tell. She saw there were camera mounts, but no cameras, and the metal was gnarled by some past trauma. In the corner was a simple cot, topped with a single blanket and no pillow, and one leg didn't touch the floor.

"All right, everybody out except the girl," Schafer said.

The troops were quick to obey, and Mila and Schafer were the only ones left in the room. He was looking at her with those digital blue eyes.

"You've got eight hours before reveille," he said. "I suggest you get to work."

The Berserker made to exit the refinery. Mila felt her heart start to beat harder, too hard. *What am I doing? I can't refine brandr. Why am I here?*

"Wait," she said.

Schafer stopped and looked back at her wordlessly.

"Eight hours isn't enough time," she said. She didn't like that her words were coming out faster than normal. "And I can't be judged on an unfinished product. I need a full rotation, maybe more."

"You have eight hours," Schafer repeated.

"It's not enough," Mila said. She tried to say it sternly, but her voice squeaked the slightest touch.

"It's what you have. If you can't do it, pray to the Allfather for a miracle, or the Matron for mercy."

Schafer continued to the doorway.

"Schafer, wait. It's impossible."

The Berserker didn't slow.

"Wait! Please, can you do anything?"

No response. He was at the door now.

Mila felt her heart beating so hard it threatened to break her ribs. Her stomach was in her chest, and her throat was tightening. A massive shock shot through her from the elerex as her arm fell limp. Her beating heart skipped and her breath was gone. She fell to a knee, trying desperately to regain it. After a deep gasp, she looked up to see the Berserker turning to the keypad just outside the door. A simple push of a button and she'd be locked away, doomed to her fate.

This isn't happening. But it was, and she knew it. This was no fever nightmare or hallucination. This was real. The cold metal on her knees was real. The stale air of the refinery was real. The char from past catastrophes was real. And tomorrow, her father would be sentenced to execution, and she'd be condemned to a life in a mine where the wretched go to die. It was too much.

"Niko!" she screamed with every ounce of breath she had left.

The Berserker's hand halted in mid-air. His soft-glowing eyes flicked to her, and she swore she saw regret in them. An apology, but one he'd never dare speak. He blinked and it was gone.

"Eight hours," he said, and pushed the button.

The doors began to grind closed, and Mila felt tears try to well in her eyes. Her mind went not to the father she knew now, but the one she'd known long ago, before he drank and cursed her existence. She thought of her mother and her golden hair, their happy life together cut too short. She wondered where she could have gone—why she had gone. A bulb above her was flickering hard, its fractional bits of light not even enough to read by. The sliver of hope she held onto flickered with it.

The doors finished closing, and Mila was alone. The light stopped flickering and went forever dark, and the sliver of hope faded into nothing.

PART TWO

CHAPTER
SEVEN

Piper DeRache heard wind whistling but could not feel it. She felt nothing but numb tingling all over her body. Opening her eyes was an obstacle she never thought she'd struggle to overcome. But in this moment, her eyelids were so heavy she thought it might be easier to die.

She managed them open and saw the whistling wind was coming in through the shattered front visor of the escape pod. She was still strapped in the pilot's chair and couldn't remember the landing. The last thing she remembered was hitting atmosphere and then... nothing. Likely she passed out, since every second after the explosion that killed Keyes and Hardy was a struggle for consciousness.

As she moved to unstrap the belts around her shoulders, she cried out as a something stabbed inside her chest. It took her a moment to find her breath, and when she did, it was raspy and wet.

Broken rib. Maybe a punctured lung. Definitely easier to die.

She moved to remove the straps again, this time more carefully. Even moving slowly, the pain was nearly unbearable. She ground her teeth together while she unclipped herself and nearly cracked them when she stood. The pain was almost enough to make her not notice the hammer pounding in her head—almost. She sighed and put pressure on her temple with her palm, praying it would ease the throbbing and dizziness.

Concussion.

Piper, holding her aching chest with one arm, stumbled to the rear of the pod. It was angled with the nose of the ship planted in the ground, so her walk was more of a climb. After painstaking minutes, she found the wall compartment marked *Supplies.* She twisted the handle to its unlocked position. The hydraulics of the compartment door hissed, and the metal plate fell away, striking the floor with a clang that threatened to split Piper's skull in two. Inside was a rope, three liters of water, a mid-range communicator, a four-person insta-deploy tent, a plasma-edged knife, a flare pistol, steel tape, and a pack to carry it all.

She took the steel tape and turned to the next compartment marked *Medical.* This time she tried to gently let the metal panel to the ground, but her free arm was much weaker than she expected, like the muscles had turned to cotton. A pain ripped through her chest and she hacked a violent cough. This sent the pain in her chest pulsing over and over and she couldn't stop coughing. Blackness was creeping in at the edge of her vision when she finally got her breathing back under control.

"Shit!" she spat, but it only made the throbbing pain worse.

Inside the medical compartment she found bandages, ointments, emergency antibiotic and pain-killing injectables, heart medications, and two adrenaline shots. She also gathered four packaged heat-reflecting blankets and chemical heat and cold packs.

Piper stumbled back to the visor, and with the steel tape and two of the blankets, sealed it off as best she could. It might have taken five minutes or fifty, she couldn't be sure. After returning to the pilot's chair and testing the shuttle power to find it completely dead from damaged systems, Piper took out another blanket for herself. She'd seen enough death to know it was near, coming to make sure she was drawn into the eternal equality, and right now her only objective was to raise her body heat. She cracked one of the heat packs and put it underneath the blanket, hoping to insulate the warmth in with her body. Then she injected an antibiotic and a pain medicine not to help ease the pounding headache and splitting chest pain, but for the horrible burning of frozen limbs warming back to life.

Her eyelids grew heavy again, and she didn't fight them. If she fell asleep, she knew with the head injury and the cold, there was a chance she would never wake. Maybe there were Jotun patrols out looking for the pod to execute survivors from the *Thialfi*. Maybe a captain who didn't go down with her ship deserved to die alone in a frozen tundra. Maybe, if she passed into the ether, the gods would be kind enough to let her into Valhalla with her crew. No, not her... not a disgraceful excuse for a privateer. There was no place for her in the hall of the Aesir. She had no right.

But maybe, if she could provide the gods with just one offering, one sacrifice, she'd see her crew again. Her frozen blood thawed into steam and she clenched her ribs hard as the pain tried to break through. She had to sleep, had to rest and regain some semblance of strength. And the thought of what she had to do told her she would wake. There was a debt to repay. It was owed by the man who sent them headlong into that trap—pinning their Sleipnir-class sprinter against the might of a Jotun capital ship. Piper intended to collect.

In that moment, she knew she would claw her way back to the pinnacle of the *VOS Gjaller*. Piper DeRache was going to kill Volkner Brandt.

◇————◇————◇

PIPER SPENT the next day trying to get the shuttle's power systems back online. She'd lined the inside of her leather jacket and flight pants with the emergency blankets. She was still bitterly cold, but at least it wasn't threatening to kill her now. When she finally got the arc array to glow up, she knew she could breathe a sigh of relief. The warmth from the humming power array and the heaters would at least let her be comfortable while she figured out her next move. Finding the long-range communication systems wouldn't even try to boot complicated things.

She'd tried a few dozen channels on the short-range communicator but received no answer. Piper had no way of knowing how close the nearest town or settlement was, or in what direction. Jotun was the largest inhabited planet in the Ymir system and had a smaller population than any beside Hod. There could be thousands of miles between her and humanity. But as she watched her water and few rations dwindle over the next two days, her options narrowed more and more.

The nights were the hardest. She tried to stay awake as much as possible, not wanting to succumb to the concussion. But that didn't stop her from drifting away and waking hours later with the horrible throbbing and stabbing that assaulted her when the pain medications had worn off.

On the third night, she made her decision. Jotun search parties would already be scouring the tundra recovering *Thialfi* wreckage. It was only a matter of time before they discovered the escape pod and the evidence that someone made it off alive. She had to get moving well before that happened.

After failing to cut through the metal with the plasma edge, discovering that it flickered on and off like a dying light, she pried the panels away from a damaged section of shuttle wall. Beneath, she found the high-density insulation she was looking for. No matter how itchy and uncomfortable it was as she stuffed her clothing full between the jacket and blankets, it was nothing compared to the frozen wind and knee-high snow that awaited her.

She let herself sleep on that last night, giving her fate to the gods once again. When she woke hours later, Piper DeRache pulled the lever to release the heavy titanium rear door of the shuttle and watched it crush the snow. Wind so cold it would make a frost giant shiver poured in, engulfing her, stinging the exposed bits of her face and burning her eyes.

"Allfather," she whispered to the wind. "Send your ravens to guide me and lend me your strength to carry through."

Piper stepped out into the white tundra. The snow was even deeper than she'd expected, coming to her mid-thigh. The land looked the same in every direction—barren and pale. She pulled out the short-range communicator and checked the channels. All of the most common were set to be tuned to with a single button click.

She looked to the sky, but only found a miles-wide sheet of lazy nimbostratus.

So, nothing to go off of.

"Where are you, Odin?"

The only reply was the whistling wind.

Piper wrapped her coat as tight as she could and made sure the bag straps were secure around her shoulders. She chose a direction, knowing not if it was north, south, east, or west, and began to trudge through the frozen waste.

<hr/>

IT HAD BEEN three days—three days of cold Piper could hardly comprehend. Even with the drugs, emergency blankets, and the survival tent, her nights had been sleepless. The bitter bite of the frozen air was too much, and so too was the shivering. Yet, at least the latter told her that her body was still fighting. When she stopped shivering, it was all over.

She'd run out of the emergency water she'd kept against her flesh to keep it from freezing yesterday. Now, she had stuffed the empty bottles with snow and let them rest against her last warm pack in the satchel strapped across her back.

Her boots, invisible beneath the snow she tread through, hadn't come off her feet in the last two days. She'd tried to dry them the first day, but quickly found the pain of her thawing feet to be too much. That first night, the tips of her toes were already tinged with purple. She dreaded to think what color the numb things were now. If she had to guess, she'd lose them if she ever reached a settlement. If she were *that* lucky.

The second day of trudging through dense Jotun snow had been cut short by a blizzard. Piper had never known any weather to be so sudden or so fierce. Even the freak sandstorms on her home planet of Tyr took time to build.

The blizzard, however, had picked up when the weather was the mildest, catching her completely off-guard. Luckily, she'd been able to deploy her tent quickly and huddle inside. Now, she noticed the weather was once again eerily calm. There wasn't even wind, but plenty of rolling clouds above.

She wasn't surprised when, only minutes later, a gust of wind howled around her, followed by a barrage of two-inch flakes. It was so impossibly thick she could hardly see her hands as she tried to pull the tent from her pack. *Come on,* she thought, fumbling through the contents with iced hands. She couldn't feel a thing she was touching; didn't even know if her thumbs and fingers would obey her mind's commands to grasp and pull.

And that's when she saw it, the flicker of a shadow through the storm. Movement by some leaping beast that blended in with pale snow. Piper felt her heart sink into her gut. She'd heard the horror stories of the Jotun ice beasts. Bipedal snow apes as large as elephants. Wolves as large as rhinos. Apex feline predators that could swallow human children in a single bite. Piper hoped it was nothing but a trick of her eyes. The hope was wiped away as the second shadow flashed a few yards from the first.

"Odin's blood," she cursed under her breath.

There was no time to set up camp now. She knew if she stopped, she was sacrificing herself to the wild beasts.

Piper sealed the pack and slung it over her shoulders, wading as quickly as she could manage through the deepening snow. When her pace hastened too much, she found herself missing a proper step with her numbed feet. The beasts just out of her view behind the stormy downfall yelped in delight.

Scavengers, then. Just waiting for me to die.

She didn't plan to give them the luxury of an easy meal. Piper was back on her feet hiking through the dense snow in a breath. She needed to keep moving. The beasts on her trail were waiting for any opening. Any sign of weakness could be detrimental. There was no room for mistakes.

It was ten minutes before her feet gave way again. The howls from the beasts beyond her vision rang out from all sides. *They're surrounding me.* Piper knew she had to get up, had to keep going, else the snow scavengers were going to strike. She pulled the plasma knife from her pocket and flicked the blade open, her thumb over the igniting button. If they struck one at a time, perhaps she stood a chance.

Piper tried to stand, but she realized she couldn't feel her legs. She looked to make sure they were still there, and they were, but they'd decided to stop obeying her.

"Dammit," she hissed. "Come on!"

But they stayed still.

No, not like this. Piper closed her eyes and listened to the wind gust around her. The yelping snow beasts were getting louder, closer, bolder. She lost herself in the darkness. There, she saw her crew. She heard Keyes and Hardy screaming while they burned to death in white flame. She saw Bronson's bloodied, smiling face looking at her from the ejection bay porthole. *Not like this.* Piper DeRache couldn't die alone, defeated in the snow, not with Volkner's debt still owed. But there was nothing she could do. Her body had given up on her mind.

Not like this.

Warmth crept in as her mind forgot her frozen body. It was a sure sign she was near the edge, about to drop off into oblivion. The howling and yelping was even closer now— too close. But she couldn't open her eyes, couldn't bear to invite the cold back in.

Her mind was on home, on Tyr, in the warmth of a desert day. It was in the haven town for rebels and pirates. She thought of her first captain, Arvid, and the day he agreed to take her on as his skyldr, an apprentice of sorts. That was in a time before he lost his life in a failed boarding of a Tyran frigate—before Captain Skuld had taken control of the *Laufey* and Piper had become their right hand. The Arvid she knew had a mid-length black beard and always wore a variety of colors. He'd given her the very jacket that was now stuffed full with ship insulation and emergency blankets. There hadn't been a day since he gave it to her that she hadn't worn it.

She saw him now, clear as day, towering over her preteen frame, blocking the sunlight with his shoulders. Except, there was something off about the memory. There was a raven perched on his shoulder and his face was shadowed. Piper suddenly felt the cold again in full force, and realized her mind was back in the snowy tundra, but her old master was still a hulking mass above her. The raven on his shoulder took flight and joined another flying above in the blizzard sky. And just like that, Arvid was gone, and Piper's eyes opened.

She rolled to quickly see the direction the ravens had flown in her vision, and in the slightest hint of sight, she thought she could make out a figure. It was a hunched, hooded man, with a long gray beard. Half his face was darkened, but she could see one eye glowed pale blue.

"Allfather," Piper whispered.

With a blink, the figure was gone, leaving Piper to question if he was ever there. But, in his absence, stood something she'd not seen before. It was a gateway surrounded by a tall, black wall with words inscribed in the Jotun hand above.

Valgrind

A town. She'd made it to civilization. She felt the feeling burn back into her legs as her body seemed to regain the will to survive. Just as she planted her first toe in the snow, she heard a too-close snarl.

Piper barely managed to enable the plasma edge on the survival knife as the beast struck. Its fur was white as the snow, broken by grayish stripes. Piper twisted around to see the lupine maw shredding her pack into bits. In girth, it was like a black bear, densely muscled. But in speed and ferocity, it was more like a lioness.

Piper plunged the plasma knife into the beast's side and ripped it toward her. Blood soiled the snow-white fur and splattered across her front as it wailed in pain. As it jumped away, collapsing in the snow every few feet to the safety of the blizzard, the second one struck. It came from behind Piper, just where she could not see or hear it. She felt the jagged claws rip through leather and insulation straight into flesh and scratching bone. That piercing pain from the broken rib was brought back to life, accompanied by an all-new terrible agony.

Piper heaved herself away from the new assailant just as it was lunging for the back of her neck. It landed in the steaming crimson pool left behind from the gaping wound on her back. She thrust the knife at it as the plasma edge flickered into nothingness. The leftover dull blade only punched the side of the beast, failing to deter it as it reset itself for another lunge. Piper was desperately clicking the ignitor, getting only moments of glowing green plasma.

Just as it was about to lunge, Piper felt herself tugged back. She felt no bite or tear, it was as if the storm itself was dragging her along. She glanced down at her foot to find there was indeed another snow scavenger beast clamped onto her ankle, pulling her through snow. In the briefest moment, Piper's mind questioned and feared why she couldn't feel it. Then, the survival instinct came rushing back, and she sat up in a violent motion, feeling her broken bones shift as she did so. With every ounce of strength she had left, she punched at the beast, at its eyes, its ears, anything vulnerable, while her other hand kept clicking the ignitor on the plasma knife.

Her vision was tunneling now and her arms were losing strength. The punching became fruitless, and she took to praying that the plasma knife would ignite. Every click of the button meant more blood lost, more darkness. She felt the teeth of the other beast pierce her shoulder and warm crimson sprayed her neck. The two beasts started tugging from either end, each claiming her as their own meal. She felt the flesh rip and the blood pour, and still she kept clicking.

Then, the plasma edge surged to life. It was a short moment, but one she refused to waste. Piper had enough energy for one last strike. She thrust the knife toward her shoulder where the beast's head sat inches from her own. It was not precision that guided her hand, but desperation honed by fate, or luck. Whatever it was, Piper welcomed it, as the plasma-edged blade found the beast's dark eye.

It roared out in agony and pulled away, ripping the knife from Piper's grasp. The other beast released her ankle, startled by its companion's sudden outcry. The wounded one stumbled back, shaking its head back and forth but losing its footing. It collapsed in the snow a few seconds later and never moved again.

The remaining beast retreated into the blizzard, apparently deciding Piper was not the easy target they thought they'd been tracking. She knew if she stayed there it would be back before long, and if she didn't move now, she'd be buried in a frozen grave. She rolled onto her belly, smelling and tasting the coppery tang of both her blood and the beasts'. Every movement was unbearable, every second dragging herself along a crucible. Still, Piper pulled herself toward the gate, toward Valgrind.

She was a few dozen yards away when the gate started to open, and she saw the shadow of a human figure. That's when her vision went black.

CHAPTER
EIGHT

HANS MESSER WAS TOYING with a Vidarin coin on Tröllaskegg's bar. He flicked it, watched it spin for a few seconds, then sighed when it fell.

"Sure you wouldn't prefer somethin' stiff?" the barman asked, gesturing to Han's glass of water.

Hans shook his head and flicked the coin again. He'd come here after they'd taken Mila, but not to drink. He'd come to avoid the silence of his own house.

"All right," the barman continued. "But if we get busy, you know I'm gonna have to free up the bar space if you ain't buying anything. You hearin' me, Hans?"

Hans didn't reply.

"Do you understand?" the barman insisted, letting the annoyance show in his tone.

"Give the whole gods-damned house a round, on me," Hans said. His words were sharp, but there was an undeniable hollowness behind them. "If your money's so important."

The barman shrugged and started pouring pitchers for the scattered patrons.

"A drunk who doesn't drink?" a voice said from behind him. It was smooth, like well-aged leather. "How curious."

Hans looked up to see the man from the poker table taking a seat beside him at the bar, placing his emerald-pommeled cane against the bar as he did so. He wore the same pinstripe suit with matching fedora, which he placed on the counter to reveal a mane of combed-back obsidian hair. Hans realized he looked both eighteen and eighty simultaneously. His high cheekbones and sharp chin reminded Hans of a hungry wolf, as did his strange gray eyes. Though, the gaunt flesh was more like bone, paler than any Vidarin Hans had ever seen.

"You," Hans said with the venom of an asp. "You're the bastard that talked me into that stupid deal."

"Stupid?" the man replied. "I made you one of the richest men on Vidar with only a few words."

Hans clenched his molars together, his fist white-knuckled around his water glass.

"What's wrong? Too high a cost?" the man continued.

Hans could have sworn he saw a glint of silver in his mouth as he spoke.

"You can't comprehend what I gave up," Hans said.

The man gestured to the barman with two fingers. A moment later, ale horns were in front of each of them. The barman uncorked a bottle and the man in the suit shook his head.

"I've got something special," he said, pulling a brown glass flask from the inside of his jacket.

He poured the contents into each horn filling them only about a quarter of the way.

"I don't want any," Hans said.

"Come now," the man said. "Have a drink with me."

Hans' nostrils flared, but he didn't reply.

"You say too high a cost," the man went on. "I say you gained the life of a king for the price of a leech."

"Watch your mouth," Hans hissed, turning on the man.

"Easy now," the man said, unflinching. "I see you're upset. A pesky conscience rattling around in there somewhere?"

"Stop pretending like you know anything about me." Hans was on his feet now, his fists trembling at his sides.

"I know everything about you, Hans Messer," the man said, taking his ale horn in hand. "I know you served in the Vidarin military under then-Major Brandt. I know about your wife leaving you to fend for your farm and daughter alone. And I know you hate yourself for being so selfish that you gave that daughter up for luxury."

Hans had heard enough. His blood roiled through his veins and he drew back a fist.

"I also know how to help you." The man seemed completely unfazed by the promise of an incoming attack, and his words were charged with conviction.

Hans loosed a breath but didn't lower his drawn fist. "What are you talking about?"

"I can help her fulfill your promise to Volkner Brandt."

Hans lowered his fist and reseated himself. "Talk."

"Drink first, then we can talk," the man replied, pushing the Hans' ale horn closer to him.

Hans lifted the horn and peered at the contents. In all his years of drinking, he'd never seen mead as perfectly golden as this. It smelled of rose and purest honey, with a hint of something else he couldn't place, though he'd smelled it before.

"Skál," the man said as he raised his horn.

Hans echoed the gesture without sharing any of the man's enthusiasm. Together, they took a sip. The golden mead tickled his throat as he swallowed. It tasted of everything he'd smelled and more. Lavender and sage filled his mouth, then shifted into the warm presence of cinnamon and nutmeg. All of it swirled in the earthy flavor of the mead's honey. When the flavors faded, however, there was one left that matched the smell he couldn't place. It was almost metallic, like he'd bitten his cheek and a touch of blood had seeped to his tongue.

"What do you think?" the man asked.

Hans pulled his head back, inspecting the liquid left in his cup. "It's... divine."

The man chuckled loudly. "Glad you approve."

Hans set down the horn. "Now, we can discuss your offer."

"Right," the man replied. "I can offer to save Mila from her terrible fate in the brandr mines, but it comes at a price."

"And how can you offer such a thing?" Hans asked.

"I have my methods, and that's all you need to know."

Hans shook his head. A feeling tensed in his gut, like a rattlesnake coiling ready to fend off a threat. "Fine," he said. *What do I have to lose?* "What's your price?"

"A trade. Your life for Mila's."

"Excuse me?"

"I save Mila from a tortured existence in the mines, a fate you imposed on her, and you forfeit your life and freedom to me," the man said.

"What are you playing at?" Hans demanded.

"A game all my own," the man replied.

Hans didn't like the man's tone one bit, and that feeling coiled tighter. "I don't know what you—"

An overwhelming sense of lightness washed over Hans, as if someone had just opened up his skull and let his mind fly free. He found himself keenly aware of every detail in front of him, from grain patterns in the wooden bar, to the minor imperfections in the bone drinking horn. He held up his hand and felt he could read his exact age to the day by examining the wrinkles.

"What's in that mead?"

"It's called many things," the man replied. "My favorite is Suttung, but most call it the Mead of Poetry. Quite a powerful drink, especially if it's your first time."

"The Mead of Poetry is a myth," Hans said.

He looked at the man and stood so violently his barstool went flying back. The barman was yelling something and the other patrons were all looking at him, but Hans didn't notice. No, his focus was entirely on the man in the pinstripe suit.

He was still a man, but not entirely. The tight skin of his face looked torn in places, letting bits of black fur poke through. Those gray eyes were iridescent, like a hidden predator's caught by a light beam. His canines were longer than they should be, and sharper.

The man clicked his tongue, and Hans saw that he hadn't imagined the reflective glimmer before, but that his tongue was actually silver and forked.

"You disappoint me, Hans."

He was staring at Hans, piercing him. Though he was still, he seemed almost to shift and vibrate so quickly Hans' eyes could barely register it. He seemed to rattle.

"I know what you are," Hans said, tripping over the fallen stool as he backed away.

"Do you now?" the man replied, taking another sip of the mead. "And what, pray tell, might that be?"

"You're the Rattle Man."

The man's forked tongue flicked out so fast Hans could

hardly register it. "I think Mr. Messer's had a bit much to drink," he said to the barman.

"Everything okay there, Hans?" the barman asked.

Hans looked around and realized no one seemed to care that the thing in front of him was wearing a human skinsuit. "Don't you see him? He's the Rattle Man!"

A chorus of laughs rose from the patrons and the barman said, "Hans, I think it's best you go on home."

Hans looked back at the barman, seeing the reason behind every tiny scar, every worry line or smile wrinkle on the aging man's face. "How can you not see?"

"Time to go home, Hans," the man said, finishing off his ale horn.

After one last glance around of desperation, Hans Messer stumbled through the mead hall and out into the cold night. Everything he looked at he saw in new, unbearable detail. He smelled kladdkaka baking down the street and knew how long it'd been in the oven and that too much sugar was mixed into the icing. He heard a distant beast cry and knew it was a piebald hare succumbing to a Vidarin nightcat. He looked at the moon and knew exactly how far it was from him and the time down to the second. It made him want to vomit.

Even disarming the biolock on the jet truck was overwhelming. As he placed his thumb against the miniature holoscreen, he was flooded with the knowledge of exactly how the device read the lines in his fingerprints and registered the sequence of his DNA. He saw his hand as not a hand, but a complex collection of nerves, tissue, tendons, and muscle. As the truck sputtered to life, he knew exactly how the fuel flowed to the rear jets and underneath thrusters. He knew exactly how much to rotate the steering wheel and how it shifted the jets.

"Odin's eye," he swore, carefully pulling the truck onto the main road. He prayed the cursed knowledge wouldn't be with him forever.

Hans made it a few miles when his enhanced perceptions started to fade. Suddenly, he was less aware of the temperature of the pre-dawn air, and didn't know the physics of his low-flying vehicle. In fact, Hans was realizing he didn't know much of anything, like the years of common knowledge were being stripped away en masse. He couldn't remember where he was going, or where he'd come from. He found his hands weren't sure how to grip his steering wheel, though he tugged at it like a toddler.

The truck wasn't about to stop autonomously, but Hans found himself powerless to slow it. He watched from his driver's seat helplessly as it veered off the main road into the steep ditch on the side. There was a violent bump as the thrusters cut out and then, when the grille planted itself in the soil, a too-sudden jolt. Hans flew forward into the steering wheel and fell into the void.

⋄———⋄————————⋄———⋄

HANS WOKE to find dull orange light creeping through the shattered windshield of the truck. There was something happening in the distance, but he couldn't recall what it was. The tip of a massive fiery orb was creeping over the horizon. He felt he'd seen it before many times, yet now he couldn't fathom it.

"The mead affects all mortals differently," a voice said from beside him.

Hans threw himself back into the jet truck door in shock, suddenly aware of the man in the pinstripe suit sitting on the bench seat with him.

"Some gain great knowledge and retain most of it. Others go completely mad. You seem to be like most—a small period of heightened perception and unlocked knowledge, followed by a long swath of debilitating dumbness." The man turned his attention from the distant sunrise to Hans and frowned. "Clean yourself up, Hans," he said, taking a bleach-white silk kerchief from his pocket.

Hans was suddenly aware of the crimson tinging the outside of his vision, the feel of something crusted on his brow, and the metallic tang in his mouth. He took the kerchief and wiped himself, looking at it to see the blotchy red. He knew that color, that liquid. What was it called?

"Tell me, Hans," the man in the pinstripe suit went on. "Do you remember who I am?"

Hans looked at him, trying his hardest to place the figure. He'd only just seen him, he was sure of it. He had shaken, vibrated, rattled.

"Rattle." It was the only word Hans could muster and he sounded like a babe. He realized forming words was no longer natural to him.

"Good," the Rattle Man replied. "And do you remember who I offered to help for you?"

Hans creased his brow and thought long. "Mi," he finally whispered, feeling something knot in his stomach. He remembered that feeling, too. He didn't like it.

"Very good," the Rattle Man continued. "At this rate, you'll have full cognitive function back within a fortnight."

Hans understood none of that. What he did understand was the sickness he felt thinking about Mila, his daughter, the one he'd betrayed.

"Mi," he repeated. A hot tear streaked down his face.

"That's right. And my offer still stands. I can help her, Hans—your life for hers."

Hans shook his head. "No, no. Can't."

The Rattle Man shook his head and let the silver tongue flick out. "Ever the coward."

There was a moment of tense silence between them.

"Tell you what, Hans," the Rattle Man went on. "I'll sweeten the deal. You offer your life for hers, your freedom to me, and I'll save her. But, I'll wait five years before I collect. That's five years to spend with your dear daughter, to make up for your crime. What do you say?"

Hans thought about it for a long minute, though it was difficult to keep his mind straight in his state. Five years felt like a long time, time even to find a way out of the deal if he was lucky. He thought of his daughter, trapped in a blackened brandr mine, every day her sanity at the mercy of some cruel foreman. Five years.

Hans found the syllables he needed for one word. "Accept."

CHAPTER
NINE

EVERYTHING in the *Gjaller* refinery was cold. The metal walls and floor, the titanium tanks and steel machinery, even the worn cot and blanket couldn't protect her from the chill in the air. She found herself craving her coveralls and wool jacket, sick of her mother's now-soiled dress.

Mila could find no instructions on operating the refining machinery, not that she had a hope of reading and understanding them in a single night if she did. The closest she found were holotablets in some steel cabinets near the first tank, but they were all busted. She did try to turn the refinery on using a control panel near the lead tank, but it was charred black and non-responsive. It was so old it had actual buttons instead of a holographic projection, and most of those buttons were either jammed or missing.

Hopeless.

After giving up on the farfetched shot of getting the refinery equipment to boot, Mila tried to get the communication intercom beside the reinforced entry doors to boot. When there was no staticky feedback nor response, she took to slamming on the doors themselves.

"Hey!" she screamed, trying to get someone's attention.

She wasn't entirely sure what the plan was if they actually opened the doors. Maybe she'd try and convince them she needed a part or ask where a lavatory was. Maybe she'd say she needed medical attention, that her heart was fluttering, and she felt like she was going to pass out. It was pretty long odds that the guards would believe her, or care enough to help her if they did. So, she went with a third option, something she felt better about lying her way through.

"I need parts!" she yelled, still pounding on the doors. "The whole array is busted!"

The hope was they'd escort her to a supply level or maybe convince Brandt to give her more time while she thought of another escape strategy. The potential plans faded as it became clear no one was going to open the doors.

Mila growled and pulled her hair at the scalp. *Come on, Mila, think.* But no alternative came.

She breathed deep, calming her racing heart, and turned her sights on the scrap pile lining the right side of the room. *Maybe something in there could help.*

As soon as she started sorting through the old scrap, it became evident how little it would help. Most of the metal and rubber pieces were unrecognizable, actual scrap in every sense of the word. Most pieces were coated in that blackened stain so present on everything else in the refinery. But, as Mila had nothing else to do, nothing else to try, she kept moving the useless pieces. She imagined the chance of finding a wide vent shaft, or some secret tunnel system left here by the builders. It was farfetched, but farfetched was all she had.

As she continued to take bits of scrap out of crates and move loose piles away from the wall, she did notice something curious about it. She'd moved just enough to make out

a carving in the swath of metal. It was barely distinguish-
able under the wall's charred coating, but she could make
out the remnants of the rune iar with the depiction of a
serpentine beast wrapped around it. Mila could tell it had
been carved by a careful hand, and she could see the outer
edge of another behind more scrap beside it.

Mila quickly started pulling more scrap away, not
caring where it landed behind her. Until she uncovered a
wooden crate labeled *OBSOLETE MILITARY EQUIP-
MENT – DISCARD ACCORDING TO GUIDELINES
FOUND IN WDTM-186-7* that she couldn't move, no
matter how much she strained.

"Odin's noose," she cursed. "Damned thing must be
filled with lead plates."

She cleared the last bits of light scrap from the top and
grabbed a slim piece of discarded steel. Mila wedged the
steel under the lip of the crate lid and pried upwards,
hearing some of the nail fasteners crank loose in the process.
She wiggled it back and forth until there was just enough
room to fit her fingers in and pulled up. It took three heavy
heaves, but she managed to pry the top completely off.

As she peered into the crate, she didn't see ammunition
shells or a crate full of outdated rifles, but instead a single
machine. It was wrapped into a tight circle, and Mila could
make out dents and scrapes down the metal siding. She
hadn't the slightest idea of what kind of machine it was or
what it was used for, but she knew she wasn't getting to the
wall behind without getting it out of the way. Using the
steel again, she started prying away the outfacing wooden
panel. After popping all the nails away, it fell to the metal
floor with a piercing crack.

Looking at the technology within, she realized it was
laying on its side, and from her current angle she could

make out the replication of a lupine face. It was a vél—an automaton usually designed to help humans with everyday activities. But Mila had read about this type of vél. It was called a Fenrir, and it was not for helping humans make tea or cleaning floors. This was a machine built for war.

They'd discontinued the Fenrir models years ago. Mila recalled reading it was because of their high price tag and a tendency for their central system to develop unique personality traits, making them difficult to train consistently. Now, only the wealthiest in any society used them as high-tech guard dogs, even though their likeness was of a wolf. This one seemed to have taken a nasty blow to the side some time ago. Mila imagined that, rather than repair him, engineers salvaged his power source and planned to recycle the body.

She crawled into the large crate to examine closer, finding she was right—his primary battery source was missing. The compartment was outfitted to receive a type II arc battery, just like most military equipment of the preceding decade. Mila suddenly remembered the metal case strapped to her thigh and took it out, opening it to see her own glowing arc battery.

"Well," she said. "I suppose I don't have much use for this anymore."

And just like that, she pressed the battery she'd spent years getting to work into the vacant compartment.

Lights glowed to life from between the titanium armor plates lining the vél's backside. They shifted from blue to pale yellow to green, then to blinking red. An error light sequence if Mila had ever seen one.

She pursed her lips and ran her fingers along the robot's side plating until she felt the smallest hint of a lip. She grabbed the thinnest sliver of scrap metal she could find, wedging it into the lip. A moment later, the plate popped up, revealing a holoscreen. It was red like the blinking lights and in the middle was typed *ERROR – Please Run Diagnostic*.

There were no visible buttons around the screen and the screen itself didn't respond to touch. That left only one option.

"Fenrir, run diagnostics," she said, enunciating clearly.

The holopanel beeped in response and the red blinked into a black boot screen. One by one, lines of text filled the screen.

Diagnostic Check in Progress...
*Power System... Normal_*
*Central Processor... Normal_*
*Peripherals... Normal_*
*Memory... ERROR_*
*Targeting System... FAULT_*
*Weapon Systems... VIOLENCE INHIBITION MODE_*
*Defense Systems... Normal_*
*GPS Software... Normal_*
Hydraulic Systems –
*Leg, Fore, Left... Normal_*
*Leg, Fore, Right... FAULT_*
*Leg, Aft, Left... Normal_*
*Leg, Aft, Right... FAULT_*
*Spine, Fore... Normal_*
*Spine, Aft... Normal_*
*Neck... Normal_*
*Exoplates... Normal_*
Diagnostic Check... COMPLETE.

"Something got you pretty good, huh?" Mila said to the lifeless bot.

There was no reply, just the blinking cursor in the lower right corner of the screen.

Mila scanned the room—the scrap heap, looking back to the bot to say, "Let me see what I can do."

She set about searching the scrap heap for parts to help repair the wolfbot. If she couldn't refine brandr and she was going to be sent off to the mines anyway, it seemed as good a thing to do with her time as anything else.

After an hour or so of searching, she'd managed to uncover three crates carrying discarded Mark IV parts. Most of them were not in working order, marred by battle-field blasts and overuse. However, she was able to find enough spare scraps to fully repair the front malfunctioning leg and part of the rear.

"Okay," Mila said, wiping the grease from her brow after a couple hours of work. "At least you'll be able to stand."

With that, Mila, having no certainty about what would come next, navigated the control panel to startup mode and pressed initiate. Motors and gears whirred to life within the previously non-functioning wolfbot as it shot up from its prone position into an awkward, off-kilter sit. Across the control panel screen scrolled in red block letters, ERROR – MEMORY CORRUPT. But the wolfbot did not panic, or go on some manic rampage. It just sat, looking for all the world like the largest metallic puppy Mila had ever seen. And just like any pet ready to be saved from a ruthless past, his visor-like eyes looked at her with adoration and thanks. Even if she died come morning, or was sent away to some hellhole of a brandr mine, she knew she hadn't wasted her time.

For a few hours, at least, she would have a friend.

MILA WOKE to the sound of grinding metal and Fen's growl warning. The bot couldn't attack if he tried, but his already defensive nature was oddly calming to her. But it wasn't enough to completely quell the sinking feeling in her stomach. The grinding was from the refinery doors, and Mila had no idea how long she'd been asleep.

"I suppose it's time," she said. "Matron have mercy."

She heard the click of hard soles on metal which seemed too light for Viking armor and too heavy for Niko Schafer's predatory pacing. She was surprised to find it was the last person on the ship she'd expected to see.

She recognized the Jotun ambassador in his fine grays and blues, though he'd forgone the stark white shoulder cape. Mila imagined that kind of thing was more ceremonial and too formal for a stroll around the ship. He stopped short of Mila's cot and cocked his head at Fenrir, who was still growling.

Mila stood and rested a hand on the wolfbot's back. "Easy Fen," she said calmly.

Fenrir's red alert lights dimmed, and he went perfectly silent, save the soft humming of his interior motors and processors.

"How in Odin's name did you come across such a machine in these few hours?" he asked in his subtle accent.

"I found him abandoned in a waste crate with the scrap," she said, gesturing toward the pile of metal lining the wall.

"And he sprang to life with what, a push of a button?"

"No," Mila replied. "I repaired him."

"Really?" The ambassador looked at the Fenrir Mark II thoughtfully, scratching his chin. "Perhaps you are something of a prodigy, after all." He took a moment to sniff the air and examine the still-dusty and cold machinery, then the pallet of unrefined brandr sitting opposite them in the room. "Though, perhaps not of the refining?"

"The equipment doesn't work," Mila replied. It could have been a lie as easily as truth—Mila didn't know. "I tried telling them—the guards—but they wouldn't open the doors."

The ambassador placed his hands behind his back and strolled to the refining equipment. His posture was straighter than any man she'd seen before, and he held his head high.

He ran his finger along the metal, leaving a long wake in the dust coating. He rubbed it between his fingers and inspected it.

"I think that's only half the story," he said.

Mila breathed deep. She was tired of whatever game this man was playing at and tired of waiting for her encroaching fate. "Can we just get this over with?" she asked, no longer trying to mask her voice with any level of politeness.

The ambassador turned away from the machinery and looked at her curiously. "Get *what* over with?"

"Whatever comes next. Just bring the guards in and tell them to take me to Volkner. Tell the president that I've failed and let him send me to the mines. Let him..." She couldn't say it. *Let him kill my father.*

The ambassador laughed, surprising Mila. "You misunderstand me, Miss Messer. I've come to help you."

It was Mila's turn to look curious. "You're going to talk to the president for me? About the busted equipment?"

He shook his head. "I think we both know that would only prolong the inevitable."

Mila maintained her suspicious glare but did not respond. No point in arguing that she could refine the brandr. Not now, not when her reckoning was so near. It wasn't worth the energy.

"I'm going to refine it for you," he said.

Any effort Mila put into keeping a stoic face was fruitless as her brows creased and she looked at him like a lunatic. Maybe he *was* a lunatic.

"Refine it for me?" she asked, unable to mask the skepticism.

"That's what I said," he responded, walking toward the refinery control panel.

"How? Better yet, why?"

"How is simple," he replied. "Refining is a hobby of mine—strange hobby, I admit, but I've been fascinated with machines and their fuels since I was a young boy."

"And your fascination makes you think you can refine *brandr*?"

"No, experience does."

Mila was floored with disbelief. "You've refined brandr into hyrrine before?"

The ambassador nodded. "A few dozen times, actually. I make it for traders from my home village. Starship fuel is hard to come by on Jotun, and even more expensive than it is here."

"Why would you not be a Master Refiner then? Why choose to be a politician? There's no chance the money is better in politics."

"True," he replied, pressing some buttons on the panel. "But, my other hobby is words, and I love my home. I can help my people more as a diplomat than as a professional refiner. Planets are going to war over refiners these days, after all. My duty is to protect."

Mila thought the story was either one of the most touching she'd ever heard, or a lie bigger than the mound of scrap lining the refinery.

"That still doesn't answer why," she said.

The ambassador looked up at her. "No, it doesn't, does it?" He took a second to survey the room before he walked closer to her and spoke more quietly than any of their conversation so far. "The truth is, you could be very useful to me, Mila Messer."

Mila backed a step away from him. "How could *I* possibly be useful to *you?*"

The ambassador straightened, creating an even more perfect posture. "Volkner Brandt believes I am here to negotiate an alliance between Jotun and Vidar. But an alliance with a violent dictator is very far from what I want. You saw how he dealt with a simple interruption, yes?"

Mila nodded, recalling the sound of Fischer gurgling and the bloodlust in Volkner's gold-flecked eyes.

"He is a man that only cares about power without reservation. An allied Jotun and Vidar would be near unstoppable, even for Idun."

"And why is that bad for you?"

The ambassador went stone serious. "I told you, my love is my home. With the might of Jotun behind him, Volkner would start a war that would kill billions, including many of my own people. An all-out system conflict would set the civilizations of Ymir back hundreds of years at a minimum. The only thing that stopped that the first time, during the invasion of Hod, was Idun. We cannot afford to see it go further."

"None of this explains why you would want to help me," Mila replied. "I'm just the daughter of a drunk fool."

"You have no idea how wrong you are, Mila," the

ambassador said, taking Mila around the shoulders and peering into her eyes. She saw now that his eyes were quicksilver, fitting of his silver-blond hair. "You are quite possibly the most important person in the entire system. As Volkner's Master Refiner, you are indispensable. Every Master Refiner he's had before has been invited into his inner circle. You will be as close as anyone to him. He discusses things with his inner circle that he shares with no one else. And he will guard you like a starving wolf over fresh meat. There are only a handful of Master Refiners left in Ymir, and none of them his. You're his key to hyrrine—the only thing left he'll need to power his Navy."

The ambassador paused, making sure Mila was following him.

"So, you want me to be your spy?" she asked.

The ambassador dropped his hands and stepped back, letting the air breathe between them. "A crude term for it, but yes. I need to know his thoughts."

"Do you not have that access?" Mila asked. "I mean, I saw the way he bent when you spoke up there."

The ambassador shook his head. "He wants to impress me—needs to. He shows me the fleet ships and defense cannons and treats me to massive feasts every night. Then he shows me his iron hand when his men fall out of line. But it is all a pony show. The only things he tells me of strategies and plans are the things he thinks I want to hear."

"And what of the guards posted outside? Do you not expect them to relay your movements to the president?"

The ambassador shrugged. "As a politician, you learn how to sway people in your favor. Some men like women. Others like the promise of future power. Most like money. Find out what they like, and promise an excess of it in the future, and they will work in your favor. The Berserker's guards are making a point to examine everything but the refinery doors right now."

Mila nodded, considering everything the ambassador had said so far. She only had one question. "How can I trust anything you've told me? I don't even know your name."

The ambassador put on a face of exaggerated appall. "Forgive me, for I have been rude." He took her hand in his, the flesh of it cool, and bowed deep. "I am Úlfljótur, and I am at your service. You may call me Úlf." He rose and rested on her gaze once more. "As for trusting me, well, I would argue you haven't another option. So, what do you say, Mila Messer?"

He was right, of course. What else did she have to lose? If she failed to refine the brandr, she'd be sent to the mines and her father executed. The punishment for treason couldn't be much worse than that. There was only one answer.

"Very well, Úlf," she said. "I'm in."

⊙———◦———◦———⊙

MILA WATCHED the ambassador closely as he navigated the vast stretch of machinery. Keeping track of every step was difficult. He moved with almost inhuman precision and speed, knowing exactly what buttons to press at the precise times. He inspected the brandr and adjusted heat and timing settings accordingly. The refinery hissed and steamed, smelling of sulfur, as it processed the raw material into bona fide hyrrine.

Mila saw enough that, if she got the chance, she could perhaps halfway replicate the process.

"This last part will take a few hours," Úlf said, rubbing his hands together as he stepped away from the machinery.

To Mila's astonishment, he didn't have even a single drop of sweat on his brow.

"You should get some rest," he continued. "Tomorrow will be a big day for you."

Mila was suddenly aware of how tired she was. A bit of sleep before seeing Volkner again didn't sound so bad.

"Thank you," she said. "For everything."

The ambassador nodded. "Just remember, you're part of something much bigger than yourself now. When the time comes, I'll need you."

Mila nodded in reply.

"Until next time, Miss Messer," Úlf said, bowing as he had before.

"Until next time."

CHAPTER
TEN

"I'll be damned," Waren said, stroking his beard as he examined the gauge on the final vat. "Take a look at this, Eber."

The older guard joined him and whistled. "Looks like little Miss Messer's the real deal."

Mila rose from the cot, wiping the sleep from her eyes. The guards weren't what woke her, it was the grinding of the refinery doors. But she hadn't wanted to look up at who entered. She had been worried everything with the ambassador had been a dream; that she was going to wake without an ounce of refined brandr to present.

Her first thought was of what seemed to be genuine surprise in the guards' voices. She guessed it must have been the other two, the young Hodian and the hairless one, who Úlf had paid off. Her second thought came along with an obnoxiously loud growl from her stomach. She realized she hadn't eaten since midday yesterday, and her body was letting her know that was too long.

Both guards seemed to hear it as they turned to her.

"Mornin', Master Refiner," Eber said. "You've pulled off quite the feat."

Mila ran a hand through her tangling hair, trying to straighten out the knots. "What happens now?"

"Well," Eber replied, "first we're gonna get you something to eat. Won't be a Vanir feast by any means; Command hasn't authorized hot rations down here. But, it should set that grumbling at ease. Then, I guess you'll go see Volky."

Mila's stomach sank at the mention of the president, though it was softened somewhat by the childish nickname. She realized Waren hadn't said a word nor really looked at her. His eyes were fixed on the vél curled up beside her cot. She'd placed him in rest mode before going back to bed. She wasn't sure how close a call it had been to shredding the ambassador to pieces and she wanted to avoid any unexpected surprises.

"What's a Mark II doing here?" Waren asked, no playfulness in the question.

Eberhard seemed to notice it for the first time, his eyes shifting wide. "Odin's spear. Haven't seen one of those in years, since—"

He was cut off as the refinery doors hissed and groaned open, and Niko stalked in. The Berserker was carrying a gray sack and little else. He gestured with a nod to the door which seemed the other guards' cue to leave. Once they were gone, and the doors shut, he tossed the gray sack onto her cot.

"These are your new clothes," he said. "You've got a set of formals and work wear. I imagine Volkner will authorize more if you continue to produce. But, for now, this is what you have, so keep them clean."

Continue to produce. "Wait," Mila started, "how did you know I pulled it off?"

Niko tapped his ear and Mila realized his hearing was digitally enhanced, and he'd likely heard the guards' conversation through the doors. Good to note.

"What's that all about?" he asked, gesturing toward Fen.

Mila shrugged. "Found him in the scrap and had some extra time."

"You realize *what* it is, right?"

"A deadly piece of Vidarin military equipment," Mila replied. "That just so happens to have a damaged aggression chip and can't exit violence inhibition mode."

Niko looked at her curiously, like he was trying to figure her out, then he shook his head. "Just don't advertise it. All the Mark II's were ordered to be destroyed a few years ago. Brandt won't like it if he finds out one survived."

"You're not going to tell on me?" Mila said, somewhat jokingly, though she couldn't deny seeing the robot tossed away like scrap would break her heart a little.

Niko ignored the question, and Mila's stomach threatened to twist into a knot again. "Get rid of the dress and change into the formals. Eberhard will be in with your breakfast in five minutes. We'll be heading to the command deck in twenty."

"Get rid of the dress?" Mila said. "I can't. It was my mother's."

Niko looked her up and down and grimaced. "It's ruined."

"It stays," Mila said, glaring at the Berserker who could likely end her life in a single movement.

Niko practically rolled his eyes. "Fine, keep it then. Makes no difference to me." He turned to exit.

"Wait, what about facilities?" Mila asked. "A bathroom? A shower? Toothpaste?"

Niko looked back at her. "There are biowipes in the bag, and there's a small head down the passageway that one of my men will show you to."

Small was an overstatement. As if the biowipe bath hadn't been depressing enough, when Eberhard led her to the bathroom, she found a tiny room barely large enough for one person. The metal vacuum toilet was freezing cold, almost as cold as the dribble of water that ran from the faucet. The shattered mirror gave her just enough reflection to see how dull she looked in the formal grays of the Vidarin government.

She missed her coveralls. At least those olive-green things showed years of character in their oil and chemical stains. She missed her shop, too, where she'd outfitted the bathroom to run with water heated off the shield battery cooling system. It was even better than the restrooms in their house, though she'd never let Hans know that.

When Mila emerged, her hair up in a knotty mess held with an elastic tie borrowed from Waren, Eberhard was waiting with a bowl of what looked to be rubbery eggs and a brown plastic packet.

"Rehydrated eggs and peanut butter," he said. "Breakfast of the truest Vikings and poorest beggars."

Mila nodded a thanks but knew her smile wouldn't pass as genuine. Even as hungry as she was, rehydrated eggs didn't sound appetizing. Still, she scarfed them down to settle her complaining stomach and managed to only gag once. She barely had time to digest before Niko was ordering her to follow him to the lift.

His stride was casual, yet precise and quick. Mila hadn't realized how fast he walked the day before. Maybe it was the shock of it all, or maybe he was walking much faster today. Either way, she found herself constantly falling a few steps behind, having to half-jog to catch back up to him. He never acknowledged it, but she could see him practically roll his eyes when he reached the lift and found her almost ten yards back. Still, he hadn't said a word.

The only sound in the lift for the first few minutes was the hum of the electromagnetic propulsion system and the beeping floor markers. Mila honestly had no idea what to expect when they reached the command deck. She felt relief that her father would be spared, at least for now, but what came along with being Volkner's *Master Refiner*? An impossibly dull wardrobe, apparently. She supposed she'd find out the rest soon enough.

"How did you do it?" Niko asked, breaking her out of her own mind.

"Do what?"

"Refine the brandr," he replied, in a tone that suggested she ought to know exactly what he was talking about.

"Oh," Mila replied. "I just did what I do every time. Put brandr in, get hyrrine out."

"You seemed pretty adamant that you wouldn't have enough time."

Mila shrugged. "Guess I underestimated myself."

Niko grunted what could have been a laugh.

An awkward gap of silence nestled between them. Mila shifted and looked around, trying to find anything in the lift to distract herself. She would see Volkner soon enough and invited anything to relieve the anxiety of that thought. No matter how happy he may be with her, no matter how kind he may pretend to be, she knew the terror that was the president.

The internal pieces of the lift were not up to the job,

however. Steel, titanium, and holopanels were only so interesting. So that left her with Schafer.

She examined his uniform, how he wore it with such casual disregard when all other officers on the ship wore theirs prim and proper.

"Why do you wear your uniform like that?" she asked.

Mila wasn't sure if he'd answer, but talking to herself was better than being alone with her thoughts. When he turned and raised a curious eyebrow, Mila felt that knot that had been set in her stomach loosen just a touch.

"Despite what some of my fellow officers might believe," he replied, "these are just clothes. Going out of your way to wear them uncomfortably is moronic, I think."

"But aren't there regulations?"

Niko shrugged. "Yes, but you'll find I don't give much of a damn about regulations. I have a job, and it's not wearing this uniform properly."

"And Volkner's just *okay* with that?"

"If I'm being honest, I think he prefers it this way. Makes his prize berserker stick out better in a crowd."

"About that," Mila said. "I thought all the berserkers were..."

"Dead?" Niko replied. "They may as well be."

Mila could tell by his short tone the conversation was over, and she couldn't help but feel like she'd crossed a line. She was left alone with those invasive thoughts of Volkner for the rest of the lift ride.

* * *

WHEN THE DOORS to the command room opened, Mila and Niko were greeted by Volkner already yelling.

"Stupid girl," he spat. "You're lucky I don't have you beheaded right here."

All of the politicians and advisors on either side of his throne were silent as the grave. He was yelling at a younger, bronze-skinned girl in a sheer red servant's dress. Mila was struck by how beautiful the young girl was, nearly flawless in every way, except for the way her back arched in her cowering pose and the way her wide eyes threatened to spew tears at any moment. Those observations made Mila's mind switch from awe to pity, and boiling anger. She felt that heat rising up her back again as the warlord hurled insults at the girl. The feeling peaked at the top of Mila's back like a molten orb just beneath the surface of her skin. Then, pain—a shock went through her that dissolved the orb, and her arm went limp.

"Shit," she hissed, stopping mid-stride on Volkner's ornate rug.

She clasped her arm tightly to keep it from flopping uncontrollably. It took her a moment to find her breath, stolen by the pain. She could also swear she felt a tinge of discomfort in her chest cavity.

"What's wrong?" Niko asked.

Mila looked up to find the Berserker's head cocked, his eyes set on the elerex. Then, his brow rose as if in understanding.

"It's nothing," Mila said, shaking her head to dismiss both the Berserker's and her own concerns. "I just need a tinkerer's screwdriver."

"Can you make it through this?" Niko asked. If Mila didn't know better, she'd say that sounded like genuine concern in his voice.

Before she could answer, Volkner called out, "By all

means, Miss Messer, keep us waiting." There was nothing but malice in those words.

Mila and Niko made their way to the foot of the throne. The military men and politicians exchanged the proper gestures, except for Volkner, who couldn't be bothered to return a simple salute.

"So, you've done it," Volkner said. "You're a *certified brandr refiner* after all."

There was no mistaking the sarcasm laced in the sentiment.

"She is, my Vini," Niko said. "I saw the gauges myself."

"I wasn't speaking to you, Schafer," Volkner hissed, his golden eyes flicking to the Berserker.

Niko didn't reply, but Mila felt like the temperature of the room rose a few degrees as the Berserker bit back whatever he wanted to say.

"Word is you produced more than I ordered," Volkner continued.

"Yes, sir," Mila replied.

"Good," the president replied. He donned a smile like a Vidarin nightcat and said, "Then you won't have an issue with me doubling the requirement tonight."

Several of the politicians and advisors stirred. Volkner's plan was clearly news to them.

"President Brandt, if I may," Úlf said, rising from his padded seat.

Mila saw the president's eye twitch, but he didn't object.

"Increasing the demand already seems a drastic step. Perhaps you should consider waiting at least a few days?"

Volkner turned his attention to the ambassador. "I appreciate your concern, Mister Úlfljótur, but we clearly have a more-than-capable brandr refiner on our hands." It seemed like he cut every word to keep from cursing at the politician. He turned his attention back to Mila. "To ensure that you haven't engaged in any trickery or lies, and to guarantee that last night wasn't some fool's luck, I expect double the amount of hyrrine come tomorrow morning. You will have the day to rest, eat, and do whatever else suits you short of leaving this ship, and then you will get to work."

There was no room for argument in the president's tone. He was a bad look away from slitting another throat, and if he decided to, there wasn't a thing anyone here could do to stop him.

As the president dismissed them, Mila's last thought was of the girl trembling behind Volkner's throne. She was the embodiment of every victim of the president's wrath. It made Mila desire to do something she wouldn't have dreamed of before.

It made her want to kill him.

⋄◦————————◦⋄

MILA'S ARM was still limp when they reached the lift. She hadn't seen a screwdriver small enough for the miniscule hardware of the elerex in the refinery. But, maybe with a little bit of digging she'd get lucky, she hoped. For now, she tapped at it, hoping to knock the adjustment screw just enough to jumpstart it.

"You know, they stopped installing those things for a reason," Niko said without looking at her.

Mila looked up at the parallel strips of exposed metal underneath his skin. "You're one to talk. I'm pretty sure they stopped making everything that's inside you."

Niko looked back at her, an eyebrow raised and his lips threatening a grin. "Getting a bit bold, aren't we?"

Mila half-laughed. "What, should I be scared? Don't I technically outrank you?"

Niko's eyes went wide, not in fear, but in almost pleasant surprise. "For now, kleizufet."

"What?" Mila asked.

"Oh, nothing," Niko replied, turning his gaze away from her again.

"No, what was that word?"

"You're pretty persistent, aren't you?"

Mila raised her chin. "I can be... when I want something. Now talk."

"It means you're very bold for someone so small," Niko replied. He looked back over his shoulder at her.

"So, it's an insult?"

Niko smirked. "It's whatever you take it as. But I do think you're already starting to understand this place."

It was either the highest compliment or most profound slander, and Niko's tone didn't tell her which. Before she could question him further, the lift stopped. Mila was surprised by the early halt only a few minutes into the ride and the cushioned braking, so different from the jarring deceleration on the refinery level.

"What's wrong?" Mila asked.

Niko looked entirely unfazed. "What do you mean?"

"We've stopped."

"Yes."

"*Why* have we stopped?" Mila demanded.

Niko looked back at her and cocked his head as he had before. He looked for all the world like a dog looking at a favorite new toy. If anyone else on the ship looked at her that way, Mila would avoid them like the plague. Yet, when he did it, it didn't feel predatory in the slightest. It felt good —like she surprised him, fascinated him—like she wasn't some farmer's daughter or a freakish prodigy, but a genuinely interesting human being. Though she knew better than to believe any of those feelings.

She read the holoscreen above the doors just before they slid open. *Sjaundi, Supply & Logistics.*

"You said you needed a tinkerer's screwdriver?" Niko asked, stepping out of the lift and gesturing for her to follow.

"Well, yeah," Mila answered hesitantly.

"Then let's get one."

Mila raised an eyebrow, but Niko was already pacing away. So, she followed.

The level was busy with fatigue-clad soldiers wielding clipboards, examining information as they walked, most of them not paying any mind to what was in front of them. Yet, none of them collided, as if they all understood exactly how to traverse the corridors blind. When Mila accidentally bumped one, the pimple-faced youth looked as though he'd been assaulted. However, his clear contempt was quickly quelled when he realized *who* had run into him and the Berserker that stood beside her. In the end, he apologized before scurrying off.

These soldiers were so very different from the grunts scattered throughout the station and the officers occupying the upper levels. They seemed actually busy, as if every one of them held information that was vital to keeping the *Gjaller* in orbit.

As they continued on, bustling men in fatigues gave way to scattered pedestrian soldiers. Some of them wore the gray Vidarin camos, but their rolled sleeves were loose and their hands in their pockets. It was the same way Niko wore his uniform. Their hair was worn in one of two ways, and Mila found nearly no exceptions. It was either very short—

shaven clean or buzzed close to the scalp—or overgrown and shaggy. It was clear this was a section of the *Gjaller* that was not inspected for any type of grooming standard very often.

The smell of machine oil and carbon solvents began to ring in Mila's nose, reminding her instantly of repairing equipment on the farm. When she noticed some men were now wearing coveralls in lieu of fatigues, she knew she was amongst mechanics. The scent of rusted parts and the sight of oil-stained coveralls made a pocket of comforting warmth open up in Mila's chest.

She was only able to savor the feeling for a few moments before they stopped at a door labeled *Mechanic Shop 12*. When it didn't open automatically for the duo, Niko pressed the intercom button beside it.

"Kord, you in there?" Niko asked.

"Who is it?" a staticky voice bit back.

"Schafer. I need a favor."

"No favors from Kord."

Niko huffed and rolled his eyes. "Come on, Kord. It's not a favor for me."

There was no reply.

"Not on the best of terms?" Mila asked.

"I'm on better terms with him than anyone on this station," Niko replied. "He's just... Kord." Niko buzzed again. "I'm not leaving until you let us in, Kord."

No response.

Niko buzzed again, and again, repeating "Kord" every time. After the sixth or so buzz, he recoiled quickly. "Tyr's bloody hand," he cursed, grabbing his thumb.

Mila caught a glimpse of liquid on the tip of it before he covered it. It was blood, but not red blood. She'd heard rumors about the blood of berserkers, about how it was proof they were no longer human. It seemed like the rumors were at least partly true. The blood on his finger was bold, cobalt blue.

Mila realized she was staring when Niko quickly tucked his hand away and his jaw tensed.

"Oh, I'm—" she started.

"It's nothing," Niko said quickly, shrugging off any conversation about the blood. He leaned in to closely inspect the intercom button. "Aesir damn you, Kord," he said mostly to himself. Looking back at Mila, he said, "He booby trapped it. Stabs you with a hidden needle if you press the button too many times." Niko laughed and shook his head as he stood back up straight. "All right, then. Plan B."

The way he spoke made Mila instinctively take a step back, half expecting the Berserker to punch the door down with his enhanced strength. When he raised a fist, she was all but certain of it, but soon found it wasn't so serious as that.

Niko pounded on the door itself and the sound reverberated through the passageway. Many passing mechanics and soldiers looked, but none dared to tell him to stop.

"Kord!" Niko yelled in a tone so command-like it was almost mocking. "As your superior officer and on the authority of Vidar's newest Master Refiner," he said, shooting a quick smirk at Mila, "I order you to open this door!"

He repeated the order once more.

"Kord! If I have to tell you one more time—"

Before he could finish, the door shot open with a hiss.

"Enough, enough!" A high-pitched yet rough voice said from within. "You bring too much attention to Kord! Just come inside."

"Well hello there, Kord!" Niko said cheerfully as they walked in. "Long time no see."

The one called Kord was stationed behind a glass-walled stand. Where the room that Niko and Mila occupied was only a few dozen square feet, the workshop stretched behind the glass was easily a few hundred. Every inch of it, it seemed to Mila, was covered in spare parts, tools, and odds and ends she didn't recognize. Every item was meticulously organized, and its space labeled, down to the last bolt.

Kord himself was the exact opposite of his carefully laid out shop. His silver-streaked black hair was thinning and grown shoulder-length, matching his unkempt, wispy beard. His forest green eyes looked in opposite directions, and neither was focused on his guests. The coveralls he wore were perhaps the filthiest garment Mila had ever seen. They were stained by grease, oil, sweat, and the gods only knew what else, and there were far more than a few visible holes worn through.

"You bring Kord's magnetic torque wrench?" Kord said, failing to acknowledge the greeting or the fact Niko wasn't alone.

"For the last time, Kord, I was ordered to retrieve that for General Ald. I don't know what happened to it after he died."

"You bring new one then?"

"No, I didn't."

"Then get out," Kord demanded.

"Come now, Kord," Niko replied. "I'll get you a new one soon, I promise. I'm not here for myself today, though."

Kord tilted his head. There was no way to be absolutely sure, but Mila thought he was now looking at her.

"Hello," Mila said, giving a little wave. "I'm Mila."

"Kord," he grunted.

"Well met, Kord."

"Mila is the new Master Refiner," Niko said.

Mila was caught off-guard when Kord cackled.

"There's no need for that," Niko said calmly.

Kord didn't stop.

"That's enough!" Niko said sternly.

"Apologies," Kord said, wiping a tear from one of the roaming eyes. "It's just that—" Kord started laughing again. "Boom!" The man seemed as though he were about to fall over, he was laughing so hard.

Niko stepped forward, poised to reach through the slot in the bottom of the glass, but Kord wrangled in his laughter.

"What you want to steal from Kord?"

"A tinkerer's screwdriver." Mila could tell by Niko's tone that his patience was wearing thin.

"Nope!" Kord replied quickly.

Niko and Kord started going in the same circle about the magnetic wrench, each one speaking a little bit louder than before. But as Mila's eyes roamed the shop behind the mechanic, their voices began to fade into the background.

She'd always dreamed to have a shop like this. Not necessarily this organized; she knew there was no hope for maintaining that kind of order in her workspace. But to have one this well-equipped would mean so many projects past done far quicker, and with less improvising and frustrated curses. With a shop like Kord's, Mila would have repaired the hoverbike battery in a day, rather than the weeks it took to source parts and tools from the pit, and the hours of straining her eyes under too-little light.

She noticed something different about the shop than she'd expected to find. Set on tall shelves in the rear of Kord's shop were dozens of toys. They were a very specific kind of toy. Tops, set on bases that allowed them to spin indefinitely via a series of shifting magnets within the tops and their bases. Mila had found one in the pit once, but was never able to get it quite right with repairs. The internal structure was as intricate as clockwork and the magnets painfully precise. Replacements were hard to find and much harder to replicate.

"All we need," Niko said, his voice escalating into a yell. "Is a gods-damned tiny screwdriver."

Just as the mechanic was about to yell back his denial, Mila said, "You like tops, Kord?"

Both men stopped talking. Niko's eyebrows were raised in a confused expression. Kord, on the other hand, cocked his head to the side and looked at Mila quizzically.

"Yes," he said. "Kord likes tops."

"I noticed your collection," Mila went on. "They're quite beautiful. And to have so many spinning is a feat."

Kord looked back at the shelves, and then to Mila. "You know about tops?"

"Oh, only so much. I find them fascinating, but they're so intricate that I never quite mastered them. One of the few things I couldn't successfully tinker."

"You're... a tinkerer?" Kord asked, almost as if he were challenging her.

Mila nodded.

Kord's brow furrowed, and his eyes shook for a moment before his frown faded, replaced with an impossibly wide smile.

"Wait here!" the mechanic said excitedly.

He scurried away from his counter to the back of his shop.

"What was that?" Niko asked.

"I saw his collection on the back wall."

Niko shook his head. "No, I mean... Kord has never—"

He was interrupted as the mechanic returned with an aged wooden box.

"Look, look," he said, opening the lid and turning it to them.

Inside was a collection of five polished metal tops and their accompanying bases. Each was a different color metal, polished to a perfect sheen. There was a black one, a blue-silver one, a golden one, a bronze one, and a chrome one.

"They're quite beautiful, Kord," Mila said.

Kord was beaming. "They were a gift from Kord's father when Kord was very young."

"And you've collected them ever since," Mila said with a kind smile.

Kord nodded happily.

Over the next several minutes, Kord showed Mila near-every top in his collection. He recalled where he'd gotten each one. Some were gifts from his parents. Some he'd bought with his own earnings. Others he'd found when he'd been deployed. There was one, a larger top the color of sandstone, that he didn't share the origins of. Mila complimented every top that was presented, and Niko's amazement never seemed to fade.

At the end of it all, Kord gave Mila one of his tops with a hue of yellow gold, along with a tinkerer's screwdriver.

"It's yours to keep," Kord said, still wearing that wide smile.

"Thank you, Kord," Mila replied.

"Also," Kord said in a much more polite tone than the one he was using when they entered the shop, "Kord must ask, what is it you need to tinker now?"

Mila rolled up her sleeve to reveal the metal plate implanted in her forearm.

Kord's eyebrows jumped. "An elerex? Kord hasn't seen an elerex in years."

"Have you worked on them before?" Mila asked.

Kord nodded. "A few, but never one quite like yours."

"What do you mean?"

Kord gestured for her to put her arm on the metal tabletop between them. Once she did, he donned a set of comically magnifying eyeglasses and began tracing the intricacies of the elerex with the tip of his surprisingly thin and nimble fingers.

"First, your elerex is more refined than any Kord has seen. This smooth plating is normally ugly iron. Yours is also much smaller than a typical device. And this," he said, pointing to the rune inscribed in the middle. "This is certainly curious."

"Runes are fairly common decorations," Niko said.

"Yes," Kord said. "But do you know this rune?"

"It's mannaz," Mila said. "The rune of humanity."

"You are almost correct. It is like mannaz in the New Futhark—the younger runes we know. But look here; these straight lines are not the new language. Mannaz has curved lines on top. No, this is one of the old runes, the Elder Futhark. Its name is Algiz."

"It is a rune of the swan... of beauty. But it also has another name."

"Elhaz," Niko said, his eyes fixed intently on the rune.

"Exactly."

Mila looked between them both. "What does that mean?"

"Elhaz is the rune of the elk, of protection. This duality of protection and beauty is what makes the rune one of the most powerful there is. Those versed in the old ways say it's divine, and not a rune to bestow lightly. They say that those blessed by this rune are watched by Heimdall himself."

The two men went so tense and quiet that Mila couldn't help but let loose a small laugh. "Is it really so serious? Probably something my father asked for before they installed it. Do you believe it's *actually* tied to the gods?"

Niko didn't reply, but Kord said, "To be watched by the all-seer is either a gift or a curse. Kord has not seen an elerex like this, nor one so young master brandr refining. Kord would not discount the gods' presence in your life just yet, Mila Messer."

Mila tried to hold her smile but couldn't. Those words were too taut, filled with too much conviction.

"I think that's enough for now," Niko said.

Kord was looking at Mila intently. "If you need anything, Mila, anything at all, you just ask Kord."

ELEVEN

BEEP.

   Beep.

   Beepbomp.

   Beep.

   Beep.

Piper DeRache was warm when she woke, both inside and outside. The outside warmth came from the radiator heater under the frosted window that dulled the white sunlight streaking in from outside. That, and the half-dozen wool blankets stacked on top of her. The inner warmth, though, was different.

No, she'd felt that warmth before—synthetic painkillers, antibiotics, and the stirrings of a low fever. Medicine. Glorious medicine. And manmade heat sources, the antithesis to that brutal cold outside.

Piper tried to shift her elbows to prop herself up only to find she couldn't really control her limbs that well.

Really good medicine.

Piper closed her eyes, fully prepared to let the tendrils of warm darkness pull her back in. She wanted to fall into that void—empty, black, wholly separate from the frozen tundra of Vidar. A world apart from the pod, the wreckage of the *Thialfi*.

Piper's eyes shot open. She didn't have time for this—lying around in bliss. She didn't deserve it, not when her ship was nothing but debris—the pieces of the carcass scattered in the snow. Not when her crew was gone, awaiting the gods' judgment in the afterlife. Not when there was a debt to be paid.

"Volkner," she whispered, the name like hot iron on her tongue.

It was the only name that mattered; the only *thing* that mattered. She had to get back to the *Gjaller,* and quick, before anyone realized she was still alive. She prayed the doctors hadn't yet discovered who she was. No doubt they knew she was an outlier since she didn't have a citizen chip, just the faint scar from where it was removed when she joined the *Laufey* all those years ago. It wouldn't take much to connect the dots that she was aboard the *Thialfi*.

No, there wasn't time for this. Piper breathed deep and gathered her thoughts, focusing on moving her arms. Her right one obeyed, but the left stayed stagnate. She ripped the blankets away and found out why her left arm wasn't moving. There was nothing there.

From the elbow down, Piper's flesh and bone was just... gone. There was a bandage around the stub speckled with bits of red-brown. The rest of her arm, along her bicep toward her gown-covered shoulder, was a sickly light purple and showed evidence of healing blisters.

Piper bit down hard and shook her head, closing her eyes only to open them and find her forearm and hand still missing. It was the gods punishing her; condemning her for being alive while her ship sat in ruin. She knew it.

Piper looked down the rest of her body, assessing the damages. She realized there were thick bandages wrapped around her chest under the gown, confirming her suspicion of fractured ribs. A small but neat and freshly-stitched wound between her ribs told her there'd been fluid in her chest they'd had to siphon out. She felt her head, finding it shaved nearly to the scalp. There were two wounds that had been stapled shut, one she remembered from the shuttle landing, the other a twisted puncture wound she deduced came from the snow beasts.

Her right arm was blistered in spots, but nowhere near as bad off as the left. Still, her normally-bronze skin was far too pale, and the limb felt almost foreign to her. She imagined that was a side effect of the drugs more than anything. It was the same feeling for her legs, which she'd yet to uncover.

As she leaned up to remove the rest of the blankets, she heard the sound of fabric ripping, and searing pain from her back broke through the drugged haze. It took her a moment to regain her breath, and even then that pain still boiled. She could smell the tang of fresh blood and knew she'd torn the stitches of some significant wound on her back. The heart monitor beside her started beeping faster and faster as she heaved heavy breaths.

I don't have time for this, she thought, and sat up again, baring her teeth in agony. She reached for the blanket with both hands, quickly realizing trying with the left was now a moot effort. With her right she managed to pull the wool blankets off and threw them onto the floor, ripping out wires tangled into them in the process. It sent the heart monitor blaring as a flat line made its way across the holoscreen. But Piper didn't even hear it, couldn't. A dulling descended on every sound and sight around her, as only one thing was in focus—her legs.

Her left one was blistered and bruised, covered in dozens of stitches in various places. It met a purple foot with only four toes. Yet, it was better than the other. Like her left arm, Piper's right leg was half gone, amputated from the knee down. But, unlike her arm, there wasn't nothingness below it. No, attached to her knee was a tarnished metal leg, the outer shell more of an abstract casing than a proper shield. All of the inner hydraulics and cords were clearly visible from the outside view.

Whether it was from the loss of blood from the wound in her back, or the shock of seeing her leg replaced by machinery, Piper couldn't know. Perhaps it was both. But whatever it was, Piper's head went light as a feather, and the tendrils of darkness took their hold.

PIPER WOKE the second time to the sound of the room door clicking shut. The room and everything in it was blurry to her, including the tall male figure that had just entered wearing a white, fur-trimmed coat with a red uruz rune emblazoned on the chest; the standard apparel of Jotun healers.

"Ah, our patient is finally awake," he said in a cheery tone that was nearly as blurry to Piper as he looked.

Piper shook her head in an attempt to dismiss the disorientation, but only succeeded in making it worse. Now she felt as if she were traversing a Tyran class 5 sandstorm in a hovership. It was all she could do to keep from puking.

"Easy now," the doctor said, his voice thick with a rural Jotun accent. "Ya've got quite the cocktail in ya'. Had to do it, though. The pain of those wounds and the mechanics may of killed ya' if not."

"What did you do to me?" Piper managed. Her voice was far too weak for her liking.

"We saved ya'. You were frozen colder than Laufey's teeth."

"My leg. My arm."

The doctor sighed. "Yeah, we had to act quick on those. Ya'd taken the frost to mid-shin, and that arm, well, let's just say it would've been easier to take more than I did. I managed to get an old aluminum one off a regular trader through these parts, though. Was plannin' to put it on yesterday before ya' had that little incident. Ya' know, to even have survived bein' out in that snow like that, you must've had the Matron watchin' close."

Not the Matron, Piper thought. She knew what she'd seen in the distant snow.

Piper breathed deep and let the swishing feeling in her head settle with her eyes closed. When she opened them, she did so slowly, carefully, not wanting to set off the dizziness again. She saw now the doctor was much younger than her, no gray showing in his short raven-black beard and matching hair.

"Biomech?" she asked.

The doctor chuckled, a deep, hearty sound. "Biomech? What kind of money do ya' think I've got lyin' around? Not enough to be makin' berserkers in my spare time, I'll tell ya' that much." He stopped to laugh again.

Piper felt a vein pulsing in her temple. She realized now the question had been stupid. Even in the smallest surgeries, biomech cost millions of marks. In more extreme cases, like limb replacements, that number was in the hundreds of millions. She'd heard from more than one source the berserkers, with their biomech-laced muscular and nervous systems, along with their titanium-infused skeletons, carried a price tag of over a billion marks each. One of the most expensive, and most lethal, weapons in Ymir; in all of human history.

"'fraid you'll have to settle for old-fashioned robotics, Miss..."

"Frida," Piper replied shortly.

"Well met, Frida," he said. "I'm called Einar."

Frida Svendottir was her most recently memorized alias. Any good void pirate worth their stardust had one, and this was as easy to remember as any other. A Tyran refugee turned modest trader after her parents had smuggled her away from the abrasive, war-happy clans of Tyr. An easy backstory to remember—mostly because it contained kernels of truth—and was just interesting enough for pity but not so intriguing as to raise unwanted questions.

"What, pray tell, brought ya' to the icy gates of Valgrind?" Einar asked.

Piper's head wasn't yet clear enough for a proper lie. So, she gathered the details she could recall from the hazy corners of her mind and made it as simple as she could.

"Fuel cell malfunction. I was headed for trade in Skadi, and when I hit atmosphere, I think I knocked something loose. Passed out on descent and woke up out in the snow."

Piper prayed to Freya for mercy that they weren't a long way from Skadi, the Jotun capitol city. Einar's raised eyebrow and knowing look told her she was way off the mark.

He was still smiling as he said, "Ya' don't say. Your navigation systems must have been malfunctionin' pretty good too." Einar looked toward the room door as if looking for a visitor, then started checking the various machines Piper was wired to. "Ya' know," he continued, "I heard the craziest announcement come over broadcast the other day. They said the *Thialfi* was shot down. Can ya' believe that?"

Piper tried to control her breathing, but it was near impossible in her state. She knew her nostrils were flaring, and her chest heaved too much.

He knows.

Einar kept going when she didn't respond. "The ship of *the* Piper DeRache. No survivors, they say."

"That's crazy," Piper managed to bite out.

"It is," Einar replied.

He paused for a moment, his pale gray eyes examining Piper's face. Every inch of Piper wanted to lunge from the bed, grab the closest sharp object she could find, and thrust it into his neck. He knew who she was, or at least the ship she'd been on; there was no question about it.

Then, Einar shrugged, as if tossing aside the entire thought. "Oh, well," he said. His eyes met hers, that smile omnipresent and warmer than the radiator on the wall. "By the way, you'll want to get a new citizen chip. Lost your old one in the amputation, I'm afraid."

Piper's defense toppled. Einar laughed softly, and she knew he could sense her confusion.

"Get some rest, Miss Frida," he said.

As he turned to leave the room, Piper found her words. "Why?"

Einar turned to her, and for the first time, his expression seemed more serious, yet still kind.

"Why do you care about Piper DeRache?" Piper expanded.

"My full name is Einar, son of Elmar. My father was Elmar, son of Eldir. My father was a healer, like me. But he was a much better man than me. He took his healin' to those who needed it most. One time, the people of Hod needed it most, when Vidar tried to invade them. He healed alongside those who fought to protect the natives."

"He was with the Iduans?"

Einar shook his head. "No, the ones that didn't fight for politics; the ones that fought for the people themselves. There were many there who did, includin' a pirate ship called *Laufey*."

A knot formed in Piper's throat as she tried to swallow.

"Only then, we did not call them pirates. *Then,* we called them rebels."

Einar let the words sink in.

"Your father sounds like a good man," Piper finally said.

"Aye, he was," Einar replied. He then paused for a long moment, looking at Piper, but not focusing on her. "His medical vessel was targeted by a Vidarin missile. He never came home from Hod."

"I'm so sorry," Piper said, and she genuinely was.

She had only just joined the crew of the *Laufey* when they allied with the rebel resistance on Hod. The Liónar Uprising, they'd called it. An army of misfits tired of the wargames between the planet superpowers who couldn't sit by and let innocent Hodians be slaughtered in a conflict that should have never been their burden. The Iduans had come to their aid, yes, and their military technology was what fended off Vidar. But they were not there, on the ground, sweating and bleeding with the Hodians. They did not stay for the fallout, to help rebuild. They did not help with the assault on the *Gjaller* while the Vidarin forces were weak. The Liónars did.

"His death is part of the past now," Einar said. "And so, it seems, are the rest of the rebels. But there are still enemies of freedom in Ymir. As I'm a healer, I can only hope to help those who would fight it."

Einar made his way to the door once more, but one question lingered on Piper's mind. "How did you know it was me?"

Einar stopped with his fingers wrapped around the door handle and said simply, "The blackeye hand."

CHAPTER

TWELVE

THE BLACKEYE HAND.

Einar had been referring to a distinct scar on Piper's shoulder. It was in the shape of a hand, with the imprint of a closed eye in the middle. The tissue of the scar, however, was not pink or pale, but permanently black. Only a handful of people in Ymir held that scar—so rare it was widely thought a myth. But Piper knew its reality, its meaning, its cost.

It was the mark of the Oracle, left behind after the crone saw one's destiny. Captain Skuld had sent Piper to seek her before giving her command of the *Thialfi*. Skuld shared the scar but had never required subordinate captains to make the pilgrimage; only Piper. She'd always wondered if it meant Skuld intended her to take control of the fleet one day, to see if she was worthy.

It was said that only the worthiest could find the Oracle, and those who couldn't find her often perished trying to navigate or escape the perils of Megingjörd, the largest and most dangerous mapped asteroid belt in the Ymiran system. Indeed, Piper had nearly died on several occasions while navigating the belt with her voidfighter. But in the end, she'd found the Oracle, and the crone had deemed her worthy of the foresight.

Religious types often said to be touched by the Oracle was to be touched by the gods themselves. It was also to give a piece of your soul to them. The scholars would call it kooky nonsense, but the small void Piper had felt every moment since the crone had touched her told her there was truth to it.

The words themselves had meant little to Piper. The Oracle had spoken of her painful past, but of more pain to come, and that just when she thought she'd known the deepest of cuts that she'd learn true disparity. She also told her she'd have a name worthy of memory, and that she was closer to the gods than she allowed herself to believe.

It had all sounded to Piper like something a common street seer would tell you for a few marks, so she'd never taken it too seriously. Still, she'd never spoken to anyone about the conversation between her and the Oracle. It was considered a sacred exchange, and no matter what she believed about the gods or religious traditions, there was no denying that black hand, nor the hole in her soul. There were some things you did not challenge.

Anyone who knew Piper's name knew she'd gone to the Oracle, so it was not surprising Einar had managed to connect the dots about who she was. She just hoped his story about his father had been true, and that he really did intend on keeping her secret. So far, it seemed his two young healing assistants had been none the wiser. They'd come in, checked her equipment, and gotten out quick. Piper had never been good at small talk, never saw the need for it. No doubt the icy quiet in the room was what made them work at a faster pace.

It had been two days since her first conversation with Einar. Their conversations now were much more professional—him giving her medical instructions and updates and her listening. He'd surgically attached the aluminum arm yesterday, its silvery metal not matching well at all with the tarnished brown of the metal leg. But, Piper had never cared much about matching colors. It was why the multi-colored dyed leather of Arvid's jacket had never bothered her. They made her stand out, drew the eyes in, made sure everyone knew she was important, that she was *the* Piper DeRache.

That jacket now sat in shreds on a nondescript chair in the corner of the medical room. The staff had cleaned the blood and gore and insulation fibers from it, but it would need a professional seamstress to repair the rips from the snow beasts. Even then, whatever they did to repair it would only do so much. The leather would always show the damage from those savage scavengers. Seyraks, Einar had informed her they were called. Piper had made a silent vow to disembowel every gods-damned seyrak she saw until her last breath.

Though Einar had told her she'd need a few weeks of attention, some negotiation with the right tone had let them settle on only a few more days in the medical building. After that, Einar said she was free to roam the village, so long as she remained in Valgrind until she was fully healed. Piper had agreed, but there was no chance she'd adhere to that part of the agreement. There was only so much time before the Jotun Navy recovery teams found her shuttle and started searching settlements for the *Thialfi* survivors. If it was discovered she was still alive—if Volkner found out about it—it could ruin any glimmer of hope she had of vengeance. No, once she was out of this ward, her only mission was to get to the *Gjaller*.

To help expedite the process, Piper had started trying to master her new artificial components. It took much more concentration than she'd ever expected to control the robotic limbs. The first time she'd managed to move the index finger, she'd forgotten to breathe and almost passed out. When she closed her fist for the first time, she'd puked. Inclining her foot gave her a migraine so vicious it broke through her pain medications. Einar had urged her not to push herself too hard, and that the function would start to come naturally as she practiced the smallest movements. It would take time for her body to adapt to the assets.

Time.

Everything just needed *time*. Whenever he said it, it was just a reminder of the time she didn't have.

Now, Piper was sitting up on the edge of the bed, having moved her leg with her still-human hand off the side. The movement had taken her nearly fifteen minutes, but she'd managed to complete it without tearing any stitches or taking her breath away from pain.

That was, until the leg itself had actually made it off the edge. In that moment, she'd been pulled nearly off the bed, and the flesh adhered to the leg felt like it was being torn away. Her drugs hadn't masked that entirely either. She knew from the intensity of the pain that, if she didn't have the medications in her blood, that feeling would have sent her into shock. It took a few minutes longer to recover from the horrible burning.

When her breathing had returned to normal and the pain had all but subsided, she focused on the metallic foot. The tendrils of throbbing began to stretch around her brain as she stared at the leg, willing the mechanisms within to move. First, it was the small toe. Then, the bigger ones wiggled in resistant response. Finally, when it felt like someone was pressing a plasma knife through her eye socket, the entire foot managed a rotation.

Piper realized there was darkness creeping in around the edges of her vision and quickly took a breath, realizing her still-mending lungs were screaming for air. The ankle rotation, if Einar had his say, was a win, and far more than most could expect to accomplish after only a couple of days with a robotic limb. He'd explained the neural and nerve connections and how the computer within the limbs relied on electrical impulses from the brain. Piper hadn't really cared to listen all that much. She only knew if her mind told her hand to punch, she wanted it to punch. If she told her foot to kick, she wanted it to kick. Simple things backed by complex science.

Right now, she was telling her leg she wanted to stand. The left leg obeyed, trying to push her up into an awkward half-stand, but the right stayed stagnant.

"Tyr's bloody hand," she cursed in a poison hiss.

The throbbing in her head was practically audible, and every pulse sent her body screaming in protest, begging her to lie back down and go to sleep.

Piper shook her head and breathed deep, as if to will away the pain. It didn't work, but it didn't matter. She needed to stand—had to. Where most had the luxury of months or years to learn the workings of their robotic parts, Piper had days.

Come on you piece of scrap, she thought through the pain and drug-riddled haze. She may as well have been smashed in the head with a brick for how horrible the pulsing was now. Death would be kinder, but there wasn't time for that either.

Come on.

The foot jerked to the side and back, as if trying to outright defy its new master. A new wave of pulsating pain flooded her mind.

Come on!

Piper bit her lip in concentration, hard enough to stain her chin with fresh crimson. The invisible shiv in her eye burned hotter than ever, and that blackness encroached once more. There was a blade dancer in her mind, severing the tissue and letting her feel every ounce of the pain.

The tang of copper filled her mouth, and that shadowy border closed tight enough she could barely make out the foot anymore. The blade dancer was joined by an artillery battalion, launching shells without cause or care. The pain was like none other—pure and omnipotent. Ruthless, unbearable, commanding her to cease her efforts. But she would not obey.

Piper screamed.

The blade dancer and battalion were engulfed in white, searing flame as her mind was set ablaze. Every inch of Piper cried out, no longer begging, just suffering.

And Piper DeRache stood.

Endorphins flooded her system, dousing the inferno of outraged nerves, gifting her the briefest bliss—a chance to appreciate what she'd done.

The door to the room slammed open, two panicked medical assistants and a wide-eyed Einar stampeding into the room, all in shock of Piper standing.

Piper simply looked back at them, putting on the most arrogant grin she could manage. Then, she had the distinct feeling of the world flipping upside down just before it disappeared into darkness.

⊲━━◆━━━━━◆━━⊳

"Ya' really are somethin' else," Einar said.

Piper was sitting on the side of the bed, regaining her breath, having just managed her first dozen uninterrupted steps. After passing out standing the first time, Piper had managed to do it again the same day. Now, two days later, she'd mastered walking. Well, she had *almost* mastered it. She could walk without the searing pain in her eye socket or the unbearable throbbing in her head. Now, it was more of an inconvenient tapping—albeit tapping with an axe blade.

She could also grab objects with a newborn's efficiency, though she knew she'd be relying heavily on her right hand for a while. It still felt strange to move the digits, as if it should be phantom, yet she saw motion she couldn't feel. Piper knew truly mastering the limbs would still take time, but she doubted she'd ever really adjust to that paradoxically absent-yet-present feeling.

"I've seen patients take months to adjust to these things, years even," Einar went on. "You're walkin' in less than a week? Astoundin'. Maybe there's somethin' to all those stories after all."

Piper shrugged off the allusion to her fame, instead asking, "Am I cleared to go out into the village now, *Doc*?"

She appreciated what Einar had done for her these past days... she really did. But right now, he was an obstacle, an inconvenience, just like her new limbs.

Einar shrugged. "I s'pose you could at least sleep somewhere other than this old medbed. I'll put in a room order at the inn."

"There a mead hall in town?"

Einar raised a disapproving eyebrow. "Drinkin' is not part of the discharge orders. In fact, in your condition, it will only hinder the healin'. Plus, if you drink too much with your medications, ya' could soon find yourself back here for new wounds."

Piper rolled her eyes. "I just don't want to be cooped up in an inn room without anyone to talk to. Mead halls make for good conversation."

Einar sighed and said, "The mead hall is next to the inn. Ya' can't miss it." He paused and gave her a knowing look. For someone so much younger than her, he acted decades older, and that wisdom shone in his look. "No more than one drink, Miss Frida, understand?"

Piper waved him away with her good hand, "Yeah, yeah, of course."

EVEN WITH THE thermals and thick coat Einar had provided, and her blood still saturated with high-potency painkillers, the bite of the Jotun wind was still unbearable. There weren't many things Piper missed about Tyr, but the warmth of the desert sun was definitely one of them. She'd be perfectly content to never see snow again after this.

Even though the mead hall was only about a hundred yards down the ice-laden street—Valgrind was only a few thousand yards in diameter as it was—it still took Piper near ten minutes to reach it. The robotic leg apparently didn't like the cold, or perhaps it was Piper's nerves that refused to work in the frigid temperature. Either way, Piper only made it about ten steps at a time before the metallic limb stopped functioning and became more an anchor than a leg. After reaching down with her still-good hand to prime the hydraulics a half-dozen times, Piper finally started dragging the dead weight behind her. She was thoroughly light-headed and out of breath by the time she laid her hand on the mead hall door handle.

The dry, artificial warmth inside was a welcome reprieve from the icy exterior wind. It smelled of Jotun evergreen, which Piper figured came from the walls, floors, tables, and bar that were all constructed of the pale white wood. There were only two patrons: an older man enjoying a toke off an electronic pipe and a hunched, weaselly man banging his fist against a malfunctioning jukebox on the side of the room.

"Ya' break it, ya' pay fer it, Harv," the meadmaster, a burly Jotun with a round belly and a massive white beard, said to the weaselly man.

"Skadi's tits, Berrant," the man called Harv cursed in a thin, but angry voice that matched his stature. "The godsdamned thing is already busted."

"Well, bust it more and it's on yer tab."

The man mumbled something under his breath that Piper couldn't make out before flipping a switch on the box. The staticky sound of an interplanetary radio announcer filled the room.

"And that brings us back to the story everyone's listening to," the smooth female voice said. "Jotun recovery teams have still only found a few pieces of the *Thialfi*. After the pirate vessel viciously assaulted the *HNV Aegir*, the capital ship was forced to respond with deadly force. The search for survivors from the *Thialfi* is ongoing, but sources from the Jotun Navy tell us that they do not expect anyone to have made it off the outlaw ship alive."

The broadcast cut out as Piper clunked her way to the bar. *It's still only a matter of time before they find the pod. I have to get out of here.*

"Ah," the meadmaster called Berrant said as Piper

approached. "Ya' must be Einar's patient. Frida, I think he said yer name was?"

"He told you about me?"

Berrant laughed with the deep jolly bellow. "Not a citizen in Valgrind don't know about the girl who bested Jotun itself. Surprised to see yer up and about so soon."

"I heal quick."

Berrant raised an eyebrow. "Aye, it seems that ya' do! What're ya' drinkin'? First one's on me, and I won't even tattle to Einar 'bout it," he said with a wink.

"Sunwater, if you have it," Piper replied, carefully taking a seat on a barstool.

"Ah, I knew ya' looked Tyran," Berrant replied. "Don't have the accent though."

"I've been on interplanetary trade freighters since before I could speak," Piper replied. "Didn't have the chance to pick up an accent."

"I see. Well, you are in luck, Miss Frida," Berrant said, the cheek skin peeking out from above his beard a happy pink as he smiled. "Harv here has just brought in a shipment of goods from Tyr. Got a dozen bottles of fresh Tyran sunwater right in the back. If ya' like, I can even spice it with a pinch of Iduan lemonsickle?"

"Lemonsickle?" Piper asked. "But doesn't Jotun have a trade embargo with Idun right now because of the Vidarin negotiations?"

"Harv has his methods," was all Berrant said before sauntering to the back room.

A smuggler, Piper thought, looking back at Harv, now carving something into one of Berrant's tables with the edge of a serrated knife. *That could be useful.*

Piper tucked the thought away as Berrant emerged from

the back and immediately yelled, "What in Odin's name do ya' think yer doin', Harvey?!"

Harv looked up, his vermin eyes wide at the fuming meadmaster.

"Get the hell out, before I show you the meanin' of Jotun rage!"

"All right, all right," Harv replied, flicking the knife closed and stowing it away in one of the many pockets of his coat. "I didn't mean nothing by it, Berrant."

"Get. Out," Berrant hissed.

Piper had fought against many enemies in her years. Some much bigger and stronger than her. None of them sent a shiver down her spine the way the meadmaster's tone just did. It evidently had the same effect on Harv as he scurried out of the hall.

Berrant shook his head and breathed deep, as if to calm himself. "If he weren't my only consistent source of supplies, I'd have banned him from this place a long time ago. He doesn't know the meaning of the word respect."

Berrant sat a full bottle of sunwater and a small bowl of yellow, powdered lemonsickle on the counter. It was a root harvested on Idun, named for its uncanny similarity in taste to old Earthen lemons. It helped take just a touch of the bite off a glass of sunwater, turning it from a pure, burning spirit into a powerful cocktail. Berrant prepared their drinks in small glasses, each with a single ice cube molded in the rough shape of Ansuz, the rune of the Allfather.

"Skal," he said, raising a glass.

Piper raised hers in response and they both sipped. Her mouth was alight with dancing notes of citrus and distilled nectar. It burned with the fire of the Surtr star and took her back to the warmth of the desert for the briefest moment.

CHAPTER
THIRTEEN

Another piece of mangled metal clanked against the floor of the refinery. Mila sat back with a huff, and examined the robotic mechanisms now exposed in Fenrir's shoulder.

"Wow, buddy," she said, looking at the busted hydraulic cylinder that was the core of the wolfbot's leg. "That's going to take some materials I can't just scrounge up here to replace."

With the help of the mechanics' tools she'd checked out from Kord's supply hole, Mila had managed to fix many of Fen's loose connectors and rusted fasteners. But the crack in that hydraulic tube would require welding at the very least. Even then, Mila knew a weld would be little more than a bandage that would need renewal every few weeks. No, the bot would have to get it replaced if it had any hope of long-term use. Except, how would she keep him a secret for that long, even if she did manage to stay alive?

Fen's head swiveled to Mila and cocked to the side, looking for all the world like a real, flesh and blood, curious dog. Then, he turned his mirrored, cybernetic eyes to the hind leg and looked back at her. Mila knew he couldn't feel emotion; he was just metal and electronic systems, after all. But the way he tilted his head again, the way he gently raised a metallic front paw off the ground toward her, it was as if he was trying to reassure her it was all right.

Mila smiled and patted the bot's head. "But that doesn't mean we're going to stop trying, now does it?"

Fen raised his chin as if in full agreement.

Mila's smile faded as she looked over at the refinery equipment. She'd gotten so lost in tinkering with Fenrir that she'd forgotten where she was—what she was supposed to be doing. Two pallets of unrefined brandr now sat on the other side of the room, the steel barrels untapped.

"What am I doing here, Fen?" she asked the bot.

Fen cocked his head in reply, those reflective eyes examining her closely.

"I mean, I was spraying mushrooms only a few days ago. Now, look at me." Mila gestured to the work uniform she'd donned after Niko returned her to the refinery earlier. "I'm supposed to be some great refiner." She sighed and continued, "I mean, what if Ulf decides not to come back? What if one of the guards tells Volkner about our deal?"

"What if he can't handle double the amount of hyrrine in a night?" spoke a voice from her flank.

The voice, which uttered almost exactly what Mila was about to say, made her actually jump off the cot. Fenrir was on his feet instantly, his right side still lame, that electronic growl loud and violent.

"It's all right, Fen," Mila said as she saw it was the Ambassador who'd uttered the words.

Strange, I didn't even hear the doors open or close. She assumed she must have been more encapsulated by her one-sided conversation with Fenrir than she'd realized. Mila breathed a little easier seeing the politician.

"Thank you, *so much*," Mila said, putting plenty of emphasis on those last two words. "I'd be halfway to a mine right now if it weren't for you."

"Of course," Úlf said, nodding his respect to her.

Mila assumed the reason he'd come again was to replicate his efforts from the night before, but a silence passed between them and he made no move. That ball in her stomach started to tighten again.

"Do you think you can manage double?" Mila asked, mainly to make sure he was planning on refining anything at all.

Úlf looked at the two pallets on the other side of the refinery and breathed deep. "That'll be a bit of a feat, for sure; but I think I can handle it. However, I must ask something of you in return."

"Of course," Mila replied. "Whatever you need, just say the word."

"I... can't," the ambassador replied, taking a deep breath and letting his shoulders sag.

Mila cocked her head. "You can't?"

"No, at least, not yet. There will come a time when I'll need something from you, Mila, and I just need your word you'll do everything you can to help me."

Mila took a step back from Úlf toward Fenrir. "A favor?"

"Of sorts, yes."

"And you can't tell me what it is?"

Úlf shook his head. "I know it's a little... unorthodox. But that's the way it has to be for now."

Mila raised an eyebrow. "I'm not usually in the business of making loose-ended deals."

The ambassador laughed. "I wasn't aware you were in the business of making deals at all prior to a day ago."

Mila gritted her teeth. He wasn't wrong about that.

"Look," Úlf continued. "I can't tell you what it is yet because I don't exactly know. I just need to know if the time comes to step up for something important I can count on you."

"Something important," Mila said, making sure her tone conveyed her understanding of how vague those words were. "You're not trying to get me to kill someone, are you?"

Úlf laughed again. "Gods above, no," he replied. "Let's leave the bloodshed to those well-versed in it already. No, I assure you the favor, whatever it may be, will be far milder than anything of that sort."

Mila shook her head and looked at the barrels of raw brandr.

What choice do I have?

Mila nodded softly.

"So, I have your word that, when I ask, I can count on you for this favor?"

"You have my word."

Úlf grinned like a fox. "Delightful."

⬦━━━━━━━╋━━━━━━━⬦

THAT MORNING WENT LARGELY the same way as the previous one. Mila was woken by Niko's guards; today it was the stoic one and the hairless one. Unlike Waren and Eberhard, these did not comment on the state of the refined brandr. Instead, the hairless guard, who Mila had learned was called Xiomar, told her to be ready in twenty minutes, and then the duo promptly left. As promised, Niko arrived to escort her to the command level exactly twenty minutes later.

"How did you sleep?" he asked, now walking alongside

her in the refinery-level passageway instead of leading her along as he had before.

Mila eyed him wearing a cocked grin. "Small talk? That's new."

Niko mirrored the smile. "Well, I can't expect that we do this walk every day in silence, now can I?"

"*Will* we be doing this walk every day?" Mila countered.

Niko shrugged. "If you keep producing hyrrine at this rate, I expect I'll be your escort for a long while."

"You don't sound as upset about being a babysitter anymore."

They reached the lift doors and Niko looked at her as he said, "Guess I'm just getting used to it."

The way he looked at her, she could almost feel the soft glow of those digitized eyes. He was standing closer to her as well, close enough for her to distinguish every note of his metallic, crisp scent. There wasn't a single part of Mila that wanted to look away from the Berserker. That was, until she felt the warmth flooding her cheeks. That made her shift her attention to the lift doors rather quickly.

She felt, more than heard, Niko give a short, low laugh as he too turned his attention to the lift.

When they arrived on the command level minutes later, Mila immediately noticed another scent, one of woodfire. Not as if someone was tending a raging bonfire, but more as if the embers of one were slowly smoldering. In a strange way, it was pleasant. Then she saw the gold and crimson garland the servants were hanging on the walls of the command deck passages, and realized the smell was fabricated, being pumped through the vents. Every soldier and politician they passed seemed upbeat, jovial even; far more so than anyone she'd seen so far on the *Gjaller*.

"What is all this?" Mila asked, taking in the festive atmosphere.

From the way Niko looked at her, she may as well have spoken another language.

"What?" Mila asked defensively.

Niko raised an eyebrow. "You really don't know?"

Mila shook her head.

"They're preparing for Freiheitstag. The ball is in only a few days."

Freiheitstag. Freedom Day. She'd heard of it on the radio, but her father had always made it a point not to celebrate. It was the day Volkner's rebellion had usurped the former government and the Governor of Vidar was executed. Back then, Vidar was close allies with Idun. According to her father, they were more like a province of the superpower planet than their own property. He'd told her that, back then, the common people prospered, but the wealthy and some of the military elite, like the president, had felt oppressed under the thumb of Idun. So, Volkner had led his coup and won, then claimed what he gave the people was freedom, and they'd given him his own holiday for it. His own *gods-damned* holiday, as Hans used to say.

"I had no idea we were so close to it," she replied.

"Did you not celebrate it growing up?"

Mila shook her head again. "My father, he always avoided it."

"Hm," Niko replied in understanding. "Not sure I blame him."

The atmosphere of the command room was different as well when the doors hissed open. She heard... laughing? And not cruel or maniacal laughter, but the hearty, celebratory type. It was coming from none other than President Brandt himself, who was descended from his throne mingling with his advisors and Úlf. She noticed they all wielded drinking horns as servants patrolled with pitchers full of mead. All except Úlf, who himself held a small glass with only a small bit of the golden liquid. As the doors shut, they noticed Mila and Niko's arrival.

"There's our girl," Volkner said, raising his hands in the air as if praising her.

The way he said *our girl* made Mila cringe, as if he were a proud father. Like she was his child, or a child of this violent court.

"Our Master Refiner's latest success breathes hope into a new era of Vidar!" Volkner continued.

"To the Master Refiner!" a portly politician called out, raising his cup and not caring as liquid sloshed over the lip and down his arm.

"Aye, to the Refiner!" another one echoed.

Volkner raised his own mead and eyed Mila closely as the others echoed the first politician's sentiment. Mila couldn't help but feel as though the jolly demeanor was a façade, and that the president was still studying her, weighing her worth. They were playing a game now. She was the wondrous refiner who had never refined anything. He was the authority that had to praise her while looking for any sign she was lying. It seemed they were both wearing masks, and it would only be a matter of time before one of them broke.

"Let it be known across the system," Volkner began, "that Mila Messer has been offered promotion to my cabinet as Vidar's official Head of Brandr Refining. She will receive all appropriate rights, respects, and compensations for the position henceforth. If anyone opposes this appointment, let him speak now or forever hold his tongue."

No one objected. Mila doubted they would even if they disagreed.

"Very well," Volker continued. "And do you accept this appointment, Miss Messer?" His gaze was like a cold iron vise around her.

Beside him, Úlf raised his chin slightly, grinning like a devil.

"I do," Mila said.

"Do you swear by Thor's hammer you will advise me and this committee in the best interests of Vidar?"

"I swear."

"Then it is settled. Praise be to Thor. Skal!"

A resounding "Skal!" echoed the president before the politicians drank deep.

A servant girl brought horns of mead to Mila and Niko. Mila thanked her, but the bronze-skinned girl simply tucked her head and backed away. She seemed small, fragile, like a pup that had never known kind words, only the crack of a whip. Mila hated Volkner for that. She made sure to meet his gaze as she drank from her horn and kept it with every sip.

I know what game we're playing.

Volkner raised his own mead to his lips, and took a long drag, also refusing to yield the gaze, as if he knew exactly what she was thinking and how to reply.

Good.

Mila's concentration was broken as she heard a small, timid voice say, "Ma'am."

She turned to find it had come from the bronze-skinned servant who only moments ago seemed terrified of Mila's thanks.

"Yes?" she replied.

The girl was looking to the side, as if she couldn't bear

to look Mila in the eyes. "President Brandt wanted me to inform you I'm to be your new handmaiden."

"My what?" Mila asked. She'd said it more sharply than she intended from the surprise and felt horrible when the girl backed away, as if stricken. "No, wait," Mila continued in a much softer tone. "I'm sorry... just, you're to do what exactly?"

"She's your own, personal servant," Niko chimed in. "All cabinet members are assigned one."

"What am I supposed to do with a servant?" Mila asked.

"Whatever you want, really," Niko replied. "Some use them as assistants, couriers, maids, any type of work you don't have time for."

"And others?" Mila asked, detecting the words unsaid.

Niko breathed deep and his lips went tight. "I'd rather not get into what *others* demand of their servants."

It was enough to make that fire roar up in Mila again as she looked back at the girl. The portrait of fragile innocence. How could someone have twisted her like this? The dangerous anger started to bubble within her; then her elerex shocked her arm and it dissipated.

Damn this thing, she thought, grabbing her arm. Luckily, it hadn't gone limp this time, just an annoying tingling sensation left in the wake of the jolt.

"What's your name?" Mila asked.

The girl looked up, the portrait of confusion.

"What do I call you?"

"I'm called Amelie," the girl replied in a tone that was almost cautious.

"That's a beautiful name," Mila said. The girl had to have only been a couple of years younger than her, yet Mila felt as though she were talking to a child.

"I see you've been acquainted with your newest asset," another voice broke into the conversation.

Even if Mila didn't know Volkner Brandt's tone, the way Amelie recoiled would have let her know exactly who'd approached. She turned to find the president strolling up to their small group with an arrogant swagger.

"The first of many benefits," he said, raising his drinking horn. "Skal."

"Skal," Mila and Niko echoed.

"You've proven yourself to be quite the asset to the Vidarin government, Miss Messer," he continued. "One of our most valuable, if I say so myself. I suppose that means I should leave Lieutenant Schafer assigned to your personal protection," he said, turning his attention to the Berserker.

"If you command it, Vini," Schafer replied.

"I do. May as well defend my most valuable asset with my most expensive soldier, even if you are in need of an update."

Mila saw Niko bristle at that, but the Berserker did not reply.

"Anyways," Volkner said, turning back to Mila, "I just wanted to offer my personal, sincere congratulations. Your father will be proud to hear the news."

Mila forced a smile and nodded her thanks.

Volkner looked as if he were about to turn away, then stopped as he seemed to think of one more thing to say. "You know, there was a time when I really respected your father. He was one of the best soldiers in my regiment. An honorable, brave man. It was painful for me to learn of what he'd devolved into, truly. To hear of him descending to gambling and drinking and lying to lenders to keep your farm afloat. I hope he hasn't passed any of that on to you."

Mila clenched her ale horn so hard she could feel the

bone trying to crack against her flesh. That roiling anger flared again, and the elerex sent out a shock. She bit her cheek and concentrated on the taste of blood filling her mouth, refusing to let the device in her arm embarrass her —not now.

"But, I shouldn't harp on the past," Volkner said with a venomous smile. "If you continue to produce brandr as you have, I'm sure you'll bring honor back to the Messer name."

There were so many things Mila wanted to do and say. So many hateful, violent things. Instead, she shook them away and matched Volkner's smile, managing, "Thank you, my Vini."

Volkner gave her one last knowing look before looking at Niko and saying, "Take Miss Messer to our grooming facilities—the one for honored guests. This is her home now, after all. Make sure she knows every luxury."

"Yes, my Vini," Niko replied.

"I look forward to our relationship, Miss Messer," Volkner said as a farewell, raising his drinking horn one final time, and finished the mead inside.

CHAPTER

FOURTEEN

The grooming facilities to which Volkner had referred
were indeed filled with luxuries. Amelie and Niko had
taken her down a level to where generals, politicians, other
wealthy elite, and special guests were lodged. The majority
of the level was unlike anything she'd ever laid eyes on. The
level was more akin to a mall for the highest of the *Gjaller's*
society, filled with high-end shops, theaters, and restaurants.
There were gardens, too, filled with greenery and pied
flowers in numbers and variations that Mila could have
hardly imagined. Its size was comparable to the docking and
supply levels but made the darkened hallways of the
refinery level seem infinitely smaller.

Grooming facilities was far too official and government-
sounding a description for the building which Mila now
found herself in. There was calming music streaming from
unseen speakers and the foyer smelled of eucalyptus and
lavender. The attendant spoke in the softest tone Mila had
ever heard. No, this was not some grooming facility,
designed for governmental efficiency as the name implied.
This was an opulent spa.

At Niko's permission, the attendant had shown Mila and Amelie to the back. Before they parted, Niko had informed her he'd be nearby and given her a transponder.

"This is a direct line to me," he'd told her. "Do not lose it. It's not easy to get these things programmed."

When she'd asked if he had a matching one, he'd only repeated that it was hard to get replacements programmed. The message was clear; the communicator was designed to communicate with *him*. Not some small electronic block like the device he'd given her, but his own internal software. Mila could tell he'd left something unsaid, but wasn't sure what. Only that he considered that communicator to be very important.

On the side of the communicator device, which was attached to a retractable strap that she could wrap on her wrist, beltloop, or anywhere else of her choosing, was a safety flap concealing and protecting a bright red button.

"Whenever you need me, press that button," he'd said. "I'll find you."

Whenever she needed him, she'd thought. Not when she was in trouble or felt threatened—whenever she needed him. She'd have thought it was unintentional phrasing, except he'd said it so deliberately—carefully. *Whenever you need me, I'll find you.*

They began with cutting her hair and trimming her nails, treatments Mila had never received from others and ones she didn't particularly care for. She'd always worn her hair for function; cutting it short herself, putting it into elastic bands as it grew, and cutting again when it got too long for her liking several months later. Her nails had mostly taken care of themselves, breaking away or staying worn down between her tinkering and farm work. The rare trim had been only that, a trim. It was never the cut, polish, grinding, and lacquering they applied now. Every tool that touched near her fingertip made her jerk her whole hand away. It'd taken numerous reassurances by her attendant to get her to somewhat trust the process.

After the trimming and polishing of both her and her nails, they were led down a hall to a room with a bath modeled to look like a natural hot spring. Once inside, the attendant instructed Mila to completely undress, to her astonishment. He then promptly left, leaving Mila and Amelie alone in the room.

"Do you need help, Meistari?" Amelie asked after Mila didn't move for a moment.

"Oh, no, thank you," Mila replied. "I just... I didn't expect to..." Mila huffed, unsure of how to word her discomfort. "Could you just turn around for a minute?"

"Of course, Meistari," Amelie replied, following the instruction.

Even with the handmaiden turned away, Mila felt every ounce of blood in her body shift to her face as she slipped off the fine gray clothes. She made her way to the edge of the steaming water, dipping a toe in to find it was just the right temperature. Hot, but not too hot. She slowly slid into the water, and what had started as one of the most painfully awkward experiences of her life, melted into bliss.

"Matron's mercy," she said, closing her eyes and embracing the warmth of the water as her muscles relaxed for the first time in... well, she couldn't remember the last time her muscles had relaxed like this.

"Can I fetch anything from the staff for you, Meistari?" Amelie asked, now standing timidly by the door.

"No, no. That's all right," Mila replied. "And what is that you keep calling me?"

Mila could tell by Amelie's frown that the girl didn't know what she was referring to.

"Meistari," Mila said slowly, unsure if she had the pronunciation right. "What is that?"

"It means master," Amelie replied.

Reality broke into the warmth-induced stupor. "I'm no one's master," she said. "Please, just call me Mila, at least when no one is around."

Amelie seemed to be thrown off-balance by the request. "I don't know if—"

"Amelie," Mila said, cutting her off. "Please."

Amelie nodded. "Very well, Mila."

Mila smiled and closed her eyes again. "You know, this is a very large bath, and I feel awkward with you just standing there. Care to get in?"

Amelie looked purely petrified. "I-I can't do that."

"And why not?" Mila asked.

"It's not for me. For people *like* me."

"And what are people *like* you?" Mila asked.

"Servants, Meis—. I mean, Mila."

"Only a couple of days ago, I wasn't sure if I would wake up a master refiner or a mining slave. We're not that different, Amelie. So please stop acting like I'm some kind of social elite and you're nothing."

Amelie nodded hesitantly. "Okay."

"Good," Mila replied, closing her eyes and tilting her head toward the ceiling. "Now please, get in so this isn't so gods-damned awkward."

Amelie did as Mila commanded, undressing before slipping into the steaming bath across from her, plenty of room separating them.

"I've never been in a place like this before," Mila said, opening her eyes and examining the room—its delicate stonework, the carved arched door frames, the abundance of plush towels. "Have you?"

Amelie shook her head. "My people tend to prefer cool baths."

"And who are your people?"

"Tyrans," Amelie replied.

That explained the deep bronze skin then.

"How did you come to be this far out in the system?" Mila asked.

Amelie looked down at the water when Mila asked the question.

"Oh, no. I didn't mean..." Mila said. "I'm sorry. You don't have to answer that if you don't want to."

Dammit. Mila thought, biting her lip.

"No, it's okay," Amelie replied. "I just... no one's ever asked me about it." The girl took a deep breath and began. "My parents were spice traders. They always bartered on Idun, the cheapest to reach in the system and the most money to be made from everyday patrons. They did it legally, more expensive than smuggling, but they were honest people. I used to stay home on Tyr with my Amma while they were away. She'd show me how to grow and dry the peppers that we'd grind for them to trade. Then, when I was old enough, they started taking me with them. My mother said I would take over the business after I served my time in the military."

"What happened?" Mila asked, engulfed in Amelie's story.

"When Idun sent its navy to reinforce Hod during Vidar's invasion, the routes between Tyr and Idun were left mostly unprotected. Our freighter was intercepted by void pirates and..." Amelie's throat tensed.

Mila nearly told her to stop, thought the girl might break if she were forced to say anymore.

"They boarded us and said if we cooperated, they'd take our goods and go. But then one of them said he was taking my mother as a trophy. My parents—both of them—were strong, proud warriors when they were in the Tyran Marines. They'd kept every ounce of that pride up until the moment they resisted the pirate, and he shot them both in the head."

Even in the steaming bath, Mila felt a very cold silence wash over the room. To her surprise, Amelie wasn't crying, she was just staring at the water.

"Amelie," Mila said. "I'm so sorry."

Amelie looked up at her and gave a smile that Mila knew was completely fabricated.

"It feels like a lifetime ago," Amelie said. "After that, they decided to take me and sold me to the first servant pusher they could find. He ended up selling me to a politician in Volkner's regime, who died only a year later. Then, I became the president's property."

"How long have you been here?"

Amelie shrugged. "Five years, give or take."

Mila shook her head. "I'm sorry."

"Why do you keep saying that?" Amelie asked.

Mila looked up and cocked her head, opening her mouth to speak, only then realizing she didn't know what her response would be. "Because I wish that had never happened to you. I'm sorry that it did happen to you."

Amelie looked back at the bathwater, entranced by the steaming surface again. "There is nothing to change it now. I learned a while ago to accept this life. Being sorry helps nothing."

Mila heard the broken tone carrying those words. It

was one of the saddest noises she'd ever heard. For as bad as her father was, at least she hadn't watched him be executed. At least he was still alive. And at least she'd never had to deal with being the captive of void pirates or slave pushers. Her life was in no way ideal but, in this moment, compared to Amelie, she felt positively Vanir-touched.

Mila wasn't exactly sure how to continue. She'd never really had to maintain conversations before. With Niko, the extended silences were expected; he was a military man, and in a strange way, they'd never felt too awkward. But with Amelie, she felt like she should get to know her better. They'd be spending loads of time together, after all. Yet, what to ask about? What subjects could she approach without risking stirring up buried memories?

If this was what I was missing with people my own age, maybe the farm wasn't so bad.

She nearly resorted to, *"What is there to do for fun around here?"* when Amelie asked, "How do you know how to refine brandr?"

Thank the gods. Mila could've sighed with relief that the girl had spoken instead of her. Yet, she'd asked her a question she was surprised no one had yet, and one she hadn't really developed an answer for.

"Well, um," Mila said. "It's not much of a story."

"Oh," Amelie replied, looking back at the water again.

"But," Mila said quickly, dreading the idea of the conversation lulling again. "I guess it started with my love of creating things."

Amelie looked up at her, giving a single blink as if expecting Mila to go on.

"Yeah, I've always loved tinkering with things, repairing them or making them better. There was this place on my father's farm... a stash of old, abandoned naval equipment. I used to pull stuff out of there that I could fix up."

"What kind of stuff," Amelie asked.

"Oh, nothing major. I fixed up our old shop with a shield generator. Once I found a radio I managed to pick up intergalactic channels on. A few holobooks here and there."

Amelie's eyes lit up for the first time that Mila had seen. "What kinds of books?"

Mila felt both shock and a bit of welcome enthusiasm at Amelie's sudden interest. "Well, mostly military stuff: equipment manuals, some historical stuff. I read them, but pretty boring. There were some about the gods, too, which were better reads, but they definitely kissed Thor's ass in most of it. The more interesting ones, for me, were the Ymiran myths. Stories about the Megingjörd Dreki, or the Howling Hills, or—"

"Or the Rattle Man," Amelie cut in, almost excitedly.

Mila smiled and waved her head, splashing hot water in the process. "No, no. I *hate* that one. How he curls his dead fingers around your soul, or pricks your flesh with a blood-ink pen."

"And how he takes your name."

"Stop!" Mila said, laughing, splashing the water at Amelie this time. She did it harder than she'd intended, as a wall of steamy water caught the Tyran right in the face.

Amelie's wide eyes spelled shock, and Mila's heart fell into her stomach.

"Oh, gods, Amelie... I'm so—"

Mila was cut off as a wall of water struck her in the face. She spat it out and cleared her eyes to find Amelie... smiling? Not just smiling, giggling, every inch the portrait of the happy young girl she deserved to be.

Mila narrowed her eyes at Amelie, her mouth a devil's

grin. "I'm not sure you know what you've just gotten your-self into, *Starscraper*."

Amelie stopped giggling just long enough to say, "Bring it on, *Moonflesh*."

What followed was splash war worthy of history. When they were finally asked to leave by the attendant, Mila and Amelie couldn't stop themselves from laughing all the way to the spa's exit.

FIFTEEN

L O

The letters carved in Berrant's table, and the 'K' the smuggler had started before being ordered out, told Piper enough about his religious allegiances.

Just like a smuggler to worship the trickster, Piper thought with an undeniable tinge of disgust. Only the lowest kinds of people worshipped Loki. But, perhaps the information could help her get on the weaselly man's good side. She needed resources, and ship passage, and since he was one of the only non-natives in this gods-forsaken village according to the meadmaster, she needed him, no matter her distaste for his kind.

Most people had a habit of lumping void pirates and smugglers in the same group, much to the disdain of both parties. Smugglers saw pirates as unrefined, lacking in finesse. Pirates saw smugglers as weak-spined cockroaches that preferred to slip between the cracks in society, rather than rebel against its rules outright. Piper was no stranger to these biases. Still, that didn't change the situation.

After braving the cold and making her way to the inn that sat only a few buildings down from the tavern, she found herself in a quaint foyer. It was the inn in which Einar had reserved a room for her. Incidentally, she expected it was also where she could find Harv. There was no way in Hel this village was large enough to warrant two inns, after all.

"Can I help you?" a melancholy voice asked.

It came from a girl behind the innkeeper's counter, who stood so slouched and unassuming Piper hadn't even noticed her.

"Yeah," Piper replied, masking any surprise at the girl's presence. "I have a room here."

Piper's too-heavy robotic leg clunked on the hardwood as she hobbled to the desk. The girl, whose long dark hair covered half of her face, looked at the leg with her one exposed eye.

"You must be the one Einar contacted me about," she said. "The girl in the snow."

Piper shook her head. "Yeah, yeah. The one who should've died. I just got the spiel from Berrant."

She was at the counter now, and was shocked by the girl's exposed half of her face. It was, in a word, flawless. Piper had never seen such spotless flesh, a perfectly rounded eye, eyelashes and lips even Iduans would kill for. Though, she could also just make out the hint of some marking peeking out from beneath the girl's raven-black hair.

"You're called Frida, correct?" the girl asked.

Piper realized she didn't have a Jotun accent. In fact, she had no accent at all that Piper could recognize. She nodded in response.

Before the girl asked another question, Piper asked, "Is Harv staying here?"

The girl flinched. "I don't divulge information like that."

Piper rolled her eyes. "I just need to talk to him about something. I'm not trying to hurt him or anything." *Unless it comes to that,* Piper left unsaid.

The girl's single exposed eye, a piercing gray that reminded Piper of the color of the clouds just before she'd been engulfed by a blizzard, set on Piper. Something about that look, even though the girl stood almost a full head shorter than Piper, and without a shred of muscle on her, made Piper recoil.

"I don't divulge information like that," she repeated.

"Fine," Piper replied, her voice cracking to her ever-lasting terror.

This girl couldn't be making *her* nervous... not Piper DeRache, who'd slain blademasters in single combat and struck deals with dictators. This girl was nothing compared to them. And yet, there was a chill that had nothing to do with the Jotun cold inching down her spine.

"I didn't catch your name," Piper said quickly, making sure to keep her voice under control this time.

"I am Kari," the girl replied, punching information into a holopad. Piper noticed she was only using her right hand to type.

"That's it?" Piper asked.

"That's what?"

"No Kari, Daughter of Kali, or something like that?"

"Just Kari," the girl replied. "Daughter of None."

Piper considered asking about the parents that the girl evidently either didn't know or didn't care for. However, there was just something about the girl that made Piper's hair stand on edge when she spoke. No, quiet was fine. In fact, it was welcome.

When she finally handed Piper an entry chip for her room, the void pirate hobbled away as fast as she could manage. Just as she found her room, another door, only two down from hers, opened. None other than the weaselly form of Harv stepped out.

His beady eyes crawled over her. "You're that girl who was in the mead hall a bit ago."

Piper's tone and short words said enough about how little she'd cared about the meadmaster's table. "We need to talk," she said. "Follow me."

<hr />

EVEN THOUGH IT had pained Piper to ask Kari anything, the innkeeper had agreed to let them use the inn's private lounge for their discussion. It was modest, a few simple leather-clad chairs and an old hand-carved coffee table with etchings of crows inlaid. But as far as Piper could tell, it was free from any prying eyes or ears.

She'd have likely opted for a booth in Berrant's mead hall instead, so that she could drink while enduring the smuggler. However, something told her the meadmaster would need a little more time to cool after Harv had started carving 'Loki' into one of his fine tables.

"Right, so what's this all about?" Harv asked, plopping himself into one of the seats.

As Piper took her own seat, he seemed to notice the pained slowness of her clumsy movements.

"You a cripple or something?" he asked without the slightest pause.

Piper bared her teeth at him. "I've brought you here to talk business, not comment on my physical demeanor."

Harv laughed and said, "it was just a question. If I thought you wanted me to talk about your body, well, I wouldn't be talking about that bum leg."

The way his small dark eyes traversed her, stopping on her bosom for far too long, made Piper's blood boil.

"You're a smuggler, right?" Piper asked, not a single hint of anything other than bitter seriousness in her voice.

Harv seemed suddenly wrenched from whatever horrible unreality he was exploring as he sat back in the chair.

"I'm a multitalented specialist. If sometimes that requires squeezing cargo through tight spaces," Harv shrugged and left the rest of the sentence for Piper to fill in on her own.

"You ever trade with the *VOS Gjaller?*"

Harv went rigid and his rat-like grin vanished. "What interest you have in the *Gjaller?*"

"I need transport there."

Harv shook his head. "I see where this is going, and no, I won't do it."

"But you haven't heard my offer," Piper said.

"By the looks of you, you don't even have enough marks to get a proper leg surgery, let alone pay me what it would take for me to smuggle someone onto the gods-damned fortress of Volkner Brandt."

"I have very wealthy friends who would pay you handsomely for such a feat." A half-truth. Piper did have wealthy friends, but whether they would help her pay the smuggler, that was more ambiguous.

"You don't understand, *girl*," Harv said as if she were no more than a toddler. "There are only two penalties for breaking laws on the *Gjaller*. Death, or time in the brandr mines. And with that choice, death is preferable."

"What will it take?" Piper asked.

"You don't have it."

"A million marks?"

Harv looked as though he'd lost his words.

"Two million?" Piper said after he didn't reply for a moment.

"There's no way you can offer that," he finally said.

"You know nothing about me," Piper replied.

Harv's eyes narrowed. "There are only two explanations for you offering me *that* much money. You're either lying and plan to ditch me or rat me out the moment we dock on the *Gjaller,* or..." Harv's head cocked to the side like a thought had just struck him in the temple. "Or you really are someone who is very important, which makes me wonder what'd you'd be doing in a miserable village like this."

Piper raised her chin. She needed him to think she was important enough to warrant the risk. She hadn't thought him sharp enough to connect the dots to who she really was, though. She didn't want to give him long enough to figure it out.

"That's my offer," she said quickly. "Take it or leave it."

But it was too late. Piper saw the realization gleam in the smuggler's eyes. "Skadi's tits," he cursed. "I thought I'd seen your face on the wanted boards before. It's beat to all hel right now, but I remember it."

Piper gave him a sideways glare. "I don't know what you're talking about."

But Harv didn't even seem to hear her. "I'll be gods-damned. They said you died, that you all died. But here you are. The Scourge of Trader's Loop herself."

Piper bared her teeth. "You'll stop talking if you know what's good for you."

Harv looked her up and down again, this time examining her more like an artifact than a specimen. "I'd say you are good for those marks, then."

"So we have a deal?" Piper asked through clenched teeth.

Harv crossed his arms and sat back again. "Well, not quite. I'll need some kind of deposit."

"I don't have any money with me," Piper replied.

"I was thinking something a bit more... physical."

Vermin. "That's not on the table."

"Table, bed, floor, doesn't make a difference to me," Harv replied. "I just want to know what it's like to be with a celebrity pirate."

Piper's nostrils flared as a hundred thoughts of how to butcher the man cycled through her head. "I'll consider your *offer*, and get back to you."

Harv shook his head again. "Sorry, but with the information I'm being forced to hold on to, I'm afraid I'll need that deposit now."

The gods-damned rat is blackmailing me?

"Look," she said calmly. "I'll agree to your terms, but only if you sweeten your side of the deal a little more."

"I don't think you—"

Piper cut him off. "I need a T-Class or higher communicator."

"A T-Class or higher?!" Harv asked. "Do you know how expensive those are? Not to mention how difficult they are to come by?"

"Five million," Piper said.

Harv's jaw dropped. "Even for you, five million—"

"Five million transferred to you the moment I can make contact with my resource."

Harv practically drooled before bringing himself together. "And the deposit?"

Piper stood and with every ounce of will in her body, enduring the wrenching pain of keeping the leg from clunking unnaturally, strode to the man. She wrapped the fingers of her still-flesh hand around his collar and pulled him close, putting her lips just next to his ear. She could smell the musk of days-old sweat and grime on him. But still, she managed to say in a voice as sultry as a siren, "If you guarantee me passage, I'll pay the deposit in full, plus interest, once you've secured a communicator. For that, *I'll* guarantee, after we're through, you'll be ruined for any other woman."

Piper felt the mousy man melt in her grasp. She pulled away to find him slowly nodding.

"How long?" she asked.

He shrugged. "A week? Maybe longer. I have to scout other villages and trading posts for the communicator."

"Make it shorter," Piper said, stroking her hand up his neck.

More nodding. "Right, yeah, okay. Just a week, no longer."

"Shorter." Piper took his own hand and placed it on her hip, guiding his touch just short of any sensitive areas.

The man was little more than a puddle now. "Three days. Three days, but it's the best I can do."

Piper took his hand and dropped it in his lap. "Three days. Don't keep me waiting."

"You're healin' up rather well," Einar said as he examined her most recent scans on a holopad.

"Well enough for you to clear me?" Piper asked.

Einar laughed. "Always in a hurry. But no, 'fraid you've still got at least a couple more weeks."

Piper groaned.

"Look now," Einar went on. "You're takin' this over twice as fast as I'd want you to. That said, you're handlin' it like no one else I've ever seen with such injuries. Don't push it."

Piper lifted her robotic hand and clenched it easily into a fist. Only three short days ago, she'd struggled to hold even the lightest of objects. Now, she worked every digit as if she'd been born with them. Three days ago, her metallic leg had rioted against her minds' control. Now, she traversed entire swaths of the village as easily as anyone else. Well, as easily as anyone could expect a fully healthy Tyran to combat the snow.

There were still moments when the pain broke through, where her head split, and the grafted skin felt like it would rip away from the metal limbs. But, they were rarer, and more tolerable. In fact, Einar had been reducing her dosages of synthetic painkillers. Not too much at once, though. That could send her into shock, after all. He wanted to get her to a maintenance dose for the extended recovery. It would take time, however. It would be gradual, safe, slow.

She hated that word more than anything in the universe right now aside from Volkner himself. *Slow.* She could not afford *slow.* But she was forced to endure.

She'd taken a great risk allowing Harv to venture out of Valgrind. He could decide to relinquish his information at any moment. She was at the mercy of the smuggler's mood. Piper prayed to the Allfather that the man cared about her promises more than his own wellbeing. A gamble if she'd ever known one. The sooner he was back, the better. Every second she spent in Valgrind was another chance for the Jotuns to find her pod, for her plan to be ruined. Gods be damned, she needed the spineless weasel.

CHAPTER
SIXTEEN

"It took you one day?" Niko asked, his expression utter shock. "One day with your illustrious new title, and you've already been kicked out of one of the top establishments on the *Gjaller*?"

Mila and Amelie had found him exiting a small, but fine-looking tailor shop in the trade sector just a few minutes' walk from the spa.

The Berserker shook his head. "I'll be hearing about that before too long, I'm sure."

"We couldn't help it," Mila said. "It just... we got a little carried away."

Amelie hadn't uttered a word, nor even managed a look at the Berserker since the conversation started. But as Mila looked at her, and the Tyran peeked up to meet her gaze, the fragile-looking girl let slip a hint of a laugh. Then Mila lost it. They were choking on laughter in less than a second, breaking the relative quiet of the trade sector.

"Gods be good," Niko cursed, still shaking his head and grabbing them both by the arms.

The grip was solid, stern, but not violent. Mila was

surprised by the warmth in his palm, considering all the metal laced into his very being.

He ushered them into a nearby unassuming gap between shop strips. There, he let them laugh until they were positively out of breath.

"Finished?" he asked, his arms crossed.

Mila thought he looked more like a disapproving parent than a military commander, and almost relapsed into the laughter again because of it. Instead, she managed to nod.

Amelie mirrored the gesture.

"Good," he said. "Now, Mila, may I have a word with you? In private?"

The tone was different than his usual, short-spoken casualness. It was hesitant, almost formal and definitely forced.

"Sure," Mila replied warily. "Amelie, I guess you have my leave to do as you please." More question than a command; Mila wasn't used to speaking to people, much less, giving orders.

Amelie simply bowed her head and took her leave, disappearing before long into the main throughway.

"Would you walk with me?" Niko asked, nodding to the main path as well.

"A question?" Mila eyed him with one dark eyebrow raised. "Normally you'd just *tell* me to come with you."

Niko laughed, and Mila noticed the dimples in his cheeks for the first time. He shrugged as he replied, "I don't give you orders anymore, not unless it's to keep you safe."

"So *I* give *you* the orders now," Mila said, crossing her arms as she put on a devil's grin.

"More or less," Niko replied.

Mila clicked her tongue. "Well then, I command you to lead the way, my pet."

"Watch it," Niko said, tilting his head and eyeing her with those piercing digitized eyes. "I'm still a berserker; don't you know we have nasty tempers?"

Mila looked up and away, waving a downturned hand like she was a royal dismissing an attendant. "Yes, yes," she said in a fake pompous tone. "You're *so* big and bad."

Niko actually rolled his eyes and huffed a breath that wordlessly said *what have I gotten myself into?* "You're going to make guarding you a massive pain, aren't you?"

Mila smiled and said, "That entirely depends on you."

DESPITE MILA'S HALF-DOZEN QUESTIONS, Niko wouldn't tell her where they were going. Even ordering him to tell her wouldn't make the Berserker budge. Eventually, she just accepted it and kept walking.

Mila had seen all the fantastic, opulent shops and services they'd passed on their way to the spa. She'd smelled the fresh breads baking and the aroma of gourmet meals drifting from the dozens of high-class restaurants. Niko had even halted his pace long enough for her to watch a troupe of street performers finish up their comedic rendition of the death of Baldur. The actor playing Baldur was painted head to toe in gold wearing only a short wrap around his waist. His outrageously dramatic reaction to the actor playing Hod hitting him with mistletoe berries left the gathered crowd nearly collapsing in laughter. Mila laughed along, but opted to leave just after. She knew what came next, and even though it was a comedic rendition, she'd always hated the way Hod was punished—killed for a crime he was tricked into committing. So much injustice in that story, no matter how much people laughed.

Eventually, Niko and Mila arrived on the stoop of a moderately-sized shop. In the windows sat all array of inter-planetary radios.

"What... what's this?" Mila asked, looking up at the Berserker, frowning with confusion.

Niko's dimples showed as he put on a soft smile. "A gift. You have your pick of the store."

"Why?"

Niko shrugged. "Thought it might cheer you up."

Mila didn't reply; couldn't find the words. He'd remembered. She'd only said it in passing, a few words tops, walking through the halls of the *Gjaller*, how much she loved music and missed her radio. And he'd remembered. Not only that, he'd brought her here and was buying her a new one.

Mila shook her head and turned on him, glaring at the Berserker with narrowed eyes. "What's your angle here, Schafer?"

"What makes you think I have an angle?" he replied defensively.

"I'm supposed to believe you're just doing this out of the kindness of your heart?"

"Yeah, that's what I'd hoped, at least. Well, that, and maybe the chance that you'd accompany me to the Freiheit-stag ball?"

Mila's mouth went slack. *He wants me to be his date?*

Niko seemed to mistake the expression as he stepped back and scratched the back of his head awkwardly. "Sorry. I shouldn't have—"

"Yes," Mila said, so softly she could barely hear herself.

"Yes what?" Niko asked as if he'd already forgotten his question.

"Yes, I'll go with you."

In that moment, the legendary warrior that made grown men quiver by just seeing him, looked to Mila like a bashful teenager, a goofy smile stretched across his face.

As if realizing it, he quickly wrangled it into a cocky grin and said, "Great. Now, for that radio."

⊱⋅┈┈┈┈┈┈⋅⊰

SHE HADN'T PICKED the nicest one in the shop. That one had a fully customizable holoscreen, volume equalizing settings, an all-new thermoion battery set the shopkeep swore would last until her hair was gray. She'd looked at it— even gotten caught up in the sales pitch for a minute—but then realized it wasn't the one for her.

Instead, to both Niko and the shopkeep's surprise, she'd wandered into the used section. It was a single shelf with no flashy marketing, just a simple sign that said "Used". The shopkeep had warned her those were sold as-is, and that he couldn't guarantee how long they'd last, but Mila didn't care. She picked one with a tempered glass touchscreen and only a few settings to customize. It had all the channels of the higher-end model, the same quality receptor module, and cost an eighth of the price. Any defects, she would take care of; a point she made clear to the skeptical salesman.

She was back in the refinery now. Niko had left her to handle some other business, though he hadn't said what exactly. Mila just assumed it was some boring Volkner-assigned task. Yet, this time when he left, he'd gone with a smile, and his absence left a pit in Mila's stomach that she was unfamiliar with.

It'd taken her only a few minutes to acquaint herself with the new radio. She was disappointed when she discovered all the non-Vidarin channels censored. That would take some trial-and-error coding work to undo, but she'd gone through the process enough times in the past that she was confident she'd figure it out. And that she did, and in under an hour.

I'm getting better at that.

She found one of her favorite old channels from Jotun that only played Old-Earthen classics. Right now, she and Fen were enjoying some foreboding guitar riffs. They were played by a group that Mila assumed must have been part of a strange religion that deified shellfish, based on their name.

One of the most welcome assets on the radio was the clock, which told Mila it was getting late.

"Think we'll get a third appearance?" she asked Fen.

Though Mila trusted Úlf to keep his end of their bargain at this point, she couldn't toss aside the feeling that their arrangement could go south at any time. There were so many factors involved, so much complexity in the Ambassador's web. If any single string was cut, everything would come crashing down.

Fen replied with a robotic bark, as if trying to reassure her. He was happily lounging beside her, his damaged back leg currently detached. Mila had asked if Niko could take the busted cylinder to Kord to be welded, and the Berserker had readily obliged.

"Yeah," she said. "I think so too."

As if in response, the great refinery doors began to scrape open.

Mila stood, still looking at Fen. "Told ya' he'd show."

"Who'd show?"

Mila's blood turned to ice as the female voice replied. Her attention shot to the girl in front of the door, wide-eyed with curiosity.

"Amelie?" Mila asked.

Amelie smiled and said, "I thought you might want some help around the refinery. With the president increasing his demands and all, it seemed like you might need an assistant."

"No," Mila said, far more sharply than she'd intended.

Amelie recoiled and quickly dipped her head, suddenly that same timid girl from the command deck.

"I mean," Mila said, softening her tone. "I have a very strict method, and it's hard to explain."

Amelie seemed to brighten. "Oh, well I don't have to do anything with the refining itself. Maybe just move barrels for you, or even fetch refreshments? Or I could—"

Mila heard Fen's mechanical limbs groan as the wolfbot slowly got to its feet and stood slightly off-kilter beside her. Amelie went pale and deadly silent as she took him in.

"It's all right!" Mila said. "Fen's a friend!"

"Fen?" Amelie asked, her voice trembling.

"Short for Fenrir," Mila clarified. "He's a Mark II."

"Aren't the Fenrir bots supposed to be... unpredictable?" Amelie asked, cautiously.

"He apparently had some damage before they stashed him down here," Mila replied, placing a hand on Fen's metallic head. "Whatever blows he took, they damaged his central processor. He's in full violence inhibition mode. Couldn't hurt a mouse, even if he wanted to."

Fen growled low and short, as if he was upset with her for sharing his big secret.

"Oh, calm down, drama queen," Mila said to the bot. "Amelie's not going to go spouting your business to the president."

Fen's response was to plop down with a loud, metallic clank, and enter standby mode.

Amelie laughed nervously.

"You mentioned something about refreshments?" Mila asked.

Amelie finally pulled her eyes away from Fen. "Right, yes, whatever you want, I can get it for you."

"Something caffeinated, perhaps?"

Amelie nodded. "I can handle that. I'll be back in a few minutes."

Mila put on her kindest and most thankful smile as Amelie exited. It was hiding the pure dread coiling in her gut. What was she going to do with Amelie? She couldn't keep her at bay all night. Dismissing her seemed to wound the young girl, but roping her into Mila's relationship with Úlf? Into the truth? No, she couldn't do that to her. Wouldn't do it. Wouldn't give her that burden of knowledge to bear.

She'd watched Úlf enough times now to at least figure out how to turn on the refiner and fill the first barrel. That part wasn't dangerous, as long as she didn't continue the process. And Amelie wouldn't know the difference between refinery equipment operating as it should and it simply being on. She'd just act it out when the girl got back, and pray to Freya that Úlf didn't show up before she had time to satiate Amelie's need to help.

When she returned with steaming mugs of coffee twenty minutes later, Mila was examining the control panel closely.

How does Úlf work with this thing? she thought, unable to decipher any words or marking indicating which button was which.

"Could you help me with a barrel?" Mila asked, determined to keep the girl busy just long enough to make it seem like she'd actually helped.

Together, they hauled a barrel of unrefined brandr onto

the cargo cart, but not without a good deal of grunting and a few swears. Mila was astounded to find they weighed more than her and Amelie combined.

"Matron's mercy," Amelie said, panting. "You've been moving these all by yourself?"

Mila shrugged, her breath mirroring Amelie's. "I've done what I needed to survive."

Together, they wheeled the barrel over to the first steel refining pot. Mila popped open the barrel seal and fetched the siphon hose from the pot, as she'd watched Úlf do on the previous nights. After feeding it in, she clicked on the power switch to the siphon pump, only to find no sign of it trying to start up.

It requires the master power, then. She'd been worried about that. As sure as she was that keeping the brandr in the first barrel would be harmless, there was no denying the creeping doubt in the back of her mind. She didn't let it stop her, as she went back to the control panel, breathed deep, and pushed the oversized, charred power button in the top corner.

Nothing.

"Nine shades of Hel," Mila cursed.

"What's wrong?" Amelie asked, peering around her to see what she was trying to do.

"Power issue," Mila replied. "Probably going to require a technician."

"What are you going to do?"

Mila raised an eyebrow at her. "Find a technician, I suppose?"

"You don't think you can fix it?" There was something almost like fear in the girl's tone.

"I've never worked on something like this before."

"Yeah, but you've worked on a lot of other things, right?"

Mila tilted her head, eyebrow still raised. "What's wrong, Amelie?"

"It's just," Amelie replied. "If you wait for a technician, you probably won't have time to refine the entire batch tonight, right? Brandt won't be happy if you're not success-ful. As happy as he was with you today, I've seen him turn. I don't... I don't want to see something bad happen to you."

Mila sighed as she looked at Amelie's doughy eyes. "All right, I'll see what I can do."

Mila followed the cord tubes until she found a long panel on the backside of the refining equipment that read MAIN POWER. Rusted screws held the panel on. They were too deteriorated to have a hope of loosening them with a screwdriver, but they broke easily when Mila pried the panel away.

Inside the underlying channel was a thick, mesh-covered cable routed down the backside of the machine. It was frayed and the bits peeking through were covered in rust themselves.

A wonder this thing was able to carry a current as long as it did.

"Looks like the power line may have just given out," she said, her eyes following the length of the cable, looking for any specific problem areas.

There were no discernable issues down the first few yards, but then, as the line approached the ninety degree turn toward the refinery wall, the metal of the channel casing started to turn black. It got darker and darker as her eyes continued until...

"Mila," Amelie said hesitantly, almost a question.

Mila saw it at the same time, the blackened foot-long

gap in the line. Evidence of a past electrical fire that left the last few feet of the cable decimated and melted. And it wasn't recent.

Mila's brow creased as she tried to work out a logical explanation to the line. *A backup power supply, maybe?* She'd seen no evidence of a battery or another line. Then how had he done it—gotten the refinery equipment to work at all.

"Mila," Amelie repeated.

Mila remembered she wasn't alone and met Amelie's nervous gaze.

"How have you been refining without power?" Amelie asked directly, her tone suddenly starker than Mila had heard before from her.

"It must've just happened," Mila lied.

Amelie shook her head. "I've been on a ship with an electrical fire before. If this happened today, it wouldn't look like that. And we'd smell it."

Mila's mind was racing almost as fast as her pulse. She was right. Absolutely right. This couldn't have happened today, and there was no backup power. *What in the Matron's name is going on?* She had nothing to offer Amelie—no lie to explain things. She didn't even understand what was happening. The massive refinery suddenly felt small, tight, like the shadows in the corners of the room were reaching out to entangle her—steal her breath, her soul.

"Mila?"

"I don't know," was all Mila could manage to reply. "I just... I don't know. It was working. Last night, it was working fine."

"You're lying to me." Amelie was withdrawing from her slowly, backing toward the refinery door.

"I'm not. Please, don't go," Mila pleaded. "Just let me explain."

Amelie shook her head. "I think I should just go. Something's wrong here."

"It most certainly is."

Amelie whipped around at the new male voice coming from the refinery entrance. Fen set into a loud, warning growl and Mila's eyes went wide. There was no one there, just the closed door, and a shadowy corner of the refinery. It seemed to loom much larger than Mila had ever noticed before.

Then, as if forming from the blackness itself, Úlf stepped forward, and Amelie collapsed.

SEVENTEEN

CLOSE. Open. Repeat.

With every repetitive motion, the aluminum alloy hand closed its fingers tight, loosened, and stretched the digits all the way out.

Close. Open. Repeat.

"Very good," Einar said. "Astoundin', actually."

"How long do you need me to keep doing this?" Piper asked, not attempting to hide the annoyed edge to her voice. She'd been doing it for at least ten minutes, possibly an eternity—she couldn't be sure.

"I think that's enough," the healer replied, checking something off his holotablet. "Now for the leg."

Piper got up and strode across the medroom. An observant eye could still detect the hesitation in her gait when she moved that right leg, but it was so subtle it could be attributed to a sore muscle. The clunk had disappeared as well now that Piper had taught herself to account for the weight. She walked back and forth a half-dozen times before Einar signaled to stop.

"Ya' really are somethin' else," he said, shaking his head. "How's the pain?"

"Feels like I got dragged behind a hoverbike across the Tyran canyons," Piper replied. Then, with a grin, she added, "so, much better than yesterday."

Einar chuckled and said, "I'm reducing your doses. Don't want ya' gettin' addicted to synthetics. Seen too many good people fall to those."

Piper nodded. She'd seen it as well after crewmates had been injured, and knew his concern was warranted. Still, she couldn't deny the idea of returning to the pain of a few days ago—both from the gashes on her back and of her adapting to the limbs—made her breath catch.

"So, how long until I can get back?" Piper asked.

"*Back?*" Einar replied. "If ya' don't mind me askin', is there a *back* for ya' now?"

Piper shrugged. "Maybe I could be of use on Hod." It sounded a lot better than the real plan. Being struck down in a blaze of glory while splattered with Volkner Brandt's fresh blood didn't seem like the type of thing you tell your doctor when you're trying to get released.

Einar nodded thoughtfully. He glanced back to make sure there were no unwanted ears before saying, "Their people owe a debt of gratitude to ya', after all."

Piper shook her head. "They're not in my debt. It's people like your father who made a difference. We did what we did because no one else would."

"It's that reason that they should be gracious. That I'm sure they still remember the name *Laufey*. You helped when no one else would."

Einar let the words sink in. Piper was back on Hod, listening to the people scream after a Vidarin missile struck a rebel hideout in a nameless village. Freedom fighters, local men and women, children, all of them, screaming. And she couldn't save them. No, she didn't deserve the Hodian's gratitude. Not like Einar's father did.

"So, how long?" Piper asked, routing the subject back to her present health.

"At this rate? Two more weeks. You're making remarkable progress, but there's always the risk of delayed rejection. Two weeks is generally the safe point."

Two weeks was too long, but Piper nodded anyway. No sense in arguing with him and risk making him wise to her plans to leave soon. Every second she spent on Jotun was a risk; a risk that her shuttle would be found, that she'd be captured. Or, worse, a risk that she'd be forced into exile, unable to return to the *Gjaller* until her name began to fade.

"Well, let me get your medicines and ya' can be on with your way," Einar said as he switched off the holotablet.

Once the door to medroom shut behind him, Piper eyed the small storage cabinet on the side of the room. She looked at the door to make sure neither of the assistants would enter for any reason, then hopped up and opened the cabinet. Tongue depressors, cotton balls, bandages, ointments, and all the general supplies lined the bottom shelf. But those were not what Piper was interested in. Her eyes were on the top shelf, where boxes labeled 'Specimen Bags' were set. She retrieved one of the boxes, opened it, and stowed away one of the auto-sealing bags in her cargo pocket in less than a few seconds.

By the time Einar reentered, she was at the door ready for the medications, which she snatched away with the briefest thanks and headed out of the healer's den.

THESE PAST DAYS, Berrant's mead hall had become Piper's favorite place to pass the time while she waited for Harv to return. Even though she hadn't any money, the burly mead-master slid her a glass of sunwater every time she sat at the bar.

"Good conversation's better than money around here," he'd said each time she'd tried to argue.

And their conversations were good, surprisingly enough. In half-truth stories, Piper told him of her time on Tyr and Idun and Hod, her focus sticking mainly to the cultures and fauna of the respective places and less her reasons for being there. He'd told her of his time as a tundra hunter and his responsibility to bring meat and fur in for the village to export.

Piper had always thought the structure of Jotun society fascinating—scattered villages organized so that everyone contributed to the success of the community in the roles they were best suited for. No one person was superior to another because they all possessed equally. Einar was equal to Berrant was equal to Kari. No exception, no argument. Civility, even though other planets like Vidar tended to demonize the lifestyle.

Today, Berrant was recalling a story about a close encounter with an odbjarn—a Jotun bearlike creature that weighed over a ton and had a vicious temper. He'd just finished telling her about it ripping his favorite coat, when the door to the mead hall opened, and a chill like death strode in from the blizzard outside, accompanied by a man in a pinstripe suit with a fedora hat and a blackwood cane.

"Welcome, friend," Berrant said. "Can I get ya' a drink?"

"Water, please," the man replied with a politician's smile.

The suit man observed the room, eventually settling on the table Harvey had sat at a few days before and making his way to it. After he sat, he removed his hat to reveal a mane of slicked-back obsidian hair—no gray despite his age.

Piper didn't recognize him. Yet, there was an eerie familiarity about the man, like some old memory in the back of her mind clawing to be recalled.

"Do you know him?" Piper asked Berrant in a low voice.

Berrant shrugged and shook his head. "Never seen 'im before."

"New patrons aren't too common here, right?"

"Not really. But of course, we do get 'em. Two in a week, though? Can't say I've seen that kind of traffic in a while."

Berrant smiled genially and Piper returned it because it was what Frida would do. But the itch in her mind demanded to be scratched. She had to speak with the man.

"Mind if I sit?" Piper asked as she approached.

The man was closely examining the side of the table, running his fingers over the letters Harv had carved.

"Some people have no class," he said, not looking at her. "To deface such a beautiful table..." he shook his head and finally looked up at Piper.

He presented that same smile; the kind you hope is genuine, but always fear masks underlying motives. Then, he gestured to the seat beside him, and Piper sat.

"There ya' are," Berrant said, setting a glass of water on the table in front of the man.

The jovial meadmaster seemed as if he were waiting for an invitation to sit, but the suit man gave no such indication. Piper raised her eyebrows at Berrant in a silent apology.

"Right. Well, I guess I'll leave ya' to it."

"Thank you, sir," the suit man said. "And, perhaps, if it isn't too much trouble, could we have some fresh bread?"

Berrant raised an eyebrow. "Might be a while. I have to get the oven fired up. Haven't lit that thing in months."

"I'm fine with waiting. And, I'll compensate you for the trouble."

The man took a pouch of coins from the inside of his fine jacket and dropped the entire bag on the table with a metallic clunk.

"Five-thousand krona sound reasonable?"

Berrant's jaw dropped and the normally-jabbering man was speechless. Piper knew five-thousand Jotun krona was likely as much money as was in the entire village. For this man to make such an offering to Berrant alone was likely unheard of.

"You really don't have to—" Berrant began.

"Take it. Use it to renovate your fine establishment or give it to the village. A gift or fair compensation for goods delivered, however you choose to look at it. But I do expect the bread to be good."

"Of-of course," Berrant stuttered. "I'll get right on it."

The bear of a man scurried away like an excitable child to the kitchen. Piper heard all manner of metal pans and utensils clanging together as he got to work.

"Now, to talk business," the man said.

"Business?" Piper asked, her head cocked to the side.

"Yes, business, Miss DeRache."

The blood flushed from Piper's face. "What did you just say?"

"Oh yes, I know who you are, Piper."

Piper kicked her chair back clumsily and nearly fell over, unused to moving so suddenly with the robotic leg. But she managed to stay on her feet, and was now glaring down at the man, her periphery noting everything she could use as a weapon.

"Calm down," the man said. "There's no need for that."

"Who are you?" Piper demanded. "Tell me now, or I swear on Odin's spear I will kill you right now."

"I'm a friend," the man replied. "A friend who wants to help you get what you want."

"And what is that?"

"Vengeance," the man said coldly.

Piper clenched her teeth together hard enough to risk breaking them. Each of her hands flexed, the human and the metal, in that same motion she'd practiced so many times already. Close. Open. Repeat.

"Please, sit back down," he said, gesturing at the chair.

"How do I know I can trust you?"

The man laughed. "You should really count yourself lucky. When I heard a drunken smuggler spouting tales of finding Piper DeRache in some snow-buried Jotun village..."

Piper silently cursed the bovine smuggler and herself for trusting he wouldn't sell her out.

"I felt that information in the wrong hands would be pretty grim for you," the man continued. "As for trusting me, well, I'd be incredibly stupid for coming to apprehend one of the system's most notorious killers on my own, no?"

"You could have the place surrounded by soldiers or mercenaries," Piper countered.

"Yes, I could. But then, that would also be stupid. You're still a master of death, and now you've nothing to lose. I have no doubt by the time they breached and disabled you, I'd already be a corpse."

"I suppose you have a point," Piper said, slowly picking her chair back up, her eyes scanning back and forth through the mead hall. They didn't stop until she sat back down. "Does my *friend* have a name?"

"Call me Atli."

"Very well, Atli. So, I don't suppose Harv will be making a return any time soon. Do I need to worry about him spreading more secrets?"

Atli raised an eyebrow and reached into his pocket, pulling out a small, clear bag containing a gray block and slid it across the table to her. She picked it up to inspect, quickly realizing it was the foldable, serrated-edge knife Harv had started carving the Trickster's name into the table with days before. Except now there was the distinct rust-brown of dry blood coating the blade and half of the handle.

Piper nodded, understanding. "That kind of puts a wrench in my plans."

"You'd have a lot more than a wrench if he were allowed to go on living."

"You want some kind of thanks?"

"Not at all. I already told you, Miss DeRache, I'm here to help you."

Piper leaned back in her chair, crossing her arms. "In my experience, help doesn't come for free."

"Nor mine."

"Then what's the price?"

Atli smiled like a fox. "A favor."

"You always this vague?"

Atli laughed. "It's easy enough to see what your plan is: get aboard the *Gjaller* and slit Volkner's throat before anyone important realizes you're still alive."

"Or gouge his eyes out, choke him with his own tongue, carve him into a blood eagle. The method doesn't matter all that much to me so long as he's dead."

"Your ruthless reputation is not unwarranted, I see."

Piper shrugged.

"I'm asking you add just a little more to your plan," Atli said.

Piper tilted her head and raised an eyebrow, silently ordering him to get to the point.

"I'll be aboard the *Gjaller* soon for their Freiheitstag celebration. During that time, I intend to destroy the entire station."

Piper sat up; her eyes wide. "Destroy the *Gjaller*?! By yourself?!"

"Yes, but I won't exactly be alone. I have people aboard the station now who I expect to help, and I hope you might be able to help bolster my numbers even further."

"How do you expect me to do that?"

"By contacting the rebels, Miss DeRache."

Piper laughed mockingly. "The rebels? Sorry to tell you, but they don't exist anymore."

"Your being here disproves that," Atli said. "And I have reason to believe the rest of them have been biding their time in the shadows."

Piper shook her head. "Look, I'm all for you taking down that hunk of metal, but I don't think I'll be able to help you."

Atli stood, the vulpine grin still present. "I'll be around the village a bit longer. Think it over, and I'll see if you change your answer. Oh, and may I just add, if you choose to aid me, the smuggler's ship is ready to go for you. If not... well, I expect finding another vessel before they find your escape shuttle may be difficult."

Piper rolled her eyes and huffed a breath.

"We'll speak soon, Miss DeRache," Atli said as he donned his hat.

The doors to the mead hall closed behind the mysterious man just as Berrant came out of the back with steaming, fresh loaves of brown bread and honeyed butter.

"Where... where'd he go?" Berrant asked, a hint of alarm in his voice.

But Piper didn't reply. Her mind was on the suit man, and though she couldn't explain why, she had no doubt he would succeed in doing exactly what he'd said.

He was going to destroy the *Gjaller.*

THE WIND TUNNELING between the stretch of Valgrind's buildings stung Piper's exposed cheeks, and the fluid in her eyes felt as though it were trying to freeze. She was walking to Kari's inn from Einar's office, where she'd just picked up injectable synthetics to last her for the next day or so. She hoped that's all she would need. Her pace was as quick as she could muster to get to Kari's inn, but the faster she walked, the threat of a clumsy trip on her awkward metal leg heightened.

When she reached the inn, she was surprised to find the suit man from the day before standing in the snow. He was in front of the inn, looking toward it, no security nor company in sight.

"Atli," she called as she approached.

She had to repeat the name twice before he acknowledged it. It was as if she were breaking him out of a trance.

"Ah, Miss DeRache," he said.

Piper tensed, looking side to side to make sure no one was around to catch him utter her surname.

"Don't worry," Atli continued. "The wind will keep our words our own."

"You wouldn't rather have this conversation inside?" Piper asked, rubbing her arms.

Atli shook his head and Piper noticed his eyes flick to the inn door and back. "No, that's not necessary. I'll be quick. And we can't trust the absence of those prying ears, can we?"

Piper grimaced, then nodded begrudgingly as she started to shiver. Atli didn't seem fazed by the cold whatsoever, even in his thin suit.

"So, the plan?" Piper asked shortly.

Atli raised an eyebrow. "You've decided you'll help?"

Piper nodded impatiently.

"I'm glad to hear it."

Atli pulled a small wooden box out of his pocket and handed it to Piper. She opened it to find it contained a biobag, and within that, a severed thumb.

"You'll take the smuggler's ship to the *Gjaller*. It's already outfitted with everything you'll need. Once there, you'll be playing the role of a Tyran trader. There's a citizen chip preloaded with your Frida credentials onboard. I will already be aboard by the time you arrive."

"Why don't I just go with you, then?" Piper asked.

"I don't travel by conventional means."

Piper wasn't sure what that meant, but judging by his tone, she knew she wouldn't get an answer if she asked.

Instead, she asked, "When do I leave?"

"As soon as you're able. The vessel is in the ship docks on the east side of the village. As soon as you're in the void, though, I need you to send that message."

"And what if they don't answer?"

"Then each of our objectives will be much harder to achieve."

The sound of whipping wind filled the gap between

them for a moment before Piper asked, "Why is it you want to destroy the *Gjaller*?"

The suit man looked back at the door to the inn and was silent for a long moment. Piper was about to leave him for the warmth of the building when he finally spoke.

"My reasons are like yours. Something was taken from me."

"By Volkner?"

Atli shook his head. "Destroying that man and his station are but the first domino. Toppling it may help me get justice for the debt owed."

Piper knew the question stinging the edge of her tongue was a risk to ask, but it couldn't be helped. "What did you lose?"

The man looked at her and that foxlike smile returned. "You should get some rest, my dear. We have a revolution to start soon."

Atli tipped his hat and took his leave. Nearly every ounce of Piper's being wanted to storm the inn and absorb the abundance of heat within. But one part of her held on to the man, watching him walk away. From the very first word he'd spoken to her he seemed like a man with a strategy—a plan set ten steps ahead of anyone else. He seemed like a conductor from the shadows. A silent puppeteer. Like the one met by many but known by few, and she knew it was by design. Yet now, as he walked tall, his back to her, she felt the suit was only a guise for some sorrow, or terror, hidden underneath.

CHAPTER
EIGHTEEN

"That was... awkward," Úlf said, looking down at Amelie's body.

Fen's bark was feral as the wolfbot tried desperately to lurch for the Ambassador. But his violence inhibition settings were too much. It was clear he couldn't move an inch with the intent to harm.

"What did you do to her?" Mila demanded, dropping to Amelie's side and checking her pulse.

Alive.

"She'll be fine," Úlf replied. "When she wakes up, she won't remember seeing me."

Mila stood, fists curled and brow sharply angled. "What is all of this? How did you do it?"

"Do what?" Úlf replied, cocking his head. His voice the epitome of nonchalance, as if he hadn't just manifested from shadow and made her friend lose consciousness.

"The refining without power," she said, gesturing to the destroyed cable. "Step through gods-damned shadow," she continued, pointing at the corner of the refinery. "And whatever the Hel you did to her!"

Úlf shrugged. "Talent?"

Mila's eyes widened in pure fury. She felt that fiery rage roiling up her spine, filling her, hot coals in her veins. "Tell me the truth!"

"Easy," Úlf replied, waving her down with both hands.

"Tell me!"

The rage was spiraling out of control. It washed through her completely, coating her nerves, her mind.

"Enough!" Úlf said, suddenly serious.

As if in response, the elerex let loose a shock like pure lightning, sucking the oxygen from Mila's internal inferno. Sharp pain erupted through her chest, the worst she'd ever felt. It forced her to her knees as she grasped her chest, her teeth clenched so hard they might crack. It was her lungs, her muscles, her heart, all convulsing in rejection of the horrible, rampaging current.

Her vision blurred, though she could hear Fen's bark. It was far away—too far. Miles. She could make out nothing but the wolfbot's raw figure, leaping toward her. Though, before he could reach her, another figure appeared. Úlf, not near the refinery door, but right in front of her, appearing like a wraith from thin air.

She watched as two of his indistinct fingers, which she now realized were just a little too long to be natural, touched her forehead. Then, she fell backwards into nothingness.

⚬——⚬————————⚬——⚬

"Mɪ?" the voice in the darkness asked. "Mi, is that you?"

"Who's there?" Mila replied into the void, her voice weak, unable to carry through the dense, viscous black.

"Mi?" The disembodied voice sounded both right beside her and a galaxy away. Mila could tell it was female, and the tone was kind, but that was it.

"Who's there?" she repeated.

Blackness. Utter, deep, endless. A hell of nothingness. A prison of shadow.

A light, far away, as far as the voice. Farther. Smaller than the tip of the sharpest needle. The hint of a hole in the hollow. The hint of hope.

"Mi."

The light was the voice. The voice was the light. But it was far. Too far.

"Mi."

⟵—•—•—•—⟶

MILA WOKE LOOKING at the flickering incandescence of the refinery lights. Every pulse pierced her mind. Gods, she felt awful, like her body was little more than a dried-out husk. It took far more effort than she expected, but she managed to sit up on her cot and examine the refinery.

Empty.

She was the only one there. Well, besides Fen, laying in standby mode beside her. She loosed a breath. *A dream. That's all it was.*

She saw the pallet at the end of the refinery still held all of its barrels.

I wonder what time it is. She assumed she drifted off listening to the radio with Fen. When she flicked on the radio to see the clock, her heart sank. *Only an hour until due time?* So her fears were confirmed. Ulf wasn't coming back again.

When she flipped her legs over the cot, she was surprised to find Fen didn't even stir. Normally he'd at least detect the motion and raise his head in greeting. *Must be as tired as I am.*

She got up to stretch her legs, refusing to let herself consider everything that Úlf's absence implied, or what it meant for her and her father. There was a single thread of hope still lingering in her that Volkner would give her one more night; just a little more time to come up with some sort of desperate escape plan. A fool's hope. A fool's hope, except...

It was full. The gauge, on the final cylinder. It was completely full. Mila rubbed her eyes and then looked at it again. They hadn't deceived her.

She remembered the still-full pallet at the other end and ran to them. They were full, but they weren't labeled brandr. *Hyrrine,* it said in stenciled letters.

Mila took a step back, unable to process the egregious amount of hyrrine in the refinery right now. Then she remembered the power line, sprinting around the refining equipment, only to find the power source still exposed—still damaged beyond repair.

"Double," Úlf said, suddenly behind her.

Mila whirled and crouched, ready to defend against an oncoming attack.

"Double the amount he asked for," Úlf continued, grinning like a wolf. "Chemists will say it's impossible, and Volkner Brandt will point to this." He gestured to the barrels.

"Where is Amelie?" Mila hissed.

"In her quarters, safe and sound. When she wakes up, this will have all been nothing more than a strange dream."

He seemed to consider Mila for a moment. "You, I wasn't so sure about."

"What are you talking about?" Mila asked, not letting her guard down.

"You had a seizure, and I believe, a heart attack, courtesy of that contraption implanted in your arm."

Mila's already-pounding heart turned into a freight train. "That's impossible. That couldn't have—"

"Couldn't have what, Miss Messer?" he interrupted. "Couldn't have happened?"

Mila didn't reply.

"I would have thought it'd be obvious to you now that *none* of this could have happened," he said, raising both hands to gesture around the entire refinery. "Yet, it did."

"What are you?" Mila demanded. "Some kind of advanced scientist? A sorcerer?"

"I'm just a humble Jotun Ambassador."

"Stop being coy," Mila said.

Úlf chuckled. "You couldn't hope to understand *what* I am, even *if* I told you."

There was weight in that sentence that made Mila's hair stand on end. The longer she looked at him, the more she realized there was something very off about the Jotun Ambassador.

The pale skin, she'd attributed to the snowy Jotun clime. Yet, it wasn't just pale; it was white and without a single flaw, as if crafted from porcelain. His smile, those teeth were too white as well. Even the symmetry of him, of his mouth, his eyes, it bordered on uncanny. And his form, he was standing completely still, yet the edges of him held the slightest blur, as if he was in a perpetual state of motion too fast for Mila to perceive. The thought made her nauseous. Whatever Úlf was, it wasn't natural.

"Leave," she said.

Úlf frowned playfully. "Don't be like that, Mi."

Mila was stricken, unintentionally taking a step back. "Don't you dare call me that."

Úlf laughed. The sound may as well have been nails scraping across the refinery floor.

"Leave," she repeated, her tone unyielding.

"And what then, if I leave? What do you gain?"

Mila didn't care about his words, whatever he was going to weave her. She just wanted him gone.

"Leave!" she screamed.

Úlf's smile snapped into a thin line and his eyes narrowed. Then, he was gone, a shadowy dust floating in his wake.

Suddenly, like a ghostly draugr chill grazing the back of her neck, Úlf whispered, "I refuse."

The words whispered in Mila's ear had her turning to throw a punch, but her wrist was caught easily by his long-fingered hand in a movement she couldn't even see. The flesh of his palm was like Jotun permafrost. Úlf twisted her arm and pain shot through her, crying out for her to get away. But he was strong—inhumanly strong. With the simple hold there was no chance of her fleeing. She was at his mercy.

His face was only inches from hers now as he said in a voice that sounded more like an adder's than a man's, "Don't forget our arrangement, Mila. You still owe me for helping you."

"I don't owe you anything," Mila hissed and spat in his face.

His eye twitched as he wiped the spittle away with his free hand and laughed again. This time, though, it was low, threatening. A promise. "Enjoy this batch, Mila Messer. Consider it a gift of good faith."

And just like that, he was gone, dissipating into the ether, leaving only that faint, dusty trace. Yet the feel of his cold hand remained around her wrist like a tether.

NINETEEN

A FEAT, he'd called it. A feat of unimaginable magnitude that will bring power and prosperity back to Vidar. Volkner Brandt had sung Mila's praises from the moment she entered the command room until the moment she left. He'd even assigned her a room on the executive level and given her two days off as a way of welcoming her into his inner circle.

Her conversations with Niko that day had been brief. He'd left her in the care of Eiji while he took care of more business. Eiji, didn't talk much. Hardly at all, really. Even when Mila asked her questions, her answers were short and mostly uninformative. Mila had managed to get out of the warrior that she was Hodian, she was eighteen, and not much else.

Not that she'd tried that hard. If she was being honest with herself, she really didn't care about Niko's soldier or her past right now. She didn't care to talk at all, actually. After what she'd seen last night, in the refinery, her mind was on one person: Úlf, who'd winked at her in the command room with all the arrogance and cruelty of a god.

She opted to spend most of the day in that newly assigned suite, leaving Eiji on post in the corridor outside. Her thoughts kept going back to Amelie collapsing, to Úlf walking from shadow, to the non-existent power flow to the refining equipment. No matter how many times her mind circled it, she kept coming back to the same conclusion—the only explanation when all other logic fails.

Fjölkyngi.

Magic.

Úlf had wielded magic last night and all the preceding ones. It made so much more sense now why none of Niko's guards seemed to know of the situation, and why they came in with that same, surprised look every single day. They didn't know. They couldn't know. Just as Úlf had controlled Amelie like a puppet and wiped her mind clean, so, too, he likely did with the Vidarin soldiers.

It raised many more questions than answers. How much of his story was true, for one. Had he lied about everything? Was there a rebellion at all? If so, what was stopping him from unleashing his magic against Volkner? But if not, what did he really want from Mila? Each possible answer came with its own unanswerable question, leaving her with no shortage of queries.

What time she spent not pondering, she spent trying to sleep. Her body still felt weak and drained from the elerex and the excitement. Yet, try as she did, rest seemed to evade her. The bed in the suite was luxurious, made for the highest in the Vidarin social structure. But the softness felt alien to her. She'd always either slept on a decades-old mattress or the rugged cot in her workshop. Plus, without Fen laying by her bed, the room felt too empty. The thought of leaving him to sleep alone in the refinery from now on felt wrong to her. Even though they'd only spent a few nights together, that bot was now her oldest friend.

Amelie made scattered appearances throughout the day, mostly to bring meals, even though Mila didn't particularly have an appetite. When the young Tyran tried to make conversation, Mila made it clear she was tired, and that silence was the best thing Amelie could provide. She knew it hurt the young girl's self-esteem to dismiss her like that, but Mila couldn't bear talking to her and know she didn't remember a second of the night before. All it did was raise those questions again, coupled with an even newer one.

Why did he let me remember?

<hr />

MILA WAS AWAKENED by Niko the next morning. She hadn't the slightest idea of how much sleep she'd actually managed to get but felt at least somewhat better than the day before. After scarfing down the breakfast he'd brought— real pork, eggs, and a fresh orange that he'd informed her was grown right on the station in the garden sector. To top it off, there was toast and spiced apple butter. Combined, it was one of the most decadent meals she'd had in recent memory, and she savored every bite after hardly eating the day before.

After that, she'd practically begged the Berserker to show her more of the ship. If she spent another day isolated with her thoughts... Well, she didn't know if her sanity could take it. He'd been more than happy to oblige her.

She didn't particularly care what he showed her, only that it was a distraction. Still, she was surprised when, instead of the market or the shipyard or a theater, they took a lift to the engine level.

"Going to show me how this behemoth stays up here?" she asked as they exited the lift.

Niko laughed, "Not exactly."

Mila cocked her head. "Well, you've certainly got my curiosity."

Making their way through the engine level corridors, they passed several areas that Mila actually did find interesting. Notably the viewing panels to the reactor rooms. One-hundred-ton versions of the same battery that powered Fenrir, and each of the dozen areas they passed held four of the humming monstrosities. And that was only in a relatively small section of the engine level. She estimated there was likely quadruple that in total. It was a truly incomprehensible amount of power, and it was responsible for the station's defense systems, life support, lights, communication arrays, and every other thing that required power to function.

That amount of power, however, came at a risk. In the wrong hands, those reactors made the *Gjaller* one of the biggest bombs the universe had ever known. It wasn't by accident that each reactor room was equipped with automated turrets, shield systems, and a detail of armored guards.

To Mila's surprise, none of the guards nor engineers on the level seemed to care much that a berserker was lurking about. They seemed to take more interest in Mila, but none of them stopped to ask what the duo was doing there.

"You come down here often?" Mila asked as they walked.

"You could say that," Niko replied.

The answer did nothing but further pique her curiosity.

She'd been so interested in the reactors themselves that she didn't notice the most peculiar thing about the level until now. On every door, there was a rune painted in fresh, vibrant red. It was Aegishjalmur, the Helm of Awe and the most powerful of the Neunorse protection runes, or so the gothar said. Mila had seen it many times, painted all over various pieces of equipment in the pit. Her father even had a few carvings of it hung on the walls in their house.

"What's with the runes?" Mila asked.

Niko frowned, but didn't break pace. "As arrogant as our president is, he still fears the gods. The gothi convinced him to take precautions against the gods' judgement after the failure on Hod, and he took it very seriously. Those are painted fresh, daily."

"With blood?"

Niko nodded. "From a goat."

Mila grimaced.

"Religious nonsense is what I call it," Niko spat.

"You don't believe in the gods?" Mila asked in surprise.

Niko shrugged. "I believe in them, I suppose. But to think we please them by slitting the throats of goats and men is ridiculous. Zealots use that as an excuse to take life. It's how wars are started and justified. Divinity is the crutch of sadists and murderers."

Mila felt the bitterness on those last words. They walked in silence for a minute after that, while Mila contemplated what he'd said. She'd never given much thought to the gods, but he was right. To think anyone had the slightest understanding of what they wanted was ludicrous.

Before long, they were out of the humming halls and moving into an area alive with the sound of active machinery. Niko explained that, while the reactors were the lungs of the *Gjaller,* creating its power, these rooms contained the hearts, pumping the power through veins throughout the station. Mila noted there were significantly fewer engineers in this section and almost no guards. The numbers thinned more and more until they were in the very outskirts of the level.

At the very end, when Mila knew they had to be close to the outer rim of the level, Niko took several quick turns that Mila thought she might have trouble remembering if she was asked to repeat them without him. They came to a nondescript door that opened with a simple push of a button. No security, no bio-encryption. Inside, there was what looked to be a long-abandoned refinery, except it was only a fraction the size of the one on the lower levels.

"They built several brandr refineries on this level during the station's initial construction," Niko explained. "Back when hyrrine was still new and everyone wanted to power everything with it." The Berserker made his way past the refining equipment with Mila close in tow. "They thought creating it closer to the engines would help reduce transport costs. But once refiners started blowing themselves up every couple of weeks, they had the refinery deck constructed far away from where the rest of the ship levels where, when there were accidents, it wasn't as much of a threat to the other levels."

There was another door in the back corner of the dark room; this one with an old-style numbered keypad.

"Most of these small refineries got repurposed to support the reactor initiative. But since the reactors generate their own power, they didn't need all the room. Eventually, the engineers and builders just stopped expanding, which left a few intact."

"And you just come hang out in abandoned brandr refineries for fun?" Mila asked.

Niko laughed—an honest, slightly embarrassed laugh

that brought out those distinct dimples. "I could care less about the refinery itself," he said as he punched in a number into the keypad. "But some of them, like this one, had cargo storage that opened directly to the void for supply ships to easily drop off raw brandr." The door hissed and crept open as he finished putting in the code. "Those spaces have their uses."

Niko gestured for Mila to lead the way. If it had been any other time, she might have mocked him for the formality. But he'd whipped her mind into a curious beast by this point. What kind of crazy, twisted, interesting thing could a berserker be hiding all the way out here? The thought even flashed through her mind that he'd brought her out here as some elaborate scheme cooked up by Brandt. But if he could smile like that while hiding a trickster's intent, well, then the stories about the berserkers had to be true, and they couldn't actually feel emotion. Mila didn't believe that.

Any speck of doubt she had about Niko or his intentions was abolished the moment she took in the room. It was smaller than she'd expected—much smaller, in fact. It was less of a cargo bay and more of a large storage closet with a windowed bay door. But it wasn't the size that surprised her. No, it was the pictures.

Pictures. Physical pictures were pasted to the walls of the humble space. And letters, written on actual paper as well. On the ground were piled blankets and pillows of all array of colors. Mila knew without asking that it probably took him quite a while to transport them up here one at a time to avoid raising suspicion. Through the windowed door she saw the violet curve of Vidar, and beyond it, Ymir. It was, in a word, magical. And not in the dark, mysterious way that surrounded Ulf. In a charming, sweet, and utterly unexpected way.

Mila didn't have words. She just gaped as Niko stepped in behind her and closed the door.

"What do you think?" he asked hesitantly.

"It's not what I expected."

"What did you expect?"

"I don't know, really. Just not this," Mila said, her eyes surfing from picture to picture.

"You don't like it?"

"Actually," Mila responded, "it's quite the opposite. I adore it."

She turned to Niko and found his wide eyes more vulnerable than she ever imagined a berserker's could be. He looked, in that moment, unlike a soldier at all. He was human, flesh and bone, even if it was laced with titanium and artificial power. It still contained him, his heart. Not the physical, shielded one in his chest, but his core. That thing that made him who he was. He wasn't a cyborg or a robot or a berserker. He was just Niko.

"Who are they?" she asked, gesturing to all of the pictures.

The varying conditions of the photos and letters told her which ones were older and which were newer. They held character in a way that a holoscreen never could. It filled her with a deep sense of sadness that most of the physical Earthen books had been burned long ago by fanatical Neunorsemen. She could count on one hand the amount of times she'd seen a physical piece of paper, in fact.

"My family, mostly," Niko replied. "I haven't seen them in several years except via the occasional holoscreen call, but Volkner limits my quota for those, so I put my money toward paper and ink for us to send letters."

Mila was examining a photo of Niko's family. Judging by the look of the paper, she figured it was one of the older ones and portrayed a fair-skinned woman with chestnut hair that matched the Berserker's. Beside her was a tall man that looked the spitting image of an older Niko. In front of them stood two young boys. Twins.

"My mother, my father, and my younger brothers," Niko said, taking a place beside her.

"Your mother is beautiful," Mila said. "Your whole family is."

It was the truth. Her eyes rolled over the pictures, watching the family grow with each one. Some were shots of them participating in various activities: the brothers wrestling with the father, the mother tending a greenhouse garden, more than one of a gift exchange at Yule. Most, however, were pictures of the entire family gathered in front of a humble-looking house.

As her eyes continued to rove and watch them grow, she came across one where Niko's father looked different. He was shorter than his mother in it—hunched, and his eyes weren't right. He seemed confused, unaware of why he was having his picture taken. In the next, he was in a wheel-chair, barely conscious by the look of things. She noticed the mother's smile in that picture as well—present, but not convincing. A lie concealing some awful sorrow. Finally, in the next picture, the father was absent entirely.

Niko seemed to track Mila's journey through the pictures and her realization. "He died last year," he said. "A brain disease caused by excessive exposure to radioactive stunners."

Mila looked up at the Berserker, both sorrow and curiosity filling her eyes.

"The last time I saw him in person was almost ten years ago," Niko continued.

"You haven't been home in ten years?" Mila asked,

every ounce of surprise carrying through in her voice. "But, you're a berserker; one of the most elite warriors in the system. And an officer to boot. You're not given time off?"

"Oh, I have plenty of leave built up. But using it to wander around the *Gjaller* for days on end isn't exactly my idea of a vacation."

"You can't go home?"

Niko shook his head. "I'm trapped here under Volkner's thumb, just like Amelie, just like you, and just like half the people on this gods-damned hunk of metal." His gaze settled on the last picture of his dad once more. "He was always the proudest of me. Even in those last couple of years when he didn't know my face. I always felt that there was a part of him lingering inside that was proud."

"I'm so sorry, Niko," Mila said.

She tried and failed to resist the urge to place her hand on his arm. He didn't pull away or recoil, not so much as a flinch. His skin was warm, but not hot. Comfortable. This close, the midnight and metal scent of him took her back the farm, to her workshop, to the father that, no matter how much she despised, a part of her missed.

"Why don't you resign?" she asked.

Niko chuckled, but there wasn't any real joy in it. "How much do you know about the berserkers?"

The question caught Mila off-guard. "Not much, I guess. The stories over the radio, mostly, and the bits you've told me."

Niko nodded as though she'd said exactly what he expected her to. Then, he sat down on the blanketed deck and reached under a stack of pillows, withdrawing a tarnished metal box with a runic bearpaw stamped into the lid. His nostrils flared as he released a long breath while he stared at the container. Then, he gestured for her to sit beside him, and Mila obliged, opting to sit a bit closer than she would to most people. The room wasn't the warmest, but being close to him warded off the chill.

He handed her the box. She opened it to find three items. The first was a military medal in the shape of a valknut attached to a bit of red ribbon, on the back it read:

Blood of Odin,
Hand of Tyr,
Blooded Berserkers
Feast on Fear.

The second was a three-inch long computer chip with a crack down the middle and rust-brown speck of some long-dried substance. There was a word stamped into the middle, but a large scratch rendered it unreadable. She could only make out the first two letters clearly: *Ba-*.

The last item was another photo. However, this one was discolored and bubbled in places. The edges were coiling and black, as if the picture had been saved from a fire. It portrayed a platoon of young men all with the same, serious look plastered onto their faces. Their heads were all shaved, including the battle-aged commander standing at parade rest on the side. Besides the grizzled leader, none of them had faces older than twenty, despite their builds being perfect, lean muscle that would take a normal adult years to hone.

Written across the bottom of the picture was *"To the Halls of Valhalla!"* It was surrounded by about a dozen illegible signatures.

As Mila scanned the faces, she realized Niko was in the top left of the group, wearing the same gray and black fatigues and stoic expression on his face as all the others. Despite the serious look, the boy in that picture looked so innocent to her. *Boy.* That was the only way to describe what he looked like in that photo—what they all looked like. *Boys.* They were so young. Too young. Mila realized Niko himself couldn't have been older than sixteen.

So many questions reared in her mind, but she wasn't sure which to ask. Wasn't sure if she *should* ask.

As if sensing her hesitation, Niko said, "It's all right. That picture is the first and only graduating class of berserkers. My class."

"You were so young," she replied.

Niko nodded. "The experimental implants were the first of their kind," he said as he knocked on the exposed metal on the back of his tattooed head. "They required the body to be able to grow with them. A full-grown adult's system would reject it and they would die."

"How young?"

"The training was six years starting just after we recovered from the surgery. I went under the knife on my tenth birthday."

"Matron's mercy," Mila said. "You were a child. How could they do that to you?"

"They did it to all of us," he said, nodding at the picture. "I hear there were hundreds of others that didn't survive the operation. Possibly thousands. It didn't matter who you were or what you were like. Tall, short, frail, sick, they took indiscriminately. We were the ones who survived the operation well enough to proceed to the training. The other children, they were either crippled by it or..." Niko drew a breath, and it didn't seem like he felt the need to finish the sentence. "Every single one of us was sixteen in that picture, and we all came from families in debt to the Volkner regime."

Mila's eyes widened with realization. "So that's why you can't leave? You're some sort of payment to Volkner?"

"A payment not freely given," Niko replied. "My mother and father fought tooth and nail when the soldiers showed up at our door. They would have died before they let Volkner's men take me. But then, they hit my father with a stunner." Niko's tone told Mila it was radioactive stunner he'd referenced before. "Then, they aimed rifles at my little brothers and threatened to take them too if my mother didn't stop fighting for me."

A tear streaked down Niko's cheek and Mila instinctively wiped it away. She withdrew her hand quickly as she realized what she'd done, but Niko simply looked at her, sizing her up as he had the day she'd arrived, a softness lingering in his digital eyes.

He sighed before saying, "But a payment all the same. Work for a debt that will never be paid; not after the bastard added the cost of becoming a berserker to my family's tab."

"He what?" Mila asked, rage prickling at her spine. "But doesn't a single berserker cost..."

"1.2 billion marks," Niko said as if he'd recited the number thousands of times. "If I never spent a cent of my salary, it would take nearly two hundred lifetimes to pay that. And with the hundred and twenty million marks of interest he tacks on every year, I think it's safe to say I'm tied to Volkner Brandt until Hel opens her gates for me."

Mila shook her head, that anger simmering at the base of her skull. "It's not fair," she hissed.

Niko raised an eyebrow.

"That brute overthrows a government and thinks it made him a god. He lets the rich run wild on this station while the people of Vidar starve. And then, when they have to look to their own government for help, it comes at a cost so steep they have to pay in their own flesh and blood?"

"That's the way of things," Niko replied.

"Someone should shove a dagger in his throat," Mila said venomously.

Niko chuckled again, this time some real humor in the sound. "I've thought about it on more than a few occasions. But there's an arrowhead missile trained on my family's home, ready to launch at any given moment if I decide to get any ideas. It was their insurance for all my brothers."

Mila cocked her head to the side.

"My other brothers," he said, gesturing to the photo. "We were the only ones who knew what we'd gone through; the only ones who knew what it was to have your humanity stripped from you and replaced by coding and machinery. They were as much my brothers as the twins."

"It couldn't have been easy losing them," Mila said hesitantly. The last time she'd brought up the deaths of the berserkers, it had stopped the conversation in its tracks.

"It wasn't," he replied.

In the long, silent pause that followed, Mila swore the room dropped a few degrees. She'd said too much, tried to dig too deep. She started to move away from him, prepared for the Berserker to say they needed to leave.

"Our first mission was two days after graduation."

The words thawed the room, and the unwelcome ice forming in Mila's veins.

"The twelve of us squashed a Vidarin rebellion like their soldiers were children with wooden guns. Almost a hundred of them, and we cut them down like sheep. So many more coups and rebellions followed, most of them destroyed before they could even gain breath. Those and the *other* missions. The ones you never hear about on the radio. My brothers and I were the definition of weapons." He paused, as if contemplating his next words. "And then the invasion came."

"Hod," Mila said.

"Hod," Niko echoed. "The war we should have never started. I was only seventeen, promoted to second lieutenant and put in charge of a landing party. We all were. Kids leading men to kill and to die in the name of Vidar." He said the last sentence as if it were a rancid taste in his mouth. "We were the first wave. We took down village after village, beating the rebel Hodian tribes back and back. We were unstoppable, which made us reckless, and Volkner bold. So, he had us drop right into the heart of Alvdalen where we knew the rebel forces were headquartered. What we didn't know is Idun was already there with them, entrenched and prepared for us." He paused to breathe, and Mila noticed a slight tremble in the sound of it. "They say one of us is worth ten thousand men." He shook his head. "But that means nothing when your enemy doesn't fight with men. When they fight with long-range missiles and pulse mines and bombers and..."

Mila could make out the muscle flickering in his jaw, the flex of tense shoulders and a stiff back.

"We weren't ready. Not for that. No matter what training we had, no matter how *legendary* they made us out to be, we were kids. Kids burdened with the death of thousands of soldiers on both sides. And my brothers paid the ultimate price."

"They said you'd all died that day," Mila said, remembering the first time she'd said it on the elevator.

"I tried to save them, and my own men. In the process, I lost them all. Well, except two."

Mila cocked her head to the side.

"You know them," Niko said. "Sauer, the one who picked you up. I found him curled up in a hole after the battle, not a damned scratch on him. The other was Eiji, though she wasn't one of ours. She was half-dead in the street beside a house hit by a Vidarin bomb. A house her parents had been inside when it struck. They started dropping them once it was clear we'd failed to take the city."

"You weren't out yet?" Mila asked, astonished.

"The Battle of Alvdalen was the first failure our dear president ever experienced, and to this day, it remains his greatest. It was meant to show off the might of Vidar and truly introduce his beloved berserkers to all of Ymir. Instead of withdraw us when it was clear we were outmatched, he tried to prove we could overcome any odds. And when we failed, he chose to bury us." Niko held up the splotched computer chip. "They didn't even bother recovering the bodies. This is the only thing left of my brothers. A single, broken memory bank I withdrew from my closest friend. His name was Barnard. He took a full volley from a Iduan chain gun. There was... barely anything left of his body."

Mila sensed the remarkable mass weighing the Berserker down. "It wasn't your fault. You know that, right?"

"I do," he replied. "And so did Commander Schmitz." He gestured to the grizzly man in the photo. "That didn't stop him from sticking a barrel in his mouth a month after the war ended. The last three of my brothers fell helping me get wounded to evac ships. I should have died with them, but I got away with just this," he said, pointing to the exposed metal on the back of his head. "Not a day goes by I don't wonder if it would be better to go the same way as Schmitz."

"Don't say that," Mila cut in. "You don't deserve to die. Clearly the gods had a reason for keeping you here."

Niko nodded slowly, unconvincingly. "I try to tell myself that sometimes too. But when I'm honest, it's really the knowledge that my family would suffer for my actions that keeps me away from the edge most days."

"There's more than your family that need you," Mila said. She left it to him decide who she meant.

A long gap of silence followed. It could have been five minutes or an hour, Mila wasn't entirely sure. But whatever time it was, it felt appropriate for the weight of the memory Niko had just shared.

Finally, when the silence felt too thick, too cumbersome, she asked, "Why hasn't Volkner created more berserkers?"

"Well," Niko said, "because he didn't have you."

"What do you mean?"

"Volkner burned most of our hyrrine reserves jumping the Vidarin fleet to Hod. Capital ships, cruisers, brigs, carriers, all jumping millions of miles at once, it's not cheap. Losing half of them, along with a hundred thousand men and almost a dozen berserkers? Brandt may be the luckiest man in the universe that Idun didn't join the rebels' efforts to take down his regime in the fallout. We were crippled. Still are. Volkner hasn't had the funds to truly rebuild the fleet or the force yet, let alone create new berserkers. And with our master refiners blowing themselves up one by one, he's been forced to buy hyrrine from other planets. Buying the most expensive substance in known existence doesn't do wonders for a military budget. But now, with a truly skilled master refiner and years' worth of brandr stockpiled, I've seen a different side to Volkner."

"You don't sound thrilled about it," Mila responded.

"Our president's mind is always on one thing: power. He still wants a Vidarin empire as much now as he did then. And with hyrrine to spare, he might just get it."

"Idun will stop him again," Mila said.

"I'm not so sure," Niko replied. "Volkner's a bloodthirsty tyrant, there's no denying it. But, he's smart. He won't make the same mistakes twice. He's already sowing the seeds of alliance with Jotun, as you've probably noticed. And there are rumors... rumors of another alliance forming with Tyr. Nothing confirmed, but his son's been gone for some time with a dwarf fleet. Brandt said it was a mission to eradicate rebel hideouts in the Megingjörd Belt. But there are whispers that eliminating rebels was only half the purpose."

Mila had the sudden urge to try and reassure Niko that the Jotun negotiations were a farce. That there were powerful people in Ymir who would see Volkner dethroned. But, then she remembered that, after last night, every bit of that hope was in question. Witnessing a man step from shadow that could refine brandr without a refinery. There were too many variables to risk talking about it now. As powerful as Niko was, she had the distinct feeling that Úlf was far stronger, and that telling Niko would only put him in harm's way.

Niko was still looking down at the picture of the berserkers—of his brothers—the evidence of that single tear still glistening, struck by the moonlight streaming in through the bay window. There were no words that could fix the damage done; nothing she could say to heal the pain. So, she saved them, offering what little else she could by placing a hand on his, holding the photo.

He looked up at her, his digital blue eyes finding hers, examining them, searching her. In the dim room, this close to him, she could make out the display array strewn across his irises. To her, it was microscopic. But she knew that, to him, it was likely a rolling feed of data that gave him super-human perception. It was also a constant reminder of the past, of the humanity stolen from him. The eyes were beautiful, yet utterly tragic all at once. The thought broke her heart.

As if he sensed what she was thinking, his eyes shifted down, resting on her forearm, on the elerex. Slowly, gently, as if not to spook her, his other hand moved toward it. She watched closely and didn't move as his fingers rested on the exposed metal. Even as her heartbeat skyrocketed, she felt calm, as if she were back in the safety of her workshop.

They were from completely different worlds. He was a warrior of recent legend and she was a hobby inventor from a no-name farm on Vidar. Yet, they were the same. They'd both had machinery forced on them. They'd both been pulled from their families. And just like Amelie, just like Fen, and just like damn near every other gods-forsaken soul onboard the *Gjaller,* they were both prisoners.

CHAPTER
TWENTY

THE SHIFT in the general disposition of the *Gjaller's* inhabitants was tangible. No, it was more than that. They'd gone wild with celebration. Politicians and soldiers laughed and joked as they strode through the passageways, drinking mead from sloshing horns. Vendors gave out free sweets, fake jewelry, and roasted meats and vegetables on sticks from their stalls and shops in the market. Bronze-skinned acrobats performed magnificent feats of balance, with flips and contortions alongside painted fire-blowers and sword-swallowers in the larger throughway intersections. Every level smelled of honeyed mead and spiced fruit. If it weren't for the crimson and gold banners and ribbons lining nearly every surface within the *Gjaller*, Mila could have mistaken the festivities for Yule.

But it was not the celebration of the winter solstice, a remnant holiday from the Old Earth. It was Freiheitstag Eve. "Freedom Day." The anniversary of the end of Volkner's coup, and the day he cut open the old Governor's back himself and declared he was president of the new Vidarin Republic. Yet, no matter how much the holiday's origin sickened her, she couldn't deny the pageantry of it all was a bit exciting. The only ones who didn't seem to care for it, she noticed, were the servants. In fact, she hadn't even seen very many of them. They seemed to be avoiding the crowds like a plague.

Unlike previous days, where her midmeal had been delivered by Niko or Amelie, today she accompanied the Berserker to a grand feast in the long hall—the largest cafeteria on the *Gjaller.* They'd arrived early, in the lull between the late breakfast eaters and the swath of soldiers that would no doubt be entering soon. There were, of course, those who'd already drunk themselves silly sprawled out on various tables and in between seats, but for the most part, the long hall was theirs for the moment.

Mila didn't mind the relative quiet in the slightest. In fact, it was a bit of a relief from the festive menagerie. The fact she could spend time with Niko talking before the long table they'd chosen was crowded with elbows, beards, and loud voices was an added benefit.

Niko had seemed about as nonplussed about Freiheitstag as the servants had. Mila had noticed the uncharacteristic rigidness in his movement unlike the normal passive predator he normally reminded her of. But she hadn't been able to ask him about it because of all the noise and celebrations; not until now, at least.

"So, not a fan of Freedom Day?" she asked with a quirky smile.

She wasn't sure if it was the tone or the smile that made him chuckle, maybe both. "How could you tell?"

"You've been walking around like someone scared of snakes who just saw Jörmungandr."

"It's just never been my kind of holiday."

His tone told Mila the drinking, the feasts, and the

festivities in the market had nothing to do with his reasons for not liking Freiheitstag. No, it was much deeper than that. A holiday based on bloodshed—a coup that led to tyrannical rule. The thought sobered any sense of awe Mila had felt about the celebrations around the *Gjaller*.

Before she had too much time to dwell on the origins of the holiday and what exactly those origins meant to Niko, figures appeared at her flanks.

"Skal!" Waren said as he slammed an overflowing drinking horn onto the faux-wood table.

"Skal!" Eberhard echoed, raising his own cup as he sat on her other side.

Niko nodded a silent acknowledgement, and both of the soldiers drank deep. Eberhard made a particularly exceptional show of it, downing his pint in only three gulps, though his beard was half-drenched in ale by the time he finished it all.

"You smell like piss," Niko commented.

"Try standing next to him on watch for a few hours," Waren said.

Eberhard laughed hard and deep. "Jotun beer," he replied. "Strong stuff, and bitter... just how I like it. But it does tend to stink like a war-camp latrine."

Mila realized this was the first time she'd seen them without their Viking-class armor on. They were wearing their fatigues as casually as Niko normally did. Most days, she imagined that would result in more than one officer lecturing them, but today it wasn't any different from what most of the other soldiers around the ship were doing.

Another pair of figures emerged from behind Niko and found their seats.

"No food yet?" the hairless Xiomar asked in short fashion.

Eiji silently took the seat on the other side of Niko, leaving both her and the Berserker now entirely flanked. She moved almost like a shadow in shifting light; quick, indefinite, unpredictable, yet fluid and graceful. Mila could practically feel the lethality emanating from the teenage girl.

"Should start serving here any minute," Waren replied, glancing back over his shoulder toward the kitchens. Mila could swear she saw a bead of drool forming at the edge of his mouth.

"Ever had a Freiheitstag feast, Mila?" Eberhard asked.

"I had breakfast this morning," she replied.

Eberhard chuckled. "Breakfast is but the warm-up."

"That's right," Waren chimed in. "The real challenge is what's coming up right now. Roast goat with rosemary and basil. Blackened kelperfish from the midnight sea with lemon and flaked salt. More golden honey mead than Thor himself could hope to drink."

"You talk about it as if it's divine," Xiomar said.

"Well," Waren said, "if you ask certain people, it is. I imagine a few mirrors have told Volkner that he's a god."

"He's no god." Everyone at the table went silent at Eiji's venom-laced words. It was the first time Mila had ever heard her talk without being coaxed into it.

"I didn't say that, E," Waren replied. "Doesn't change the fact he acts as if he's one."

"Gods do not bleed. Volkner will."

"Eiji!" Niko hissed. "That's enough."

"She's not wrong," Xiomar said, taking a sip from his glass of clear liquid that Mila suspected wasn't water.

"That may be, but we cannot speak like that. Not here."

"Oh give 'em a break, Lieutenant," Eberhard said. "You of all people should hate this brutal holiday."

"Stop," Niko snapped, violently cutting the older soldier off.

Eberhard's eyes went wide. It was clear he wasn't used to Niko taking that tone with him.

"This discussion stops now," Niko continued.

"What did you mean by brutal?" Mila asked cautiously.

Niko took a deep breath, then his lips pulled into a tight, thin line. "It's nothing."

It was as if the alcohol and joy had just been sucked from the table's inhabitants. After a moment of tense silence, Waren finally said, "Have you all ever heard the story of the Megingjörd Dreki?"

"You've only told us a thousand times," Xiomar replied.

"I haven't heard it. At least not your version," Mila said. She had read the story before, but she wanted the group's focus to shift as much as Waren clearly did.

Waren propped himself up like the most esteemed skald.

"I saw from the bow, scales like beryl,
their shimmering surface set with peril.
I knew the Dreki was near.
I heard the Megingjörd silence stark
in the void's vast vexatious dark.
I felt the Dreki feel my fear.

THE TEETH TETHERED in its maw
filled my crew and clan with awe.
The helmsman swung to sheer.
Our flagship proved to be a feast,
in the belly of the hungry beast.
Our fate was coming clear.

· · ·

VALHALLA'S HALLS hold dead men now,
      they were taken from our bow.
      The Dreki delivers drear.
      By godly drollery, I draw breath,
      to know the Dreki harbors death.
      My wrath approaches swift with spear."
Mila had become so entrenched in Waren's flowing words that she hadn't noticed the long hall filling up.

"Ah, time to eat like heathens," Eberhard said, knife and fork already in-hand.

As if in response, the first servant arrived, placing a platter piled with roasted vegetables in the center of their table. In quick fashion, more servants appeared, placing other plates of roasted meats, fresh cheeses, warm breads, and, of course, overflowing pitchers of mead. It was without contest the most food Mila had ever seen in a single place before. She wasn't even sure how enough livestock had been raised to slaughter like this. Only very few farmers had successfully maintained goats, swine, and poultry on Vidar. She hadn't the slightest idea where they possibly came up with this quantity.

"Biolab," Xiomar said, as if sensing the question in her eyes. "Science level. They've had a cloning operation going for a few years now—they just grow the tissue though. None of the animals are live."

"They can produce this much?" Mila asked.

Xiomar nodded.

"And more," Eberhard added, a large bite of pork in his mouth with a steaming roll not far behind.

"Enough for the people of Vidar?" Mila asked.

Eberhard shrugged. "Not sure about all that. But more than enough for this ship, that's for certain."

"Why don't they distribute it?"

"They say the cloning process is too expensive," Waren said, rolling his eyes.

"You don't think so?"

"I think Volkner and his staff place a high value on lining their larders. Even the troops only get treatment like this once a year."

Mila loosed an agitated breath. "Well, it would be nice to eat something other than mushrooms every now and then."

"At least you have food."

Mila was caught completely off-guard by Eiji's razor tone. And when she met the teenage warrior's eyes, she found the fury of a thousand blades piercing into her.

Waren groaned. "Not this again. Look, E, we're all sorry about what happened to Hod, but you shouldn't take it out on Mila."

"No," Mila said before anyone else could reply. She was still holding the young warrior's gaze. "It's all right. I want to know, Eiji. What do you mean by that?"

Everyone else at the table went quiet despite the raging feast all around them. Even Eberhard and Waren stopped eating. Well, they at least slowed their pace and opted for quieter foods.

"The people on my planet have no way to grow food," Eiji said, her voice cold steel.

"Because of the war?"

"The clans of Hod have never seen eye-to-eye on anything. We warred with one another since the discovery of Ymir for land, resources, slaves, everything. But with time, things began to change. My people began to realize the rest of the system was leaving us behind, and so they began to ally themselves. I was born into the symbol of that unity— Alvdalen—the first city to welcome all, regardless of their former allegiances. I grew up there, and watched my brethren learn how to work together for our common benefit. Then, just as we were ready to rejoin the other planets in the modern age, your people decided to blow up Alvdalen, and half my planet along with it. Now, the clans are more brutal than ever. The soil of Hod died after the invasion, ridden with radioactivity. The few places left that are safe to live are ravaged by other raiding clans looking for food and other resources like animals. The price of living on Hod now is not suffering inconvenience or living under oppression. The price is blood."

There was a too-long span of silence following Eiji. Her words lingered like a storm cloud above them.

"Nine bloody steps," Waren cursed. "You really know how to work a room, E."

"Eiji," Mila said with enough force that everyone at their section of the table, as well as some of the adjoining ones as well, looked to her. "What happened to your planet was a crime."

Both Waren and Eberhard's eyebrows rose. Xiomar remained stoic, but there was no denying the curious glimmer in his eye. As for Niko, he tilted his head and let one brow arch. Eiji just held that cold, damning stare.

"I don't know what influence this new position with in Volkner's staff will give me," Mila continued. "But I swear to you, I will use whatever platform I'm given to push for aid to Hod."

"My people don't need any more Vidarin *help*."

Mila didn't flinch. "That may be true. And I may know nothing about war or politics, but I know right from wrong.

It was my people who did that to yours, and I will do anything to help make it right."

Mila only then realized how quiet their section of the long hall had gone. Every soldier in their section of the long hall had stopped eating to listen to her. Most seemed too drunk to even have fully comprehended what she'd said. Others looked curious and intrigued. Mila didn't see any of them. Her eyes were still transfixed on Eiji's.

Until finally, the girl raised her chin. Mila had to make her own determination on what that meant. But it seemed that she'd gotten through to the Hodian on some level.

They heard a comment come from a few tables over. "Those greasy savages can rot in their glowing bomb holes."

Every one of the soldiers who had been looking on, including Niko and his charge, snapped to the source of the voice. Eiji shot to her feet and whipped around, drawing a black, rune-engraved dagger from somewhere within her loose-fitting fatigues.

"Eiji, stop!" Niko commanded, rising to his feet as well. He was ready to leap the table to grapple her, and there was no doubt in Mila's mind he would succeed if it came to that.

"Let her come, Lieutenant." Mila saw the source of the voice for the first time and her hands curled into white-knuckled fists. "I'll put the rabid bitch down."

Every member of their table section, including Mila, were on their feet now, tensed for a fight. Two tables away, wearing a sadist's grin, was Sauer, with a new golden captain insignia pinned to his collar.

"Watch your tongue, Sauer," Niko hissed.

Sauer stood. "I'm afraid you can't speak to me like that, Lieutenant."

"I don't give a damn about that piece of scrap metal. You will not talk about my soldiers that way."

"I'll talk to your rag-tag band of outcasts any way I see fit," Sauer replied.

"Have you forgotten just who it was who pulled you out of that gods-damned hole on Hod?"

Sauer laughed, but there was no humor in it. "I remember you running past the bodies of your own men to save a foreign runt."

Niko was bristling. Mila could practically feel the rage filling the air around them. She felt that same anger rising in her that she'd felt so often lately, but it was dimmer this time, in the shadow of another feeling, fear. The long hall was too close to finding out the meaning of the title "Berserker."

"I order you both to stand down," she yelled, making sure they and every other soldier in the long hall heard it.

Niko seemed to snap out of the bloodlust so evidently coursing through him. He looked at Mila and nodded.

"Who in Hel's name do you think you're talking to?" Sauer demanded. "Only a few days ago I was scraping you up from amongst the fungus."

"I said stand down," Mila repeated.

Sauer opened his mouth to speak again, but Niko beat him to it.

"I recommend you listen to her, Captain. She outranks both of us, after all. Wouldn't want that shiny new rank to be tarnished."

Sauer bared his teeth before standing straight and replying, "You're not worth it, Schafer. I won't waste my time fighting a traitor. Who knows, maybe someone else will kill you before the day is done anyway."

Sauer strode from the long hall without another word. They all found their seats again, and after a few seconds, the long hall was filled with the sounds of laughing, drinking, and feasting.

"Bastard," Waren said. "You'd think he'd at least show some thanks for what you did."

"He's a coward," Eberhard said. "The thing a coward fears most is being called cowardly. That's why they lash out and talk big, but only fight when the battle is easy."

"What did he mean by that?" Mila asked. "The last thing he said, about someone killing you before the day is done. Was he threatening you?"

The men at the table shifted uncomfortably. Eberhard and Waren were suddenly especially interested in their mead, and Xiomar was examining the edge of one of his daggers very closely. Even Eiji seemed to be trying to occupy herself with anything but that question.

Niko shook his head and forced a smile that Mila knew was fake. "It's nothing," he said. "Just loud words spoken to anyone who will listen."

Mila gave him a look that made sure he knew that she knew he wasn't telling her the whole truth. She would have dug in further, if not for someone saying her name behind her.

She found Amelie dressed in a short crimson and gold dress, the same most of the other servant women were wearing. The few there were to be seen, that was. After overloading the tables with food and drink, most of them had disappeared once again. But of what she had seen, none looked so deathly beautiful in their dress as Amelie did in hers.

"I was wondering where you were," Mila said, smiling. "You look stunning!"

"I concur," Waren said, turning to look at Amelie as well.

Eberhard even gave her a little clap.

Amelie blushed as red as the crimson of the dress. "It's nothing," she said. "All of us are given them for Freiheitstag."

"But none wear it so divinely," Waren said, rising from his seat. He bowed low, took one of her hands in his, and planted a soft kiss on the top. "Waren Haas, at your service."

Amelie seemed speechless, but forced an awkward, polite smile.

"Matron's mercy," Eberhard said. "You'll have to excuse him. He's a hopeless romantic."

"If you can call it romance," Xiomar said.

"I take offense to that," Waren said, releasing Amelie's hand and returning to his seat.

"Take it however you want to," Xiomar replied. "As long as it's your mind that's offended and not something else."

"Easy," Niko said. "I think we've had enough insults hurled around to hold us over for at least a few minutes."

"So, what's going on?" Mila continued to Amelie. "Come to join in the feast?"

"Um, no," Amelie said. Mila realized she still looked and sounded nervous.

"Is everything all right?"

Amelie seemed to realize how she was acting and put on a smile. "Yes, of course! I just came to let Lieutenant Schafer know he's been requested."

That same uncomfortable silence that kept falling on their table washed over it once more. *What is the deal?*

Niko nodded and rose from his seat, as if knowing exactly what the servant was talking about.

"Will someone please tell me what's going on?" Mila asked, but everyone seemed to look to Niko, so she turned to him. "What is happening that no one will tell me about?"

"It's nothing," Niko said. "Just a stupid tradition I have to participate in."

"What *tradition*?"

"I'll explain later. For now, just enjoy the feast and take the rest of the evening easy. Amelie could take you to the spa again. Or whatever you want to do. Just have them charge it to my tab."

"The last thing I need from you is money," Mila replied. "I just want to know what all this is about."

"I'm sorry," Niko replied. "But I have to go. Like I said, I'll find you later and explain."

That was the end of it, as Niko took his leave from the long hall.

Mila looked back to the group at the table, but before she could demand answers, Waren said, "Yeah, I think I'm about as stuffed as a Yuletide hog." The soldier started to stand, and the others mirrored him.

"You guys, too?" Mila asked. "What is going on that no one wants to tell me?"

"Sorry, Miss Mila," Eberhard said. "Can't say. Don't want to betray the L.T.'s trust."

And just like that, it was just her and Amelie.

"So, to the spa?" Amelie asked.

"Odin's eye," Mila said, shaking her head. "You're going to hide it from me too, aren't you?"

Amelie's eyes were wide and apologetic, and Mila knew she wouldn't talk without some serious coaxing.

"Fine," Mila said. "You can all keep your secret."

"Secret?" Mila heard from behind her.

Her blood went icy cold. She hadn't heard that voice since the Ambassador walked from the shadows a few nights ago and brought an obsolete refinery to life. Sure enough, she turned slowly to find Úlf standing there, wearing a set of ambassador's clothes even finer than his normal set.

"I do love a good secret," he said.

Mila could have sworn she saw a flicker of silver in his mouth as he spoke.

"It's nothing," Mila replied.

"Oh, well then if it's nothing, how curious you would mention it." When Mila didn't reply, he smiled and said, "No matter, it's none of my business. Anyway, tell me Mila, are you going to the show?"

"The show?" Mila asked.

"We were actually going to the spa," Amelie cut in.

"The spa, on Freiheitstag Eve?" Úlf asked. "Nonsense! You'll come with me to the performance."

"What performance?" Mila asked.

"Oh, you don't know?" Úlf replied. "Well aren't you in for a treat."

"It's really nothing," Amelie said. "A silly, historical thing."

"Silly?" Úlf asked, laughing. "I dare say you'd never utter such a thing in front of your president. It's his own, special way of concluding the day. You simply have to see it at least once."

"Really, Mila," Amelie started. "It's—"

"I'll go," Mila said. "I want to know what it is."

"Splendid!" Úlf said. "I promise, you won't be disappointed."

TWENTY-ONE

THE AMPHITHEATER on the central level of the *Gjaller* was easily the largest venue Mila had ever been in. The only other times she'd gone to see a show were just after her mother left, and those were in the town theater that sat maybe fifty at most. If the figure Úlf gave her was to be believed, this sat a half a thousand times that.

Úlf had led her to a side entrance for those deemed too important to sit amongst the rabble where a servant then led them to their box seat. It was the farthest forward on their side, protruding from the wall and almost overhanging the stage. Below them, and looking far up into the upper levels, every single one of the ten-thousand seats was filled. Their occupants were nearly exclusively soldiers, with a few merchants and foreign visitors scattered throughout. Most, if not all of them, held some form of charred meat on a stick in one hand that was being distributed by numerous tray-carrying servants, while in their other hand they bore drinking horns. They were not shy about their thirst.

The crowd noise of the theater was a monotonous roaring from which the occasional nearby drunken laugh or profanity emerged. That was, until a disembodied voice came over a loudspeaker.

"Please find your seats," the voice said. "The performance will begin shortly."

To Mila's surprise, the rowdy crowd did seem to settle down and take their seats. The roar dulled to a low, rolling murmur. That was, until the curtains in the elevated box seat directly across the theater from Mila and Úlf opened, revealing Volkner, clad in the finest crimson and gold dress uniform she'd ever seen. There was a woman on his arm in masquerade. She wore a dress to match his, except the gold and crimson were reversed, the gold shimmering in the theater lights. Mila felt suddenly underdressed in her drab politicians' apparel.

The crowd roared again, and Mila saw more than one punch thrown as soldiers spilled drinks in excitement or unleashed too much spittle in their rallying cries. She heard some of them scream the president's name. Some yelled "Savior," some "Guardian." She swore she even heard one politician in an adjacent box seat cry out that Volkner was the vessel of Thor himself. All of the various calls eventually converged into one, single, repeating chant. "Vini."

"Vini."

"Vini."

Volkner didn't stop them. Not yet. He entertained their praise—basked in it.

"He acts as if he's a god," Mila said, disgusted.

"Many down there would say he is," Úlf replied.

"And what would you say?"

"I would say he knows nothing of the gods." There was venom laced in those words.

"You still wish to see him dethroned?" Mila whispered.

Úlf turned toward her and cocked his head, looking at

her with those quicksilver eyes. Something about those eyes reminded her of a snake.

"Nothing would please me more, Miss Messer."

Mila pulled her eyes away from the ambassador, focusing on the stage below. "I hope that's true," she said. *But I don't know what I can believe anymore.* "Who's the woman?"

Úlf shrugged. "One of his countless courtesans, I imagine. Volkner never stays with one long, as I understand it. Not after his wife passed."

But the woman did not seem to Mila to be just any mere woman of the night. No, she stood and sat with purpose, every movement deliberate, careful, deadly, like a prowling nightcat.

Volkner finally waved the crowd off and they withdrew into their low murmuring once more. He took his own seat and Mila caught his gold-flecked eyes watching her, his face set with the coldest smile. Mila didn't look away. She held the look and fought his chill with a thousand embers burning through her own stare. Everything Volkner did was to test her, she knew that. She wouldn't fail his test.

Volkner finally raised his chin with a smirk and turned to whisper something in the masked woman's ear. Her only response was the curl of her painted lips into a knowing smile. Mila had the distinct feeling it was something vulgar about her, or Volkner, or both of them.

The voice came back over the loudspeakers to announce the beginning of the production. The murmuring of the crowd ceased, leaving the amphitheater as quiet as her workshop on the nights she couldn't pick up a radio signal. It was unsettling in such a large space filled with so many people, like a black hole was left behind in the wake of the joyous laughter and conversations.

The theater lights dimmed, the audience becoming a sea of dark, faceless figures. The stage itself was still concealed by a thick, scarlet grand drape. Two spotlights from some unknown source in the upper mechanics of the room centered on the drape, where the Gothi, wearing his own ornate crimsons and golds, stood holding what appeared to be a scroll of real paper.

He began by unrolling the scroll and making a show of reading it carefully. When the priest spoke, the sound emerged from all around Mila, clearly the work of hidden speakers.

"Welcome, sons and daughters of Vidar and her allies, to a night of celebration. We have convened to remember and honor our noble and just leader, President Volkner Brandt, on this Freiheitstag Eve. Were it not for his courage and determination in the face of tyranny and oppression, we would not enjoy the prosperity and freedoms we possess today." The man paused for a few moments to allow the crowd to applaud. "Tonight, we will relive the road to freedom and rejoice in our fortunes. It will be a tale of hardship and perseverance, heartbreak and victory. Let it serve as a reminder of why we are here, and why we are resolute in our campaign against those who would reign over our people with terror."

Another round of applause echoed through the theater, this one a little more rambunctious than the last, but still tame compared to the outrageous outcries earlier.

Mila couldn't help but shake her head.

"Problem?" Úlf asked, though Mila could tell by his tone he likely knew exactly what she was thinking.

"Do they even know what he is? Any of them, besides the generals and politicians?"

"They know blood and bullets and steel," Úlf replied.

"Most of them are raised their whole lives believing they must die fighting the good fight so they can go to Valhalla."

"And what, fight for the rest of eternity drunk and eating pork every night?"

Úlf chuckled. "It sounds so unfulfilling when you put it that way. But yes. It's the same thing every warrior in this system strives for. The chance to die a death worthy of the gods. Although, I must admit, these fellows are a little bit fanatical about it. Still, they're nothing compared to some of the Hodian warbands, or the Tyrans for that matter."

"They're worse? Worse than this?"

Úlf nodded. "The Tyrans are born and die with a rifle in one hand and an axe in the other. Their whole entire society revolves around perseverance through military might. The Hodians, well, they're little more than animals at this point, and will claw out each other's throats for pretty much any reason."

"And *he* wouldn't?" Mila looked across to Volkner so there could be no mistake who she was referring to.

"His goal is peace," Úlf replied.

Mila whipped around at that. "What did you say?"

"You heard me right," Úlf replied. "What Volkner wants is peace."

Before the ambassador could go any further, the Gothi began to speak again.

"Our story begins in the year one-hundred and twelve of the Universal Ymiran Calendar, with the outbreak of the Tyran rebellion. And so, I present to you, the Tyran rebels!"

Doorways around the amphitheater opened as if on command. The crowd began to boo as through the doors walked single-file lines of men and women clad in Tyran silks, all wearing shemaghs to cover their faces. A few of the men in front carried crude handaxes and wooden shields.

As they proceeded, the crowd began to heckle them relent-lessly. More than a few soldiers yelled slurs like "Sand Rats" and "Cloth Heads." Before long, the procession was being pelted with food scraps. Many of them recoiled when hit, but kept walking. One girl struck by a thick turkey bone fell to a knee, which made Mila start to her feet, anger threat-ening to consume her.

She was stopped when Úlf laid a hand on her forearm and said, "There's nothing you can do now. Besides, we don't want your elerex acting up."

"How did you—"

Úlf stopped her with a finger over pursed lips. Mila ground her teeth, but obeyed.

The line of Tyran-garbed individuals walked until the rows were filled, and the armed men were directly in front of the stage. The priestly herald onstage cleared his throat and began reciting a tale.

"We find our fair Vini, young and green, above the shifting sands of the Tyran wastelands. Still long from being our savior, the then-Corporal was on the eve of first glory. For it was this day, so many years ago, he would spill blood for the first time. Dropped in that desolate degraded place, our intrepid Yfir would do our Iduan masters' bidding by violence with bullet and blade. At the end, only he and a dozen comrades would emerge from the vile blót. But it was in that battle—that crucible of searing sun and rancid gore—that the roots of a hero took hold."

The Gothi paused to savor the silence of the bewitched crowd. Every person below was on the edge of their seats, waiting for some coming cue.

"And so, ladies and gentlemen, I give you our first event of the night: the Bloody Battle of Holbaek!"

The crowd roared, piercing the trance of the skaldic

premise. The sudden sound made Mila's heart jump. As the man rolled up his scroll and trotted from the spotlight, four of the armed men in Tyran silks made their way to the stage. The curtains slowly began to open, and the sound of far-off drumbeats began to sound from the concealed speakers around them. The sound was hypnotic for the crowd below and they went starkly silent.

The stage was set with a backdrop of a burning city, its buildings of tan sandstone collapsing. On the stage itself, rubble was strewn about, betwixt the pieces lay lifeless, bloodied mannikins. In the middle of the stage stood two men. The close-shaven sides of their heads that revealed runic tattoos told her they were most likely Vidarin soldiers. The absence of their Viking-class armor they no-doubt wore regularly left them in more traditional warrior garb of wars very long past. Each was clad in chainmail vests set over leather and cloth, with laceless boots and a metal helmet tucked under the arm. On their backs were attached thick, iron-bound wooden shields that made the Tyran characters' own look little more than playthings. In their other hand each bore a weapon—one a thick-headed hammer and the other a short, double-edged sword.

The drums were louder, closer now as the Tyrans took their places facing away from the audience. The Vidarins donned their helmets and shields. Mila saw plasma auras spark to life around the shields and weapons as the duo activated some hidden switches. Something about that broke Mila's perception of them. They were no longer ancient Viking warriors on some far-off battlefield. No, they were here, now, dressed as ancient fighters but entirely present. And they were using modern weapons. Not polished replicas, but actual plasma-imbued weapons.

The drumbeats were even louder, drawing nearer and nearer with every second.

Mila looked to Úlf, whose eyes were fixed on the stage. She didn't think she'd seen the mysterious man this entranced before.

"Úlf," Mila said. "Why would they need plasma weapons for a reenactment?"

Úlf's quicksilver eyes flashed to her. He didn't have to say a word.

The drumbeats were upon them, drowning her voice, her thoughts. But it wasn't enough to quell the realization.

Mila shook her head. "Wait, you're not saying— They can't be about to—"

Mila's words were cut as the drumbeats ceased, and the amphitheater held its breath. The silence served as the signal for the six figures on the stage.

Begin.

Another drumbeat began, much faster but far subtler than the first. The four Tyrans spread out, moving slowly but not like honed fighters. No, it was far more like a group of timid pups.

Opposite them, the soldier with the hammer made a show of cracking his neck, while the other swung his sword in a lazy circle. The Tyrans moved closer, slowly, terrified. Until one stepped too close.

The hammer-wielder launched himself at his silk-clad prey. The Tyran raised his shield, ready to block the attack, but the soldier swiped it away with his own. Before the Tyran could move his sword to block the blow, the soldier was already halfway through his next move.

The crowd went wholly maniacal as the blood sprayed, but Mila couldn't hear it. Her entire world was white noise, and the perception of the so slow yet so quick uppercut swing of the plasma hammer. It was a flawless strike, unchallenged, and it made contact under the victim's chin. Mila didn't know what the trauma from a blow to the chin with a plasma hammer looked like up close, but from her position in the box seat, she'd be surprised if the Tyran still had a jawbone. Of course, that didn't matter so much, as the Vidarin soldier followed swiftly with another blow to the felled man's face, leaving no room to wonder if he was still alive.

"I need to go," Mila said, rising from her seat.

"You can't," Ulf said. "The show's only just beginning."

"I don't want to watch this."

A roar emanated from the crowd and Mila looked up long enough to realize the swordsman had just taken down his first adversary with a blade through the gut.

"You must," Ulf replied.

"Who do you think you are?" Mila hissed.

"Someone who holds all the cards," Ulf replied. "Someone who knows Hans Messer, and exactly where to find him."

"Is that supposed to be a threat?"

Ulf rolled his head back and laughed. "Why, of course it's supposed to be a threat."

"You're overestimating my affections for that man."

"So, you'd see him killed?" Ulf's tone was deathly stark.

Mila tensed. There was no denying now that she hadn't the slightest idea whose side Ulf was on. But that conviction. He was either an incredibly gifted liar, or he was telling the truth. Mila knew it was likely both. Though, as much as she hated her father, the thought of him being slaughtered by this *man*. Ulf knew exactly where to strike.

She took her seat once more and grit her teeth as the

Vidarins downed the two remaining Tyrans in short order. The display was more an execution than a battle.

There was only one Tyran left alive, just barely, crawling toward the edge of the bloodstained stage. The swordsman walked to him like a stalking jackal and kicked the pulsing wound on his back. The man wailed—a horrible, desperate sound. The audience responded with laughter.

Monsters.

The swordsman bent down and grabbed the back of the man's shemagh, pulling it off and presenting it as a trophy to the now-cheering room. The removal of the garment revealed not a tan skinned Tyran warrior. Mila was utterly horrified to realize the person bleeding to death on the stage was little more than a boy, malnour-ished and pale. A servant, starved, with tears streaming from his eyes.

Mila felt her own tears rising hot in her eyes. She real-ized all the concealed faces in the single file lines belonged to servants, forced to adhere to this barbaric tradition against their will.

The crowd's cheering dulled into a chant of, "Kill."

"Kill."

"Kill."

The swordsman stomped on the wound again, and once more the boy cried out, loud enough for Mila to hear the word he screamed clearly. "Mamma!" The accent and pet name for his parent were unmistakably Hodian. The boy was pleading for mercy and love and safety. Between crimson coughs and pained sobs, he begged for his mother.

Mila's tears escaped and her heart felt locked in a vise grip. She was going to be sick with anger and frustration and utter, depthless sorrow. That rage flared hot as white steel, but before it could peak, Úlf grabbed her arm around the elerex and squeezed. It felt like the weight of a starship crushing her arm.

"Let me go!" she demanded.

"Calm down," Úlf replied. "Now is not the time for you to lose your temper."

"You don't give me orders!"

Úlf squeezed harder. "Not now. Save the anger, for later, when we can use it."

Mila's nostrils flared and she bore into Úlf with her glare, but his quicksilver eyes were unflinching. There were so many things he knew that she didn't—that he wasn't telling her. The thought of each one pissed her off more than the last.

The crowd's chant was overbearing now, but broke into a cheer as the swordsman satiated them with the blood they so desired. In a single, downward strike, the boy's pleas were silenced forever.

<hr />

THE BATTLE ENDED with a prayer of tribute from the pointed-beard priest, asking for Thor's blessing of strength, and for the dead's safe passage into Valhalla. Mila thought it a joke that any gods would look favorably on such a display. This wasn't a death in noble battle or the ritual tribute of willing zealots; this was blood sport. Their bodies weren't honored. They were dragged and piled on the side by other unwilling servants. A brutish spectacle for a violent crowd, nothing more.

The following battles were much the same. The curtain would close, the Gothi would read a new poem, then the curtains would open again to a redecorated scene and a few Vidarin soldiers, always more able than the last, standing on the stage. More servants, at first Tyran-dressed and later wearing more traditional Iduan clothes, would take their places opposite them. Then, the soldiers would slaughter them like cattle to a cheering crowd.

Mila's fingernails peeled away the waxy coating on the wooden arm of her chair, her body still begging her to leave. But she stayed, though not because Úlf told her to. She stayed to watch every single drop of innocent blood spilt. She stayed to let that anger simmer in hot coals at the base of her spine. She stayed to remind herself, with every scream and tear, that she hated Volkner and his war-hungry cult.

She didn't look away. Not once. Through the Tyran Battle of Holbaek and the beginning of Volkner's rebellion against Idun with the taking of Trier, she didn't look away. Over a dozen more innocent servants—some men as old as her father, some boys too far her junior—were cut down in those two displays.

By the time the Gothi took the stage to announce the final chapter, Mila had unknowingly clawed through to wood and was stripping splinters of it away. She didn't even notice her fingertips were bleeding.

The pointed-beard man coughed to clear his throat. "Ladies and gentlemen, we have seen strife and struggle, hardship and perseverance. Now, let us experience triumph! Let us remember why we celebrate this day!"

The priest basked in the crowd's cheers as though they were adoring him and not the subject of his stories.

"On this day, twenty years ago, bold Volkner's forces marched on the gates of Bonn where the then-governor hid in his tall tower. Our liberators fought for one day and one night then, in the dawn of a new day, they took the city by the force of will, passion, and patriotism alone. It is a day that will live in our hearts forever. A day the gods feasted in Valhalla with the bravest of Vikings. So, without further ado but infinite admiration, I am proud to present the final stage of our fair Vini's rise. I give you the Battle of Bonn and the beginning of our freedom!"

This time, when the heavy curtain behind the man swayed open, he did not move. He stayed still, the spotlight upon him. The scene revealed behind him was not rubble and bodies and burning buildings, but an elegant backdrop of blue and silver banners embroidered with the symbol of the Iduan peoples—an apple set within a laurel wreath.

"As tradition dictates," the Gothi began. "This bout shall be of two blades. The felled shall die honorably as the Governor did..."

Úlf spat a humorless laugh.

"...while the other shall have the honor of representing our Vini until he, too, is eventually felled in Freiheitstags to come. Many of you vied for the position of challenger this year, but, as we all know, there can be only one. So, I present to you, this year's challenger."

One of the largest men Mila had ever seen entered from stage right. He was massive in every sense of the word, his shirtless tattooed torso wrought with hard, bulky muscle, and standing what seemed to be nearly double the announcer's height. The runes of Thor strewn across his flesh indicated he was not a servant, but in fact a Vidarin soldier.

"That one's got jotun blood in him," Úlf commented.

"He's not Vidarin?" Mila asked.

"Oh, I imagine he is," Úlf replied. "I mean actual giants' blood."

Mila knew it was just a metaphor, but the fact Úlf spoke with no sense of exaggeration made her shift in her seat.

The behemoth of a man had his head shaved to the scalp, but sported a braided and oiled beard grown to his navel. He wielded no shield, but rather a warhammer in each hand; the same style as the soldier from the first bout. Turning to the crowd, he let out a roar like a raging bear, which they adored as they screamed back their admiration.

As the crowd's cries fell, the zealous herald spoke again. "And now, the main event. I present to you, my fair comrades, the reigning avatar of our Vini!"

The crowd did not cheer nor yell nor boo. They didn't say anything; not any words in any language that Mila recognized. Instead, they began to hum a beat.

It started low at first, barely discernable as a uniform noise. Then, after a few moments, the beat became one, as present as the drumbeats during the preceding fights, but more primal and ritualistic. Mila looked down and saw the shoulders of every soldier heaving with the rhythm of the sound. A knot formed in Mila's stomach, one she'd mistaken for dread in the past but now understood was instinct. Whatever was coming to that stage, she didn't want to see it.

But it didn't matter.

She had to watch, to remember that rage, the silent promise she'd made to herself the moment the first servant boy cried Mamma.

The humming stopped, and every ounce of that rage shifted into wild confusion and fear. The theater watched —*she* watched—as the reigning Vini took the stage, his predator's gait and lean build immediately recognizable.

Niko.

CHAPTER

TWENTY-TWO

THE LAST BERSERKER walked onto the stage with a lethal calmness. Though the room had gone utterly silent, there was no sound from his steps echoing through the amphitheater. In fact, there was no sound at all, as if everyone in the room was holding their breath.

His apparel was the same as the man standing on the opposite side of the stage, except where the man wore nothing from the waist up, Niko wore a black wolf's pelt draped around his shoulders. His cloth pants and boots were black as well. He wielded no shield and a single weapon—the rune-inscribed handaxe that he always wore on his belt.

Niko did not stop to face the crowd. Instead, he walked straight up to the man opposite him, who Mila now saw stood a full head and a half higher than the Berserker, and extended an arm. The man returned the gesture, his own burly limb dwarfing Niko's as they clasped each other's forearms. A sign of respect between warriors.

After that, Niko found his spot and finally turned to face the crowd, peering over them, inspecting them, telling them everything that was about to come without speaking a syllable. They kept holding their breath, watching, waiting.

Mila whirled on Úlf. "I am not watching this."

"Yes you are."

"I've played your game long enough. I'm leaving." Mila started to her feet.

"You're running."

"From what?" Mila hissed. "The sight of barbarism?"

"From the truth."

Mila started to reply, but couldn't find the words fast enough.

"The truth," Úlf continued. "About your boyfriend... about what he really is. About what they all are."

She could have corrected him, set him straight about the purely professional nature of her and Niko's relationship. But at the moment, that seemed so... trivial.

"But why? Why do you care so much about what I think?"

Úlf shook his head and clicked his tongue. "You still don't see it. Fair enough. I suppose it has only been a few days."

"See what?" Mila's fists were curled tight, every inch of her taut.

"That this, all of *this*, you are the key to dismantling it. You always have been."

You always have been. Mila thought he was exaggerating. Promising something grand as he always did to keep her interested. And he was nothing if not a brilliant liar. Still, there was not even a hint of deception in those words. The thought of them made the flesh along the base of her back prickle.

"Enough talk," Úlf said. "You'll learn everything you need to in due time."

With that, any hope of continuing a conversation was doused, as Niko faced the audience, and rose his handaxe above his head.

The crowd went rabid, cheering and yelling and screaming. Some shouted "Vini" while others chanted "Schafer." Some just bellowed out non-words and war cries. They were all on their feet, desperate to watch the Berserker work.

A spotlight settled on Volkner's box seat, where the president was standing, ready to give his blessing for the battle to commence. With what appeared to be the same care and demeanor the man would have deciding a dinner dish, Volkner raised his hand to his chest, hushing the crowd for the briefest moment, and laid his fist on his chest in a lazy salute.

When Mila looked back to the stage, she found Niko was not watching his opponent. No, those soft glowing eyes were set on her. Mila looked away. She didn't want to give the Berserker any false perception. She wanted to hold his stare and tell him how disappointed and mortified she was that he was a part of this. But she couldn't. She knew it'd be a weight unlike any other.

This wasn't staring down soldiers in the long hall or even silently challenging a tyrant with her eyes. This was Niko, who held all the pain of a lifetime in eyes that had only seen a few more years than hers. And that pain was too present when she'd met his eyes just now. But it didn't excuse any of it. It didn't negate what he was about to do.

When Mila finally looked back up, she found Niko and the giant man circling each other like predators. Niko had shed his wolfskin cloak, and now every perfect, lean muscle of his tattooed arms and torso flexed and shifted in the stage lights. Unlike the man opposite him whose bulging muscles,

Mila suspected, served to better move boulders than traverse a battleground, Niko's build promised a balance of deadly speed and true power.

His tattoos were unlike his opponents as well. Unlike any of the soldiers she'd seen besides him, in fact. Where theirs were all clean and new, inked by machines that could follow the lines of their body precisely, Niko's were beautifully imperfect. Where theirs portrayed the symbols of their military units and those of Thor and Odin, Niko's appeared more as letters. Like those cascading down the shaved sides of his head and his arms, those on his chest and back portrayed runes that Mila didn't recognize. They looked older, rawer, though sequenced like a story. And the occasional crooked or curved edge to the symbols made it clear they'd not been inscribed with a machine, but likely by hand. That made them unique.

The two men continued to circle, the crowd growing more and more chaotic, desperate for action. But Mila only knew that by the sound of them. Her eyes were glued to the stage, to every exposed and vulnerable inch of Niko.

The large man lunged first. It was surprisingly precise, considering his build. One might expect a man like that to rampage forward bullishly, which he did. What one would not expect is for him to halt and pivot so effectively, which he also did, when Niko sidestepped out of his way.

The bear of a man's following strike aimed for Niko's exposed ribcage. Even though Niko wasn't facing him, the Berserker seemed to predict the move and spin back out of the way, opposite his opponent's momentum. The man did not relent, whirling on Niko with a heavy strike from his offhand. Niko parried it with ease.

The man roared in rage, splitting the noise from the crowd. He swung again, and again, each time Niko parrying and sidestepping. Where the bullish warrior's movements were powerful and trained, Niko's were instinctual, automatic, and entirely effortless. There was no mistaking who the superior fighter was. The Berserker's opponent was trained for battle, but Niko, he'd been designed for it.

The hammer-wielder struck and struck, and with each strike Mila saw his shoulders heave more and more. He was running out of energy fast, his all-out assault fading.

One strike came within an inch of Niko's short beard. The Berserker responded with an inhuman leap back, putting a half-dozen yards between them. He sat on his haunches, one hand on the ground, his gaze evaluating the warrior opposite him.

The other man took a moment to catch his breath. Even from their elevation, Mila could see the streams of sweat rolling down his entire body. Niko, still as a statue, wasn't even winded.

The few-second reprieve ended as the hammer-wielder rolled his head back and roared, "Observe, Aesir! Be spilt the blood of mine or my foe! Open your gates and slay the boar! A true Viking feasts in your hall this night!"

To the screams of the audience, the massive man charged. His movements were like Thor himself really had reached down and imbued him with godly lightning and thunder. The sheer momentum of him would fell a man, even one so strong and resilient as Niko. But the Berserker didn't flinch. He remained crouching, watching, though his gaze was not considering his opponent. No, once again, they were on Mila.

Pay attention, idiot. He's going to kill you!

Her fingernails were bloodied, embedded in the wood of the chair arm. Her jaw was clenched so tight she risked breaking a tooth. She wanted to yell, to scream, to tell Niko to get his cybernetic head out of his ass. But any words would be drowned by the crowd. All she could do was watch him throw his life away, watching her.

The bear of a man was over him, his hammer swinging down fast... too fast. There was no time for Niko to leap to safety now, nor a chance of blocking a blow that powerful. This was the end.

Mila could hardly perceive what happened next. With his offhand, Niko caught the man by his wrist, stopping the blow as easily as he might a child, drawing a gasp from the crowd. Then, in series of precise movements so fast they seemed as one, he snapped the limb, disarming his opponent, and planted his axe blade in the behemoth's throat.

The man stumbled forward and fell to his knees, no longer in control of his body. The blade had gone deep enough that there was no question it had severed his vital arteries. It was less than a second later the man fell face-first onto the stage, and didn't move again.

The crowd didn't cheer. It was as if their breath had been stripped away by the promise of a bloody struggle unfulfilled.

On the stage, Niko rolled the giant man over and closed his eyes, muttering a prayer that the room could not hear. Then, he pulled his axe free and stood, facing the audience. But he did not acknowledge them with a war cry or gesture, nor a salute to President Volkner. Instead, he was looking at Mila.

The crowd's quiet slowly gave way to disgruntled mutterings. Some of the men made sure their opinion that the bout went too fast was known. Others even demanded a new opponent take the stage. A few outright booed.

None of it fazed Niko, who simply continued to watch Mila. But she'd only met his gaze long enough to know he was looking at her. She didn't want to see him longer than that, to admit she recognized the emotion swimming in his digital eyes.

She didn't bother saying anything as she got up to leave. And Úlf didn't try to stop her. There was nothing left to see —no more brutality to share with her. He'd made his point in the most painful way possible. But, it had been effective.

Mila exited the booth as the curtains closed, and was completely gone by the time the Gothi took the stage to try and calm the audience, now a budding mob of drunken and disappointed soldiers.

With every step, she tried to forget all she'd promised herself to remember. With every step, she realized the memory would forever be a scar.

MILA WAS HEADED to the refinery, the only place on this gods-damned ship she knew she could find a friend. Everyone she thought might become a companion had just lied to her. They'd hidden the truth of Freiheitstag; the truth of its twisted rituals and of Niko. Even Amelie had known and hadn't told her.

She'd almost made it to the lift when Niko caught up to her.

"Mila."

She kept walking.

"Mila, wait!"

She picked up her pace.

"Mila!"

This time, when he said her name, it was pleading, desperate, and much closer. She turned to find him, still shirtless, only a few feet from her. It was clear he'd tried to hastily clean himself, but there were still patches of the felled opponents blood smeared on his flesh.

The passageway was eerily barren, save the two of them. The pedestrians of the main floors were still occupied at the theater, watching the closing scenes.

"What do you want?" Mila asked, any hint of flirting or excitement that might have been in those words an hour ago entirely absent.

"I just want to explain."

"Explain what? The dozen innocent people I just watched be killed? The man you just butchered?"

"I didn't butcher him," Niko replied, a muscle in his jaw feathering.

"What do you call it then?"

"A fight, one he volunteered for, knowing full well that only one of us would come out alive."

"That wasn't a fight. That was an execution."

"A sacrifice, yes. But one he was willing to make."

"And what about all of the others?" Mila demanded. "All the servants that never stood a chance. Don't try to tell me they were all willing sacrifices too."

Niko swallowed. "No, they weren't. But I would have never killed one of them."

"No, just some random comrade."

"His name was Berinhard," Niko growled. "He wasn't a random comrade. He was a soldier I've known for several years. He volunteered for that battle because he believed dying by my hand—being a blood sacrifice to the gods— would take him to Valhalla."

"You called that religious nonsense," Mila snarled. "You said we know nothing of the gods or what they want. What was it? Oh, I remember, 'divinity is the crutch of sadists and murderers.'"

"Careful, Mila," Niko said through clenched teeth.

"Or what? You'll murder me too?"

"I'm not a murderer."

Mila scoffed a laugh. "You're delusional. With one breath you claim you don't think killing a man pleases the gods, but with the next you slaughter one and call it justified."

"I never said it was justified," Niko said. "It's not. None of this is," he said, raising his arms, gesturing all around them. "But he believed in it, and he willingly died for that belief. I'd fight and kill a man volunteering to die for what he believes in a thousand times over if it meant I didn't have to spill another drop of innocent blood."

"But when all of those servants were screaming and bleeding under Vidarin blades, *that* you could just stand by and watch?"

Niko recoiled. His normally fluid posture was rigid and tense. Finally, shaking his head, he said, "You know absolutely nothing about it. You've been on this station for less than a week. Who in Hel's name do you think you are to judge me? To assume you know a gods-damned thing about killing someone? I thought after sharing... what I shared with you, you might have a touch of empathy. Might care about what I have to lose if I refuse *him*."

Mila crossed her arms, the feeling of them acting as an extra barrier between her and the Berserker comforting. She could deny neither the permanent stain on her memory of seeing those people slaughtered, nor the logic behind Niko's words. Still, it didn't matter. She wanted to go be alone with Fenrir in the cold refinery, far away from the cultish festivities. She needed to get away from them. From Niko.

"You disgust me," she said, little more than a whisper.

Without another word, she took the small, matte black

communicator he'd given her, the one that routed directly to him, and held it out.

Mila barely managed to look up at the Berserker, to see the vulnerability; the hurt in his expression. It made her stomach twist and her heart want to stop beating. But, she'd said the words, and made the gesture, and there was no taking it back.

Niko breathed deep and wiped the damaged expression from his face. "It doesn't matter. I'm still the head of your personal guard. I won't take that back, especially since you likely won't want me around for a while. It'll be even more useful."

The feeling that welled within Mila was a mix of pulsing pain and deep sorrow, but beneath it, that toxic anger boiled.

The elerex let loose a shock, trying to jolt her arm, but she wouldn't let it move her. He wouldn't see her pain. The elerex shocked again. This time, the arm tried to go limp, but she managed to keep it held up. Though she couldn't prevent her fingers from spasming. She lost her grip on the communicator, and it struck the ground with a resonating clang.

Niko looked down at it, and for the first time, she saw his shoulders slump. Giving back the communicator would have been a powerful strike. But dropping it... dropping it felt more profound. It was the kind of insult that words could never convey, only actions. She hadn't meant to do it, but it didn't matter. She wasn't going to pick it up, wasn't going to give him hope that she still trusted him. No matter how badly she wanted to.

Niko bent down to pick up the device, then looked back up at her, meeting her stare with those soft digital eyes. It was suffering and regret that swam within them. Every fiber of Mila's being petitioned for her to forgive him for what he'd done, for who he was. To apologize and act like none of the conversation had ever happened. Even as he saluted her and turned and walked away, she wanted to call out to stop him.

But the words never came.

CHAPTER

TWENTY-THREE

MILA SAT on the cot in the refinery, Fen's immensely heavy
head in her lap. The wolfbot had acted like an excitable pup
on her return and had only just now, after a near half-hour
of frolicking, decided to settle down. It occurred to her how
terrifying it must be for him when she left, after being abandoned for so many years in the refinery, conscious but not
allowed to live. Every time she left promised a possible
return to isolation—a feeling she knew all too well.

Her elerex was on the fritz again, apparently unsure
what to do with the chaotic mix of emotions she felt after
dismissing Niko. Fumbling with the adjustable screws only
provided a few minutes' relief before she had to go at them
with the tinkerer's screwdriver again.

She expected Úlf would be showing up at any minute
now, not to refine, but to lecture her. The thought of the
ambassador made that burning rage in her flicker, which set
the elerex off again. It sent a shockwave through her that
would have killed her if her heart were weak.

"Shit," she hissed, grasping her chest.

Fen looked up at her, cocking his head in concern.

"This thing's going to be the death of me, Fen," she said. "Seems like I might have to choose between it or my arm before long. What kind of refiner would I be then?"

Fen barked softly, as if acknowledging the sarcasm in the last few words.

Mila leaned her head back on the cold metal wall. "I want to go back to the farm." The irony of the sentence made her laugh. "How sad is that? The one place I was trying to escape my entire life is now the only place in the universe I want to be."

Fen cocked his head to the opposite side, this time a look of curiosity instead of concern.

"You'd like it on the farm, I think. Lot of places for you to explore—not cooped up in this Hel's abode all day. Maybe, one day, I can take you there."

Maybe. But Mila knew, in all likelihood, she'd never see the farm again.

MILA WAS HALF-ASLEEP, falling into a dream world when the refinery doors groaned open. She jolted awake, ready to unleash her rage-laced words on Úlf or Niko, whichever was brave or stupid enough to face her first.

Instead, she found Amelie, the girl's doughy eyes brimming with regret.

"You've been requested," she said.

"Tell whoever requested me they can wait until tomorrow," Mila replied.

Amelie shifted uncomfortably.

"What?" Mila demanded.

"I can't do that," Amelie replied. "I'm so sorry."

"And why not? Just who requested me?"

Mila realized the answer before Amelie spoke, but hoped she'd be wrong. Dread coiled in her gut as Amelie spoke, and she discovered she wasn't wrong.

"Volkner."

THE ROUTE AMELIE led Mila through was not straightforward nor simple to remember. They took several different lifts to corridors that Mila had never seen. She knew they had to be close to the command deck, but beyond that, this area of the ship was a maze.

The farther they went, the less people there were. The few they did pass were warriors that Mila recognized as the Honor Guards—Volkner's personal elite soldiers clad in their crimson-accented golden Viking armor complete with horned helmets.

Mila had always had a fairly sharp short-term memory. But by the time they reached their destination, an oversized, elegant door with a massive carving of Mjolnir on it, strewn with the same colors as the six Honor Guard standing post at its flanks, Mila knew the only way she'd make it back to the main throughways was with Amelie as a guide.

Truth be told, she was surprised how easily Amelie navigated the twists and turns. She had to have walked the path a hundred times. Maybe more.

The guards said nothing, only assessed them through their masking visors like eyeless sentinels. This was no warm welcome like she received most days from Adel on the command level. Only cold silence.

"I present Master Refiner Messer to meet with the president," Amelie said in a strict, formal tone.

Mila had never heard her speak so assertively, directly.

"Of Thor's goats, which did the runner break his leg?" the guard challenged.

"We shan't know," Amelie replied. "But Thialfi shall run in its stead."

A code? Is this really that serious?

The guard who'd spoke the challenge turned and spoke into an intercom on the wall, announcing the Master Refiner and her servant had arrived. The reply instructed Mila alone to enter, and she recognized the voice as Adel's.

The guard gestured Mila forward, stopping her just before the door.

"Arms out to the side," he instructed.

"A search?" Mila asked, taking half a step back. "Is that really necessary?"

"All visitors to the private quarters are subject to searches," the guard replied.

"Private quarters?" Mila looked at Amelie, whose eyes spelled regret.

Mila was suddenly fully aware this was no ordinary government business, and every instinct she'd felt to run from Lieutenant Sauer on the farm reared again. But this time she fought it. Instead, she raised her chin, straightened her back, and put her arms out. The guard began patting her down. It wasn't gentle in any sense, but it was also in no way intrusive. Mila didn't know if that was only because of her title, or if the Honor Guards were actually more honorable than the average savage soldier. She suspected the former to be more likely.

The guard buzzed again to let Adel know she was clear, and the door hissed open, revealing what appeared to be a minimalistic bedroom.

"And you'd do well to remember your place in all this," she heard Volkner saying as the door opened.

When she stepped inside, she found Adel standing stagnant by the doorway, the picture of a professional, stoic guard. He didn't greet her. Not even a smile or a look in her direction. He was not, however, who Volkner had been speaking to.

No, his words had been directed at the Berserker standing a few feet into the room.

Niko?

Niko's back was to her, and she didn't know what their conversation had been. But she could tell by his rigid posture it was taking everything in him to hold back what he was thinking.

Volkner was wearing casual clothes: a pair of silken pants with a crimson wrap pulled tightly around him. The dictator had freshly shaved skin around his thick beard, with a small bandage on his neck, likely covering a nick from the grooming. Mila got the sense Volkner Brandt was not the type of man who would trust another person with a blade close to his throat.

The room itself was relatively modest, to Mila's surprise. The loudest thing about it was the runic eye over the large bed backed to the far wall. Other than that, the room held no holoframes nor screens, no eccentric decorations, no evidence of an endless string of bed guests. Yet, there was a certain detachment to it. Mila knew Volkner had a son and was recently widowed, yet not a single thing in the room depicted their likeness.

The president's golden eyes flicked to her as she entered. "Ah, Miss Messer, you've finally arrived."

Niko glanced back over his shoulder at her. The half-second glimpse of his digital eyes confirmed every insight she'd made about his posture. The Berserker was dangerously close to a rage, and her presence only seemed to throw fuel on his flames.

"You're dismissed, Schafer," Volkner said.

Wordlessly, Niko turned and took his leave. He flashed a look at Mila as he passed her, but she did not meet it. She hadn't forgiven him. Not yet. Maybe not ever. So, she missed the anger in the look, the rage. She also missed the fear.

"You may go as well," he said, this time directed at Adel.

"Sir?" Adel responded, clearly not expecting the command.

"You heard me."

There was hesitation in Adel's voice as he replied, "Yes, Vini," with a salute.

The doors hissed shut behind Mila, and she knew she and the president were alone. She suddenly wished to be anywhere else in the universe besides right here. There was no guise of courtly protocol, no ambassador to impress. No physical or figurative shields to protect her. There was only him.

"Drink?" he asked nonchalantly, gesturing to a small bar cart tucked into the corner of the room. He started to walk to it before she answered.

"No, thank you," she replied.

"Smart. Good to keep your wits about you, eh Mila? May I call you Mila?"

"I expect you may call me whatever you'd like," Mila replied, carefully watching his every move.

Volkner laughed. "I expect you're right. Still, it's respectful to ask, is it not?"

Two oversized ice cubes clinked into a fine, crystal glass before Volkner bathed them in golden-brown liquid from an equally fine crystal decanter.

"Why have you brought me here?" Mila asked.

"To talk. I thought that might be obvious."

"About?"

Volkner smirked and cocked his head. "You're awfully bold for someone who's worn a high-ranking title for less than a week."

"You know what they say about the bold," Mila asked. "I imagine you're an expert in the saying, Vini."

Volkner waved her off. "None of that. I hate those useless titles. Call me Volkner."

Mila shifted, uncomfortable with the idea of addressing the man as if they were friends. The president didn't seem to notice as he took a seat in a tufted chair near the bar cart.

After taking a slow sip, making no effort to hide the satisfied 'ah', he said, "I suppose you're right. I've been accused of being many things, but meek is not one of them."

Mila was still on-guard, but with the president sitting, she felt it all right to take her gaze away from him to explore the room once more. Maybe something would be there to let her into the mind of the madman.

"Feel free to look around," Volkner said, apparently noticing her wandering eyes. "Though, I'm afraid it's a rather short tour."

"You didn't have larger quarters built when the *Gjaller* was constructed?" Mila asked.

"Despite what you may have heard about me, I'm a man of very simple tastes. And so was my wife. All we wanted was a place to ourselves far away from the headache of politics."

"There are no pictures of her," Mila said. "Your wife."

Volkner swirled the ice in his glass and took another sip. "We enjoyed one another's presence while she was here. But, now she's gone. Pictures would only serve as a constant reminder of that which I lost and will never regain."

"You don't think you'll see her again when you *die*?" Mila made sure to put special emphasis on that last word.

Volkner laughed, louder this time, as if genuinely amused. "Oh Mila," he said, shaking his head. "It's no secret there are only one of two places I'm going when I die. If I'm lucky, I'll go to Valhalla, where I'll join my ancestors in glorious feasts and battle until the end of time. But, I expect I'll most likely be tucked away in a dark corner of Hel's realm, doomed to walk in darkness for eternity. My wife, she was neither a warrior nor cruel. I've no doubt she basks in the light of Freya in Fólkvangr."

"That's awfully bleak."

"I see no sense in lying to myself about it," Volkner replied. "Either everything I've done—every person I've killed or ordered killed—I've done so for the greater good, as has always been my wish."

"Or?" Mila said when he paused.

"Or, the rebels and Hodians and Iduans are all correct, and I really am the black-souled bastard they say I am."

Mila wasn't sure to make of the conversation, of this apparent vulnerability. It felt like she was treading very dangerous waters, and that one wrong word could land an axe blade in her throat.

Volkner looked at the runic eye above his bed. "But, that's for the gods and their wisdom to decide."

Mila slowly paced the room per his invitation, but found very little that gave her a window into Volkner Brandt. "And what about your son? No pictures of him either."

"Just as I enjoyed my wife's presence while she was

here, I'll enjoy my son's when he returns. No sense in dwelling on him while he's gone."

"Where has he gone?"

"He commands a tactical fleet assigned to eliminate rebel threats in the Megingjörd Belt."

"Seems a pretty mundane task for the son of Volkner Brandt."

Volkner didn't respond, so Mila turned to him to find his head cocked and his mouth peeled in a knowing smile.

"You think I've sent him somewhere else?"

"I never said anything like that," Mila replied.

"You didn't have to. You know, I didn't overthrow Idun's hold on our people with brute force alone. It took a lot of clever planning and careful manipulation. I wouldn't have succeeded if not for this," he said, pointing at his temple. "I'm very good at reading people, Mila. I can fill in the blanks like pieces of a puzzle."

"What puzzle blanks are you filling in now?"

"That you suspect my son is not where I say he is, and that there's only one person who I think would discuss potential military movements around you." Volkner took another sip.

A chill crept up Mila's spine. She was toying with Volkner—trying to play his game of words, and already she'd made an error and exposed information Niko had shared with her in confidence.

Volkner's smile was lupine. "It doesn't matter. Lieutenant Schafer doesn't know the whereabouts of my son any more than any other lowly soldier in my ranks. In fact, I expect you'll know more about our operations than him before long."

"And why's that?"

Volkner seemed as though he were about to answer the

question, but was interrupted by a thought. He sat back in his chair again, looking as comfortable as anyone lounging at the end of a long day.

"You know, I remember serving with your father, though it feels like a lifetime ago. He was a brilliant soldier. Shame what happened to him."

Mila gritted her teeth. She knew it was bait, but it was good bait. "What do you mean?"

"I guess he wouldn't talk about that time too much," Volkner said. "Tell me, did he ever tell you about Greta?"

She recognized the name, though her father had only uttered that name in drunken, incomprehensible tantrums. Mila just shook her head.

"She was like a sister to him when they served. People even called them the twins. Then, everything changed, when I sent them into those damned tunnels."

"Tunnels?"

Volkner nodded. "They were part of an expeditionary force under my command, assigned to clear wilderness for habitation. But there was unusual seismic activity in the area, tied to instabilities caused by a tunnel system carved deep into the crust. Your father and Greta led a team in to collapse the system and calm the activity. They were supposed to set explosives and get out. Instead, the unlucky bastards got caught inside when they started detonating."

"So, you had to, what, dig them out?"

Volkner jumped to his feet as if suddenly excited, pointing at her as if she'd just asked the perfect question. "That's the thing. We lost comms with their unit and sent in rescue engineers to excavate the rubble to get to them. But, when they got there, every single one of their squad was safe in their camp at the mouth of the system. Unconscious, but safe. All except your father."

"What? Where was he?" Mila asked, suddenly hooked by the story's twist.

Volkner walked to the end of the bed and looked up at the eye. "I haven't the slightest clue. But I do know I lost two of my best warriors that day. Greta deserted and went off to gods-know where. Your father... well, I thought him dead. So, imagine my surprise when two of my officers send up a report that someone by the name of Hans Messer wanted to sell his master refiner daughter to my cabinet. And what's more, they reported that he lived on a farm on the same plot of land I thought we'd lost him to so many years ago."

The hair on the back of Mila's neck prickled. Her thoughts raced to the pit, to the abandoned military equipment she'd salvaged scrap from her entire life. Hans, her father, he was a part of the group that had left it there? And his and Volkner's history... Volkner hadn't paid Hans and retrieved her from the farm out of desperation—hadn't entertained the thought that a random farm girl would somehow miraculously possess the skills to refine brandr. He'd sent men with a holoscreen to verify it was truly Hans. And he'd taken her... why? What was her role in all of this?

Volkner finished his drink. "Now what do you make of a story like that?"

"I think it sounds like my father gave you the slip and opted to live his life peacefully outside of the military."

Volkner nodded. "That was my first thought as well. But your father... he's no idiot. A sad, drunken fool, yes; but he is clever. Or, at least, he was. If he were a deserter, he'd have known better than to stay there."

"It was the last place you'd expect to find him."

"True, perhaps. But we thought him dead. Going elsewhere, ripping out his civilian chip and replacing it with a black market one, changing his identity. That would have been his move. Instead, he stayed there and made no effort to mask who he was when he went into town. The only reason he wasn't discovered sooner is because no one there had a reason to know who he was. A great soldier, yes, and popular amongst his own units. But renowned, he was not."

"You clearly have your own theory," Mila said carefully.

Volkner turned to her. "I do."

The president walked toward her, slowly. She could smell the bold spices and spirits wafting from his breath and now-empty glass.

"I think your father is tethered to that place."

Mila flinched. "As in emotionally?"

Volkner shook his head, those gold-flecked glinting as they caught the overhead lights. "I mean very literally. I don't think he can go beyond your farm or the local village."

"That's crazy," Mila said before she thought the words through.

Volkner laughed a true, humor-filled laugh. "Is it? Tell me, Mila, what do you remember of your mother?"

"That's none of your business," Mila hissed.

"I expect you remember very little of her. You might even say you can barely remember her at all."

Mila went tensely still. As much as she didn't want to admit it, she could barely remember anything about her mother. Scattered memories of happiness and flowing blonde hair. But she couldn't remember the smell of her, or her name. She couldn't even remember what her face looked like.

"I was young..." she said with too-little confidence.

Volkner clicked his tongue. "The soldiers we found unconscious couldn't remember anything either. They all recalled going into the cave, but beyond that, they were blank. We had them put under psychiatric observation for weeks after the incident. They all spoke of strange dreams. But that wasn't the interesting part. No, it was what they dreamed about... every single one of them. Do you know what it was?"

Mila managed to barely shake her head.

"It was a woman. A woman of purest beauty, according to most of them. With hair like the sun, but a face she always kept hidden behind piercing light. The doctors called it a form of shared psychosis that the men developed after the trauma of almost dying in the caves."

"What happened to the men?" Mila asked, unsure if she really wanted to know the answer.

Volkner took a deep breath and clenched his jaw for a moment. It looked almost like regret. "We had them committed to permanent psychiatric care, all in different hospitals around the planet. Their dreams and the thought of the woman consumed them. They'd try to draw or paint her until their palms bled. When they ran out of paint, they'd just use the blood. Lunatics, all of them. I didn't give them another thought after that until... Well, until I discovered you." Volkner gestured to the scratch on Mila's arm. "We ran your DNA to make sure you're actually Hans' daughter."

"And?"

"You are, undeniably. But, the other half of your DNA, your mother's, that didn't appear in any Vidarin registry. In any Ymiran registry, in fact."

Mila's couldn't stop her eyes going wide. Her mother was a draugr? A ghost in the system. One who'd never had a chip assigned?

Volkner didn't say anything. He only watched her with peeled eyes and reveled in her realization. He was so close to her now, like inescapable night about to overtake her. But her head was spinning, her heart racing. She'd known her father lied to her about her mother dying, and that he'd worked to corrupt Mila's own chip, but this... she never knew who the woman who bore and birthed her was in the first place.

Just as it seemed Volkner might crush her with the sheer weight of his presence, he changed course, opting to return to the bar cart and refill his drink instead. Mila took the opportunity to remind herself to breathe. She focused on the carpeted floor trying to remain steady, though the influx of confusion made her dizzy and the room swayed. She felt her elerex trying to act up, but it never released a charge, only teased with small shocks, as if unsure what to do with her in this state.

The crimson, white, and gold of the carpet looked almost fluid to her, a sea of shifting colors. She barely noticed the speck of blue staining the fine fabric. It was cobalt, the same color as...

Niko's blood.

Mila's swaying confusion gave way to that burning anger she'd felt so often these past few days. What had Volkner done to him before she'd come in? Hit him? Cut him? It didn't matter that she hadn't forgiven Schafer yet; didn't matter she wasn't sure if she'd ever be able to completely. But the sight of his blood, the blood of one she might have called friend, that overrode everything.

The anger flared, but the elerex was quick to react, sending that heart-stopping shock through her chest, illuminating every nerve in her body. Her vision went black for a moment, and Mila counted herself lucky she didn't end up on the floor. The rampant anger was subdued for now, but still burned in hot embers against the elerex's lightning wall.

Either not noticing or not caring, Volkner turned and continued speaking as if everything was completely fine. "If there's one thing I'm certain about, it's that your family is very interesting, Mila."

It pained Mila to speak, but she managed, "The men. Have you spoken with them since you discovered me?"

"I sent inquiries to the hospitals. From what I can gather, most of them died, either killing themselves by blood painting, insomnia, or some other crazy behavior. A few are alive, but constant narcotics have fried their minds to the point they're little more than empty vessels. One of them, the nurses tell me, managed to cut out his own tongue so he couldn't speak to doctors and broke all of his fingers over and over again so they couldn't make him write."

Mila was horrified, but dealing with the lingering pain made it easy to conceal her shock.

"I think your father could be the key to something very important, Mila. And you're the key to him. Or, so I hope. And with you just happening to be a master brandr refiner, I think it's clear the fates willed our paths to cross." Volkner downed his freshly filled glass in one swig. "I think we'll do great things together, don't you?"

Mila nodded weakly, still reeling from the elerex's shock.

"Fantastic!" Volkner said, raising his hands in the air. "Then I see no reason not to move forward."

"Move forward with what?"

Volkner shook his head. "You're slow to the finish sometimes, aren't you, girl? Go back to the refinery and create one more batch; the largest yet, for us to power up my personal capital ship. The hyrrine you create and the secrets swimming in your blood will be exactly what we need to return Vidar to her former glory. You will be the driving force behind our empire, the one to train other brandr refiners and launch the great Vidarin conquest, starting with that miserable, savage-run planet Hod. Tomorrow you will accompany me to the Freiheitstag Ball. There we will announce, for all of Ymir to hear, we are to be wed."

There was no anger, no confusion. There was no hate, nor regret. There was no Hod or Idun or Jotun or Tyr. There was no Vidar. There was only her, alone in a room with Volkner Brandt. Her father, Niko, Amelie, Fen, and the mother she did not know were all galaxies away. There was only the sense of sudden descent, the lurching feeling of stolen footing, as the *Gjaller,* and the universe, fell from beneath Mila's feet.

PART THREE

CHAPTER

TWENTY-FOUR

MILA'S SHOP smelled of midnight dew and rusted metal. The provisional radio in the corner of the room played the remnant tunes from the old Earthens, not the electronic folk so loved by the Messer paterfamilias. It wasn't turned up loud like he liked, either. In fact, he could still hear the occasional howling wind as it made the shop sway.

Hans sat, listening to the sounds of guitar chords and unaltered vocals in the dim light of the shop. The singer sang of a hotel, one so lovely and surreal that it seemed more like a dream than a true memory.

Hans was sober, as he'd been all week. After the mead of poetry, or whatever in Hel's name that cursed man had given him was, he didn't expect to ever touch alcohol again.

Retained snippets of the knowledge and perception gained during the episode bounced in his head, but they were in no way welcome. Hans knew from the flow of his blood and the lack of rasp in his chest he really had been spared from the edge of death for the time being. He knew his jet truck would need a full engine rebuild soon from the rhythm of its putter. Most of all, he remembered things from his past he'd long drowned in spirits. It was those thoughts, and the regret of condemning Mila to a life amongst tyrants, that returned his gaze to the loaded plasma revolver on the workbench in front of him.

Beside it was a flickering holoscreen depicting him and a six-year-old Mila. They were laughing, happy, gesturing for the photo-taker to join in. She hadn't made it in time, though. The only evidence of his wife's presence there was the golden-tan arm peeking in from the left border as she tried to beat the timer. The next picture—the one that would have had her in it—showed up as 'Corrupted File.' Every time it cycled back to that missing picture, it felt like rounds as real as those loaded in the gun on the desk pierced through his chest.

"Shame," a voice said from behind him.

The revolver was immediately in Hans' hand as he spun his chair around to face the sudden threat. When he saw the tell-tale pinstripe suit, it didn't matter he was facing the Rattle Man, that he knew plasma rounds would be useless. He kept the gun aimed carefully, precise, the instincts of soldierly youth rearing their head in his soberness after too many drunken years.

"I bet she was a real beauty," the Rattle Man said, unfazed by the barrel two feet from his face.

"Get. Out," Hans hissed.

"That's a bit rude, don't you think?"

"Where is she?"

"If I tell you, will you stop looking at me like that?" The Rattle Man asked, adjusting his tie mockingly. "I really don't care for confrontation."

A muscle flickered in Hans' jaw.

"Fine. Your dear daughter is doing well. I did what you asked and refined the brandr for her."

"And?" Hans bit.

"And what?"

"You said I'd have five years with her!" The gun started to tremble in his hand. "I gave my life to you for that. Five years! Do you have any idea what that means? For me to forfeit *my* life?"

"I know *exactly* what that means," the Rattle Man said, his silver tongue glinting between words. "Your daughter is safe, Hans. Better than that, actually. She's Vidar's Head of Brandr Refining now, and if the rumors are to be believed, she may wed Volkner himself soon."

"She what?" Hans' body went slack, though the gun was still raised.

"That's right. We could soon see a new First Lady of the Republic. And so long as she continues to make her promises, I will continue refining, and the fairy tale can go on."

"Her promises?!" Every inch of Hans was taut immediately, every fiber of him screaming to pull the trigger. "She shouldn't have had to promise you anything. I gave you—"

"You gave me your life so I'd save her," the Rattle Man interrupted. "And so, I did. I refined the brandr into hyrrine that same night and saved her from a life in the mines. I made no promises for following nights. That, I left to her."

Hans squeezed the trigger once, twice, click. Both shots rang out as the molten plasma slugs flew, only to hit the opposite wall of the workshop as the hammer fell on an empty chamber.

The Rattle Man had simply vanished as if made of shadow. Though his essence was still thick within the workshop air.

"Nine heavens and nine Hels damn you," Hans said,

dropping the now-empty revolver. "All the Aesir and Vanir damn you."

The Rattle Man's disembodied reply was like a voice pulled from darkness. "Your daughter's fate is in her own hands. Fear not, though. I hear there's chatter amongst the rebels about something happening to the *Gjaller* soon. You may yet see your daughter again soon... *if* she survives."

"What do you mean?" Hans asked to the empty room. "What's going to happen?!" He yelled. But he couldn't feel the Rattle Man's slithering presence any longer.

Hans' blood was boiling with fear-fueled anger. He whirled on the workbench and swiped everything onto the floor in an impulsive fit. Spare parts, tools, the radio, and a whole menagerie of other odds and ends crashed to the floor.

Hans pulled his hair and growled, his chest heaving. Then, the futility of it set in, and he found himself regretting taking out his aggression on Mila's things. He was left with only the sound of the humming reactor battery outside the shop, the passing wind, and his own red-filtered thoughts.

He crouched to the floor and started picking them up, one by one, until he grasped a holobook that had flipped on when it struck the floor. The current page flickered inconsistently, and the bottom right edge was dark. He knew he'd likely damaged the projector array inlaid within.

"Dammit," he said, flipping the tablet-like device over in his hands, finding the damage points. "I'll fix this Mila," he whispered to himself. "I'll fix all of this. Somehow." *But I don't know where to start* he left unsaid to the darkness.

As if in response, the screen on the device stopped flickering. Hans knew the holobook immediately. It was *The*

Nightwalkers. That cursed book of dark fairy tales he'd carried with him to read to his soldiers for entertainment all those years ago. He'd read every single story within it at least a dozen times over. And the one that displayed now had always sent the darkest and coldest of chills down his spine. Now, he felt that same chill as his mind weighed the coincidence of *that* story showing up. Of Mila having salvaged *this* holobook. The title stared at him like an omen. A single word, but now with more meaning than he'd ever known then.

Rattle.

Hans sat slowly into the chair, reading that title over and over. As his eyes narrowed on the words, the tip of his tongue stuck out just the slightest touch. The stories weren't real, or so many believed. But even if they were tall tales, it was wise to assume there was always a touch of truth to them. Knowing what he knew, that touch of truth terrified Hans Messer. Finally, with a breath of determination, he read the rhyme in whole.

In night black, cold and rain,
comes a man without a name.
Lost souls knock upon your floor,
when he's standing at your door.
Slither lips and silver tongue,
hear his words, too late to run.
Your given call to him is chattel,
never give your name to Rattle.

When the holobook wouldn't flick to the next screen, likely due to the damage, Hans read the poem again. And again. And once more. It had always been a scary story, but that's all it was, a story. But now... Now it felt more like a warning.

...never give your name to Rattle.

The last line echoed through Hans' mind. Over and over and over again still.

...comes a man without a name.

Hans, brow creased, pondered every last element of the nursery rhyme. Every period, every pause, every rhyme. But all he came back to each time was the name.

It was a hunch at best, but it was all he had. Hans picked the radio up from the dirty ground and blew it off. The damage wasn't bad, considering it'd been near broken already. Thankfully, it still worked. Now, if he could just get it to transmit. He knew it was possible given the type of radio array she'd used—military, designed for communication, not listening to galactic radio stations. The fact she'd figured out how to get it to pick up those signals, another pang of regret hit him as he realized how little credit he'd given her for so many years. He'd been a master of mechanical and electronic repair in his day. But she'd taken everything he'd taught her and amplified it to surpass him in every way.

Hans removed the backplate and examined the wiring. He reached into that knowledge from his past tucked away in dusty memories, following the connections and seeing exactly how they needed to be reoriented for sending. The few bits of fraying or rusted wiring he was able to replace quickly enough with scrap wire Mila kept in jars on the back desk. So resourceful, his daughter, ready for any repair or improvement at any time.

After an hour of adjustments, replacements, and repairs, it was ready. He knew he'd have no way of knowing whether or not the message reached its destination. He also knew getting the message to the *Gjaller* without it being flagged would be an impossibility. So, he'd have to send it on blind hope to the one person he knew who could encrypt it and smuggle it in digitally. The one person he knew who hated Volkner Brandt more than him.

He set the destination codes and tuned the channel, hoping they were still the same despite all the years that had passed. But those codes had always been *their* codes, direct to their private radios so they were never stranded when military equipment and communication arrays went down, and they vowed to one another they'd never change; that they'd always have each other's backs, like brother and sister. That hadn't stopped him from tucking his radio away years ago into a now-dust-covered box. Now, he could only pray she hadn't done the same.

With an anxious breath and a prayer to whatever god would listen, he began. "Greta, this is Hans Messer. I need your help."

CHAPTER
TWENTY-FIVE

MILA DIDN'T SPEAK a word for several minutes as Niko and Amelie escorted her out of the maze that led to Volkner's sleeping quarters. They'd asked her what happened. Or, at least, she thought they had. Everything and everyone still felt far away from her, like a dream or a memory. It wasn't until they reached the lift that she really heard them.

"Mila," Niko said, placing a hand on her shoulder and shaking her a bit.

It was the hand that jolted her back to the now, and she recoiled from it. Niko quickly withdrew, his eyes wide with the hurt of realizing what his touch did to her. But Mila knew it'd only been the shock of being touched that made her do it, not the feel of *his* hand. As much as the thought of him slaying the warrior on stage to the cries of a ravenous audience haunted her, there was still so much of her that wanted to forget what'd she'd seen. Forget what he'd done. But she hadn't. She couldn't. And she knew she shouldn't.

"Mila?" Amelie coaxed softly.

"Did he hurt you?" Mila asked in an impossibly low tone. It was all she could muster.

"What?" Niko asked, baffled. "No, he didn't— Mila, what happened?"

"I saw the blood," Mila said.

"What blood?"

"Your blood... on the carpet. I assumed he must have done something to you."

Niko shook his head. "I'm fine. But we need to know what he said to you."

"He said I'm going to be the driving force behind Vidar's return to glory."

"And?" Niko asked.

"And... I'm going to be his date to the Ball."

Niko's posture tightened and she saw his fists clench, but he said nothing.

"There's something else," Mila continued. "He said... he said we're going to get married."

"He what?!" Niko practically yelled. The Berserker's eyes were like glowing coals in a forge basin suddenly struck with a bellow's gust.

"You can't be serious," Amelie said.

"Completely," Mila replied.

"Rotten bastard," Niko hissed as he turned back toward the way they came. "I'll put a stop to this."

"Niko, wait," Mila said, reaching out to grab his steel-like arm.

The touch stopped him still.

"Don't."

"He's crossed the line," Niko replied.

"He's making a political move," Mila said.

"She's right," Amelie agreed. "If another planet stole his master refiner, that's grounds for sanctions and negotiation. Steal his wife, that's grounds for war."

Niko's shoulders heaved. "So, what? I'm supposed to just let this happen?"

"Yes," Mila said. "Think of what will happen to your family if you just barge into his quarters and try to tell the most powerful man on Vidar he can't marry me."

Niko's shoulders slumped as he considered the thought. "And what of the millions who will die when he has enough hyrrine to jump a fleet, or has sold enough to build more berserkers?"

"If I'm his wife, maybe I can help stop things."

Niko turned back to her, his digital eyes searching hers for something. She wasn't sure if he found it or not when he finally said, "I swear to you I will free you from him."

"You'll swear nothing," Mila replied. "I'm not going to have your family's blood on my hands."

"Whatever I do, whoever's blood is spilt by my actions, that has always been and always will be my burden to bear."

❖─────◆─────❖

Even with Amelie standing beside her, Eiji and Xiomar armored and stoic as ever in the corner, and the ambient heat of Fenrir's hydraulics wafting toward her, the refinery felt colder than she'd experienced yet. But Mila knew that had little to do with the temperature. It was the feeling of certain hopelessness. It was the same feeling she'd spent the first night in the refinery.

She'd put on a brave face before. Telling Niko she was okay with wedding Volkner was better than the Berserker going on a bloody rampage and getting his family killed. He may believe the burden would be his and his alone, but Mila knew their doom would always reside in her conscience if that happened.

"What will you do?" Amelie asked.

Mila shifted her chin in curiosity. "What do you mean?"

"To make things better. You said you'd help stop things. How?"

"Oh," Mila replied. She rubbed the back of her neck pensively as she said, "I guess I'll try the diplomatic approach first. Try to talk the bastard down. If that doesn't work then... well, I imagine I'm my own best bargaining chip. If he loses his Master Refiner, he loses any chance of winning a war."

"You mean you'd kill yourself?"

"If it came to that," Mila said, her voice threatening to trip over the words. Amelie's concerned expression made her quickly add, "but only as an absolute last resort. I won't let him win so easily, but neither will I doom an entire planet."

"You might be trading Hod for Vidar," Amelie said. "If he can't prove his might with a successful conquest, he might take it out even harder on your population."

Mila bit the inside of her cheek. "I hadn't considered that. I don't suppose you have any ideas?"

"Stab him in his sleep," Amelie replied in what seemed to be only a half-joke.

Mila chuckled. "Could work, except I don't think I'll be allowed a blade anywhere near him." She took in a breath and huffed it out through her nose in frustration. "Why is it so hard to topple an empire?"

"A tree is not felled by the first blow, but neither can it fall without it." It was Eiji who spoke.

When Mila looked at the young Hodian, she did not expect to be met with an unyielding glare. But that's exactly what she found.

"I've heard that phrase before," Mila said. "My father used to say it when he was... Well, when he wasn't speaking clearly."

"It comes from the Níu."

"What is the Níu?"

"Rebels," Amelie said before Eiji answered. "It's treason to speak those words here; you should know that."

"I expect it is also treason to say you'll stab the president in his sleep," Eiji replied.

"We weren't serious," Amelie replied, suddenly sounding like she was retreating into her former timidity.

Eiji took a step forward. "Treading on treason's doorstep is a dangerous game, even if you don't enter its home. Someone could push you in."

Amelie stepped back like a nervous puppy.

"Are you suggesting something, Eiji?" Mila asked, both out of curiosity and in an effort to take the focus off of Amelie.

"You cannot topple the tree yourself. But you could deal the first blow."

"Are you actually suggesting I try to kill Volkner?"

"I suggest dying as a warrior is better than just dying. And if you can take him with you, all of Ymir would be better for it."

"And then what?" Amelie asked. "He'd just be replaced by his son, or one of the countless corrupt politicians he keeps around him. Killing Volkner would only cause more chaos. It would have to all be taken down and rebuilt, but for that you'd need an army."

Mila suddenly remembered Úlf and the forces conspiring against Volkner Brandt, though she still couldn't know what his motives were or if he was still lying to her.

Still, she might have brought it up, if not for the refinery doors grinding open.

It was Niko entering at an urgent stride, a garment bag slung over his shoulder.

"What is it?" Mila asked, reading his posture and pace.

Niko laid the bag on the cot and surveyed the room to make sure they were the only five present. "I received a message."

Mila raised an eyebrow.

"It came *specifically* to me. And it's for you."

Mila hesitated, confused, before asking, "From who?"

"It was heavily encrypted so I can't know where or who it came from. But they have to know I'm your personal guard, and that I wouldn't go directly to Volkner."

"I don't know who off this station would know something like that."

"Someone with spies," Xiomar said.

Niko nodded.

"Well, what did it say?" Mila asked.

"It was short, and I have no idea what it means, but it said *A man without a name - find the name.*"

"Cryptic," Eiji said.

"Do you have any idea what it means?" Niko asked.

Mila creased her brow, mulling over the words, but shook her head.

"If someone went through this much trouble and made this big of a gamble to get you the message, it has to be important."

"I'm sure it is," Mila replied. "But I still don't know what it means."

"Do you know anything about a man without a name?"

Mila shook her head again and said, "No, nobody like

that. I've only heard about people like that in stories and fairy tales."

As she said the last two words, a chord reverberated in the back of her mind.

"Actually, I've only heard of *one* story like that." Mila turned away from the group and thought about the nursery rhyme. More to herself than the group she said, "Your given call, to him is chattel. Never give your name to..."

The room started spinning. Mila suddenly felt light-headed as every memory of every interaction with Úlf stormed her mind. How he'd walked unseen past guards, emerged from shadow, refined the brandr into hyrrine without a single blip of power. How he'd done everything in exchange for *favors*.

Mila knew exactly what the message meant; knew exactly what the person who'd sent it wanted her to know. Úlfljótur was no ambassador. He was not from Jotun. He was not a miracle worker or a force for good. He was not Úlf at all. He was something else entirely.

He was the Rattle Man.

"What is it?" Niko asked, clearly sensing something was off.

Mila slowly turned back to face them, finding concerned looks on Amelie and Niko's faces, and even a hint of curiosity on Eiji's.

"It's going to sound completely mad," she said. "But I don't think Úlfljótur is who he says he is."

"The ambassador?" Niko asked. "What does he have to do with anything?"

"Everything." Mila closed her eyes and took a deep breath to relieve the knot forming in her throat. "I can't refine brandr."

"What?" Niko asked, vocalizing the confusion on the faces of all in the room.

"I haven't refined any of it. Not a single drop. It's all been him."

Niko shook his head. "That's impossible. I've had guards posted outside the doors every night. It's the only way in and out." He whirled on Xiomar and Eiji. "Unless my soldiers have been letting him through unchallenged and have failed to report it."

"No," Mila said. "They wouldn't have seen him. Or at least wouldn't remember it if they had."

"What do you mean? How is that possible? Some kind of drug weapon? Why wouldn't you have said anything about this?"

"No, no drugs," Mila replied quickly. "But possibly something worse. I don't really know." By the looks on everyone's faces, it was clear they weren't drawing the correct conclusions, if any at all. "Here, let me show you something."

Mila went to the section of cord channel where the damaged power line was. Everyone else huddled around her, watching intensely. Even Eiji and Xiomar had ditched their generally stoic, disinterested personas to come see what she had to show them. When she removed the panel, the cable was still as evidently mangled and burnt by a fire long past.

"That's the main power," Xiomar said.

"Has it been running it off of a backup?" Niko asked.

Mila shook her head. "The system is completely powerless."

"I don't understand," Niko said. "How did he possibly refine things without power?"

"Magic." Amelie's eyes were like saucers, just as they

had been the first time she'd seen the damaged line. The memory Ùlf had wiped from her.

"Don't be ridiculous," Niko said.

"She's right," Eiji said. "It's not ridiculous. There are things in this universe we can't understand. The man, he must be using some kind of sorcery. This thing would be impossible if not."

Niko looked at Eiji incredulously, then turned to his other soldier. "Xiomar, what do you make of all this? Surely there's something we're missing."

Xiomar shook his head. "That is the only line running from the machinery. There can't be another source, and this can't run without power. They're right. It's either a miracle or magic."

Niko released an agitated breath. "Well, this day just keeps getting more and more interesting. How to hell do I explain to Volkner there's a sorcerer on his station?"

"He's not a sorcerer," Mila said, provoking confused looks all around once more. She stood and said, "He's the Rattle Man."

Niko groaned and Xiomar cocked a smile. Amelie's eyes went even wider, which Mila would not have thought possible. Only Eiji kept her composure the same.

"The Rattle Man's a myth," Niko said. "A story to tell little kids to stop them talking to strangers."

Xiomar started humming the rhythm of the nursery rhyme.

"All myths come from some truth," Eiji said.

"How proverbial," Niko said. "But let's try to be serious here. We have a real problem to deal with."

"Yes, we do," Mila said. "It's the Rattle Man."

"How are you so sure?"

"The message," Mila said. "It made everything make

sense. Ulf has been helping me in exchange for future favors. All the old stories talk about how the Rattle Man trades for promises. I couldn't figure out how he could do the things he does, or why he'd deign to help me. He said it was to give him eyes within Volkner's inner circle, but it seemed strange to me he would just happen to know how to refine brandr. Now it lines up. They say the Rattle Man can do anything in exchange for favors."

"If your theory is true, and he is the Rattle Man," Niko said, "then making those promises was the worst thing you could have done."

"I realize that," Mila replied, slouching a bit. Then she straightened and said, "But there's no use brooding on that now."

"You have a suggestion?"

"I do," Mila said. "We have the will to change Vidar, but lack the resources, the allies, and the weapons. I say we use him."

"Absolutely not," Niko said.

"I agree," Eiji said. "That is a risk we cannot take. If he is the Rattle Man, he will take the name of whoever makes the deal. You're lucky he has not taken yours yet."

"What does that even mean, taking a name?" Mila asked.

"It means he'll take your soul," Amelie said quietly.

Chills ran down Mila's back.

"There is no worse fate than to have a soul stolen," Eiji said. "You will be like this armor," Eiji tapped the metal breastplate of her Viking suit. "But without the person to fill it. Your essence will belong to him."

"So be it," Mila said.

"Mila," Niko said, a hint of desperation in his voice. "You can't seriously think that's okay."

"He'd own my name or my soul, but we'd bring Volkner down. We'd take all of this down. The Vidarin people could prosper, if only I'm willing to pay the price. It doesn't seem too steep if you ask me."

"But what if it's a trick?" Niko asked. "What if he traps you into this imprisonment and you can't even ensure he makes good on his word?"

"How is that different from the life I'm already doomed to?"

No one replied.

"I have a chance to make a real change here. And who knows, maybe he does really want to take Volkner down for some reason. Maybe he'll simply help us?"

"That's a fool's hope," Eiji said.

"She's right," Niko said. "You can't trust him; not a word of anything he says. And no one should make another deal."

"It's still worth trying," Mila said, unyielding. "Let me talk to him. Tonight, when he comes to refine again, I'll figure out his intentions. I already owe him favors, but I won't promise any more and I won't let him take my name."

"No," Niko said. "It's too risky. When he realizes you know who he is, what's to say he won't just kill you. Or all of us, for that matter?"

"He won't kill me, and I doubt he'd harm any of you. He says he needs me, that it's not a coincidence I'm here."

"Volkner said a similar thing to me," Niko said. "Earlier, in his room. He spoke of you being the key to something, and it didn't seem like he was talking about brandr refining."

"I haven't the slightest clue what it means, but it might just protect us," Mila said. "I don't think he'll harm any of you either. He would have already killed Amelie if that were the case."

"What?" Amelie asked. "Why me?"

"Because, you've seen him do unnatural magicks before. Do you remember coming to the refinery with me last time?"

Amelie started to shake her head. Then, her brows creased, and she said, "Wait, I remember walking down here with you... or starting to. But the rest, I can only remember bits and pieces of the refinery. Other than that, I remember waking up in my bed, thinking it was a bad dream I'd already mostly forgotten."

"It wasn't a dream. Ulf—the Rattle Man—came in after we'd found the damaged line. He did something to you that made you fall unconscious and said you wouldn't remember any of what you'd seen. If he was wholly malicious, why would he have not killed you?"

"We have no idea how powerful he is," Eiji said. "For all we know, rearranging and wiping memories could be as easy to him as breathing. And we cannot know what his motivations are."

"Eiji's right," Niko said. "If he is what you say he is, we can't know what he really wants. He's dangerous."

"He is," Mila agreed. "A foe not to be taken lightly. Or an ally that could help us change everything. I intend to speak with him tonight. None of you can stop me from doing that unless you go to Volkner himself. If you have to stay with me to protect me, so be it. But the meeting is happening."

Niko sighed. "Fine. We'll have your meeting. But I will protect you if necessary with every weapon at my disposal. And if he charges another favor or asks for a name, it will be mine."

Mila nodded in agreement, though she already knew it was a lie.

TWENTY-SIX

THE STATIC WHITE noise of the communication system taunted Piper, but she wouldn't cut it off. No rebels had replied to her message. She didn't even know if they'd received it. And even if they did, she wouldn't receive a reply from the Níu in time to alter her path.

With or without them, Piper's mission remained the same. Despite what Atli had asked of her, the core focus never changed: kill Volkner. If the rebels showed up and exploited the weak points in the *Gjaller,* fantastic. If not, then she'd just have to pray for Odin's guidance.

Even though the smuggler had been Loki-worshipping scum, she had to admit he'd stocked his ship well on his Tyran run, and he'd kept up his codebook with the tenacity of a bureaucrat. The silken Tyran robes, dyed with a menagerie of reds, golds, purples, and blues, complete with a jeweled shemagh, would do nicely to help her blend in amongst the *Gjaller* rabble once onboard. Then it'd just be a matter of navigating her way to the Great Hall, where they'd no doubt be having their Freiheitstag feast. That would be her chance.

The white noise continued without interruption.

"Dammit," Piper cursed to herself. "Come on."

Something flared in her back that sent her head screaming. Before she knew what she'd done, Piper punched a flat length of the pilot console with her metallic hand, leaving the metal mangled and dented. She gritted her teeth and pulled out one of the injectables Einar had left her. It hissed as she plunged it into her thigh, releasing the sweet synthetic within. Piper threw her head back in thanks to Einar and the gods as she felt the pain withdraw.

She inspected the pouch with the injectables. *Three left. Have to be careful how I use them.*

The pain from the still-raw wound on her back, the nerve connections to the robotic limbs, and the dozens of other bruises and cuts healing all over her required a dose of that medicine every twelfth hour, or so Einar claimed. However, Piper found that after only the second hour the pain was rearing its head again. That meant she had six hours until she used the last dose, and eight until the pain returned for good. She highly suspected she would be dead before it was ever an issue again.

Piper took a breath and listened closely for any last-second break in the white noise. Any indication at all that she'd been heard. But it didn't come.

Piper punched in the coordinates to *Gjaller,* which the ship's system was equipped to predict. That made things easier on her; no tedious math. One bright spot before the world of darkness she was so near to entering. The numbers glowed at her like an invitation, or a warning. Her finger hovered over the engagement switch, but it felt like someone was tugging a rope tight around her chest.

"Witness me, Allfather," she whispered to herself.

Piper had never been overly religious, and she prayed to Odin only because it was what those around her had always done. But she'd seen and felt enough things she could not explain. She knew there had to be some truth in the gods, even though it was a truth she knew she couldn't understand. And it was that truth that let her finger touch the switch, flipping it to engaged.

The console and overhead lights shifted to red, indicating that the jump formula was processing, and any inhabitants of the ship would only have a few seconds to strap into their seats before the ship plunged into the yawning void.

A yellow light blipped on, letting Piper know it was time to cut power to the secondary and auxiliary systems. She flipped each off, leaving the communications array for very last, giving the static sound every chance to break. Just as she reached the switch, it did.

It was impossibly brief, even more so than her own message. But she knew it was to make sure no one could know what it meant if intercepted and decrypted. It was only four words total, spoken by a rough, female voice. Yet it told Piper everything she needed to know.

"We are the axe."

A smile tugged at the side of Piper's lips as she flipped off the communication array and allowed the ship to make the leap.

———◇———◇———

It'd barely been two weeks since she set eyes on the *Gjaller*, but it was still as astounding as ever to look upon the station. The longbow cannon turrets alone were each the size of the smuggler's craft she was in, and there were hundreds of them. Not to mention the *Tarnkappe* shielding she knew encased the station unseen.

It was too risky to attempt another communication to the Níu at this range. She had to trust that the short reply was confirmation they knew the plan. Her only communication now was to the behemoth station, requesting docking access and providing the shuttle credentials. Judging from the reply, even the on-duty landing officers had dipped into the mead. That was good.

Within a matter of minutes, Piper docked in one of the dozens of trade ship bays. A young officer with a cocked service cover half-tripped up to her holding a holotablet.

"Business?" he sputtered, squinting at the words on the tablet.

"Trade. I have a shipment from Tyr of spices, spirits, and fabrics," she said, reaching to her roots for a flawless Tyran accent.

"Chip." The officer held the tablet out, implying she should hold up her arm for him to scan her citizen chip.

Piper did so without hesitation, holding up the robed arm and pulling back the fabric to reveal her wrist. The officer held the scanner over it, waiting for it to register. Piper knew full well it would transfer nothing to him, since her chip had been removed years ago when she joined Arvid's crew.

"*This makes you a ghost,*" Skuld, then Arvid's first mate, had said. "*No one can track a ghost.*"

The officer's brow creased in drunken concentration. He tapped the side of the holotablet, but even if Piper did have a chip, it wouldn't have done anything. There were no moving parts to knock free in holoscreen devices.

"Is there a problem?" Piper asked.

"Your chip may be malfunctioning."

"Aesir be damned," Piper cursed. "I was afraid of this. I had an accident recently and, well," Piper pulled up her other arm's sleeve to reveal the robotic limb. "They said the chip appeared fine, but there was always the chance it could malfunction with non-Tyran scanners."

It was a believable enough lie. It was true all the planets had their own styles of equipment for reading citizen chips and the chips themselves differed in both design and programming. Governments claimed this was primarily in an effort to protect citizen information from being easily spread to other planets, but the common suspicion was that it was actually to protect captured spies. Fortunately for Piper, Vidar and Tyr were on good terms politically, so there would be little reason to accuse her of espionage.

"I see," the officer said. "In that case, I'll need to escort you to admin for vetting."

"Is that really necessary?" Piper asked. The only part of her face that was uncovered was her eyes, and she made a point to use them by fluttering her lashes more than she'd have done in any other situation. "I'm really dying to get settled so I can participate in the night's festivities, and admin can take so long."

"I'm afraid so," the officer replied, covering his mouth with a fist to conceal a hiccup. "Can't make exceptions just because it's Freiheitstag."

Piper stomped a concealed foot playfully, loud enough for him to hear. "Oh, all right. But if I'm late to the ball, I'm holding you personally accountable, mister..."

"Huber. Lieutenant Huber."

"Strong name. Old name," Piper said. "I imagine you come from a rich history of Hubers."

The officer's posture straightened, as if adhering to the

idea. "My father says our lineage traces back to the Vikings of old, that my ancestors were landowners and proud farmers who took up sword and axe against any who would threaten what was theirs."

"I suspected as much. That family tree helped give you those strong arms, no doubt. I wonder, will I be able to find the strapping Lieutenant Huber at the Freiheistag Ball?"

"You will," Huber replied.

"And will he have a companion on his arm?"

Huber shook his head.

Piper took a slow step closer to him. "Perhaps, if you let me forego the admin nonsense, I could fill that gap?"

Huber's pale cheeks went rosy, and he tried to keep his smile under control. "I suppose we could work something out."

"Good," Piper replied. "Meet me outside the Great Hall a half hour before the festivities begin. That way we can get a good seat."

Huber nodded dumbly, handing her a visitor badge. Piper ran a finger down his arm, then made her exit before he had a chance to think twice about agreeing.

She'd been inside the *Gjaller* before, but only once, and only long enough for her conversation with Volkner. However, she'd looked at schematics of the station more times than she could remember. She knew exactly which lifts to take to find the reactor level and knew how many guards she'd have to pass along the way. Getting them to let her pass, though? That would be near-impossible.

It was good, then, that the reactor level was not the foremost level on her target list. No, that honor went to the Great Hall, where President Volkner Brandt would be sitting at the head table enjoying the celebration of his bloody ascent to power. The perfect spot to show all of humanity that Volkner Brandt made a mistake by crossing Piper DeRache, and that he would never make that mistake, or any others, ever again.

CHAPTER

TWENTY-SEVEN

"Does he always take this long?" Niko asked, pacing the area in front of the refinery door.

They'd been waiting in the refinery for near two hours since Niko had agreed to Mila's terms. The room had been mostly tense silence broken only by the sounds of Mila adjusting Fenrir's various screws and plates trying to finish up the repairs on the wolfbot's outer shell. She had only one piece remaining; an armor plate for his hind thigh that she'd been unable to scrounge up from the scrap pile.

Eberhard and Waren had joined them in the refinery as well, but Amelie had left at Mila's suggestion. If things did go bad, and a fight broke out, she didn't want the servant getting caught up in a massacre.

"It varies," Mila replied. "But he's definitely kept me holding my breath before."

She glanced at the garment bag laid beside her on the cot. Niko seemed to notice as he said, "Oh, right, I'd forgotten. That's for you."

"For me?" Mila asked, looking at him with a brow raised. "What is it?"

"I think it's more customary to open a package, rather than ask the sender what's inside," Niko said with a hint of a smirk.

Mila returned the smirk and rolled her eyes, allowing him to see the playfulness in the gesture. She hadn't gotten completely comfortable with him again. Not yet. But she'd started to realize it may have been harsh to jump to conclusions. After all, she'd been in this world for a few days, and already she felt her innocent predispositions fading into thoughts of war and revolution. He'd been woven into its very fabric for most of his life. She couldn't fathom how someone, especially a berserker, could have retained their humanity after that.

She wiped the oil from Fenrir's repairs and gently unzipped the bag. Her breath caught in her throat as she saw the fabric within. She recognized it immediately, well before the entire piece was exposed. It was a dress. Dazzling white trimmed in emerald green, complete with a sash as gold as Freya's tears. Her mother's dress, absent any damage or stains caused by her arrival to the *Gjaller*.

"How did you..."

"I figured you'd stuffed it away, too stubborn to discard it. So, I took the liberty of finding it and having it fixed up. I'd hoped you'd wear it to the ball, but..." Niko hesitated, seeming to wince with a touch of pain. "But I imagine Volkner would prefer you in his colors."

Mila inspected her hands to make sure she'd wiped away every speck of oil or debris. Then she ran her fingers across the fabric, fighting back the tears threatening to spill. She never thought she'd see it in its former glory again.

"Then I suppose we'll just have to throw our own ball," Mila said, smiling at the Berserker.

"I'd like that."

"You want us to step out?" Eberhard said from his post in the corner. The old man was grinning like an imp.

Mila had half-forgotten they were there, and it appeared Niko had too as he suddenly straightened.

"The way the room just heated, you'd think the refining equipment turned on," Waren said, his cheeks rosy with laughter.

"You two happy with yourselves?" Niko asked.

"Happy? Of course not," Waren replied. "Thought that was the whole point of talking to the magic man and trying to change the planet, make us all happier."

Niko closed his eyes and shook his head. "Sorry about those two. They're the oldest in the room, but the least grown up."

"It's called wisdom," Eberhard said. "You live as long as I have, you learn you need to take time for a laugh."

"And I'm just a hopeless romantic, so please excuse my partner's interruption and continue. I'm waiting for the part where you sweep her off her feet, Niko."

"Or perhaps I'll sweep you off yours, Waren," Mila said with fabricated venom.

Every one of the soldiers' eyes widened, even Xiomar and Eiji's. Waren seemed especially caught off-guard, but Niko simply chuckled.

"The refiner has a warrior's spirit," Eiji said.

"Or a bard's tongue," Waren said. "Either way, she's deadly."

"Are you sure you're protecting her, Niko?" Eberhard asked. "Or are you protecting everyone else *from* her?"

Niko shrugged. "I guess we'll have to wait and see."

The group shared a quiet laugh, and Mila imagined this was probably what life was like for most people who'd grown up with friends. She liked the feeling, and never wanted it to go away. Even though she'd only just met them, and though they were seasoned warriors decked in advanced military equipment, she knew she wanted to protect them.

"Well, since we have no idea when our guest will arrive, let's help Mila find her last piece for Fenrir," Niko said. "Everyone, start digging."

Fen barked as if in appreciation.

Mila explained what to look for and all of them set to scrounging through the pile, though, not without a fair amount of groaning from Waren. Mila went to the far end of the heap, the section she had explored the least for parts. Luckily, the portion near the front of the room had held a fair share of parts from decommissioned Mark IVs, so she hadn't had to dig in too far. Well, not farther than she was used to, having spent so many years digging through the pit on the farm.

After shuffling through the pile for a few minutes, and with plenty of loud clanging as the men threw aside various pieces of metal, Eberhard stopped them.

"What's all this?" the aging soldier said.

"You found something useful?" Niko asked.

"I don't know about useful. But definitely interesting."

The group walked to where Eberhard had been digging, about halfway through the pile. The massive hunks of scrap thrown out of the way was a testament to the old bear's strength. The space he'd opened gave a clear view of the wall behind.

There were carvings in it, much like the iar rune Mila had found toward the edge. Except these were not carvings of runes. This was an artwork, the wall its canvas, though, even in the large hole Eberhard had made, there was only a portion of it revealed. The part they could see depicted a massive, bound wolf biting off the hand of an armor-clad man.

"That's Fenrir," Eberhard said.

Fen stood and started making his way to the group.

"No, not you, Fen," Eberhard said kindly. "The real Fenrir. It's the story of when the gods bound him with Gleipnir, and the man who's hand he's biting off is Tyr."

"There's more," Waren said.

"Clear it," Niko instructed.

"How much?" Waren asked in a way that implied he didn't really want to know the answer.

"All of it."

It took them the better part of the next hour to haul away the bulk of the scrap, piling it by the evac door at the far end of the refinery. Through the whole process, there was still no sign of the Rattle Man.

Moving the parts and spare metal revealed an expansive carving lining nearly the entire wall. Starting near the entrance was the rune that Mila had seen before—iar. It was surrounded by other runes, some representing a wolf and others death. Moving left, the carvings transitioned into a carving of a man and a woman, the man in simple armor and the woman in robes. The woman stood a head taller than the man, and from the way they faced each other, hands intertwined, it was easy to see they were lovers.

Next to that was the man, absent the woman, with three children. The first, a boy, had a snake wrapped around his body, much like the iar rune, though, it seemed more like his pet than a predator. The next, a girl, had a body bisected. Her right half was soft-featured and beautiful. But her left, though part of the same frame, was largely scratched out. The last child was a nondescript boy in simple clothes, a boyish smile etched onto his face. A wolf pup sat at his feet, curled and sleeping peacefully. The man was standing behind the three, smiling much like the boy.

"Ragnarök," Eiji said. The young warrior was already looking at the end of the string of carvings.

"She's right," Eberhard said. "It's the entire tale of Ragnarök." He pointed at the carved mural. "That's the Loki and the giantess Angrboda. And there, their three children, Jörmungandr, Hel, and Fenrir. The divine feared the three children because of a prophecy that they would bring about the Twilight of the Gods. So, they banished them," he said as he pointed at a series of carvings. To the first and second, a carving of a bearded man in a winged helmet with the boy and the snake and again the bearded man with the bisected girl, he said, "Odin took the World Serpent first and cast him into the seas. Then, he sent Hel to Niflheim, charging her to be the eternal caretaker of the damned." The next picture they'd already seen, of the wolf and one-handed god. "Then, they took Fenrir, the massive wolf but still little more than a boy in age. They tricked him into playing a game and bet him he could not break their chains. They bound him in all of the strongest chains they knew, but Fenrir-wolf broke every one. So, they turned to the dwarves in desperation, who wove the ribbon Gleipnir from impossible things, and it was impossible to break, even for Fenrir. They locked him away beneath the soil of the world, and pierced his jaws with a sword to hold them open for eternity."

Mila noticed something Eberhard skipped. The man from the earlier depictions, Loki, on his knees in the background of the images, his hands clasped and tears dripping from his face.

Eberhard continued to the last picture, a busy work filled with dozens of figures, including all three of Loki's children, giants, the gods, and the trickster god himself. "And finally, Ragnarök, the day Fenrir will escape his bonds and join his siblings to strike down the gods and destroy Asgard."

"Good riddance," Eiji said.

"Watch it," Waren said. "Those are the Aesir and the Vanir. You want to be cursed dropping into battle?"

"I don't seek the blessings of gods who fear children."

"They were protecting themselves from doom," Waren replied. "Would you not do the same to save your people?"

"They did not protect themselves. They ensured the doom. If Fenrir were never bound, he wouldn't have anything to break free from. The prophecy could not have a hope of being true without the gods acting as they did. They are fools."

"Eiji!" Waren snapped.

"Waren's right, young one. To slander the gods so brashly is unwise," Eberhard said.

Mila couldn't help but admire how much Eiji seemed to have thought about these things. For being a few years younger than Mila, she seemed to have the wisdom of decades more. What's more, Mila couldn't help but think there was truth in what she'd said.

"Eberhard," Niko interrupted, still examining the mural. "You've been on this station longer than any of us. What was this level used for before the refinery was moved down here?"

"Brig," Eberhard replied. "Full on prison, pretty much. They had cells, a cafeteria, recreation areas, even areas to convene for worship. Why?"

Niko carefully considered the room, examining the wall, then other charred-over surfaces. "I believe this was one of those areas of worship." He gestured to the wall, to a rune half-covered in char, one Mila would have never thought twice about had he not pointed it out. But now she recognized it as the rune kaunaz, and it was placed high above any other inscriptions. "I believe it was a shrine to Loki."

It wasn't the presence of the rune that made Mila shudder, but rather the stark silence as it seemed like everyone else held their breath.

"Why would anyone build a shrine to the trickster?" Waren asked. "Nothing but bad can come of that."

"I don't know," Niko replied.

"Makes you wonder if all the master refiners before Mila were cursed because they worked in this place," Eberhard said. "Their fortunes grew so large, so fast, but their lives were so short."

"Enough," Niko said. "I was just making an observation. There's no need to get superstitious about it. We have one focus tonight, and these carvings don't change that. We need to—"

Niko went abruptly silent, and his digital blue eyes seemed distant.

"Niko?" Mila asked.

"He's receiving a message," Waren said. "Always goes still like that when they come in. It's kind of creepy."

The pause lasted only as long as Waren spoke, as Niko's eyes refocused and he said, "We're being summoned. Me and my squad."

"By who?" Mila asked.

"Volkner." Every inch of Niko was taut.

"What?" Waren asked. "At this hour?"

"Waren's right," Eberhard said. "He's a bastard and doesn't care about anyone's time but his own. But this late?"

"Something's wrong," Eiji said, looking intently at Niko.

Niko nodded. "You're all right. This is out of the ordinary, even for the president."

"Can you pretend like you didn't receive it?" Mila asked.

"I could, but he'd know I was lying. Not once has a message failed to get through to me while on the *Gjaller*. All the berserkers have a direct connection to the station's communication array. It's why whoever sent that message was able to route it to me."

Mila loosed a long breath. "Then you have to go."

"What?" Niko asked. "I'm not going. Not if *he* could show up at any time."

"You have to," Mila repeated. "Or else we risk being found out."

"She's right," Eiji said. "Volkner is paranoid. He'll suspect something immediately if you don't answer his call."

Niko scowled, mulling over the situation. Mila knew the Berserker was likely exploring all the different ways he could turn down Volkner and not jeopardize their newly formed strategy.

He finally said, "Fine. I'll go, but I'm only taking Waren and Eberhard. Eiji and Xiomar will stay here with you. He won't be suspicious about me leaving soldiers on guard for the Master Refiner."

The soldiers nodded their understanding, and Waren and Eberhard checked their rifles.

"If it's some kind of trick," Waren said, "we'll do what we've always done and blast our way out of it."

"Just don't be too quick on the trigger," Niko said. "I don't want to have to save you from Volkner's wrath yet again."

"You'll never let me forget the past, will you?"

"It's because of the past we're with the crazy bastard,"

Eberhard said. Then he looked at Mila and said, "Don't worry. We'll get the boy back safe and sound even if he tells us we're off to fight the Megingjörd Dreki."

Eberhard and Waren made their way out of the refinery, and the remaining armor-clad duo took up their posts by the door once more.

Niko waited an extra moment, standing only a foot or so from Mila, but in that moment she wished he'd stand just a little closer.

"I'll be back as soon as I can," he said. "If he shows up before we return, please promise me, no favors."

Mila looked up at him, refusing to let the fear of the thoughts of what could happen in the coming hours show through. She knew it was a promise she might not be able to keep. She knew if it came down to it, she would make a deal with the Rattle Man to help them succeed in their plot. But there was no use admitting it, no use giving the Berserker that weight to bear.

So, she replied with a single word. "Okay."

TWENTY-EIGHT

MILA'S MIND WAS SPLIT. On one half, she was rolling through scenarios of what could happen when the Rattle Man came. The other half was consumed with Niko.

It'd been five hours since he'd left with Waren and Eberhard. She'd tried the communicator, but had only found static on the other end.

"The command level has a blocker for communicators that aren't using the ship's systems," Eiji had explained. "Prevents any potential spies from reporting in real time."

It made sense, and the sentiment was supposed to help ease her mind. But it hadn't.

With every passing minute, it felt like the refinery closed on her a little bit more. They were dangerously close to reveille now, and every moment without the Rattle Man present was time lost to negotiate with him.

Eiji and Xiomar had taken to sleeping in two-hour shifts so one was always on guard. They'd seemed surprisingly comfortable racking out on the metal refinery floor, even turning down Mila's cot when she'd offered it. Mila hadn't been able to sleep with the worry. She'd just sat on the cot, examining the carvings once concealed by the scrap pile. Her thoughts shifted between Niko, then the Rattle Man, then to Eberhard's tale of Ragnarök. It was a clockwork cycle, and none of it gave her any peace.

Xiomar was on watch now, and was on his feet instantly as they heard a noise like the thud of something heavy falling in the hallways beyond the refinery door. It sounded far off, so it wasn't surprising it didn't rouse Eiji.

"I'll take a look," Xiomar said, his hands instinctively checking the hilts of his various sheathed blades.

Mila nodded, and the door ground open, then shut again as he exited, leaving Mila the only conscious person in the room. She was surprised that Eiji still hadn't stirred, but knew it was likely because she'd had to sleep in and around much louder things. For a brief moment, her thoughts were only on Eiji, curiosity swarming of the life the teenager had to have lived already. The possibilities were both amazing and utterly tragic.

The thought dissipated as Fen jumped to his feet, erupting out of sleep mode into full alert. Mila stiffened, that familiar cold slipping through the refinery.

"Eiji," she said, trying to rouse the young warrior. But she didn't move. "Eiji!"

"Oh, that won't be necessary," that too familiar, yet now strangely foreign voice said from the shadows. "She'll be sleeping a little while longer."

Fen's barks reverberated off the refinery walls, stopping only long enough for him to growl.

The Rattle Man, in the form of Úlf, stepped from the corner of the room, out of pure shadow. "Apologies I'm so late."

"Where were you?" Mila said, now on her feet, her eyes blazing.

"Oh, somewhere else, arranging things," he replied casually. "But I'm here and ready to help."

"Do you have any idea what time it is? And how much brandr needs to be refined?"

Úlf looked at the half-dozen loaded pallets set near the first vat. "Ah, our Volkner is getting a bit greedy, I'd say. That will be a bit of a challenge to refine in an hour."

"I know you can do it," Mila said, not breaking her fiery gaze.

"Oh? I've earned your confidence?"

"I know you can do anything in exchange for favors."

Úlf cocked his head, his eyes narrowing and lips curling. "What exactly is it you think you know, Mila?"

"In night black, cold and rain," Mila said. "Comes a man without a name."

Úlf raised his chin, his grin widening. "And what does that old nursery rhyme have to do with me?"

"It's about you. You're him. You're the Rattle Man."

Úlf laughed, and the sound felt like ten thousand ants crawling all over her skin.

"What a strange conclusion to come to," Úlf replied. Then, in the tune of the rhyme he said, "Slither lips and silver tongue, hear his words, too late to run. Tell me, Mila, how did you come to such a bold conclusion?"

"I thought about it," Mila lied. "When you revealed your magic, I knew you weren't just a Jotun ambassador. You kept asking for favors. That's what all the old stories say the Rattle Man does."

"Believable," Úlf said. "But a lie. I can taste your lies, Mila. No, I suppose someone tipped you off that I was here. That annoyance Hans, if I had to guess."

Hans? Mila thought, failing to keep herself from flinching at the name.

"You're surprised?" Úlf asked. "Didn't think dear Papa was clever enough to figure it out?" Úlf shook his head. "There is so much about your family you do not know."

"Then tell me," Mila said. "Tell me why you keep saying I'm so important. Anyone could have been your master refiner. You could have gotten anyone into Volkner's inner circle. You could have gotten there yourself, I'm sure. Why am I so gods-damned important?"

Úlf clicked his tongue. "If I am who you say I am, and you know the old stories, then you also know that's not how things work."

"Name your price," Mila hissed.

"You know my price."

Mila shook her head. "Not that."

"Then you'll never know the secrets I hold about you, your father, and your mother."

Mila didn't respond, only maintained her boiling gaze.

"Look, I understand it's a big decision, giving up a name," Úlf said as if he were selling her a new hoverbike. "Take some time to think on it. Just promise me one more favor, and I'll refine the brandr for you to keep the tyrant happy. Then, after the ball, we can talk more about your parentage."

Mila's brow creased as her mind cycled through thoughts of her father and mother. Volkner had said such things about Hans, things that would seem crazy to the normal person. She knew hardly anything about her father's past, despite near two decades of living with the man. And she knew far less about her mother, the woman who'd left them; the one who Mila could only remember in blurry silhouettes.

Then, her mind went to Niko and Amelie, to Eberhard and Waren, to Eiji and Xiomar. It went to all the servants held on the *Gjaller* against their will. It went to the brandr mines overflowing with the sweat and blood of the damned. Mila knew, not for herself, but for all of those held under the thumb of the Brandt regime, that she must choose justice and liberation, by whatever means necessary.

"I'll do it." Mila said.

For the first time, Úlf seemed surprised.

"My name. I'll give it to you." Mila continued. "But the deal has to be sweetened."

"Name your terms, Miss Messer," Úlf said coolly.

"In addition to refining the brandr and telling me about my parents, you have to help us overthrown Volkner's regime."

Úlf cocked an eyebrow. "That is no small demand."

"It's my price."

Úlf gave her a clever sideways look, as if he were trying to figure her out.

"First the brandr," Úlf said. "Then, we'll rip Volkner's regime apart. We'll make our move at the ball, when the fool's army is drunkest. After that, I'll tell you about your parents."

"Tell me about them first."

Úlf shook his head. "No."

"Why not?"

"It's my insurance, and the thing you want most, more than saving this planet even. It helps me make sure you won't waver."

"You're wrong," Mila hissed. "Saving the Vidarin people from Volkner and his corrupt cronies is my highest priority."

"Stop lying to me, Mila."

Mila bared her teeth at him, and tried to ignore the guilt creeping in the back of her mind that he might be right. No, that he *was* right. She wanted to save Vidar more than she'd ever wanted almost anything. But the thought of knowing who her mother was and why she was so important, and why her father had always been so stoic about her... That, no matter how badly she wanted to deny it, was something she wanted just a little more.

"Fine," she said. "I agree to your terms."

"Oh no, Mila," Úlf said. "It's not that easy, not for a deal like this."

From out of the air itself, Úlf produced a scroll of cream-colored paper, real, tangible paper, and a silver pen with a sharp point, which he held toward Mila.

"If you would kindly," he said.

"You want me to sign. Like a contract?"

"Not *like* a contract. It *is* a contract."

Mila's jaw tensed, and her hands seemed to move slower than she commanded as she took the pen from him.

"Where do I sign?"

Úlf wagged a finger. "First, the ink."

Mila raised a brow, not sure what he was instructing.

"Your blood, Miss Messer. Stab the point in your flesh and it will do the rest."

There was suddenly a loud pounding on the refinery doors, and Mila could barely make out Xiomar's voice yelling something from the other side.

"We haven't got long," Úlf continued.

Mila examined the silver pen. It was nothing special; nondescript in every way except its cool, rounded silver and razor-like head. Yet it felt entirely too heavy in her hand.

The pounding continued, joined by the sound of Fen barking. It was as if the wolfbot were telling her not to do it. No, not telling. Begging.

But the sounds faded away. There was only silence, her

and the pen in her hand. The blade poking through her flesh felt like a wasp's sting, and she could feel her blood flow into it. It was her or Vidar. She knew what she was giving up, knew the memories yet to be made that would be wiped away with the stroke of a pen. But it was her future, her life, her name, her soul, in exchange for prosperity, peace, and safety for all of Vidar. For the new friends she had and the ones she would never know.

With a few strokes, the deal was done, her blood lined across the bottom of the scroll.

"Good," Úlf said, and for the first time, she saw the silver forked tongue flick within his mouth. "Now, for that revolution."

The pounding and Fen's bark were all around her, drowning her in noise. Then Úlf snapped his long fingers, the sound of it deafening, and Mila's world went black.

CHAPTER
TWENTY-NINE

"Mila?" the voice said in the darkness.

There was a light, too far away. Golden, and bright, but little more than a pinhead.

"Mila?" the voice said again.

It was a kind voice, soft, ethereal. Comforting.

"Mila."

"Mila," she repeated the word to herself. That's all it was... a word.

She was floating in the absence, the Yawning Void. The Gaping Abyss. Ginnungagap, the empty space between all things.

It was cold here. Colder than Vidarin nights. Colder than the refinery floor. Colder than any cold she'd felt. Loneliness.

"Mila," she said again. "I knew that name once."

"Mila," the faraway voice said again.

"Whose name was it?"

"Mila!"

The voice was closer now. Very close. And so was the

light. Bright. So bright. Blinding. Golden, like the Ymir star, and every bit as powerful.

"Mila!"

It was no longer the voice of kindness and comfort. No longer beckoning.

No, it was the voice of despair, a compass, trying to guide her somewhere. But where?

The light was upon her now. "Mila!"

She saw a figure. a woman, walking toward her, though she could decipher nothing more. Only her dress, angelic white and green-trimmed, a sash of purest gold.

"Mila!"

The voice was around her, but it did not belong to the light. It belonged to someone else, someone far away. Someone who needed her.

"I'm sorry," Mila said, as she willed her body to turn away from the light. "I must go."

"Mila!"

———◦—•————•—◦———

She woke gasping for air, her throat too tight and her mind fuzzy.

"Mila. Thank the gods," the girl with the black hair and sun-soaked skin beside her said.

"What happened?" The other demanded, this one a man without hair, only pale and scarred flesh.

"I—" she began. But she couldn't remember.

"Mila, look at me," the dark-haired one said.

There was a thing behind the girl. A large thing, made of metal, with glowing eyes. She knew this thing.

"Fen," she whispered. She looked at the girl. "Eiji." She looked at the man. "Xiomar."

The armor-clad duo knelt over her exchanged worried glances.

"Do you remember what happened?" Xiomar asked, this time more gently.

She creased her brow. "Mila."

"Yes," Eiji said. "That's your name."

"My name?"

"Matron's mercy," Xiomar said. "Say you didn't."

"Mila," Eiji said. "Did you see the Rattle Man?"

She nodded, slowly, unsure.

"What happened?"

She thought long, searching through the abyssal darkness to find herself in the murky fog before. To that time when she still had a name.

"Everything," she managed. "He's giving us everything. We're... we're going to do it. We're going to take it all down."

"What did it cost you?"

Mila dropped her head, closing her eyes to hold back the fear and confusion trying to overrun her. It was explanation enough.

Xiomar rubbed a hand over his bald scalp. "Nine bloodied steps, Mila. What have you done?"

"Oh, Mila," Eiji said, resting a ginger hand on Mila's arm, a gesture gentler than anything she'd imagine from the warrior. "I'm so sorry."

"Niko's going to have our guts for this," Xiomar said. "Whenever he gets back."

"Niko," Mila said. "Where is he?"

"Haven't heard from him since he left last night with the dunce twins," Xiomar said. He shook his head. "This entire plan is as broken as that refinery equipment."

"I'm sure they are fine," Eiji said. "It does us no good right now to jump to conclusions. Odds are he was given some assignment—shit work Volkner reserves for our team."

Though Mila's heart felt like it was in a vise, she managed, "Eiji's right. Where they are doesn't matter. They aren't here. We still have a plan to carry out."

Eiji and Xiomar nodded in agreement.

Mila began to recall everything from the night, as she sat up and searched for the hyrrine. She sighed with relief to see plenty of barrels set at the end of the equipment.

"How long until the ball?" Mila asked.

"You were out for a long while," Xiomar said.

"How long until the ball?" Mila repeated.

"Four hours," Eiji replied.

Mila's eyes went wide. "You're saying reveille was six hours ago?!" *And we've heard nothing from Niko?* Is what she left unsaid.

Eiji nodded. "We need to get you upstairs, in fact, so you can get ready. We were about to carry you."

"Get ready?"

"A bath. Hair, make up." Xiomar said.

"We don't have time for that," Mila hissed.

"You have to," Eiji said. "For the same reason Niko answered Volkner's call. You... we have to avoid any suspicion."

Mila nodded. "Okay." She looked at the wolfbot, his digital eyes seeming to sparkle with relief that she'd woken. "But Fen comes too."

THEY'D FOUGHT her on the decision to bring Fen along. Even after she'd argued that they didn't know what would happen after the ball, that he might get stuck in the refinery alone again for years on end. That Volkner wouldn't decommission his bride-to-be's robotic companion, not on Freiheitstag. Or that, even if he did, it would be a better fate than solitude.

In the end, however, the best argument she could make was that she still technically outranked them. Until their coup was in full effect, at least. The decision had resulted in an expedited trip to her room through the most backward, low-traffic corridors, peppered with off glances from a few drunken pedestrians, and more than a little stress for her escorts.

But they'd made it. She was in her assigned room, Fen by her side with Xiomar and Eiji each standing against opposing walls. They were waiting for her pamperers to arrive, or so she called them. Going to a spa was one thing, but what she imagined she was about to endure... that was a special kind of hel that made the refinery seem like paradise.

"They'll make you look like a princess," Eiji had said, knowing full-well it'd get under her skin.

Mila had responded with a dramatic eye roll, and, "I'm happy you still have your humor at a time like this."

When the pamperers did arrive, two well-dressed servants and an aging tailor, they were shocked to see the massive wolfbot lying like a pet dog beside Mila. After the shock subsided, they politely asked Eiji and Xiomar to step outside. The duo resisted for a moment, but with a nod from Mila, obliged.

"We'll be just outside," Eiji said.

"Call if you need us... for *any* reason," Xiomar said.

"Will your, ahem, *pet* be staying," one of the servants asked.

"He's not a pet," Mila replied coolly. "He's my friend. And yes, he will be staying."

The trio didn't question her, and calmly went about their duties. First, the tailor took measurements around her. She wasn't used to people being this close to her, but he was calm and gentle, and his face held a genuine smile to match his kind eyes. He left the room after his measurements, leaving her to the mercy of the remaining two.

The first, a short woman with a Jotun accent, armed with a satchel of cosmetics, asked, "So, what kind of look would you like? Soft, like the petals of a flower? Or fierce, like the wolves of Odin?"

Mila considered it. "Gold," she said. "Gold like the burning Ymir star. And green, green like an emerald."

"Oh," the servant said hesitantly. "I have the gold, but the green... I'll have to check. I brought mostly reds because, well, red and gold are President Brandt's colors."

"No red," Mila said. *That will come later.*

After fishing a palette from her satchel with shades of blue and green, one she swore over and over again she did not know she owned, the duo went to work. It took over two hours for them to finish. But when they were done, Mila could hardly recognize herself. They'd concealed every blemish, accentuated her eyelashes and lips, and outlined her eyes with the green that faded seamlessly into gold.

Her dark espresso hair they'd curled on top and swept to the side. It reminded Mila of a herd of horses stampeding through a shallow river. On the other side, they'd knotted her hair into two braids flush with the scalp. Together, she thought it looked like a style a Valkyrie of Odin would wear.

"What do you think?" The makeup artist asked. "How does it make you feel?"

Mila didn't need to find the word. It was there, in her

reach, just like the entire gods-damned Brandt regime. A single word, uncomplicated and true.

"Powerful."

―――――・――――――

THE TAILOR RETURNED JUST as the beauticians left. He brought with him a garment bag, not unlike the one she'd laid on the bed behind her.

"I believe it is all ready," he said. He started to say something else, but stopped when he saw Mila's face. "Ah, I see."

"What do you see?" Mila asked, genuinely puzzled.

"I could have saved myself some trouble."

Mila cocked her head.

"This dress is no use to you, is it dear?" he asked, patting the garment bag in his hands. "I know because I finished fixing a dress with those exact colors only yesterday for a man who seemed very excited to pick it up."

"You're the one who repaired my dress?" Mila asked.

"Mhmm," the man replied with a wide grin. "Quite possibly the finest materials I've ever had the pleasure of working with." His grin faded as he said, "May I ask why it is you're not donning the President's colors? He requested this dress specifically."

Lies and explanations bounced around Mila's head, but none felt right.

"That's all right," the tailor said. "Forgive a nosy old man for overstepping."

"No, it's not that," Mila said. "It was my mother's dress. And Niko—Lieutenant Schafer—went through the trouble of bringing it to you. Even though I'm not going with him tonight, I just..."

"Say no more," the tailor said. "I was young once,

though I don't look it now. I just hope you know what message you're sending by not wearing his colors."

"I do," Mila said.

"Good."

It wasn't the response Mila expected. She'd expected him to pity her or scold her. Instead, he seemed happy about her answer.

"I've lived on this station a long while now," the tailor said. "Long enough to see Volkner Brandt grow from a bright-eyed revolutionary into a xenophobic tyrant."

"You think he was a good man?"

"Yes, he was. But that was then, and things have changed. Perhaps it's time for them to change again. I think we need new bright-eyed revolutionaries. Who knows, maybe this time they'll truly change Vidar for the better."

"What's your name?" Mila asked.

"Waldo."

"Thank you, Waldo. For the dress, and for your words."

"No, thank you, Miss Messer," he said, placing a gentle hand on hers. "Not for what you have done, but for the things you will do."

CHAPTER
THIRTY

After the tailor had left, Mila sat in silence, pondering the old man while she waited for her guard duo to reenter. A few minutes went by, and she knew it had to be close to time for her to make her way to the great hall. She stood to go check the door, just as someone pounded on it.

Fen was on his feet growling immediately.

"Master Refiner!" A voice said from the other side, a voice she recognized, but not as one of her friends. "It's time to go."

"Where are my guards, Sauer?" Mila demanded.

"They've been reassigned," Sauer said. "I've been tasked with escorting you to the ball."

"On who's authority?"

"The president's."

Mila could hear her too-fast heartbeat echo in her head. She withdrew the small black communicator which she'd stowed away in one of the dress' hidden pockets.

"Niko," she said, praying for a response.

But there was only static.

"I don't like this, Fen," she said to the wolfbot looking up at her. "I don't like it at all."

"Miss Messer," Sauer repeated, the call like poison on her ears. "I must insist you come on."

Mila didn't want to think of the countless things that could have happened to all of them. Didn't want to imagine what Volkner did to usurpers. But if they had been found out, if they were the government's prisoners, there was only one way to save them now.

"What do you say, boy," she said, placing a hand between Fen's shoulder plates. "Are you ready to make an entrance?"

Fen growled in approval.

When the door hissed open, Mila found Sauer and a detail of six Viking-armored and heavily armed guards. All of them flinched when they saw her, and the massive vél stalking beside her.

"That *thing* cannot come," Sauer spat. "And *you're* not wearing the dress made for you."

"No," Mila said. "I'm wearing the one you and your men nearly ruined. It's been restored. But don't think for one moment I've forgiven you for tarnishing it. As for Fen, he comes, unless you want to try and stop him."

Even though Fen could not actually harm anything, it didn't stop the bot from taking a step forward, making Sauer's already pale skin turn a shade whiter.

"Fine," he said.

The officer stepped out of the doorway for them to pass. Mila took a breath, but kept her eyes hard and constant. There was a well of fear within her, but now she could not show it. No fear, no regrets. There was only room to show strength now. Strength and dangerous defiance.

Still, that didn't stop her world from slowing when she walked through the doorway, and saw servants cleaning fresh bloodstains only a few feet away.

THE DOORS to the great hall towered above her. They were shut, leaving her to examine the two massive twin depictions of Thor, one on either door. The storm god had been carved in full armor and flowing cape, with a broad chest and arms as thick as logs. In his hands he held the short-handled Mjolnir, the greatest weapon ever forged. A war hammer said to be unstoppable, one that would fell any foe. Mila couldn't help but wish she had such a weapon right now.

On the other side of the doors, Mila could hear the crowd already in festive mood. There were songs playing, men singing, and the smell of mead and ale wafting from every direction.

She'd been the last to arrive, which was fitting, considering she was to be announced as Volkner's newest prize. A little trinket, soon to be forgotten, as Sauer had said on their walk to the great hall. If their plan succeeded, by some miracle, she silently swore she'd cut Sauer's tongue out herself.

"They're about to announce you," Sauer said without an ounce of compassion. "Don't trip."

Mila breathed deep and closed her eyes, imagining every one of her friend's faces. Imagining all the people she intended to save. All those she'd given her very name for.

Her name. Something that felt so hollow and distant now. A sentiment from a life past. Something taken. A name placed upon her soul when she was born, and one removed with a flick of a silver pen.

A name that sounded both familiar and foreign to her when the herald announced it, and the great hall doors began to creep open.

CHAPTER

THIRTY-ONE

Piper DeRache sat in full Tyran silks by the already drunken Huber, in a hall full of equally drunk and utterly obnoxious men. She'd allowed her crew the pleasures of spirits and certain substances on occasion, but never in extreme excess and never at a time when it could jeopardize the *Thialfi's* safety. And if they ever let those luxuries get the better of their judgement, her justice was swift and unyielding.

At one end of the hall were massive double doors. They opened every few minutes and a herald at a podium in front of the head table announced the arrival of some honored guest. He'd just announced a portly general by the name of Grobe with his much younger Hodian wife. Then came a man called Voight, a famous merchant, and one Piper personally knew to have his hands deep in the blood money on the black market. More names were called, some she recognized, others she didn't. None did she particularly care about.

She cared only about the head table, where Volkner sat drinking wine and smiling like the smug snake he was.

There was an especially high concentration of armed guards along the walls close to the head table. Piper knew Volkner was a cautious man, but she counted at least three dozen armor-clad guards within a fifty-foot radius of him, far more than she'd expect him to post at an annual celebration. Behind the table was a massive viewing window, but its blast shields were deployed, blocking any view out in to the void.

The men around her though were loud and cocky bastards, most of whom couldn't retain their decency through even a single drink. Piper suspected it was the side effect of a culture that prized warring over everything else. A culture where young boys learn they can have whatever they want, so long as they're bold enough to take it. And that boldness came with mead and ale, as did the groping hands and shameless speaking. They made Piper sick.

"Miss Frida," a voice said from behind her.

She turned to find Atli in a suit the same style as that she'd met him in, though this one was more adorned for festivities. Well, he had a pin of mistletoe on, at least.

More something for Yule. But the thought was fleeting.

She stood from the table, glad to get away from the drunken soldiers. Her date was so slack faced that he didn't even seem to notice her leave.

"Good to see you made it," Atli continued.

Piper nodded. "Easy enough with these morons," she said, low enough none around would hear; not that anyone looked even remotely interested in their conversation.

"Did you manage to get your message out?"

Piper nodded again.

"And?"

"I think they received it. Beyond that, I can't say what to expect from them."

Atli raised his chin and put on a pensive look. "I predict we'll get quite the show tonight."

Piper shrugged. "We'll see. And your side of things?"

"I have people where they need to be," Atli replied like a true businessman.

"How will I know when to strike?"

"When your friends arrive, there will be chaos. In the initial confusion, before his guards have the chance to usher him away, you'll get your chance for vengeance."

Vengeance. The word was like honey on her ears. Her revenge on the tyrant bastard was so close. But she had to stow the eagerness, the excitement. She had to be logical, smart, and patient.

The doors opened and the herald announced Mr. and Mrs. Roth, the head of the family in charge of overseeing most of the Vidarin brandr mines. That shameless name had profited off the forced labor of others for decades.

"Ah, I believe the festivities will begin soon," Atli said. "Best find my seat. You should find yours as well and pay attention. They're announcing the Master Refiner soon. She's quite something."

Piper, who'd stolen a glance at the Roth's, turned back to find Atli gone. His sudden departure left a chill in her bones.

As she sat back down, the herald took the podium in front of the head table again.

"Your attention once more, please," the stout man said.

Once again, a sobering silence fell over the expanse of soldiers and guests.

"Announcing our honored guest," he said. "Master of all Vidarin brandr refining, the honorable Mila Messer."

The great doors opened, and what walked through was not what Piper had expected. The gasps and enduring, shocked quiet of the crowd told her it was not what they'd expected either.

It was a girl. She wore a dress of purest white with verdant accent. Tied around her waist was a sash of astonishing gold. Beside her prowled a Mark IV Fenrir vél, matching her pace perfectly.

She walked with her chin high and her eyes straight, and Piper thought she looked every bit like the old descriptions of the Vanir. Piper also noticed the girl's unwavering gaze was set on one person, and one person only. Piper knew that gaze. It was not one of admiration or trust or friendship. It was the same look she knew adorned her own face when looking upon someone who'd crossed her. It was a look of promise, unmistakable in its meaning. A promise of a debt to be collected. And it was set on one person; the very debtor Piper intended to collect from.

Volkner Brandt.

Piper suddenly grabbed her leg as searing pain shot through it. She could hardly breathe, it was so intense. The drunken fools around her didn't even notice. They were too busy gawking at the girl in the middle of the room.

"Nine bloody shits," she cursed under her breath, squeezing the flesh where it met the robotic limb as hard as she could.

It was delayed rejection, the very risk Einar had warned her about and the reason he wanted her to stay on Jotun the full two weeks.

Piper withdrew a syringe from within the flowing silks. She'd only just taken the previous dose a half hour ago, but the pain was too much. Her body was quite literally fighting her robotic leg. Every nerve sang with pain as the flesh tried to separate. She wanted to scream, to drop to the floor and beg someone to help her. But she couldn't do that. She couldn't throw her chance away. Not now. Not when she was so very close.

Piper plunged the syringe through the robes into her thigh. She knew the danger of the action: the possibility of overdosing. But if she was going to be captured or die anyway, it was well worth the risk if the drug had any possibility of giving her the chance to cut Volkner down.

It was mere seconds before the sounds of the room began to fade, as if she was getting farther away from the festivities without moving. All the conversations melded into a single dull roaring. The lights seemed brighter now, and her movements felt delayed.

She grabbed a glass of water on the table and drank it down in a single pull. This wasn't good. She wasn't fully in control of herself now. The pain of the limb trying to rip away from her body was masked, but the cost was great. She'd be going up against Volkner at an even greater disadvantage now. That was if she ever got the chance at all.

CHAPTER

THIRTY-TWO

No one spoke a word as Mila and Fen strode down the long red and gold carpet toward the head table. Volkner, who'd grimaced at first, had relaxed his face into a clever smile. He was making his moves in his mind, as was she. All Mila could hope for was that her entrance had thrown off course whatever his plan for the night had been.

She took the seat on his left, Fen sitting behind her on the stage. The seat to his right, however, was still vacant, even though she was supposed to be the last guest.

"Quite the entrance, Miss Messer," he said, taking a sip of blood-red wine.

"Fitting of the future bride of Volkner Brandt, I hope," Mila said, making sure he heard the false courtliness in her voice.

"Indeed. I would expect nothing less than bold. And coming in with a weapon so erratic and unstable that we ordered them all scrapped—that's certainly bold."

"Where's your other guest?" Mila asked.

"Oh, they'll be along shortly, I imagine. No need to wait though."

Volkner gestured to the herald who signaled that the feast, and the night's festivities were to begin. The doors from all around the room opened, with well-dressed servants carrying platters of all arrays of food from across the system entering. Entire roasted boars, game birds, bowls of steaming vegetables, vats of ale and wine and mead. There were plates of fruits and baskets of breads set with butter and honey. There were even shellfish that Mila did not recognize, likely smuggled in from Idun or Hod. It was the biggest feast of the holiday yet to match the biggest night of Freiheitstag.

"Isn't it impressive?" Volkner asked. "All these people, all with drinking horns overflowing and more food than they can hope to finish. It's as if Valhalla is here tonight instead of in Asgard."

As he spoke, a group of performers took to the center of the room. They were the same troupe Mila had seen in the market. Acrobats and jugglers with flaming axes. A contortionist with a skin-tight suit and face paint to make her appear as a serpent. The feats and flips and tricks they performed were truly magnificent, both in the square and now.

"It is something," Mila replied. "Though I wonder how so much food can be here; enough that it cannot possibly be eaten by all these soldiers and guests, and yet the people on the surface of Vidar are resigned to the most basic of foods to survive."

Volkner laughed. "There was once a time when I would have wondered the same thing. But now, I find it fruitful to reward those close to me with treasures. It attracts more to my ranks, and makes Vidar stronger."

"A well-fed people would make Vidar stronger as well."

"Vidar the planet, possibly."

"What other Vidar is there?" Mila asked.

"Vidar the ideal," Volkner said. "An empire unquestioned by the system, full of food and drink enough for all Vidarins to never go wanting. But for that, I need loyal soldiers, and as much as they disgust me, politicians."

Mila said nothing.

"What I don't need," Volkner continued, "is a few drips of poison causing earthquakes. Toxic ideas, if given breath, can threaten the very fiber of what we've worked so hard to build. Do you agree?"

"I agree," Mila said. "A great tree cannot be felled by the first blow." She saw Volkner's eyes narrow as she spoke the words. "But nor can it fall without it. And if it is a tree that blocks the view of many from seeing the sunrise, then others will line up to cut it down."

"Yes," Volkner said. "Very bold, indeed."

Other acts followed the troupe. The first was a bard reciting tales of the gods. Mostly the ones that showed Thor in a pleasant light, the stories where he defended Asgard from giants or put a stop to his brother, Loki's, trickeries.

The next act was a single girl, wearing simple, traditional clothes crafted in the style of the Vikings of old. She sang in the old language as well. Volkner explained it was the tragedy of Baldur, and his accidental death at the hands of his blind brother, Hod. Mila knew the story well; the same displayed by the actors in the wealthy district, albeit without the melancholy of the current interpretation. The story of how the Trickster had taken advantage of Hod's desire to be a part of the godly games, and given him an arrow infused with mistletoe—the only thing that could kill the near-invincible Baldur.

Though she couldn't understand her words, Mila found them absolutely beautiful. Her voice and soft tone put all conversations in the hall to rest, as everyone lent her their ears. Mila thought there was something very tragic about her voice here, amongst these people. This was a horrible place. It was not the place for beautiful voices or words. It was not the place for angels.

As the girl's song came to an end, many of the guests, and even a few of the soldiers, had to wipe their eyes. Hers was the only performance that ended with an applause.

As if the girl's finale were his queue, Volkner stood.

"Greetings, friends and comrades!" the president announced. "Skal!"

The room boomed with a resounding "Skal" in response.

"I am so honored to be amongst such great warriors on this night, Freiheitstag. Every year, we convene to feast and drink in celebration of the day we took back our freedom from the clutches of a foreign power. But this year, I am pleased to announce we have much, much more to cele-brate!" Volkner reached a hand toward Mila, who hesitantly accepted it and rose beside him. "First, our hyrrine supplies grow like drips from Draupnir every day, thanks to our newest Master Refiner."

The soldiers cheered, many of them spilling drinks in the process.

"And to show my gratitude for her diligent work, I have decided to reward Mila Messer."

Mila braced for the marriage announcement, the flesh over her entire body crawling with a thousand ants.

"I am going to absolve her of her duties and allow her to return home, retaining all benefits and compensations of the highest presidential staffers until her last day."

The room's cheers died into a confused, murmur-laced hush. Mila looked at Volkner, who shot her a quick grin like a fox. Then, he gestured for her to return to her seated position.

"I am also disappointed to announce," Volkner continued, "that we discovered a group of rebel sympathizers on board this very station plotting a coup d'état."

The crowd's murmurs grew louder, shifting into alarm.

"Rest your minds, brothers," Volkner said. "We have already identified and detained those involved."

The doors to the great hall crept open to make way for a massive, rolling object. It was a small stage, pushed along by over a dozen servants. Behind the stage, gagged, bound, and bloodied, escorted by a dozen armed guards, were Xiomar and Eiji.

On top of the stage, there were two poles, a man chained by his arms in between them. He had no shirt on, and Mila recognized the old runes tattooed down his muscled flesh. He was gagged as well, and the chains holding him were far thicker than any one would expect for a single man. His glowing, digital eyes wove the promise of fury if he ever broke his bonds. Just as Fenris-wolf would one day break free from Gleipnir and return to kill Odin in Ragnarök, so, too, if those chains ever failed, would Niko Schafer return to take the life of Volkner.

The crowd booed as the traitors were escorted in. Many threw food and drinking horns, unconcerned with the expensive carpet or the servants tasked with moving the stage. More than a few items found their mark on Niko's arms, his torso, his head. But his eyes did not shift once. They were not on Volkner, promising the repayment of a debt owed, as Mila's had been. Instead, they were focused on Mila, another promise being made. Yes, if he broke from those bonds, there was a promise. They would kill Volkner,

and they would dismantle it all, with or without the
Rattle Man.

Mila's chest felt tight, and that burning, feral rage
rushed through her. The elerex shocked, fighting it back,
but Mila drowned it out. She put that pain in the void
where she'd floated when she'd lost her name. Far away. It
would not touch her here. Even if she couldn't use her arm
and the electricity threatened to stop her heart, she would
not release that anger. Not now.

"Tonight, we will bring justice to these insects," Volkner
said, gesturing toward Niko and the other prisoners. "In the
old ways. The lessers shall be thrown to the void. And the
Berserker, he shall know the greatest of punishments. For
those festivities to come, I give you a taste."

Volkner raised a hand toward the blast panels behind
him, which hissed and groaned as they began to open. They
revealed the great viewing window spanning the length and
height of the hall. One of Vidar's moons was in view, and a
cut of Vidar itself. But neither were the focal point.

Mila covered her mouth as tears stormed her eyes. She
heard Niko scream, muffled through his gag. There was a
commotion from the guards around Eiji and Xiomar as well,
as they were tackled to the floor and beaten. The rest of the
room clapped and cheered. And Volkner smiled.

Outside the viewing window, chained to the *Gjaller* so
they would not drift away, were the frozen, lifeless bodies of
Waren and Eberhard.

THIRTY-THREE

The drinking horn Mila held cracked in her hand.

"You're a monster," she hissed at Volkner.

"I'm a leader," he replied. "Protecting my people."

Though the cheers continued, Mila saw that Niko had stopped screaming. Now the Berserker was hanging limp in his chains, staring at the stage beneath him.

"I believe I've broken his spirit," Volkner said, unenthused. "Shame, I thought it'd last just a little longer. I wanted to see if his body or mind would go first in the blood eagle."

Mila was on her feet instinctively. "You can't."

"Oh, but I can, Miss Messer. And I fully expect to. Lieutenant Schafer will serve as a shining example that no one, no matter how lethal or how expensive, is above my law."

Volkner turned to the crowd and raised his hands. "My brothers!"

The cheering faded so the patrons could hear their leader.

"I must admit, I could not have discovered these filthy

rebels alone. I have my faithful servant, and newly appointed spymaster to thank for that."

The Great Hall doors opened once more, revealing a single figure. A girl wearing the crimson and gold dress Mila recognized from the night in the theater. The figure was the same as well. It was the one who'd been on Volkner's arm that night. The woman who'd moved with such calm confidence and lethality. The one in the mask. Though, now she wore no mask, and her face, it may as well have been a mistletoe arrow through Mila's chest.

Amelie.

The crowd clapped and sang her praises as Amelie strode to the head table. Mila met her eyes and found them untimid, and unapologetic. It looked like Xiomar had been knocked unconscious by the guards, but Eiji was bucking again, spouting unintelligible curses at the girl. Niko simply looked at her as she passed the stage and shot a smug smile his way. That smile shifted to Mila for the rest of the walk, all the way until she took a seat in the empty seat on Volkner's right flank.

"Hope I didn't miss anything too fun," Amelie said, her tone unlike any Mila had ever heard from her. It was cunning, mocking, and comfortable in its cruelty.

"Nothing much, my dear," Volkner said as if Eberhard and Waren's corpses were as uninteresting as the chains binding them to the station. "The real festivities are only beginning."

"Have you enjoyed the night so far, Mila?" Amelie asked.

"You're a snake," Mila replied, maintaining the inferno of rage swirling through her veins. Her eyes on Volkner, she asked, "Has she always been your pet?"

"She's been a valuable asset to me for some time now,"

Volkner said. "She's told me so many interesting things about you and your *friends*. I have an even deeper interest in that ambassador now, especially."

"What did she tell you?"

"I told him enough," Amelie said.

"I wasn't asking you," Mila snapped. "I won't stoop to talking to a serpent in the grass and let it bite me again."

"You don't have to stoop to be bitten," Amelie said. "A crafty snake will find a way."

"You're such a disappointment."

Volkner laughed. "I could listen to you two go back and forth all night! But it's time for dancing."

Volkner took Mila's hand in his own and prompted her to the empty space in front of Niko's stage. She'd never danced before, not with someone else, and the fact her first time was with Volkner Brandt... that was a memory she'd be haunted by for the rest of her life.

A band with traditional instruments: a simple drum, a lyre, flutes, horns, and a bagpipe—style woodwind—began to play a slow tune from their stage on the far side of the room.

Volkner led and Mila followed well enough, though every second his hands were on her the urge to rip his throat out became more and more unbearable.

Before long, they were joined by dozens of soldiers and their dates dancing drunkenly. The band shifted from slow into staccato and jaunty. Mila caught glimpses of Niko and Eiji, both who held promises of death and violence in their eyes. Whenever she saw Amelie, the girl had a pretentious, arrogant smirk on her face, and Mila made sure her eyes told the story of every horrible way she wanted Amelie to die, both for what happened to Waren and Eberhard, and what would happen to Eiji, Xiomar, and Niko.

A point came when dancing partners switched. Mila was passed to an aging lieutenant with a massive moustache first, and then to a private so drunk she had to help hold him upright. After that, there was a man nearly a foot taller than her, and another a foot shorter. Then, she was passed off to someone she did not know, but who felt intensely familiar.

The man seemed old, older than her father or Volkner even. Yet his slicked back hair was obsidian black without even a suggestion of gray. His ensemble was an old, earthen-style three-piece dinner suit, the kind you simply didn't see anywhere anymore. It was tailored to fit him perfectly. His movements in the dance were smooth and strong, more direct than any others she'd danced with so far.

"Hello, Mila."

It wasn't his voice or his look that told Mila who he was. It was the *way* he said her name, and the silver tongue he said it with.

This was the Rattle Man.

"You decided to drop the ambassador routine?" Mila asked.

"Recent developments rendered that form a liability, wouldn't you say?"

"So, you knew then? That something was wrong?"

"Of course I did. What do you think I am?"

"You could have saved Eberhard and Waren. Niko and Eiji and Xiomar are going to die now because of this mess."

"None of them are my concern. We have our deal, and I have but one objective at the moment, to help you take this all down. Your friends' lives are inconsequential."

"So then what is your plan?" Mila asked through clenched teeth.

"I thought that'd be obvious. I'm going to destroy this station."

Mila's eyes went wide. "What? You can't do that!"

"And why not? It's the most direct way to bringing about the change you want. Volkner and all of his cronies and higher-ups are stationed on this station. Don't worry, I have an escape already arranged for you and I."

"There are also thousands of innocents. What about the servants and the traders and vendors? What about my friends, who are trying to help us?"

"I already told you," the Rattle Man said. "Inconsequential. You'll learn soon enough how miniscule their lives really are in the scheme of things."

"You can't do this. Not like this; this was not our deal."

"Our deal was very simple, but very unbreakable. You gave me your name, and in exchange, I agreed to refine last night's brandr, tell you about your parents, and overthrow Volkner and his regime. Methods of doing these things were not discussed, so I can achieve them any way I choose."

Monsters on every side of me.

She gathered herself, trying to think of a way out of this horror. "How do you plan to do it?"

"Not that it matters, but the reactors."

"You're going to destabilize them?!" Mila said, her mouth wide with astonishment.

"With a little help from some allies."

Mila noticed him eyeing the servants lining the walls of the Great Hall.

"An army ready for their moment to be provoked," the Rattle Man said. "An army that would rather die than live out their days imprisoned here. We're going to give that to them. We're going to be their salvation."

"I won't let you," Mila said, starting to pull away from him.

The Rattle Man clicked his silver tongue. "Ah, I'm not quite finished with this dance, Mila."

It was as if an invisible force pushed Mila back to him. She tried to pull away, but her limbs would not respond.

"Have you already forgotten you owe me?" the Rattle Man asked. "I own you, Mila Messer."

Mila sneered at the man. "I'm going to stop you."

The Rattle Man laughed. "And how do you possibly imagine you'll do that?"

Mila thought and thought, but no solution came to mind. She didn't know the answer. She didn't know how she could possibly stop him, how she could possibly save all the innocents aboard the *Gjaller*.

"Nothing?" the Rattle Man asked. "Pity. I was really curious to hear what you'd come up with. Of course, no matter what it was, it wouldn't work. After all, I do already own your name."

My name? Mila thought, remembering how empty the mention of it made her feel. But the thought shifted into something else, something knocking in the back of her mind. *In night black, cold and rain, comes a man without a name.* The old nursery rhyme, the one that had told her who Úlf was. The one referenced in the message... the message... *Find the name.*

"Úlf," Mila said intently.

"You should know better. That's not really my name."

"*I know,*" Mila said, narrowing her eyes on him.

The Rattle Man's brows raised. "Ah, I see. So, you do have a plan, then?"

"Hammond," Mila said, trying to gauge his response. "Heinrich, Hann, Harry."

The Rattle Man laughed again. "You'll be at it for quite a while with that approach. Still, quite a creative thought. I wish you all the best of luck with it. While you rattle off names, just know I don't make deals lightly, and you will not stop me from delivering on ours." The Rattle Man leaned close to her ear and whispered, "And one other thing. You shouldn't believe everything you hear in stories."

"But they all contain a kernel of truth," Mila replied.

The Rattle Man gave her one last devil's grin and said, "Good luck, Miss Messer."

With that, Mila was released, and the Rattle Man seemed to disappear into the crowd just as the music came to an end. Mila continued cycling through names in a whisper, hoping one would catch. *Find the name.*

"Klaus. Kelby. Kellen."

"Everyone," the herald at the podium announced. "Please return to your seats. The night's main event will begin soon."

The main event. The executions. Niko's blood eagle. She didn't have much time, as the Rattle Man made it clear his move was not going to be made in time to save them.

"Len. Leon. Leopold."

She walked slowly, staring at the floor in stark concentration. He was right, this would take her too long. But what other choice did she have?

"Webber. Wendall. Wilber."

"Now, my brothers!" Volkner announced. "I satiate your warrior's thirst with blood!"

A hooded man armed with a runed archaic hatchet took the stage. Mila knew the weapon. She'd seen it on Niko's hip every day since she'd arrived.

"We've administered special drugs to the Berserker to slow his healing, allowing us to perform the sacred ritual in the way the gods intended!"

"Orlin. Otho. Otis."

"This is our greatest offering to you, almighty Thor! Take this traitor's blood as tribute! Weave your will into our hands and give us your strength as we look back across Ginnungagap, to the savage planet Hod. Show us the path to victory. The path to glory. And let those who fall feast in Valhalla!"

The crowd yelled and chanted, the soldiers acting as if they wanted to deploy in the very moment to slaughter all in their way.

No god wants this. No god would entertain this malice.

"Penn. Pepin. Poldie."

"Commence the ceremony!"

Mila watched in horror as Niko's eyes widened in pain when the blade of his own axe carved into the flesh of his back. Her time was up. She couldn't afford to keep spouting the names in hopes she may stumble upon the right one.

She could see the Rattle Man now. He was sitting on the inside edge of one of the long tables. The only one in the room, besides Niko, looking at her, smiling like a Cheshire cat. She hated him, hated the man—the thing—for what he'd done to her. Done to them. What he was going to do to everyone aboard the station. She hated that he had her name. She hated that he'd tricked her into believing he could refine brandr into hyrrine. Hated that he'd tricked her into offering favors before she could hope to know their gravity.

Tricked.

He'd tricked her. Úlf, the Rattle Man, had tricked her. He'd tricked all of them, from the very first people to write his tale in a storybook. He'd tricked them into believing that in the dark came a man with no name. He had a name. He'd always had a name. Yet he'd *tricked* them.

"Loki Laufeyson!"

Mila was standing, pointing at the Rattle Man, her blood boiling and her conviction resolute.

Every eye in the room found her. The soldiers, the guests, Eiji, Niko, even the hooded man and Volkner beside her. All of them looked at her, most of them confused, some chuckling drunkenly. But some, namely her friends and the president, looked intrigued, waiting for the explanation for such an outburst.

"Loki Laufeyson. *That* is your name."

The Rattle Man was not smiling anymore. No, his gaze was that of a wolf. No, a viper. No, his gaze was the promise of death. Or perhaps it was all three.

He stood and walked to the center of the Great Hall, armed with a walking cane in his left hand, in view for all to see.

"Congratulations, Mila Messer," the suit-man said.

"What is the meaning of this?" Volkner demanded.

"Mila has cracked the code. She's discovered the Rattle Man's true name." The suit-man replied.

"Who are you?" Volkner said, now standing as well.

"Are you deaf, old man?" The man's form began to shift then. First, it was into that of a servant woman. Then, into the silver-haired ambassador. Finally, he began to grow, his skin stretching too tight. "She's just told you. I am the Warlock of Asgard. The Trickster of Old. I am the one with poison in his eye and in his heart. I am hate incarnate."

He grew nearly a foot taller than the tallest man in the room, as his tightened skin began to rip, revealing obsidian fur beneath. His eyes turned silver, matching the forked, silver tongue flicking from between his lips when he spoke. His shadow was darker than any other shadow in the room. Darker than any shadow there'd ever been. A shadow as black as death.

"I am the blamed, the bound, and the discarded. The stolen babe. The broken, belittled link between gods and giants. I am the father of many, the seed of Ragnarök."

The cane stretched into a black-shafted spear with a polished, leaf-shaped blade. His true form was in full view now; a bipedal, humanoid wolf with vicious claws and elongated limbs.

"I am Loki."

CHAPTER
THIRTY-FOUR

PIPER WAS on her feet instantly, as were most of the guests, save a few soldiers who were simply too drunk to comprehend what was happening. Everyone was backing away from the wolf-like creature that had just emerged from what was formerly Atli.

"*I am Loki.*"

That's what he'd said, just after the Messer girl had stood and declared it. And then he'd turned into... *this.*

All bets were off, all plans altered. She suddenly knew, even if the rebels didn't show up, people were about to die. Not just Volkner, stabbed through the heart in Piper's glorious revenge. But a lot of people—soldiers and innocents alike. These were uncharted waters. She'd come face to face with evil before on plenty of occasions. But this... at best, he was a boogeyman straight out of a horror story. At worst, he really was Loki, and he was angry.

"Get to the docking bays," she said to servants frozen in place nearby. "Go now! Tell every servant you see along the way to go too. Get off this station any way you can!"

She didn't know if the rebels would show up. She didn't

know if any of the servants could pilot hijacked ships or if traders would board them and flee the *Gjaller* before things went bad. But she did know that now was their only chance to get away before blood was spilt. She could worry about everything else later.

She repeated the order to those near her and several began to understand and act. Soon, they were vacating the Great Hall en masse, the Vidarin soldiers far too distracted to stop them. One belligerently drunk officer who didn't seem to realize there was a god standing in the center of the room tried to stop her speaking. She promptly snapped his neck using the ridiculous strength of her robotic arm and took the plasma pistol on his hip.

Rebels, soldiers, servants, gods. No matter what else emerged in the Great Hall tonight, Volkner Brandt was still going to die.

———

Mila felt strength and purpose surge in her blood as the thought of her name no longer felt foreign. He was Loki, the Trickster. She'd spoken his true name, resolving her debts and regaining her name, just like all the old Rattle Man stories. And according to those stories, knowing the true name gave even mortals power over him.

"I command you to leave this place," Mila said, noticing the servants already starting to exit the room.

"Oh, Mila," Loki said, his voice rough like gravel, but still clearly articulated. "Didn't I tell you? You shouldn't believe everything in stories."

Mila felt something in her gut tighten as he spoke free of any supernatural restraint.

"True, your little revelation made me drop my disguise

and release your name. But to think you have power over me?"

There was a single Vidarin soldier who'd stumbled forward while everyone else backed away. The unlucky bastard was just within reach of Loki's long arm, as the god's clawed hand wrapped around his head. Then, to make his point that Mila had no power to stop him, Loki crushed the man's skull like a grape.

Loki stretched his neck, and Mila could hear the vertebrae cracking.

"It feels so good not to hide anymore," he said, licking the fresh gore from a finger. "Now, I can take this disgrace of a station down for good."

"You'll do no such thing, Trickster," Volkner said.

"Watch me, false king."

His movements weren't even a blur. They were virtually non-existent. Before Mila could blink once, Loki had appeared close to the nearest group of soldiers, piercing one through with a spear and gouging out another's throat with his razor-like claws. Their dates and plenty of others around them screamed. And then all chaos broke loose.

The soldiers who'd had weapons on them, along with the guards, began firing without hesitation. A hail of thousands of glowing plasma rounds descended on Loki. Many struck him, in his back, his chest, his head. Some found the tables, the chairs, the walls. But far too many found allies and the innocent dates and traders too slow to hit the ground before the gunfire broke loose.

"Fen, let's go!" Mila shouted to the wolfbot behind her.

Volkner had thrown the table over and drawn not his pistol, but the plasma-edged handaxe at his side. Amelie sat speechless and still, and Mila had the brief desire to punch her in the teeth, but there wasn't time for that. She and Fen had to get to their friends.

The first volley of shots ended with dozens of Vidarins, and guests wounded or killed, and Loki consumed in a smoky haze. Mila and Fen used the brief pause to sprint the length of the Great Hall. By the time they got there, however, Eiji had already killed one of her guards while the others had charged into the action and was finishing undoing her bonds with his keys. Mila watched as Eiji walked to the hooded man hiding behind the stage, kneed him in the groin and punched his throat, then disarmed him and cleaved Niko's handaxe into his skull.

The move was so casual and smooth Mila thought the teen could have done it a thousand times. Perhaps she had.

"Here," Eiji said, tossing the hooded man's keys to Mila. "Get Niko. I'll get Xiomar."

Mila ascended the stage as Fen growled and barked toward anyone foolish enough to get close. Niko was still slumped as she unlocked his chains.

"Did they get him?" he asked.

Mila looked to where the haze around Loki was beginning to clear. "I can't tell. I think... wait."

The shroud finished clearing, and Loki came into view, utterly unharmed, and his smile lupine.

"Matron's mercy," Mila said.

"It would take Thor's lightning to kill him," Niko said.

"We're fresh out of that at the moment," Mila replied as she undid the final lock, and the chains fell limp. "Can you walk?"

Niko nodded, standing slowly.

"We have to get off the ship, now."

"I can't," Niko replied. "Not yet. I can't leave until Volkner is dead, or else I put my whole family at risk."

"What?!" Mila asked. "What are you talking about? Loki is going to take the whole station down!"

"No, he's not. He would have done it already, but he can't."

"The wards," Mila said, suddenly realizing why Loki had needed people to help him in his plot. "The runes on the reactor doors. He can't get past them because he's a god."

"Exactly. He won't take down the station. But we will."

"Niko," Mila said. "There are thousands of innocent people on board. We can't just blow it up."

Niko looked around the room, his jaw clenched, and nostrils flared. "Then I'll have to kill Volkner here. And stop Loki."

Mila thought about arguing. Thought about dropping any sense of higher cause and begging him to flee with her. The people weren't their responsibility. Not really. Her mind knew it, but she didn't really believe it.

"Okay," she said. "Do what you must to kill Volkner. But after that, we have to go. If Loki can't blow up the reactors himself, then it doesn't matter. We can leave."

Niko nodded, then gestured to Eiji for his axe, who tossed it up. Xiomar was on his feet now as well, battered and bloody, but conscious and moving of his own ability. They'd each collected plasma-edged blades from nearby bodies.

"You all go," Niko commanded. "Get Mila out of here."

Mila smiled and said, "Ignore that order. None of us leave until we all leave."

"Yeah," Xiomar said. "You thought we'd just tuck tail when Volky owes us such a steep debt."

"We're with you until the end," Eiji said. "For Waren and Eberhard."

Niko nodded. "Very well. Then let's see who can reach the gates of Hel first."

⊰————◦———————◦——◦⊱

PIPER THREW her silken Tyran robes aside so she could move easily in her leathers hidden underneath. Volkner was walking toward the wolf-beast armed with a plasma handaxe. She wasn't about to give that *thing* the satisfaction of taking her kill.

The pistol in her left hand and a war hammer she'd swiped off a distracted soldier in her right, she leapt a table and broke into a sprint. She navigated the crowd as nimbly as she could, but running with the robotic leg was awkward and unnatural. Not to mention the drugged haze from so many narcotics coursing through her system. It was enough to make running around people too inconvenient. So, instead, she simply started knocking them out of her way.

She broke through the last line of soldiers as their volley of gunfire ended, and they were forced to reload. The wolf-like figure was wholly concealed by haze and smoke, but Piper knew there was little chance it—whatever *it* really was—had survived.

Her sights were on Volkner—the tyrant snake. There were mere meters separating them, and no one and nothing in between. He was focusing on the haze around the wolf, and nothing else. That would not do. She raised the pistol. Her rage-laced blood coursed at the sight of him, the bastard that sent her into a trap that took everything from her. He was all that she could see in her tunnel vision.

If Piper would have stopped for just a moment, taken a breath, she would have noticed three things. The first was the warmth of the liquid dripping down her back from the wound she'd reopened jumping the table. The second was Volkner's expression, wide-eyed with both wonder and fear. The third was that the haze had dissipated, and the monster stood without a single singe.

But she saw none of that. She only saw Volkner in the glowing iron sights of her pistol. As she screamed out her debtor's name, watching him and all around him shift their eyes to her, she saw the briefest look of realization on his face. He knew who she was, and what she was about to do. And she did it. Piper pulled the trigger.

Once, twice, three times. The first round hit the president in the shoulder, burning through his dress wear. She'd already predicted he'd have some sort of armored exosuit on underneath, so her aim shifted. The second shot grazed his exposed neck, making his empty hand start to move toward the wound in instinct. On the third shot, she pulled the trigger so hard with her mechanical hand that it snapped. But the shot went off, and hit her target in the center of his forehead.

The last shot sent Volkner crashing into the table behind him, falling prone on the other side, out of Piper's sight. She dropped the plasma pistol and fell to her knees, not caring at all about the half-dozen pistols and rifles now trained on her. There'd have been many more, if not for the massive wolf standing only a few feet from her.

"Good, Piper," it said in that gravelly, non-human voice. "Now go to the reactors. Finish the *Gjaller*."

Piper was suddenly aware of the pain pulsing from her back and how wet her clothes were.

"I'm finished," she said, her breathing ragged. "He's done."

Her vision was darkening around the edges. Even if she wanted to destroy the *Gjaller*, to kill thousands of soldiers and innocents indiscriminately, she didn't think she would have the strength to make it to the reactor level and fight off all the guards she knew she'd have to face along the way.

"We had a deal, girl," the beast said as it shred a soldier with its claws as easily as one might chop a fish with a butcher's knife.

She perceived enough to know most of the soldiers were fleeing the Great Hall now. There were a few left, either too drunk or too proud to run from a fight. One, an older man in the gold and red armor of the elite Presidential Guard, was leaping the table to get to Volkner. All the others were tucking tail after seeing the ineffectiveness of their guns on the self-proclaimed god. Though, having withstood a barrage like that...

"Are you really him?" she asked. "Are you Loki?"

"I am," he growled. "And I'm growing impatient with you. I don't take broken deals lightly, DeRache."

Piper laughed, feeling dangerously close to collapse. "What are you going to do? Kill me? I'm already dead."

Piper could barely perceive the god's movements. He seemed to shift unnaturally and constantly. But it was like looking at a fan blade. You could see him in motion, but never exactly know where every part of him was at a given time. One moment he was a half-dozen yards away from her, and the next he was so close she could feel his impossible heat on her face.

She felt his claws dig into the back of her neck as he picked her up by her head. She grabbed his wrist with her robotic hand and squeezed, but he didn't flinch.

"You may be dying," he said, his forked, silver tongue flicking out in the pauses. "But I can make your death last an eternity."

Piper suddenly wished she'd breathe her last breath at

that moment before he could impose whatever terrible punishment he was implying. But, just as she wished it, another voice yelled from behind Loki.

"Hey, horsemother!" it said.

Loki sneered and dropped Piper. When she hit the ground, she saw the Berserker and the two who'd been in shackles sprinting toward the god, weapons ready, like true Vikings ready to join Odin's table at Valhalla. That's when the darkness finally took her.

CHAPTER
THIRTY-FIVE

Niko Schafer looked every bit the picture of a legendary warrior charging into battle, flanked by his noble vanguard. Though Mila felt helpless in the moment, there was something about that sight that sparked the smallest bit of hope that maybe, by some miracle they could make it out of this.

But then things changed. Before they reached Volkner, a woman appeared, seemingly out of nowhere, and shot the president. Mila watched as he fell, shattering drinking horns and glass as he tumbled over the table behind him, lying limp on the other side. She saw Adel jump to his side within seconds, but her focus quickly switched back to Niko and the others.

Loki had moved as well, just in front of the woman, and was holding her by her head. Niko had shifted course, and now he and Eiji and Xiomar were running—running right for... Loki?

"No!" Mila screamed.

She didn't know what Loki was capable of exactly, but she'd just seen him shrug off a thousand plasma rounds as if they were less than flies. Even if Niko's healing capabilities weren't subdued by drugs, he was still no match for that. They were running head-first for a god.

She leapt from the stage, Fenrir joining at her side, and together they sprinted toward the action, utterly unsure of what she'd do when she got there. Fear had replaced the anger boiling in her; fear of not being able to save her friends. Thoughts raced through her head, searching all her memories for what she knew of the gods. For any weaknesses.

But nothing came.

Niko was upon the god now, yelling "horsemother" as his axe made contact. To Mila's infinite surprise, Loki actually cried out in what seemed like anger, and pain. Niko withdrew his axe—that runed, archaic hatchet—and struck the stunned Loki again. Eiji and Xiomar were there now too, their movements as graceful as dancers, but lethal as assassins. Except, when their strikes with their plasma-bladed weapons made contact they bounced off.

Loki was ready for Niko's third attack, as he swiped the Berserker away with the back of his hand. Niko flew over a dozen feet and crashed into the same long table where Adel was checking Volkner's pulse. Niko tried to get up but grabbed his back and stumbled forward to his knees. Something was wrong. Had he been at full capacity, Mila knew he'd have jumped up from a blow like that. But right now, it was impressive he was still breathing after such an impact.

Eiji and Xiomar leapt away from the god, who'd stopped to inspect the two bloody wounds in his shoulder.

"Where did you get that axe, boy?" he spat.

Niko's shoulders were heaving, and he wiped the blood trickling from the side of his mouth and smirked. "What's wrong? Did I hurt you?"

Loki was upon him in a blink, his clawed hand clenching the Berserker's throat. "Tell me where it came from, or I'll murder you, your friends, your lover, and then your family."

Niko's eyes were flickering closed, and Mila knew if Loki squeezed just a little harder, he'd snuff out the Berserker's life for good. The sight of him, on the verge of death once again, made that rage rush back in a full inferno, and with it a shock like a tidal wave from the elerex. She fell to the ground, clutching her chest as the elerex released its fury. This was too much. Far too much. Every inch of her was tensed, every pain receptor reporting, her heart threatening to stop.

Was this it? Was this what happened? The reason the elerexes were banned? Yes, there was no question about it. This was it, that moment, the one she'd always suspected would come, but wished it wouldn't. The elerex was going to kill her. Unless...

"It would take Thor's lightning to kill him." That's what Niko had said, just before they rushed into the fray.

She had to get the elerex out of her. Now. Even though she knew she'd lose her arm because of it. She was going to die otherwise. And if she could get it out, it might become the only weapon they could hope for in this fight. She might not have Thor's lightning, and she could not kill a god. But, perhaps she could stun one.

Mila forced her near-immovable hand to the elerex, digging her fingers into the flesh around it, the agonizing wrenching pain of it a boon to the already phenomenal agony filling her entire body. She forced her fingertips deep enough to find the lips of the device, then, she started to pull.

The elerex protested, sending another more intense

shockwave through her. She jolted, but kept pulling. Another shockwave, even more intense than the last. This one made her collapse all the way to the littered carpet and lose her grip on the device. She didn't have the strength left to move her arms again—to move anything. The elerex was too much.

She'd fallen in a way that allowed her to see Niko, who Loki held up by his throat, so his feet weren't touching the ground. She saw them, but she couldn't move or speak to help them.

"Answer me, insect!" Loki growled.

Niko's head was near limp rolling around in the god's grasp. But he found the will for his response, as he spat in Loki's face.

That was it. Mila knew it. She was too late.

Loki planted his spear through the carpet into the metal floor of the *Gjaller*. Then, he raised his empty, clawed hand above his head, prepping his death blow. But before he could deal it, he was thrown backwards, as it felt like the entire *Gjaller* was hit by a battering ram.

Alarms sounded and the lights shifted to red. A voice came over the intercom system announcing "Battle stations! Battle stations! We are under attack! All crew to battle stations!"

Mila heard dozens of explosions elsewhere in the station. Though they weren't from within. They were impacting from the outside.

Loki was getting back up, his grimace like that of a child taken away from a favorite toy. She didn't know what was going on out in the void, but whatever it was had given her the only second chance she'd get.

Her lungs were vise-like, any hope of taking a deep breath gone. She closed her eyes and thought a prayer to the matron. Then, as she found that void, that Ginnungagap in her mind's eye, she slowly, painfully, moved her arm again, managing to get to her feet in the process. Mila screamed like a siren as she plunged her fingers once more into her arm.

"No!" Loki yelled.

She opened her eyes to find him looking, wide-eyed and panicked, directly at her. She grinned a devil's grin, and gripped the device tight. With all the might she could muster, Mila Messer ripped the elerex from her flesh, her blood reflecting off the screw-like pointed barbs that had fastened into her flesh for nearly a decade. Then, her arm seized, and she dropped the device.

Mila lost all control. The rage that had been crashing against the elerex's electric wall was suddenly free. It wasn't confined to her spine now. No, now it was in her head, her feet, her arms, her hands. It was in all her bones and her muscles. It was woven into her very blood. So much unhindered anger and something else. Something feral unleashed. Something she could not control.

Power.

It was too much. She couldn't contain it, whatever *it* was. It erupted from her, from her fingertips, her palms, her eyes. Light. Pure, burning, radiant light consumed the room, as the bound fury was unleashed like a rampant flood, a flood with a mind, and a target.

Mila didn't know what was happening, much less how to control it. But the light, whatever it was, seemed to know who she wanted dead, as the greatest concentration of rays blasted into Loki, sending the god toward the far wall. He splintered every table along the way, eventually connecting with and denting the titanium bulkhead.

Mila's fury, her light, was not finished. It was like a

captive nightcat released to the wild for the first time, wanting a fill of everything it'd missed—everything withheld for so many years. So, the light kept crashing into Loki, rendering the god completely immobile. It kept going even after his eyes had rolled into the back of his head and his body turned to a ragdoll. It kept going even when another massive explosion rocked the *Gjaller*. It kept going until there was nothing left to give, and her light of the brightest sun faded into the flicker of a candlewick.

CHAPTER

THIRTY-SIX

PIPER WOKE FROM DEEP, cold blackness to the brightest light and most intense heat she'd ever experienced. Light as bright as the Ymiran sun. Brighter.

She got to her feet quickly, the fatigue of near-death wholly absent from her now. In fact, she felt amazing. There was no pain around the connections to her robotic limbs, nor was there any from her back. She was entirely healthy. *How* was she entirely healthy?

The light started to fade, and the heat with it, until she could see its source. The girl, Mila—it was coming from her. As the light withdrew completely, she watched Mila collapse to the blackened and burnt rug around her.

She heard a thump, as something large hit the floor behind her. She turned, her eyebrows rising and hair standing on end, to find it was Loki. He'd fallen to the floor in a sizzling heap, the metal far above him on the wall glowing orange. He did not move.

Around the room, others were starting to stand, but not all of the bodies. Those who had died would remain dead. But those who'd clung to life had been given a second chance. None stuck around to test fate a second time. That left her, the girl, and the three that had saved her from Loki's final judgement.

Suddenly, an explosion struck the *Gjaller* so hard it nearly knocked her on her back. She wasted no time rushing to the viewing window behind the head table. There was a full-on war going on out in the void. She counted ten, fifteen, over twenty ships marked with an axe sigil. There were Dainsleif-class gunships, Gungnir-class brigs. There was a handful of Hofud frigates, and even a Mjolnir-class capital ship. The capital ship she recognized and knew very well. It was the *Laufey,* the pride of the rebels, captained by Arvid's own protégé, the legendary Skuld.

The Níu had come. They'd heard her message and come. And they'd come with a fleet. It wasn't near the size and power it was during the Hodian invasion, but it was three times as large as anything she'd expected. A feeling welled inside Piper at the sight, something she hadn't felt in some time. Hope.

The thought was ripped away as she heard a plasma pistol report, and a searing round collided with her arm. She rolled to the side, turning in the process, to find Volkner Brandt firing another shot at her, the only sign of the plasma bullet she'd hit him with a small, black smudge on his forehead.

A million explanations raced through her head of how he'd been unharmed by the round. The most likely, and most logical, was that he was wearing some new advanced form of armor that was near-invisible to the naked eye. That, or the bastard really was blessed by Thor.

"Piper DeRache," the president hissed. "They told me you were dead. Seems I can't trust anything the Jotuns say."

"Sorry to deliver the bad news," she replied, breaking

into a sprint toward a nearby body, praying the soldier had been armed.

Piper leapt back and forth in her run to avoid the shots until she heard his pistol click on an empty chamber, and the president tossed it aside.

She found a short-handled warhammer lying amongst the destruction and picked it up. Turning to face her enemy, she saw he, too, was prepared for a melee, with his plasma-edged axe.

"So, tell me, Piper. Why would you come back?"

"You owe me a debt," Piper said, her voice like Jotun ice. "I've come to collect."

The two warriors charged, each crying out like the Vikings of old. Only one was walking away tonight. The other would either dine in Valhalla, or rot in Hel's depths. Either way, one of them was going to die.

———✦———✦———

Niko leapt up as the light faded, his body miraculously healed and his lungs no longer screeching for air. Eiji and Xiomar were already at Mila when he got to her. She was conscious, but barely, and her body was far too hot.

He slid to his knees in front of her and held her in his arms.

Mila didn't seem to have the strength to speak, so he had to settle for a faint smile. He didn't know why he did what he did next. The relief he felt made it almost instinctual. Niko cradled her head in his hand and kissed her forehead, her flesh threatening to burn his palm and lips.

"Thank the gods," he said, pulling away.

"I'd be careful with that phrasing," Xiomar said.

In his concern for Mila, Niko had almost forgotten the

circumstances surrounding them. That was Loki heaped against the far wall. The Trickster himself. And Mila... Mila had just released some power unlike anything he'd ever seen.

"What was that?" Eiji said, asking the question on everyone's mind.

"I don't know," Niko replied. "But we have to get her out of here, now."

"Niko," Mila said, barely a whisper, as she reached for his hand.

The Berserker took it gently, but firmly. He wouldn't let it go until she wanted him to.

She didn't say anything else, just gave the lightest squeeze. She was trying to tell him everything he needed to know with the touch, and he understood it thoroughly.

"Lieutenant," Eiji said, nodding to the far side of the room.

Niko turned and saw the pirate, Piper DeRache, who they'd just saved, standing at the viewing window. Behind her, a gun raised, was Volkner Brandt.

"Shit," he hissed, looking back at the group. "Get her to the docking bay. That's Piper DeRache, which means I have a pretty good idea of who's attacking the station right now. They wouldn't just destroy the station with all the innocents aboard, so I'd wager they're trying to extract. Get on one of their ships. Get her to a healer."

Eiji and Xiomar nodded, understanding there would be no belaying the order this time.

He turned his attention back to Mila, who seemed to be fighting consciousness, but still maintained her hand in his. "Mila," he said, "I have to do something. Eiji and Xiomar are going to take care of you for a little bit, but I'll catch up soon."

Mila's head swayed, her eyes trying to close, but she was able to squeeze his hand once more before letting go. "Niko," she repeated, almost too soft for even his enhanced hearing to catch. She managed to look up at him. "Don't be late, kleizufet."

Niko couldn't help but smile. It was a silent promise, but not one he was entirely sure he could keep.

Xiomar and Eiji hefted Mila up, each putting an arm around their shoulders. Fen barked urgently, as if telling them all to hurry. As they started to hobble toward the massive doors of the Great Hall, Niko turned and, armed only with his axe—the axe that had made a god bleed—he set his sights on Volkner Brandt.

⊲·———·—·⊳

VOLKNER AND PIPER's bout began with finesse. They exchanged blows, parrying and blocking, jumping back and in. They had the same fighting style—aggressive. In favor of powerful swings, they would risk openings in their defense. Against a careful, patient opponent, this would be detrimental. But in a battle of fury, it was inconsequential.

Their weapons met again, and again. It didn't take long for Piper to start to feel the fatigue of all-out barrage. Yet, Brandt seemed to not be slowing down at all. Even for someone fit and healthy in their prime, that kind of stamina was unbelievable. But for him, at his age?

When his bodyguard came to his aid, Piper really felt the tide of the skirmish turn against her. Her aggressive style withdrew into defense. The war hammer was too bulky and awkward to perform effectively. It was a weapon made for breaking bones, not for deflecting and blocking.

She had to resort to using her metal limb as a shield against the presidential guard's attacks.

There was a time when Volkner Brandt would have told his man to stand aside. A time when he was too honorable to accept help in a one-on-one fight. But not now. His gold-flecked eyes glittered with blood rage. It was clear he didn't care how he killed her—just him or him and a thousand men, it didn't matter. As long as she died.

She was slowing down, doubting how much more her robotic arm could take. The older guard, though an unquestionably able and furious fighter, was breathing heavily as well. But Volkner was still as fresh as when they'd started. She made a risky move and grabbed the older guard's wrist with her robotic hand, wrenching it to the side so his axe fell from his grasp. But, in doing so, she missed the body on the ground, directly behind her as she backed up.

Piper stumbled, giving Volkner just enough time to strike the handle of her hammer and send it flying from her grasp. She quickly raised her arm, trying to set some semblance of a defense before his next strike. But before he could execute it, a force like Thor's own hammer crashed into him, sending the president flying. Piper quickly realized the force was Niko Schafer, the Berserker.

Not letting the distraction linger, she launched herself at Volkner's guard, her robotic fist colliding with the underside of his chin, knocking the man out cold. Then, grabbing his axe, she leapt toward Niko and the president. Niko had rolled away and gotten to his feet, his axe ready to strike. Volkner was only slightly slower to recover, but it was just a little bit too slow.

The president looked up, but Piper was already there, her axe swinging down and cleaving into his shoulder.

Blood spattered from the wound, but the axe blade did

not sink as deep as it should have. It seemed to hit something that stopped it dead, sending a painful vibrating sensation cascading through Piper's hand. She pulled the axe back and withdrew before Volkner could retaliate. She was standing side-by-side with Niko now, and they both saw it.

The blood running from Volkner's already-healing wound was not red, but cobalt blue. And the skeleton she cut to was not bone. It was metal.

"You're a..." Piper started.

"...a berserker," Niko finished, filling in the pause.

Volkner laughed, glancing at the healing wound on his right shoulder. "That's right," he said. "I have to admit, your shot to my forehead twinged a bit."

"How long?" Niko asked.

"Oh, a few years after the trial was a success."

"The trial?" Niko growled, every muscle on him taut and shaking.

"Yes, your little platoon. You were the testers to make sure the human body could withstand the stress of infusions. I had it performed again on people closer to my age, of course, but that took much longer. The human body gets so brittle with age."

Niko launched forth with a beast's fury and speed. Piper followed, but could not hope to match his pace. The two men, the true Berserker and the false, collided. There was no grace in Niko or Volkner's movements. No finesse. Their fighting styles did not open risk to attacks in favor of power strikes. No, it went farther than that. It was only fury-filled blows, a barrage of them, exchanged without even the faintest hint of self-preservation.

They struck without discrimination. When an axe arm was recoiling, a punch was thrown, then the blades clashed again. They blocked, punched, kicked, but neither retreated. Blue blood sprayed from their noses, their lips, gashes in their arms and torsos. Both stood their ground, their movements so fast and erratic Piper's eyes could hardly keep up.

Piper realized in that moment she was not the only one in the universe who Volkner owed a debt. The unrelenting violent volley Niko unleashed without care or concern of anything else around was evidence of a man scorned. She knew she had to let them go, let this fight be Niko's, for his honor.

The frenzy continued, both men pushing far past the limits of any normal person. More strikes landed. More wounds opened. Volkner's dress uniform was falling off of him in damp ribbons, exposing gashes in his flesh continuing to try and heal. Niko's fist met his forehead, in the exact spot Piper had shot him mere minutes ago, and the president stumbled as if stunned for the briefest moment.

In that impossibly brief span, Niko made his move, kicking the inside of Volkner's knee with the strength of a rampaging bear. Piper heard the metallic crack of breaking metal as Volkner's knee bent out to the side unnaturally, his lower and upper legs moving in opposite directions, and the president fell, catching himself on his non-broken knee.

The shock of it was enough to allow Niko to disarm him, sending Volkner's axe spinning away on the metal floor. Piper was at his side in an instant.

"You gods-damned bastard," Niko said, his hands trembling. "You had no right. You stole our lives from us, turned us into your toys, then threw us away."

Volkner looked up at the pair of them. "Everything I've ever done has been for the good of Vidar. Everything has had a purpose."

"You're sick," Piper said. "You may have once wanted that, but not now. Now, you're only interested in power. And you're willing to take everything from everyone in order to get more of it."

"I don't expect you to understand, pirate," Volkner spat, his mouth dripping with blue blood.

Piper crouched to be level with him. "It was you who branded us pirates, not us. I am, and always have been, a Níu."

Volkner sneered. His gold-flecked eyes, which Piper now realized had the smallest pixels intertwined, were locked on her. "I was once a rebel too."

Piper stood, looking down at him. "You were. Then you became worse than the very thing you rebelled against."

Volkner's narrowed eyes and grimace began to retreat. He seemed to be thinking, as one tends to do when faced with certain death. "I won't apologize for what I did. Not any of it. But I do hope you do things differently. For Vidar."

Volkner started muttering a prayer under his breath. Piper and Niko looked at each other and knew what was next. They raised their axes high above their heads and, with the full view of the Níu fleet behind him, collected all of Volkner's debts.

CHAPTER

THIRTY-SEVEN

THE WALK to the lift was long and slow. It was everything Mila could do to stay conscious and keep at least some of her weight off Eiji and Xiomar. Luckily, most soldiers were too busy running to various battle stations and responding to orders to notice them. The few that came too close Fen dismissed with a not-so-subtle growl.

They'd just exited on the docking level, and the sight was one to behold. Rebel ships had landed in the docking bays with full platoons of freedom fighters set up in defensive positions. Behind them, servants, traders, and civilians were being uploaded en masse onto transport ships.

"Allies!" Eiji yelled. "We are the axe!" She and Xiomar raised their free hands to show they weren't a threat. "This one needs medical attention!"

A rebel officer waved them forward and they started making their way across the bay. There were a few dozen people in front of them, all civilians. Mila breathed a sigh of relief knowing so many innocents were making it to the escort ships.

They'd made it only a few steps when suddenly a voice like gravel spoke from behind them.

"Where do you think you're going?"

The trio turned to find Loki, singed and scabbed, standing like the suffocating picture of death above them.

"Go!" Xiomar said, leaving Mila to Eiji while he turned to face the god.

Xiomar was fast, his movements like water. He drew a plasma-edged dagger that he'd lifted off a felled guard, wielding the glowing blade in his left hand. With his right, he pulled something small and metallic, specked with drying blood, from his pocket. The elerex.

The blademaster leapt forth and withdrew quickly, showing all watching exactly why he'd garnered renown for his fighting. To an untrained eye, it might have seemed like he was toying with the singed wolf. But it was not so arrogant as that. Xiomar was probing Loki's defenses, searching for a weakness—any opening where he could sweep in and plant the elerex in the god's flesh.

The blademaster narrowly escaped two swipes from Loki's claws, but the injured Aesir was still far too fast for the mortal man. His third strike, the backhand of his second wide swing, struck Xiomar in the ribs, sending him across the *Gjaller* floor like a ragdoll.

Loki lunged and was upon Eiji and Mila in less than a heartbeat. Eiji raised an arm to protect Mila, but his strike snapped the limb like a twig and threw the teen Hodian a dozen feet away.

Without strength left in her legs, Mila fell, but was quickly picked up by Loki. His silver tongue and sulfur breath were all she could perceive as she waited for him to squeeze the last bits of life from her.

"You're mine, Mila Messer," the god seethed. "You, and

your drunk father, and your whore mother are mine. You will give me back what was stolen."

Mila couldn't reply. She could only hang like an empty vessel.

The same voice that had announce the battle stations blared from the loudspeakers around the station along with a new siren alarm. "Danger. Reactor meltdown imminent. Evacuate immediately." It repeated the sentence over and over.

"What did you do?" Mila asked weakly.

"You think you were the only seed I had planted here?" Loki clicked his tongue. "This station is filled with desperate souls willing to do anything for the promise of salvation or strength."

"The servants," Mila said weakly, realizing the key ingredient of Loki's plan that they'd all overlooked. "That's why they were so scarce tonight."

"It's really too bad," Loki said, his grip tightening on her, threatening to crush her bones into dust. "Oh, how I wanted to see the look on your face when I told you all the horrible truths of your parentage. How much pain your father, and your mother, have caused."

This was it. Her body had no strength to resist, her muscles empty of even the most desperate of will. And then, Loki dropped her.

The god wailed in pain, and Mila spun away from him in free fall, her golden sash coming free on Loki's claws. She slammed into the cold *Gjaller* floor, looking up to find Loki desperately reaching his long arms behind his wolfish form, clutching the air for something. But he wouldn't find it, as Niko had already withdrawn his axe from the god's back, and was preparing for another strike.

Loki whirled on the Berserker, his limbs swinging

wildly, like a feral animal. Mila recognized something in those movements—something she'd never expect from one of the Aesir. Fear. Loki was scared of Niko. Or, more accurately, the god was scared of the Berserker's axe. Mila knew Niko may never get the chance to strike the wolfish god again now that he was alert to the mortal's presence.

Loki snarled as he struck again and again, narrowly missing Niko each time. As fast as he was, Niko could not evade forever. One small misstep, and he'd be done for.

"Get her out of here!" he yelled.

It was then that Mila realized Xiomar and Eiji had made it back to her flanks, Xiomar grasping his ribs and Eiji cradling one arm.

"Let's go, Mila!" Eiji ordered as she and Xiomar clumsily helped her to her feet.

Together, they began to hobble away, but it was not soon enough, as they heard the horrible crack of flesh on bone and metal. Mila looked back to find Niko skidding across the landing deck floor, a trail of blue blood in his wake.

There wasn't time to react as Loki charged the hobbled three. A few of the distant rebels let loose plasma rounds at him, but they were less than fleas to the god. There was nothing left to protect them; nothing to stay the deity's wrath. Nothing except the Mark II Fenrir that growled at their side and lunged with its jaws wide in an act of all-out defiance against its violence inhibition protocols.

"Fen!" Mila screeched, her body seizing at the sight of her vél leaping forward.

The scene of the god holding her limp, hissing promises of death in her face, had triggered something in the bot. An override to his inhibitor. He'd launched himself onto the god, sinking his teeth into Loki's arm, his bite a death lock.

"Fen!" Mila cried out again as Xio and Eiji pulled her away as fast as they could manage toward the rebel ships.

The rebels were yelling for them to hurry, that there wasn't much time.

"We can't leave them!"

"This place is going down," Xio replied hastily.

"I'm not leaving them!"

Mila looked back, trying to rip away from the duo hauling her along. It was just in time to see Loki fling Fen away. The vél was back on his feet in an instant, except... that back leg. The weld in the hydraulic tube had broken, and steaming fluid coated the metal down the limb. He was having trouble supporting himself. Still, even with the limp leg, he growled at the god defiantly. Then, he let loose a howl worthy of Geri and Freki, and launched himself forth yet again. He was fierce and fearsome, but just slightly off-balance. When he made the jump, his aim was too far left, but not out of Loki's reach. The god grabbed the wolfbot and slammed him on the ground. Parts and armor flew in every direction, but he was not wholly defeated. Not yet.

Fen forced his head back, splitting wires and metal along his neck as he did so, and Mila saw blue sparks emit from his teeth. It was a bite of lightning, one of the Mark II's most effective weapons, and the perfect thing to paralyze a god.

His teeth made contact, and Loki went taut, hissing through clenched teeth. Niko was stumbling toward them as an explosion erupted from the lifts in the center of the docking bay. It threw the Berserker even more off-balance, but Fen managed to hang on. It was just long enough for Niko, bruised and bleeding, to raise his axe, and plant it in the Trickster's chest.

Another explosion, larger than the first, raged from the

lifts, engulfing Loki whole and sending Fen and Niko tumbling across the metal floor. Niko was back on his feet in a slow second, but Fenrir did not move. As he lay prone, his digital eyes were looking at Mila, still bright but dimming. The next few moments suspended themselves in time, as Mila refused to break her gaze away from her brave wolf. He never looked away either, not once; not until the soft glow of his proud eyes went out entirely.

"No!" Mila's scream was like the wail of a mother watching a child fall from a cliff.

"Take her!" Eiji said, handing Mila off entirely to Xiomar.

Xio carried her together toward the last transport ship and beckoning rebels. But Mila was looking back, at the two warriors, neither of which were running to escape the doomed *Gjaller*, but instead toward the lifeless Mark II.

⊙—•————————•—⊙

THE LAST TRANSPORT was only a few hundred meters from the *Gjaller* when the first reactor blew. Piper, Eiji, Xiomar, Niko, and Mila all watched as escape pods launched toward Vidar and military ships detached from their dockings, still-attached fuel and supply lines ripping away in the process.

The other reactors followed in quick fashion, each an immensely bright light, though not near as bright as Mila's light had been. Before long, the *Gjaller* was ripped into two halves, each half littered with subsequent explosions from failing systems.

They all knew the magnitude of what they saw in that viewing window, but none of them said anything. There were no cheers, no hugs or handshakes. They'd done it, but it had not come without sacrifice. There were three bodies that would never be burned on pyres, and a chip module in Mila's hands—a cost that was far too high. And yet, they knew, all of them, that this was only the beginning. There was still so much blood to be paid.

There was still a debt owed.

THIRTY-EIGHT

AFTER THEIR TRANSPORT docked into the *Laufey,* Mila, Niko, and the others were immediately put into jump protocol as the capital ship made the leap into the void. The moment the leap was finished, Mila was rushed to a medical bay and put into a bed. She wasn't given sedatives or synthetics, but the immense, empty tiredness she felt consumed her the moment she was in the linens.

When she woke, Niko was asleep in the chair beside her bed. The second she stirred, the Berserker sprang awake, looking ready to fend off Loki himself again.

"It's just me," Mila said with a soft smile.

"Thank the Matron," he said, relief washing over his face.

"What's wrong?" Mila asked.

"Nothing! It's good, you're awake!" he said quickly.

"But?"

Niko sighed. "But, they don't know what happened to you. And they had no idea when you'd wake up."

Mila took a moment to examine herself. She was in a hospital gown connected to all manner of IVs and wired monitors. However, her flesh told no tales of trauma, and her body felt no aches. In fact, she never felt better, as if a weight had been lying on her back her entire life. There was only one flaw in her skin, and it was where that very weight had lived for so long. It was a jagged-edge scar in her forearm, a forever reminder of the shackles that bound her.

"How long was I asleep?" she finally said.

"Five days."

The number hit Mila like a rock. "Five days? It feels like I just went to sleep!"

"It wasn't really sleeping," Niko said. "Not according to the doctors."

"Then, what was it?"

"They said it was more like... hibernating. Your body went into a state of incredibly low energy to preserve itself and build back up."

Mila's brow furrowed, trying to make sense of what had happened to her. But she knew no explanation would come any time soon. Instead, she decided to ask a question Niko might actually be able to answer. "Have reports come in from the *Gjaller* yet?"

Niko nodded. "Some. Top half is still in orbit, but there's not a soul alive on it. Vidarin crews are scouring it for bodies. The rebels have people on the inside that have confirmed some fairly high-profile deaths, our dear Volkner included."

"What about the bottom half?"

"The explosion was intense enough to send it into atmosphere. They're saying it created one hell of a crater."

"Any survivors there?"

"Not sure yet," Niko replied. "But, it's doubtful. Crews haven't been able to douse the flames, and the area is incredibly radioactive. If there are survivors, they won't have an easy life."

"What about Kord, and Adel?" Mila asked.

"I don't know about Adel. He was near-unconscious last time I saw him. But he's a resourceful bastard, and they say nearly a thousand escape pods managed to launch before the meltdown. I wouldn't put it past him to have made it on to one. As for Kord, well that piece of work made it onto a rebel ship. They're holding him for questioning now, like all the deserters, to make sure he doesn't have lingering allegiances. I put in a good word for him though." Niko winked.

"Might want to put in two words," Mila said. "I don't imagine Kord's taking the loss of his workshop all too well."

Niko nodded, "Yeah, you're right about that. As much of a living hell that hunk of metal was, it did have its small joys."

"Oh, Niko," Mila said regretfully, suddenly remembering his nook on the engine level. "I'm so sorry..."

"It's all right," Niko said with a small smile. "I keep Barnard and the others, their faces, their voices, all stored in here," he said, pointing to his temple. "Same with my family, but I expect losing the paper pictures and letters is a small price to pay for Vidarin liberation, and the chance to actually see them again."

That thought made a ball of warmth form in Mila's chest. She didn't particularly want to see her father anytime soon, but she did have so many questions for him. And meeting Niko's family—if he *wanted* her to meet them—that didn't seem so bad either.

"There's something else," Niko said hesitantly. The words cut Mila's comforting thought short. "The rebels managed to apprehend several Brandt loyalists off the *Gjaller* and are holding them as prisoners. They've given them the option to defect and join the rebellion, but many have refused. They said they'll give them a few more days, but then trials will begin."

"Okay," Mila said slowly, an eyebrow raised. "That's good? But what aren't you saying?"

Niko took a breath and met Mila's eyes. "They have Amelie."

The name was like an ice dagger though Mila's heart. She gritted her teeth, but waited for Niko to continue.

"She hasn't denounced the Volkner regime yet. They've already asked me and the others about her."

"And?"

Niko raised his chin. "And we've all asked that she be punished to the fullest extent of their laws."

"Execution?"

Niko nodded slowly.

The feeling that swirled within Mila was one of raging anger and... fear. She was angry for what Amelie had done. Waren and Eberhard died because of her deceit. Yet, she still remembered those little moments with Amelie; the perception of the Tyran girl as a scared servant. Some irrational part of her still felt like that girl was her friend, and she didn't want her to die. The feeling was nauseating, but it changed nothing. Amelie had dug her own grave. It wasn't Mila's place to stop her from laying in it.

"All right," was all she said on the matter.

Another question lingered in Mila's mind. It was the one person—the one *thing*—she needed to ask about, but it was more difficult to form the words than she expected.

Niko seemed to notice the perturbed look and said, "You want to know about Loki."

Mila nodded. "Do you think he's dead?"

Niko leaned back in his chair and swept a hand through

his hair. "Can gods truly die? In the stories they do, sure. But what happens in reality? We're in truly uncharted territory here, Mi. The only thing I'd ask is do *you* think he's dead?"

"No," Mila said softly, and the word hung heavy between them.

Niko nodded in agreement. "I think you're right. I don't think we've seen the last of Loki Laufeyson."

The med bay doors hissed open and the voice of an excited Eiji sliced through the tension in the room. "She's awake!"

The girl looked more like a teenager than Mila had ever seen. She wasn't wearing Viking armor or any military wear. She was wearing a simple set of loose coveralls over a plain tank top, her broken arm hanging in a sling. Xiomar, behind her, wore an all-black casual outfit, fitting for the blademaster. She could see evidence of thick bandaged wrapping his torso bulging from beneath his shirt. They both seemed... relaxed. Mila was happy to see them this way. It was strange, of course, having only seen them as finely-honed killers before. But, still, it made her happy.

After them came two dressed much differently. The first was the woman Mila now knew was the legendary void pirate Piper DeRache. Her hair had been cut, closely shaven on the sides and neatly combed up on top. She wore a colorful leather jacket with a myriad of fresh stitches and patches. Beside her was another woman with graying hair cut similar to Pipers, but her dress was that of old-patterned military fatigues.

After smiling and greeting Eiji and Xiomar, Mila looked at Piper. "You're Piper DeRache. I'm sorry I didn't introduce myself before, but I've heard all the tales about you."

Piper laughed. "It's a pleasure to meet you, Mila. That

was some seriously insane shit you pulled on the *Gjaller*. I'm gonna count myself lucky we're on the same team. As for the stories, trust me. I'm not half as bad as they make me out to be. Her on the other hand," Piper said, gesturing to the woman beside her. "The horrible stories about Captain Skuld are all true."

"Captain Skuld?" Mila said, astonished. "But you're..."

"A woman?" Skuld finished for her. "Yeah, I get that a lot. And don't believe a thing this one says."

Skuld made her way to the foot of Mila's bed and sat. "It's an honor to meet you, Mila," she said. "Your father is one of my oldest friends."

"My father?"

Skuld nodded. "Though, he probably wouldn't know me by Skuld. We served in the military together, a long time ago, so he would know me by my real name, and it's the same you can call me. I'm Greta."

Mila's world felt like it started to spin. She was the one Volkner had spoken about—the one who defected. Little did he know she'd gone on to be the most notorious rebel in all of history.

Greta spent the next few hours talking to Mila. She told her of leaving the military to join a group of goodwill missionaries who sent aid to planets and colonies in need. Then her later return to the fighting life organizing rebels to rise up against the injustices of Volkner. Finally, she told her about the message she'd received from Hans; the same one she'd smuggled onto the ship to Niko based off information from one of her most reliable spies, Eiji. That part had astounded Mila almost as much as the revelation that their force now consisted of nearly two hundred thousand rebels, carefully cultivated over the last decade in secret.

"But now we've revealed ourselves and struck a blow

that will be heard around all of Ymir," Greta said. "It's time to topple this corrupt Vidarin system and install one that will help unite the planets instead of divide."

"And what about the gods?" Mila asked.

"That's something I was hoping you all could help me with. You're the only ones I have who have seen a god in action. And now you may have killed one."

Mila suddenly remembered Niko's weapon. "Your axe! How did it..."

"We don't know," Niko said. "We've discussed it in length, but I don't know why it could harm Loki. It's an old family heirloom, passed to me from my father, and from his father to him. I know it had been in the family since we left the Old Earth, but beyond that..." Niko shrugged.

"Where is it now?" Mila continued.

Niko breathed deep at that. "Last I saw it was stuck in the rotten bastard's chest."

"No," Mila said. "You can't mean it went down with the station."

Niko nodded regretfully.

"Unfortunately," Greta cut in, "we don't have much time to sit on these woes. We'll have to be ready for possible repercussions, both of upsetting the Vidarin hierarchy and of revealing a god to the system."

"That's where we come in," Niko said, looking at Mila. "We're some of the best fighters in the system. And you... we have to figure out what that power you unleashed was."

Mila nodded. "Maybe start with teaching me how to fight normally?"

Niko smiled. "You sure you're ready for that?"

"When training starts," Mila replied, smiling back devilishly. "Just don't be late."

"We'll give you a few more days to recuperate and make

proper arrangements," Greta said. "Then, you'll receive initial training onboard the ship before we send you on your first mission."

"Mission?" Mila asked, surprised she was being given orders.

"That's right. You're one of the Níu now, should you choose to join."

Mila looked around at each of her friends. Eiji was, of course, already one of the rebels.

"I told her I'd have to wait until you woke up for my answer," Niko said, smiling playfully. "Xio felt the same. You are in charge, after all."

"Well," Mila said, "if that's the case, then consider us enemies of the system. What's our mission?"

"You'll be going to the Megingjörd Belt," Greta said. "Piper will be escorting you with a squadron."

"What's in the Belt that warrants such a renowned escort?" Mila asked.

"The Oracle." It was Piper who spoke this time. "We expect she may be our best chance at knowing what to expect in the war to come. We also hope she can tell us what in Hel's name the power you unleashed on Loki was."

"The Oracle," Mila repeated, mostly to herself.

Only days ago, she was a farm girl desperate to escape her simple life. Now, she lived in a universe where gods were real, and she was a weapon against them. It was a world where answers did not come from books and schools, but from fairy tales and myths, psychics and seers. There were obstacles ahead unlike anything they could imagine. But they, all of them, would tackle them together.

Tiny smoke wisps swirled each time Mila Messer touched the tip of the soldering iron to the wiring connections on the motherboard. Greta had supplied her with all the parts she needed to build a Fenrir Mark II, but it meant nothing if she couldn't get the chip module to function. It would be a Mark II, but it wouldn't be Fen. The power indicator light on the board would be the telltale sign there was hope. But it'd been days, and she hadn't gotten it to light once.

There was a knock on her shop door. The shop was a generously sized mechanic shop in the *Laufey's* upper sectors that Greta said had been unmanned for some time. It was Mila's to do with as she pleased. So, already there was a radio in the corner and plenty of junk. She'd have it looking just like the shop on her farm in no time at all.

"Come in," she said to the knocker.

"Any luck?" Niko asked.

She shook her head. "Not yet. But I can be persistent."

"Oh, I know," Niko said sarcastically. "I got what you wanted, by the way."

He placed a few pieces of paper and a pen on the workbench beside her.

"I can mail it to him as soon as you're finished," he continued.

"Thank you," Mila replied, forcing a smile.

The rebels had informed Mila and Niko that they'd sent retrieval teams to Vidar to get both of their families off the planet before the assault on the *Gjaller* started. They'd sent word ahead. Niko's family was secured and en route to the *Laufey* as they spoke. Hans, however, had refused the invitation. Despite what Hans was, Mila still couldn't forget *who* he was. He was the man who had sent her away to a life of darkness. He was also the man who'd sent her the message that saved her life. Most importantly, he was one of her best chances in the universe to learn who and what she actually was.

"Are you ready to see them again?" Mila asked.

"I don't know," he admitted. "It's been a long time. Things have changed. Gods know I've changed."

"Well, get ready," Mila said. "I'm meeting your family this week either way, so I can tell them how much of an ass you were to me on the *Gjaller*."

Niko laughed, then fell into pensive silence.

Mila stood and placed a hand on his cheek. "Hey," she said, "they still love you. It's going to be okay. Even if you've both changed, you'll always be family."

Niko nodded.

"When do they board?" Mila asked.

"Six hours."

"Okay, let me work a little bit longer here and then I'll meet you at the mess hall so we can eat before they arrive."

"Okay," Niko said, smiling as he left.

Mila sat back down at the bench, and carefully went about making the necessary connections. The paper taunted her in her periphery. There was so much to write, so much to say. So much to ask. How could she sum it up in just a few pages?

Oh well. Best to not dwell on it now. I have a few days to write it, after all.

She forced her focus back to the motherboard. Her eyes were narrowed on it, the tip of her tongue peeking through her lips. She made each connection with a guardian's care, making sure not to scratch or break anything. Too much pressure would break a connection. Too little, and it wouldn't be strong enough. The motherboard and chip module was a sophisticated, specific, careful design. Only sophisticated, specific, careful repairs would do.

Mila made the final connection, the deciding piece. She waited a few seconds, then a few seconds more.

"Come on," she said to herself.

But there was no light.

Twenty seconds had gone by. Thirty.

Nothing.

Mila closed her eyes and breathed deep. "Please."

She opened her eyes. Forty seconds. Fifty.

She felt a tear forming. If this didn't work...

But then, before the thought even had the chance to finish, that pale red light began to glow.

EPILOGUE

A FLEET of rune-addled ships floated just outside the Tyran atmosphere. It was a small fleet, consisting of only a dozen assault vessels and support ships. Not a fleet prepared for total war, but more than enough to escort their flagship, the Vidarin capital ship called *Magni*. The handful of ships looked like specks of pepper against the golden-red curve of the planet.

The young leader of the *Magni* had many titles and names. On ship, he was Admiral. On planet, he was General. Amongst friends and faithful zealots, he was savior. To enemies, he was Gríma. Now, in the sandy arena far below his fleet, sprayed with the blood of his fresh-slain foe, he was Champion.

The Tyran negotiations had been rocky, the terms of the alliance hard-fought. This was the final test. The General could have sent his flagbearer to serve Vidar in the duel in his stead, as the Tyrans had, but he did not want there to be any question about his commitment to a unified cause. The Tyrans valued fighting prowess and a battlefield mind above all else, after all. This was the best way to secure their loyalty in the wars to come.

The arena was not filled with adoring fans, as the theater back on the *Gjaller* might have been during a duel. But then, this was not intended to be a spectacle. This was purely business, which is why only three Tyrans stood watching the now-finished bout. Each of these tan-skinned envoys, swathed in colorful Tyran silks, had but a single title. The first was the Master of Land, the highest officer of Tyran terrestrial and sea forces. The second was the Master of Air, the highest officer of in-atmosphere aerial warfare. The last was the Master of Void, the highest officer of off-planet operations. Together, they comprised the Three Pillars of Tyr, the foremost authority of all the desert planet.

"I will have your answer now," the General said, looking up at the three leaders of the Tyran war machine.

Just then, a Tyran servant entered the arena, hurrying to the Master of Land and whispering something in her ear. The Master's expression remained stoic, unchanged. She only nodded.

"Your answer," the General said again, his nostrils flaring, and jaw muscles flexed.

"You'll have our answer soon," the Master of Land replied, her voice like a blade on a whetstone. "There has been a development that requires our discussion."

"What development?" the Master of Void asked, his voice like gravel and shale.

"It is better not discussed here, in the presence of outsiders," the Master of Land replied. "We will take a reprieve and make our decision in due time."

The bloodstained General spat on the sandy arena floor. "You'll do no such thing. I'll have your answer now. I killed your champion. By your law, you must—"

"Silence!" the Master of Land demanded. "You forget your status as guest here, General."

The General sneered, his gold-flecked eyes wide.

"Though," the Master of Void said, "the young General is correct."

"I concur," the Master of Air said, his voice more ethereal, like the wind. "He has adhered to our customs. Our laws are like Gleipnir, unbreakable."

"Very well," the Master of Land replied. "Then we shall discuss here." She set her emerald gaze on the General. "There is news from Vidar. The great *Gjaller* is no more."

The General flinched, but the two other Masters did not so much as bat an eye.

"And Volkner Brandt, what of him?" the Master of Air asked.

The General's grip on the handle of the shortsword he wielded tightened.

"Dead. They say he was killed by the hand of Piper DeRache, and of his own Berserker."

There was a crack like breaking bone as the wooden handle of the sword shattered, and cobalt blue blood dripped from the General's hand, staining the arena sand. For the first time, the three Masters' brows shifted in a small semblance of surprise.

No matter what Volkner Brandt was, no matter what people called him in the sun or shadow, and no matter the nature of the memories they shared, the General's blood boiled.

Piper DeRache. Niko Schafer. They were going to die.

And it would be none but he, Haldor Brandt, who would avenge his father's death.

NEXT INSTALLMENT
COMING SOON

Mila & Company will return soon. Sign up for updates at
ehgaskins.com/newsletter.

ACKNOWLEDGMENTS

I could not have written this book without the support of loved ones and the guidance of several people who I now consider some of my dearest friends.

First, to Allie, my wonderful fiancée, my biggest critic, and my most devoted fan. We've weathered some tough storms over the past few years, but we've conquered every obstacle together. I could not have done this if I hadn't had you there pushing me forward every step of the way.

Second, thank you to my parents who never doubted my dreams – not even for a second. You taught me the value of hard work and unyielding determination. You inspired me with stories from your youth and showed me that imagination is a gift that should not be squandered.

To everyone that backed the *Rattle Man* Kickstarter, it's because of you that I'm able to share this story in so many formats. You guys are true Vikings, and I've been so incredibly humbled by your support. I hope the story lived up to your expectations!

To the Western Colorado University Graduate Program in Creative Writing faculty, thank you so much for giving me this opportunity. To Rick Wilber, my patient Thesis Advisor, your mentorship has been invaluable and working with you has been an absolute joy. To Fran Wilde, I've marveled at your knowledge of writing since my first day on WCU's campus three years ago. To the genre fiction professors and other department professors I've worked with, thank you so much for showing me the ropes of both the craft and the industry of fiction. An especially deep thank you goes to those professors and faculty members who showed nothing but kindness and understanding during some of the hardest months of my entire life.

To the rest of my friends and family, thank you for always showing interest in my work and celebrating my milestones, especially when I forget to take a moment to do so myself. A special thank you goes out to my Dungeons & Dragons companions, who constantly provide valuable inspiration and have proven their patience when I'm on a deadline. I can't wait to accompany you all into new worlds, full of fresh stories, laughs, and the occasional tears.

Lastly, to my graduating cohort – Ruthie, Liza, J.D., Cammy, and Elan. We made it! We've finished the sprint and now the marathon begins. I can't wait to read the great things you all write in the years to come!

ABOUT THE AUTHOR

Raised on *Lord of the Rings, Star Wars,* and *Dungeons & Dragons,* it's no surprise that Ethan (E.H.) Gaskins adores everything science fiction and fantasy. He holds his M.F.A in Creative Writing from Western Colorado University and his B.A. in Philosophy from East Carolina University. Originally from the Carolinas, Ethan currently lives in Denver with his fiancée and four rambunctious pets. He's a jack of many trades, desperately trying to master at least one. That's why, while he's worked in marketing, a retail pharmacy, and even spent several years as a tanker in the Marine Corps Reserve, his heart lies with creating the most wondrous fictional worlds and characters he can.

Keep up to date with Ethan's writing by visiting www. ehgaskins.com/newsletter today!

facebook.com/ehgaskins

twitter.com/EthanGaskins

instagram.com/ehgaskins

goodreads.com/eh_gaskins

amazon.com/E-H-Gaskins/e/B09YKQ7LHB